SHADOW HAWK

BLOOD & SHADOWS BOOK 5

BOOKS BY ALIANNE DONNELLY

BLOOD AND SHADOWS
Blood Moons
Blood Trails
Blood Debts
Blood Hunt
Shadow Hawk

THE REBEL COURT
Catch Me
Dearest Love
Sweetest Kiss

DAWN OF RAGNAROK
The Royal Wizard
Dragonblood
Prince of Deceit

THE BEAST
Bastien
The Beast

OTHER TITLES
Wolfen
Virtual
Function: L1VE

ALIANNE DONNELLY

SHADOW HAWK

BLOOD & SHADOWS BOOK 5

To all the unimportant side characters who appear out of nowhere, disrupt all my careful plotting, and refuse to shut up and let their story go untold. Come at me. See what happens.

I have lived long enough. My way of life
Is fall'n into the sere, the yellow leaf,
And that which should accompany old age,
As honor, love, obedience, troops of friends,
I must not look to have, but in their stead
Curses, not loud but deep, mouth-honor, breath
Which the poor heart would fain deny and dare not.

-Shakespeare (*Macbeth*, Act V, Scene III)

1

October 18, 3036 – Hadran City, Anamtaigh

Laura Belden was going to be a widow.

"Are you kidding me?"

William _shushed_ her. "You might want to lower your voice."

Laura gritted her teeth and hissed, "So you just decided to go off on your own and not bother including your wife in the decision-making process?"

Sixteen kids and five other teachers had come on this excursion to see the Crooked Tooth Ski Resort Music Festival. They'd barely arrived at their hotel in Hadran City, and her husband chose _now_ to share this bit of news.

William grabbed two bags from the hoverbus storage and put them on the luggage levpad with undue care. "Correct," he replied with his signature stubbornness that always came across as a royal decree. She blamed his aristocratic accent. "It's my life and my choice to make. I already booked my passage. I leave in four days."

Which would explain why he'd packed a full suitcase for an overnight trip. He was planning to leave straight from here and let her break the news to everyone back in Karsengale Valley on her own.

Yep. Forget Blue Skies. She was going to kill him. "It's _our_ life, William. That was the deal we made when we got married. And if you're not feeling well, you're supposed to tell me, not check yourself into a long-term care facility behind my back!"

She might as well have been a lowly peasant annoying the high lord. William had a unique way of staying calm and composed under any circumstance, and it always pissed her off so much, the way he never got rattled. Always a rational counterargument delivered with conversational wisdom in the face of her fury.

He was about to deliver one now but cut himself off when Rusty ran up. "Laura! Kyle took the snack pack, and he won't give it back. Can I hit him?"

Laura took a deep breath for patience. "No, you cannot. Kyle, get over here."

Instead, Kyle and his accomplice, Amaya, hoofed it straight across the street moments before the light turned green and a steady river of transports blocked the path. He did a little victory dance over there, and Laura understood where Rusty's animosity was coming from.

"I'll get them," William said.

"No, you save your strength," Laura retorted. "I'll get them."

She couldn't look at her husband right now. Their marriage wasn't perfect, but their partnership was about so much more than just the two of them. They'd founded their school together, for crying out loud. He was the kids' favorite teacher. And, to make matters worse, most of them were orphans. The last thing they needed was for a father figure to abandon them without a word.

This was very badly done.

Hadran City was a metropolis unlike any other on Anamtaigh. Where most of the planet's communities limited the height of their buildings to no more than three stories, here, they towered taller than sixty. The spires stretched and narrowed toward the sky, creating a cityscape of elegant spikes set against the backdrop of a stunning snow-capped mountain range. Mountain Road, the largest street running through its center and the one Laura was about to cross, marked a straight line toward Crooked Tooth, the iconic tallest peak. Its crystal art installation at the top reflected sunlight like a beacon.

Laura had looked forward to exploring the city—she'd never been there before. Now, all she could think was how much she wanted to be back home, away from everything and everyone, including her husband.

When traffic came to a stop, Laura ran across the street to fetch the kids. Kyle saw her coming and took off up the block, Amaya on his heels. It started a stampede. Half of the kids from the hotel side ran for him, too, and four teachers followed. Alexis was eight months pregnant; she should not be running anywhere. Laura would have yelled at her, but there was no need. Alexis' husband, Miguel, was already doing a fine job of it, following at her heels.

"Don't be upset with him," Noemi counseled, putting an arm around her. The telepath didn't usually pry into people's thoughts, but she sometimes picked up on loud ones, even when her shields were in place. "He's doing what he thinks he should."

Laura shook her head. "This wasn't the plan."

"It wasn't *your* plan, you mean."

"Because it doesn't make sense!" William was two years shy of forty; he was in the prime of his life and should have been out there, exploring all the universe had to offer. Instead, he was about to check himself into a place he would never leave again—and for what?

Yes, William did have a degenerative disease that would eventually kill him. But, unless he was somehow holding back the truth about its progression, he still had years before he would need the kind of care Blue Skies offered.

Victor, their newest telepath addition, ran up to Laura's other side and mirrored Noemi. "It does if you think about it from his side."

Laura glared at him. "Shields. Now."

"They're up! I can't help it any more than Noemi can."

"Try harder," she growled.

He dropped his arm from around her shoulders and distanced himself a bit, his cheeks flushed.

"Was that necessary?"

"Probably not." But right now, Laura was so angry she couldn't think straight.

Noemi sighed. "Listen, William doesn't make spur-of-the-moment decisions. He's been planning for this eventuality for years. If he thinks it's time, you need to let him go."

Laura stopped Noemi on the sidewalk and looked straight into her dark brown eyes. "Is it time?" She wasn't a mind reader like Noemi. All she saw in William was that he'd made up his mind and wouldn't be swayed from his decision. He was determined to get on that shuttle four days from now and, short of Laura ordering him not to go, nothing and no one would convince him to stay.

It was a blatant breach of privacy for Noemi to answer. She didn't like being forced into the middle of an argument like this and usually went out of her way to avoid it. That she wasn't snapping at Laura for asking said much more than any revelation.

A sharp pang hit Laura straight in the chest, and her breath caught.

It was time. And she hadn't noticed.

"What am I supposed to tell the kids?"

"Nothing. Not yet. Let them enjoy the festival. Maybe we can stay an extra night to give them more time with him. Once we get back to Karsengale, we'll put together an assembly."

Noemi was always a rock in a crisis. Laura appreciated it more than words could ever say. One day, she hoped to be as self-possessed and clear-thinking as Noemi when emotions ran high. Laura still had a temper, which tended to complicate things more often than she cared to admit. She was working on it, though.

Isla whistled from across the street, pointing up the block. The kids were swarming toward a novelty candy shop on the corner, leaving their teachers in the dust.

Laura rolled her eyes. "Good lord, that's all we need. Sixteen kids on a sugar high." She was about to go after them when Noemi caught her arm. The telepath's fingers dug in so hard it brought her up short, and she frowned at the woman who'd gone ashen. "Noemi? What's wrong?"

"They're here," Noemi said, barely making a sound.

"Who's here? What are you…?"

The sky above darkened by degrees until the streetlights turned on overhead. What looked like a storm cloud quickly took on a blacker, more solid shape—a massive shuttle unlike anything Laura had seen before.

A cold chill seeped from its belly, spreading frost over the high riser walls and freezing Laura's heart. She didn't have to ask anymore; she knew what that shuttle contained.

Her palms became clammy with memories of cold, hard-faced men sitting in the audience at her high school play, stalking down the aisles like sharks through a school of fish afterward, invading their celebration backstage to take her best friend "for a chat." The way he'd spoken to her the next day—the way he'd looked straight through her—still hurt to remember.

And on the heels of that pain came wrath.

How dare the Shadows show themselves back here? Laura brought down her shields, ignoring the clouds of color that immediately formed around her to focus her will on the shuttle. She didn't need to read thoughts. All she needed was one receptive mind up there to take direction. Laura could be very persuasive when she put her mind—

Noemi yanked on her arm hard. "Don't! You'll cause more harm than good."

"But I can—"

"No, you can't."

Isla and Victor came running, shouting, "Get down!"

Noemi hauled Laura sideways, and they crashed to the ground beneath the awning of an upscale fashion store as the top of the spire next door exploded. The ground shook, and debris rained down on the street. Automated transports came to a stop, and Laura watched helplessly as their drivers got out to see what was happening. Some ran for cover, while others froze, watching chaos descend on the street around them.

She blasted out an order as far as her power could reach, telling everyone to get off the street, get inside. Most of them obeyed, momentarily turned into automatons under Laura's directive. It got them moving, but not with forethought or strategy. They ran a straight line, heedless of the giant metal and concrete chunks raining down onto the street. Not all of them made it to safety.

A gray haze of indecision saturated her mind, thousands upon thousands of intentions—and lack thereof—crowding out her own, and Laura froze. She couldn't think, couldn't move. All she could do was watch as her people ran for the hotel, adults carrying the smallest kids, herding the bigger ones, keeping their heads down, not daring to glance up as the Shadow shuttle pivoted toward the next target.

She saw where it would hit; she knew the weapon they were about to deploy. It would leave a two-mile-wide crater and level an entire neighborhood.

So much happened so quickly. The greatest tragedy to ever befall

Anamtaigh, and Laura was stuck, unable to do anything about it. But she saw it all with perfect clarity.

Noemi untangled herself from Laura and stepped into the street like a sleepwalker, gazing up toward the sky.

Alexis was on the ground up the block, screaming, clutching her belly, with Miguel lying unconscious next to her.

Across the street, Semi and William crouched in the hotel entry, hugging three kids each. She couldn't see their faces clearly, but she could read their intent. Semi wanted to get inside. William's only thought was to regroup. He wanted to risk making a run for the kids farther up the block.

Isla stepped into the street, weaving among the transports to join Noemi. She took the other telepath's hand, and they gazed at each other in silent conversation for a moment before nodding in agreement.

As one, they looked at Laura—no, not her. They wanted Victor. The twenty-year-old boy wheezing somewhere behind Laura, terrified out of his mind, hurting, wanting desperately to get away. He'd had a taste of war, and his courage had abandoned him.

But the women kept staring, patient, unrelenting, and Victor sniffled and went to them, taking their hands to complete the circle.

Alexis screamed again. Rusty had made it over to her with a tall stranger whose chin was black from the edge of his lower lip to his neck. He talked to Alexis while he checked Miguel's pulse. Rusty was so pale, staring at her hands covered in blood.

Semi and William were arguing. Their group of kids was already inside, but William hadn't moved from his spot.

And then another chunk of concrete came falling down. Kyle saw it first and pulled Amaya and Jamie away from its path straight out into the street.

No! That was the wrong way to go. Laura lurched up onto all fours.

Miguel had come to. The sidewalk quartet of misery was heading toward the hotel, Rusty leading the way, Miguel bracing Alexis' belly, and the tattooed stranger keeping an eye on the sky.

None of them saw the kids in the street.

William did.

Laura felt his decision almost before he made it, and both of them ran out toward the kids at the same time.

—*Laura!*—

The telepathic blast speared through her brain, stopping her in her tracks long enough for everything to go horribly wrong. No-emi dumped a jumbled mess of knowledge into Laura's mind with no rhyme or reason, except for one unifying thought binding it all into a chaotic ribbon: —*The safest place anywhere will be far from everywhere. Hide!*—

The hairs all over Laura's body raised on end as she saw William throw himself at the kids in the street, bowling them back toward the sidewalk, and then there was a flash of light behind them. The pressure wave swept everything in its wake, picking up transports and hoverbuses like toys. One of them slammed into her, taking her along for a ride.

The last thought that went through her head before it struck a solid surface was, *I wish Finn was here…*

~

Laura came to in the shade of a transport leaning against the wall at her back. Her body was a knot of agony from the top of her head clear down to her toes, but she was still alive. Couldn't stay put; the transport didn't look stable. It could collapse on top of her at any moment.

She pulled herself out by her elbows and emerged into a different world. The sky above was swirling with streams of unnatural color, curls and eddies of them mixing, spreading apart in a glorious display that made a mockery of death. The air smelled of smoke and chemicals; she tasted blood and metal on her tongue. Laura struggled to sit up as the world tilted and pitched under her.

The silence was absolute. When she touched her right ear, her fingers came away bloody.

She blinked hard to focus through the dust. All color had leeched into the sky, leaving buildings, transports, trees, and people covered in shades of gray.

The spire across from the hotel was sheared off in the middle. Pieces of it littered the street, but most of its height had collapsed inward, leaving a gaping hole straight through to the next street over. Transports had been blown every which way. The northern mountain vista was smoking. Crooked Tooth was gone, and an avalanche of boulders spilled down into the valley, burying the ski resort and everyone in it.

They'd failed. Noemi, Isla, and Victor had tried to push the Shadows beyond the mountain range, but something must have gone wrong. Laura looked for them in the street. Their bodies were scattered like broken dolls on a pile of transports blown back in the explosion.

William—the kids…

Laura struggled to her feet, gasping for breath as her vision blacked out for a few seconds. Undeterred, she hobbled up to the mound at the edge of the sidewalk. Her throat felt raw with the tears she swallowed back again and again. Her kids needed her. William needed her. She couldn't fall apart now.

She dropped to her knees before the human pile covered in dust and reached out a shaking hand. Her fingers were crooked, out of alignment. Someone else took hold of her husband to lay him out on his back. A stranger took hold of her wrist to stabilize her hand as she watched William cough his way back to consciousness.

Several people pulled apart the kids, tossing away the tattered remains of a snack pack to make room on the sidewalk, and Laura didn't breathe or blink, watching three little bodies get laid out side by side. She watched and waited for them to wake up. Seconds stretched into minutes, into eternity, and none of them moved. They looked wrong. Not children anymore, but puppets collapsed in heaps with their strings severed.

The people who'd separated them now rearranged their limbs and covered their unseeing eyes.

Much later, when the worst of the pain dulled to nearly bearable levels, Eskel would tell her she screamed her throat bloody as they dragged her across the street and into the hotel lobby.

Laura didn't hear it, and she didn't feel it. She didn't care that her vocal cords were shredded—she had nothing to say.

It would take months for her to recover enough to wonder…

Had Finn been there, after all?

2

Rowe, Rowe Rowe your boat…

Laura's hypnotic voice echoed off the walls and assaulted Finn like a blast of down feathers through his brain. Stuck in total darkness, he couldn't tell how far she was, but her voice shaped the width and length of a hallway lined with metal—one much too familiar.

Lightweight footsteps in hard-heeled shoes thumped on the floor a fair distance off. Finn blindly reached out one hand in front and one to the side, tracing the wall so he could follow the sound of her retreat without walking into something. What the hell was she doing here? It wasn't safe.

…gently down the stream…

His hand slid off the wall into empty space. A hard grip on his arm yanked him into dust-borne dusk. Finn blinked, coughing to clear his airways. Explosions and gunfire assaulted his ears. He felt the soldier shaking him but couldn't see his face clearly enough to read his lips. "…the fuck is your problem, Rowe? You callin' it quits, or what?" Another explosion shook the world as the soldier pointed behind him and said something Finn didn't catch. "…and I don't see a 'shoot on you." Another hard shake. "Answer me, trainee!"

Finn looked behind him. His heels were two feet away from a sheer drop-off into a gorge. He shook his head hard and slapped himself to wake the fuck up. "Where's the rest of the unit?" There should have been fifteen of them, all as sleep deprived as Finn felt.

The soldier yanked him around to face a scorched hole in the ground, still smoking from the heat of the blast. Nothing left but scraps of cloth and red blobs of flesh scattered around the rim. "Where every soldier goes when his lookout falls asleep."

Finn felt invisible bands pull taut around his chest, tugging him backward alongside the gorge to escape the sight. The soldier yelled after him, but the whistle of a falling warhead cut him off short. He looked up, cast Finn a quick, regretful glance, then dived head-first into the gorge.

Between one backward step and another, Finn found himself in the pitch-black hallway again, the sound of footsteps beating a gentle rhythm through the ringing in his ears. His legs were shaky, and the scent of smoke and death clung to him, but Finn followed those footsteps, tripping over his feet.

If Miss Laura should command…

His foot caught on something, and he went down face-first into mud. Burning pain bloomed in the side of his face, and his left hand throbbed, swollen, and discolored.

A robotic voice shouted a status report over the loudspeaker as, next to him, John Wayland laughed at the sky. "Good call, diving for the mud. Not even God would find us in this mess."

Finn rolled over and sat up. His abdomen ached with internal injuries. "Last resort of a desperate idiot." He coughed to clear dust and smoke out of his throat.

Wayland shrugged. "Can't argue with that."

"How many down?"

Wayland snorted, sitting up on his heels. His uniform was burned away from the left shoulder down, the skin of that arm red with the effects of whatever caustic material had blasted him. "More like how many out. Half, at least."

Finn swore.

A beep from Wayland's com band sounded a new message alert. "The fuck?"

Finn checked his own, but it was silent. "Something goin' on that I don't know about?"

"Just says 'Classified.' I'm supposed to report to the strategy room in ten."

Finn raised a scorched eyebrow. "Better haul ass, then."

"Yeah. Come on, old man, let's get you cleaned up."

"Motherfucker, who you callin' old?" But he did take the offered hand and allow Wayland to haul him to his feet. Of course, the son of a bitch sent him stumbling on his way—

—straight back into the pitch-black hallway.

If Miss Laura should command, life is what you dream…

Finn leaned against the wall, breathing hard through the pain of accumulated injuries. "Laura!" She should not be here.

The rhythm of her footsteps didn't change at all. She was getting farther.

Finn lurched away from the wall and followed at a trot while she kept singing that goddamned song he hated to love. Half chasing her, half running from the din of war nipping at his heels, he felt as if the hallway was filled with water. The floor stuck to his boots, slowing him down, making him fight for every single step forward.

Rowe, Rowe, row your boat—

"Laura, get the fuck out of here! Run!*"*

—gently down the stream…

He was on all fours, exhausted, fading, crawling forward inch by maddening inch, while 'round and 'round his head, a repeating chorus sounded out the beat to her song: It's not safe. Not safe. Not safe…

If Miss Laura should command, life is what you dream.

The footsteps stopped and hushed all other sounds in their wake.

Finn held his breath, waiting for another round, another step—anything to tell him she was still alive. Please be alive. *"Laura!" he shouted at the top of his lungs, but the darkness that had lovingly conveyed her voice in endless echoes swallowed his.*

A metal latch screeched free a hundred yards ahead, and a heavy door swung open on groaning hinges. Light blazed into the darkness, illuminating white walls that faded to black a foot in front of Finn. He squinted at the silhouette of a woman as she turned sideways to look his way. She might as well have been a shade, for all he could see of her features.

"Wake up, Rowe," her familiar voice called back in a gentle command that wrapped itself around his brain in a warm embrace to ensure compliance. "You've dreamed long enough."

～

June 25, 3039 – Just outside Hadran City, Anamtaigh

Finnegan Rowe jerked awake, grabbing the hand on his shoulder, but stopped himself short of twisting it broke when he recognized the bright orange hat of a flight attendant. It took him a second more to clear his mind enough to release her.

The woman whose name tag read BECKA smiled, despite her eyes rounding with fright. "Sir, we've landed."

Finn looked around. The shuttle cabin was empty. He was the last one still in his seat. "Right. Sorry." He unbuckled his seatbelt and got up with a groan of remembered injuries. Aside from a bit of stiffness in the joints, he was perfectly healthy, but God damn those memories.

Nodding his farewell to the flight attendant, he took his bag and marched down the aisle heading for the exit. He pretended not to hear the woman sigh her relief behind him.

There were no crowds in the shuttleport. Pretty standard for a middling, no-nonsense planet like Anamtaigh, but even so, Finn would have expected a steady stream of people moving around. Instead, he saw a handful of 'port attendants in uniform and piles of debris shoved against the walls. No holosigns anywhere. Passengers looking for their gates wore transparent screens over their eyes, and those disembarking followed printed arrows attached to the walls.

The lines for ID check had dwindled to a couple of stragglers by the time Finn arrived. He scanned his chip on a pad in front of the clerk who looked like he'd seen better times. The droop of his fleshy mouth gave him a distinctly amphibious look that went well with his deep croak of a voice. "How long will you be staying?"

"Don't know," Finn replied.

The man looked up from his screen to give Finn a once-over.

Finn did his best to strike a casual pose, but he was still too raw from the nightmare to marshal his blank expression. "I don't remember this place being so run-down," he said to break the tension.

The clerk huffed. "How long since your last visit?"

Too long. "Twenty years, give or take." His missions had brought him into the planetary neighborhood plenty of times before, but he hadn't stepped foot on Anamtaigh's soil since taking off for Shadow training. "I was born here," he added for no reason whatsoever.

Something changed in the clerk's expression, looking uncomfortably close to pity. He broke his stare and busied himself with some rapid-fire typing to hide an obvious slip of his give-no-fuckness. "Well, you ain't coming home, that's for sure. Whatever this place used to be…" He paused as a haunted shadow crossed his gaze. Shaking it off, he gave Finn a bitter half-smile. "It's a whole different kind of place now. Welcome to Anamtaigh, Mr. Draven."

Finn nodded, smoothly slipping into the skin of Jonathan J. Draven, a Gray Dublin police officer looking for some peace in the countryside. "Where can I rent a transport vehicle?"

The clerk snorted. "Your best bet is the taxi service out front. All we got left to rent are some old wrecks from decades ago. Been sitting there for years 'cause no one can drive 'em without a nav no more."

"I can drive them." He could drive anything and everything with a digital interface. His training had seen to that and more. "Which way?"

With another toad-like croak, the clerk reached for a tray of black, T-shaped rods. He stuck the long end of one into a hole in his console, typed in a few commands, and then handed the rod to Finn. "Good luck."

Finn nodded his thanks and walked away from the counter to let the harried-looking woman with a toddler on her hip push in. Settling the long end of the rod over his ear activated the screen across his eyes, and a fine, light blue sheen fell over his vision, with blinking red arrows on the floor pointing the way to the transport rental garage.

A half-hour later, he drove out of the shuttleport and stopped dead at the first intersection.

His memories of leaving Anamtaigh were as fresh as if he'd lived them yesterday. The world before him now looked completely different. Instead of lush, green fields, scorched earth and crashed shuttles lined the road leading away from the 'port. Where the tall spires of Hadran City used to point the way to civilization, spiky remnants jutted up from what looked more like a landfill than the vibrant city it'd used to be.

Crooked Tooth, a mountain landmark in this region, had been sheared straight, and a hill of rubble the size of entire buildings now littered its base—the former location of a touristy winter resort.

With inter-world communication still patchy at best, news traveled slowly and sometimes not at all. Finn hadn't expected Anamtaigh to come through untouched by the Shadows, but this…

The taxi behind him beeped loudly to get him moving.

Finn stuck his hand out the window and waved, pretending to be an idiot who didn't know how to operate the rental vehicle, then haltingly set off again.

He hoped the damage was confined to this region, it being a hub of travel and activity, but as the hours dragged on and he passed through region after region, Finn saw the same level of destruction everywhere. And the more he saw, the more his shoulders tensed until his back spasmed, and a headache pounded in his temples.

Finn wasn't a hero by any stretch of the imagination. Hell, after everything he'd done and been made to do, he couldn't even be classified as good or decent anymore. He had a slew of excuses to offer in his defense, but none that would stand up to scrutiny. In the end, Finn had chosen to sign over his life to the Shadows. That was all that would ever matter.

For three years, Finn had roamed the worlds alone, hiding from the Shadows as much as the well-meaning telepaths who tended to get a little too comfortable around him for his own comfort. The people he'd been told were the enemy had helped him heal from the damage done to him by his own unit. In return, he'd helped them turn the tide of war. Now that the Shadows were no longer a threat to him, Finn was officially out of reasons to stay away. It was time to go home.

What about Laura? Wayland's voice hammered inside his memories. *Is she still alive? When was the last time you saw her?*

Some sins were harder to confront than others. Finn had had parents once upon a time. He'd had cousins and friends, too. But he'd never mattered much to them, so they'd never mattered much to him. The only one he'd ever truly cared about was Laura McNally.

It was Laura who loomed like a specter of judgment in his conscience, reminding him that no matter how much good he did, it would never be enough. By signing on with the Shadows, Finn had betrayed Laura in ways he hadn't fully understood until it was too late.

The Shadows had been trained and conditioned to fight against one thing: the telepath threat to all mankind. Every hour of every day, nicely or forcibly, they'd been fed the lie that they were doing the right thing—the *righteous* thing—by standing guard over humanity's God-given free will.

In that battle, Laura McNally was the poster child for Senator Griffith's ideal enemy. She and Finn had spent so much of their childhood in each other's company, her telepathic presence had simply become a part of Finn, and he hadn't questioned it a single time. Until a Shadow recruiter had explained to him how a persuasive telepath could manipulate people to their will.

At a very young eighteen years of age, to be told that someone he loved had been controlling his thoughts and actions the whole time had done a number on Finn—precisely as they'd intended.

It hadn't occurred to him until he'd thought about it later that Laura had never once made him do anything he wouldn't have done on his own. She'd never once made him think anything he hadn't heard from his parents or others in the community his whole life. But by then, he'd been in too deep, with too many Shadows watching his every move. Resistance and disobedience of any kind had not been tolerated.

And while the Shadows had held Finn on a tight leash, fighting their secret war, Laura McNally had lived a full life without him.

It was almost sunset when he entered what should have been Avencore, a village a hundred and fifty miles west of Karsengale. He could have gone on and reached his childhood home in an hour and a half, but after two decades of radio silence, Finn doubted Laura would invite him in for dinner if he showed up on her doorstep unannounced.

With only his transport headlights to illuminate the road, Finn navigated a maze of buildings that had seen better days to the Thane & Owens Inn, where a flickering holosign advertised V ANC ES.

The lights were off, and the door locked when he walked up to the entrance. He pushed the button to announce himself, but it sparked and crackled. Not a good sign. Finn rapped his knuckles on the door. "Hello! Anybody home?"

A window above creaked open. Finn stepped back and craned his neck to look up. No sign of a proprietor poking his head out to see who had awakened him. Only the barrel of a weapon sliding out and pointing down.

"Oh, shit." Finn held up his hands. "I don't want trouble. I'm just looking for lodging."

"You one of those red soldiers?" a woman called from her hiding place.

"No." Shadow uniforms were dark-blue and black. "Police officer. Jonathan Draven from Gray Dublin, Earth."

After a few silent seconds, the gun retreated and the window closed.

Eight minutes later, the lights in the entry turned on. He heard the clack and rolling rumble of a lot of locks, bolts, and bars being shifted around, and then the door finally opened on a woman who Finn assumed owned this friendly establishment. Her face couldn't have been older than thirty, but the shadows under her eyes and the white in her rumpled hair aged her an additional fifteen, if not more.

She also held a gun down by her thigh as a prudent precaution. "You got credits?"

"Depends. How much do you charge?"

The woman snorted and stepped aside to let him in.

Despite the building looking pathetically run-down on the outside, the inside was clean and cozy. Doors and windows were framed in golden wood, the floors were covered with plush carpets, and here and there, hand-carved wooden accents adorned the walls.

The woman noticed him taking stock. "I run a proper business," she told him with a mixture of pride and warning. "Rooms aren't much, but the beds are soft, and the bathrooms are clean. Pay upfront, and I'll even throw in breakfast on the house."

"How much?"

Still wary, the woman rounded a desk and pulled out a leather-bound ledger from one of the drawers. She made a show of leafing through the pages and asked, "How many nights?"

Finn had no idea what he'd be driving into tomorrow. He might be back here by noon and heading for the shuttleport the next day. He'd need to recon the situation for a while and gauge Laura's condition and state of mind before he tried to approach her. "About two weeks." Anamtaigh's orbit around its sun, Vexa, gave it an even four-hundred-and-twenty-day year, with twelve months consisting of five Earth-standard seven-day weeks. If he couldn't figure his shit out in fourteen days, there'd be no point in staying any longer.

The woman turned a couple more pages. "You're lucky. I got a whole crowd of folk coming on July sixth that'll keep this place full-up for a month."

Sure she did. "I'll be out of your hair on the fifth."

"That'll be sixty-four credits a night, plus a cleaning fee."

"I won't need room service."

"I'll still need to clean the room after you leave," she returned sweetly, then added, hard-faced, "Fee's non-negotiable. You want it or not?"

Did he have a choice? Finn smiled and held out his wrist. The chip embedded there stored his identification and was linked to his bank account. When scanned, it would process payment instantly.

The impossible woman moved just her eyes to glance at his proffered arm. "Cash only."

Finn gritted his teeth, keeping his smile plastered in place. Cash was a rare commodity these days. Only the most backwater establishments demanded it, either because they weren't accredited by the Business Bureau to carry out virtual transactions or because they didn't have the equipment and connectivity to do so.

He set down his bag and dug out the cash wallet he kept on hand for bribes. He didn't keep too much on him to avoid attracting attention. Most of his emergency stash sat in innocuous-looking parcels at post depots on multiple worlds. All he had to do was submit an order, and they'd be shipped to his current location in a matter of days.

"Sixty-four a night for fifteen nights." Finn counted out the bills. "Let's see, that's—"

"Nine hundred and sixty," the woman said quickly. She'd done that math in her head. "Round up to a thou' with the cleaning fee."

Finn counted out a thousand credits, then added a few more. "I'll give you an extra fifty for some information."

The hungry stare she had trained on his money turned wary as she looked up into his face. "I ain't no snitch, copper."

Understandable. Finn had chosen his identity as a police officer, fully aware that they weren't the most trusted profession at the moment. In far too many cities, the cops who should have been on the front lines, protecting their citizens and herding them to safety, had been the first ones to run for the hills when the fighting had started in earnest. Some had turned informant, reporting the names and locations of known telepaths to the Shadows to save their own necks.

"I'm not a spy Miss…?"

"Thane," she said.

"Miss Thane, I'm really not here to cause trouble. All I want is for you to tell me what happened here, and which road will take me to Karsengale without running into a downed shuttle wreck."

The proprietress unclenched, and her shoulders drooped. "That's a long tale to tell."

Finn handed her the stack of bills. "I've got nothing but time."

She shrugged. "Not like I need the sleeps. All right. First thing you need to know: there is no 'Karsengale' anymore…"

3

June 33, 3039 – What's left of Karsengale

Laura had been wide awake for hours by the time the rooster crowed out in its pen. From his room above, Darax muttered a filthy curse, then hollered at the top of his lungs, "_Rusty, if you don't shut that bird up, I'm cooking it for dinner!_"

Laura folded back her blanket and sat up, rolling her head and shoulders to work out kinks that never seemed to loosen lately. Anamtaigh had a twenty-eight-hour day, and somehow it still wasn't enough.

Three doors down, Rusty slammed out of her room and yelled up to Darax's window, "Don't you touch him, you animal!"

More voices chimed up, grumpy adults and giggling children all voicing their opinions on being awakened at the crack of dawn.

Laura unraveled her long, chestnut braid and reached for her comb without looking into the mirror. She ran the sturdy teeth through the length of her hair before plaiting it back into a long rope.

As the compound woke to life, she dressed in yesterday's clothes—they were still clean enough, and laundry soap was expensive—then sat back on the edge of her bed to stare at her shoes. They were the same shoes she'd worn for years now, broken in and as comfortable as a pair of work boots could be. But for some reason, they'd been chafing her with every step the last few days. It wasn't a physical flaw, either. Laura had inspected them inside and out, looking for frayed seams, deteriorating soles, and stray pebbles. She never found a thing, and her feet never showed any wounds or marks at the end of the day.

Laura shook her head and stuffed her left foot into its boot. She winced as she tied her laces. Something didn't fit, and she couldn't put her finger on what it was. Nothing there that shouldn't belong and nothing missing, but somehow, it felt like both at the same time.

She'd dwell on it later.

After shaking out her pillows and blanket, she pulled back the rag drapes to let in some light and opened the window. "No one's cooking the rooster," she decreed at the top of her lungs.

"Aw, come on," Darax whined above her. "It doesn't even lay eggs."

Outside, the fourteen-year-old spitfire they called Rusty for her reddish-brown hair stomped her foot. "He's my friend." She was all arms and legs at the moment, but Laura could tell the girl would fill out into a heartbreaker one day. Maybe when the supply lines got re-established, and they managed to free up some funds for proper food.

A gal could dream.

Feeling more tired than ever, Laura checked over everything one last time, then gently knocked on the door connecting her room to William's. He never bothered answering anymore, so she poked her head in without waiting.

Her husband smiled at her in welcome. "Good morning. How do you fare this fine day?"

Laura entered, closed the door behind her, and countered, "How are you feeling?" His drapes were always open, as was his window. He liked being able to see and hear what happened out there in the world.

William sighed and braced his elbows to sit up.

Laura was at his side immediately, helping to prop a bigger pillow behind his back.

"Oh, don't fuss. You know how I hate it."

She knew. But she did it, anyway.

Another loud, shrieking bird call rose outside.

Laura shook her head, billowing up William's blanket to straighten it. "That rooster's days are numbered. I don't know how long I can keep Darax from stuffing it into his metal press."

William chuckled. "I rather enjoy him, myself. He's a bit of life and color in this dreary world of mine." He caught her hand while it smoothed down the edge of his bed sheet and made her look at him. "You didn't answer my question."

He hadn't slept well, and it showed. The dark circles had deepened, sinking his bright blue eyes into his skull. The irises would glow like jewels if it weren't for the gray tinge to their whites. Yet, somehow, he still retained so much of his aristocratic allure. His features were simply too elegant to be marred by disease.

"I'm fine," she said.

He dipped his chin to look at her from beneath his dark blond brows, a wry smile tucked into one corner of his mouth. "Then why don't I believe you?"

"I don't know. I should think a husband would trust his wife implicitly."

He laughed weakly, then winced, resting an arm over his abdomen. "Oh, I do hope, once I'm gone, you will find someone who can fully appreciate that droll wit of yours."

"Oh, knock it off. You're gonna outlive us all."

As if she hadn't spoken, William looked out the window with a haunting look of longing. "It may be sooner than either of us think."

Needing to break his dour mood, she asked, "What would you like for breakfast? Eggs are still off the menu, but I can offer you some lovely stale rolls, a cup of burnt coffee, and maybe even a selection of artificial cheeses."

"Now you're being cruel, wife. You know very well the only brewed liquid I put in my mouth is tea."

Laura bent to kiss the top of his head. "Tea it is, milord. And I'll see if I can ferret out some biscuits to go with it."

She was at the door when he said, "Would you be a dear and hand me my shaving kit over there?"

Laura froze. They didn't have any electric shavers left. The last ones'd had to be broken down for parts to rebuild Eskel's medical tools. All William had in his kit was a bit of dry soap, an old-fashioned brush, and a six-inch blade. "I need to get the rabble settled, but I can come back to help you shave later."

"Laura," he warned.

"What?" she snapped and instantly regretted it.

William's foreboding expression softened. "Darling, you are very good at commanding all and sundry to your will. But even you aren't strong enough to stop death in its tracks when it comes for me."

"That doesn't mean you have to hasten it along." Then, because their discussion was getting too morbid for her peace of mind, she said, "Do you seriously expect me to put a sharp blade into a grip that shakes worse than Eskel's centrifuge?"

William raised his bony hand and held it suspended over the bed. "Steady as a rock."

That's what I'm afraid of. "I'll be back to help you later," she insisted. "Save your strength. We're raising the storage house walls today. If they stay up this time, we're gonna be drinking tonight, and everyone will expect to see you there."

He smiled. "How could I possibly refuse such an invitation? Now go. I heard tell there's some rabble needs settling. It sounds like they're in dire need of your unflappable leadership."

The kitchen wasn't big enough to fit everyone in their ever-growing household, but they all gathered there anyway. This morning, Sisa had porridge bubbling away in a huge pot on the stove, Reemy was portioning out sugar and cinnamon from their dwindling supplies, and everyone else stood around with bowls and spoons in their hands, waiting.

Laura greeted the group with, "You're all aware there's a perfectly serviceable table out in the hall, yes?"

"Yes, Laura," Darax said, rolling his eyes.

She glared at him. "You still have soot on your face. When's the last time you washed?"

Darax grinned as the others snickered. "I'm doing my part for the community by conserving water. I thought you'd be proud."

She pointed out the door.

With a sigh, he set his bowl and spoon on the counter and sulked out to the bathroom. Forty-seven years old and a wizard with metals, but you wouldn't know it from the way he acted. It hadn't always been part of his charm. The fallout had affected them all in different ways. Darax seemed to be regressing in maturity. He forgot his manners often these days and sometimes had trouble controlling his emotions which made Laura fear that one day, he'd overreact to something so badly he'd hurt someone.

"As for the rest of you, hands out."

Fifteen pairs of hands stuck out for her inspection, child and adult alike. Laura went around and inspected each of them, keeping a firm hold on her stern expression despite their giggles. She put on the Mother Hen act for their benefit, but the reasons for her fussing were sound, and they all knew it. A bit of comedy never hurt in a situation as serious as theirs.

Once she passed everyone, she continued to Sisa at the stove. Laura looked over the young cook's hands as she stirred, then casually dipped her finger into the pot to steal a taste and laughed as a barrage of offended shouts assaulted her ears.

Darax ran back in, his face still red and his hair wet from washing. "What? What did I miss?"

"Nothing," Laura assured him, patting his shoulder on her way out to the drinks station. "You're just in time."

Immediately, everyone picked up their bowls again and lined up to get their share of breakfast. Their eagerness was as much a joy as it was a pain to see. Laura had instructed Sisa to cook up something tasty with their few remaining supplies. If their shipment still hadn't come by nightfall, she'd have to take some extreme measures.

Worry about that tomorrow, she told herself. There was plenty else to worry about today.

William's teacup was the only one of its kind in the cupboard, and no one touched it but Laura. It was a relic of the old world, fine porcelain with a chipped saucer and a tiny silver spoon to go with it. Laura put a measure of dried tea leaves into the black pot and poured hot water over them, allowing them to steep while she looked for biscuits.

"Any breakfast left?"

Laura turned around, hiding a small pack of sweets behind her back.

Quinn grinned down at her. "You have something on your lip there." At six feet, eight inches, Quinn was a giant among them, with a deep, menacing voice to match, but his heart was pure gold—and physically failing.

Laura wiped crumbs from her lip and flushed with guilt as she chewed and swallowed the rest of the biscuit. "Don't tell anyone," she said softly.

"I wouldn't dare," he whispered back, then raised his voice to a normal volume. "Especially since I know you haven't had breakfast yet."

She frowned. "You don't know that."

"Kitchen's still full. That means you haven't eaten. You never eat until everyone else is fed."

"They need it more," she said.

Quinn raised an eyebrow. "No, they don't. What they need is to *learn some manners.*" He shouted the last part toward the kitchen, causing the noise level in there to drop. And then he waited, big arms crossed over his chest.

A moment later, Darax walked out with a full bowl and spoon. He offered both to Laura, bowing his head in contrition. "Here. We saved you some. We would never forget about you."

Glaring at Quinn, who remained stubbornly unaffected, she accepted the bowl. "I never thought you would, dear." She sent him back into the kitchen with a smile that wavered as she glanced down at the bowl. They'd been more than liberal with the toppings.

"Don't you dare shed a tear over it," Quinn warned. "It's not charity or kindness. It's your due."

"Oh, go eat, will you? Wall raising at ten."

"I'll be there. Not like you lot can do jack without me."

Very true. Quinn's unique genetic glitch made him ten times stronger than the average man. If he put his back into it, fifteen to twenty times stronger. Rumors said he'd come from a rich family somewhere on Jericho, but they'd shunned him when his abilities began manifesting in puberty. Quinn had been on his own, making his way through the worlds all by himself ever since.

Her heel chafed in her boot. Laura set aside the bowl to check it, but, as always, no obvious flaw revealed itself. "I should just get new shoes."

And new clothes while she was at it. And a mattress and drapes, and why not a whole new house?

Wake up, woman. Dreams are for those who can afford them. You live in the real world.

And in the real world, William's tea was getting cold.

~

Seven days were usually more than enough time for any half-decent Hawk to gather intel.

Not these days, and not on Anamtaigh. With the whole planet cut off from major networks and databases, precious little information moved in and off-world, and even the most basic search brought up familiar glitches hinting at Shadow interference. Someone was controlling the flow of information—which tracked with what Ms. Thane had told him about the "red soldiers" terrorizing the countryside.

But it wasn't only information they controlled. Finn got a tail on his ass the first time he stepped out of the inn. They never engaged, but three men in civvies now followed him all over Avencore, subtle as porcupines. Two had made camp in the house across the street the first night. Not Shadows, then. At least, not the Shadows he knew. They would have brought him in immediately to answer for his desertion if they were.

Whoever they were, they seemed not to know who they were fucking with. Finn was tempted to go deliver a housewarming gift of apple pie and a few broken bones. He resisted. Barely.

Nevertheless, their presence forced him to constantly readjust his strategy to keep one step ahead of them. Rather than driving up to Laura's front door, he'd made several recon trips into the region on the pretext of exploring the countryside on foot. After the first two eight-hour hikes, his tails had gotten lazy and stopped following, which allowed Finn to venture farther into the valley.

He'd watched the compound for three days in a row, and the more he saw, the more Laura's situation troubled him. Her community was totally isolated. Without getting inside, Finn didn't know how many people lived there, but he estimated somewhere around twenty-five, adults and children combined.

The compound consisted of two buildings and a rough, industrial work shed. The main house looked like three different structures stacked one on top of the other resembling a step pyramid with garden plots on two sides of the bottom and middle tiers. The second building was smaller and didn't appear to get much use.

They had little in the way of resources. A cornfield across the battered road seemed to yield some food, but it only covered about a third of the available plot. The produce gardens had as many dry, dead plants as live ones.

No livestock except a rooster.

No conveyances, either, except a beat-up old levpad.

In the three days he'd watched the valley, Finn hadn't seen a single vehicle pass through. No one came to the compound, and no one left.

This was a siege.

Shadows didn't employ long-term assault strategies like this, except in special circumstances when the goal was to break someone into compliance. But why would they bother with it in Karsengale? It wasn't as if Laura's compound housed any high-priority targets.

Except maybe Laura herself.

Finn recognized her through his binoculars, and from that moment on, she dominated his attention whenever she was in sight. The girl he'd left behind had grown out of her whimsical phase of rainbow dresses and hair ribbons into a no-nonsense woman of purpose.

A married woman of purpose.

Finn still winced every time he thought of it. The local databases had stopped recording events when the war began three years ago, but he'd found enough from the years prior to know Laura McNally was now Laura Belden, a name that fit her like a bad shoe. She and her husband, William, had founded a boarding school for orphans and children in need, and both had an active role in its operation.

The database listed the Belden School as "closed" three years ago, but it looked to Finn like it had never stopped operations, only redefined them. Instead of a school for children, Laura appeared to be running some sort of a refugee shelter, and not from the sidelines.

A clear leader to her people, she involved herself in every aspect of daily life. She never passed someone without stopping to exchange a few words or lend a hand. He watched her get her hands dirty repeatedly, treating every task, no matter how important or menial, with the same matter-of-fact approach, leading by example.

And her people loved her for it. Men stood straighter when Laura was around. Women smiled more. Children approached her without hesitation, and she always spared them a bright smile and a touch or a hug. No need to use telepathy to manipulate these folks; they obeyed her naturally because, with every action and every word, she showed them how much she cared.

Finn couldn't look away. As much as Laura's people basked in her presence, he felt it from miles down the road. Seeing her at a distance made him want to get closer, to hear her laugh and watch her eyes crinkle when she smiled. It made him forget he wasn't welcome in her world.

Laura was mesmerizing.

And she was in danger.

This morning, he'd parked the rental closer than ever, out of sight in a copse of trees three miles down the road. It was time to stop stalling. He got out of the transport, double-checked that it wouldn't be readily visible, stepped out onto the broken roadway, and stopped.

He was nervous.

Seventeen years with the Shadows, and his heart was pounding faster than it ever had before a mission. He was hyperaware of the sun's glare, the steamy heat of the day, and the road's uneven surface. He kept looking for signs of movement in the landscape, expecting an enemy to jump out at him any second. His palms were sweating, for fuck's sake.

Finn shook out his hands and slapped himself across the face a couple of times to get his shit together. No more stalling. One last paranoid look around, and he set off down the road toward Laura's compound, measuring his pace to just short of a soldierly march.

A mile or so from the main building, he noted a rise in activity outdoors. To be expected. They had a building site set up with frames and pulleys. Some kind of construction project they were getting off the ground.

A half-mile later, he frowned, watching as they started physically raising one of the walls.

And then he ran like hell.

4

At ten o'clock, all the men and a few women gathered around their wreck of a storage warehouse. Laura didn't waste time or energy thinking about all the supplies they'd lost in the last attack nine months ago. It was ancient history. Now, the foundation platform was clear, and along each of the four sides was a wall-and-roof panel laid out on the ground, ready to be lifted into place.

They'd built a rough frame as placeholders for them, and a pulley system was already strung through with ropes to lift them one by one. As proud as Laura was of their achievements, she couldn't help a twinge of disgust at how low they'd sunk. Frames and pullies, like people had used in ancient times when all the rest of civilization out there had robots and machines to construct buildings automatically in less than twenty-four hours. The walls that were about to be raised and welded into place now had taken six months to construct. Well, three, but the first set had collapsed beneath its own weight within hours of being raised.

Quinn went around to each wall, tugging on the ropes to make sure they were secure. He took his place on the far side while the rest of them lined up along the top of the first wall to go up. But no one moved until Darax tested his welding torch and checked every corner of the frame to ensure they were solid. Once Darax gave his nod of approval, Quinn took hold of the rope he'd be using to pull up the wall, looping it around his arm and his waist for leverage.

"Ready!" he shouted.

The rest of them each stepped up to their part of the wall. With the sloped roof portion in the way, they couldn't take proper hold until it lifted at least a foot or two, but they had to be prepared to step in as soon as that happened. Once everyone was in position, Laura shouted back, "Ready!"

Quinn counted off and then grunted, pulling on the rope. The top of the panel rose several inches, allowing those who were pushing up to get under it and add their strength to the effort. Quinn walked backward, hauling the bulk of the weight as the rest of them pushed, with Darax keeping a careful eye on the alignment. They needed it to go up perfectly straight so the base could slide down into its brace channel. If they were off by more than an inch, they'd have a hell of a time maneuvering the panel into place.

"Hold!" Quinn called when the wall was slightly over forty degrees or so upright. "I'm running out of room."

Laura had been afraid of this. Across the foundation, the opposite wall laid out on the ground was only a few feet away from the infirmary. Quinn needed a certain distance from the central pulley to get enough leverage, which didn't leave much extra room to walk the rope back.

"Can you hold it steady on your own for a count of three?"

Doubtful. Ten of them propped up the massive panel from the underside, and all of them strained beneath its weight. It wouldn't take much to break them. But what choice did they have? "Darax, get over here," Laura ordered.

He didn't hesitate, adding his strength to theirs. "Ready."

"I'll count off. On one, I'll slacken the rope to unloop my arm and get a grip closer to you. Four steps, max. Just hold on until then."

Butterflies in her belly. If this didn't go to plan, all of them would be crushed.

"Three."

Laura licked the sweat off her upper lip and braced her feet.

"Two."

Her hands felt clammy. What if they slipped?

"*One!*"

The weight of the wall increased tenfold, and a panicked gasp escaped Laura as she felt the solid slab inch lower. She quickly counted the seconds, waiting for Quinn to heave it back, and instead heard him shout in alarm.

Three seconds turned into seven, then ten, as they all strained to hold the wall in place. The women whimpered, losing their stamina. The men growled and grunted, trying to pick up the slack, but it was too much, and the wall inched lower still.

"Quinn!" She pushed with all her might, but her boots kept slipping in the soft earth.

"Hold on!" he roared on the other side of the wall at the same time as another person joined their ranks next to Laura, throwing his shoulder and weight against it. With their combined effort, the wall resumed its upward path, and Laura pushed harder to get it vertical. A few degrees short of that, it wobbled and then, with a screech of metal on metal, dropped into its slot.

Everyone cheered and embraced as Quinn rounded the fully erected wall at a run, wide-eyed and red-faced, rubbing his chest. "Everyone alive?"

Shaking out her arms, Laura nodded. "We had some extra help," she said, turning to thank the newcomer.

Blood drained out of her face at the sight of him.

Towering a head taller than her, with broad shoulders blocking her view of everything behind him, the man ran a sheepish, four-fingered hand across the top of his shaggy brown hair and winced something almost resembling a smile.

Laura wavered on her feet, feeling as if she'd just plunged two decades into the past. She was sixteen years old again, pleading with her best friend and soulmate to stay while her heart shattered, knowing he wasn't going to.

Twenty years ago, Finnegan Rowe had left a stupid, reckless boy. Today, he'd returned a man with serious eyes, thick stubble shadowing his jaw, and lines bracketing his mouth.

And all he had to say was, "Hey, Laura."

Of all the reactions Finn had imagined and prepared for, none had involved this. Laura stared at him with an arrested expression, the blush of strain quickly draining from her cheeks as her jaw went slack.

She didn't say a word, which left Finn at a total loss as to how to proceed. He shoved his hands in his pockets, skin prickling with the weight of a dozen judgmental stares. "You look good," he said, trying for a smile. It felt wooden and awkward.

She did look good. Maturity and hardship had chiseled away the plumpness of youth, carving her into something new, stronger, and more confident. Despite her harsh circumstances, Laura hadn't wilted. On the contrary, she'd risen to the occasion, not a damsel in distress but a hero in her own right, getting shit done as only she could.

Finn already knew he'd fucked up by leaving her the way he had. But standing in the crosshairs of her shocked stare, he felt the full weight of what he'd put her through, and it was so much worse than he'd ever imagined. It hurt to meet her gaze. The hazel depths he'd thought about every time he'd awakened from one nightmare into another now brimmed with nightmares of her own—and the pain of heartbreak that he hadn't been there to help her fight through them.

Seventeen years of spying had never prepared him for facing the monster he'd become in the eyes of someone he'd used to love. Finn had no strategy for dealing with it. There was so much he wanted to say to her that words failed him, and all he could do was stand there and wait for her to deliver the *coup de grâce*.

I missed you, he thought. *Every day since I said goodbye. Even when I didn't know it.*

The man who'd watched the wall raising from the inside stepped up to Laura's left. "And who might you be?" He was wiry, as most of Laura's people were. This one stood out by the smell of burning metal wafting out of his clothes and the grayish-blond hair sticking up from his head.

Finn felt the big guy step up behind him and toed his feet apart for better balance in case they decided to jump him. He'd never seen a feat of strength like the big guy had demonstrated minutes ago. If push came to shove, one strike from him would probably take Finn's head off.

"I'm an old friend of Laura's," he said.

"Friends of Laura's are always welcome to lend a hand," the metalsmith said.

Behind Finn, the deep-voiced giant added, "But she doesn't look too happy to see you. Laura, can you vouch for this guy?"

Laura closed her mouth, and a small, unintentional hum escaped her throat. She looked at the metalsmith, then the giant, before returning her gaze to Finn as if she couldn't believe he was standing there.

Just when he thought she was about to speak, Laura whirled on her heels, her long braid whipping around to slap the metalsmith across the body, and walked away, leaving him surrounded by a good number of hostile glares. Three women, nine men, all equally haggard, almost sickly, but all of them ready to lay Finn out if necessary.

He'd watched these people and the others in the compound for days. Aside from the big guy at his back, none of them appeared to have any special abilities, physically speaking, but they might still be telepaths.

"I didn't tell her I was coming," he explained with an apologetic shrug.

The metalsmith shoved his hand out. "Darax."

"Finn." There would have been no point in trying to maintain his fake identity. Laura would have outed him sooner or later, and he didn't want to start off with her people on a lie.

With a firm grip on Finn's hand, Darax yanked him around to face the giant and gave him a shove. "You take center. Quinn pulls, we push. Hop to, friend of Laura's. We got three more walls to raise."

~

Laura couldn't catch her breath. She came in from the bright day and stopped past the threshold. She was in the temporary storage room, where they kept all the crates that would need to be moved into the new storage house once it was ready. Stacked as they were, the crates looked like a bounty of supplies. Too bad a good third of them were empty.

She had about six feet of distance to pace from one end of the room to the other. Nowhere near enough to shake off the maelstrom swirling through her head. All of the old resentment boiled up to the surface, bringing with it all of the hurt, too. Her chest physically ached as she struggled to hold it in, to shove it back into the past where it belonged, but it wouldn't go.

The day Finn had left, Laura's world had shattered. She'd gone from the teenage high of a first kiss to having the boy she loved look at her with pure hatred overnight. To this day, she still had no idea what the Shadows had told Finn to make him so eager to leave with them. But she would never forget his parting words. "I know who I am, and I won't let you change me, no matter how hard you try. I'm going to go out there and do something that'll actually matter. Maybe one day you'll grow up enough to do the same."

The walls were starting to shrink down on her. Laura marched out of the room and toward the back of the building. Rusty's pet rooster took to the air when she burst out into the open again. Bracing her hands on her knees, she stared at the muddy ground and forced herself to breathe down the lump in her throat.

Her physical reaction to Finn's presence was the least of her problems. Colorful sparks were dancing around her field of vision, fireflies flitting about before fading out and reappearing elsewhere. Visual manifestations of intent lingering in the air minutes, sometimes hours after the person they belonged to had left.

Her shields were down.

They hadn't failed like this in years—she'd made them just about impenetrable after the attack in Hadran City. Plus, she only used persuasion when necessary these days, and it hadn't been necessary for a month now.

Laura closed her eyes and began a meditative breathing rhythm, struggling to clear her mind enough to rebuild her mental protections, piece by piece. Only when she was able to look around again and see nothing but the physical world did she trust herself to stand up straight and walk back into the house.

The kettle still had water in it. She set it to heat again and retrieved a small, clean face towel. William wanted a shave, and Laura needed something to do that would keep her out of sight.

"How goes the wall raising?" William inquired. He was sitting up on his own, a book in his hands. His smile was as welcoming as ever but didn't quite reach his eyes. His window faced the rooster's pen. He would have seen the bird spook but with his headboard to the wall where Laura had burst outside, he wouldn't have seen her freak out.

"Small hiccup, but we're managing. I needed a break and thought you could use the company."

"I see."

She busied herself at the dresser, setting out the shaving kit on its tray, ensuring the soap was mixed properly and the face towel was soaked through, warm but not scalding. When she brought it to the bed, William marked his place in the book and set it aside so Laura could put the tray in his lap.

He didn't object when she placed the hot towel on his face, but he watched her the whole time she honed the razor on its sharpening strap.

"I think the walls will hold this time," she said to fill the silence. "Darax did a good job with the welds, and the stabilizing slots were a stroke of brilliance."

"Yes, and now we shall have an entire building to store all the things we don't have."

And a strong emergency shelter in case of an attack. Hope for the best but always plan for the worst was Laura's go-to strategy.

But some things no rational person would ever think to plan for. Like a twenty-year-old nightmare rising up to haunt her in the light of day with a banal greeting and an awkward smile as if he wasn't a mortal enemy who'd waged a three-year war to exterminate people like her and everyone who allied with them.

She pulled the towel away from William's face and swirled the brush in its soap dish. "I'm going to call the Ulster brothers again to confirm delivery. The shipment should have been here by now, but they could have been delayed, right?"

William pressed his lips inward as she applied the soap there. "Are we hoping that wishing will make it so?"

"I'm trying to remain an optimist." Desperate and in denial, more like. Finished with the soap, Laura set it aside and picked up the razor blade. Her hand shook so badly, she had to set it down.

"Laura, what's going on?"

She couldn't meet his gaze. "It's nothing. Probably a little muscle strain. The walls are a lot heavier this time. We barely got the first one up."

William took her trembling hand in his. "It took all of you to raise one, so you left them a shoulder short for the other three to keep me company? That doesn't sound like the Laura I know. Tell me what chased you into hiding."

The patient way he waited for her to gather herself was enough to break Laura. She met his gaze, so full of kindness and encouragement, and blurted out. "Finn is back."

William blinked. "Ah."

"He just showed up like, 'Hey, Laura. You look good.' And what the hell am I supposed to do with that? He's a Sh—" She couldn't say it out loud. Lowering her voice to a whisper, she leaned closer to William. "He's a murderer."

"You can't know that."

"Can't I? He left with the Shadows the second he turned eighteen." The morning after their school play. Two days before his graduation ceremony. "You weren't there. It was like he suddenly became a different person, and I…" Deep breath. "For all we know, he was piloting their shuttle in Hadran City three years ago."

William raised an eyebrow. "As I recall, that shuttle crashed into Crooked Tooth and exploded. Are we assuming he has some mythical ability to reconstitute out of his own ashes?"

She stared. "Are you defending him?" He couldn't possibly.

"I am simply providing some perspective."

"Why?"

"Because you sat down and said, 'Finn is back.'" When she signaled her utter lack of comprehension with silence, he sighed and explained, "You, Laura Belden, fierce protector of our ragged little flock, left the man alone with your people. You didn't react with the alarm of someone confronted by a Shadow threat. You didn't chase him off or make him stop breathing where he stood. You came in here, sat down with me, and said, 'Finn is back.'"

Laura started to argue, but he cut her off. "If he were truly as dangerous as you're trying to make him sound, we would not be talking about it right now because you'd be too busy burying his remains underneath the new storage house, and you know it. Whatever he was in the past, whatever he might have done, you're not afraid of him now."

"No, I'm too pissed." And hurt. And ashamed. She *should* have made him stop breathing the second she turned around and saw his face.

"As well you should be—for how he treated you."

She couldn't believe what she was hearing. "But not for what he did for the Shadows?"

"What did he do for the Shadows?"

"I think we can safely assume he wasn't baking cookies to raise money for their cause!"

William gave her a look.

He didn't know the whole story. Laura had never told anyone what Noemi had shared with her before she'd died. Most of it hadn't made sense at the time, but in the days and weeks afterward, Laura had connected enough random bits and pieces to give her nightmares for months.

The Shadows had been building up their forces for decades before they ever stepped into the light. And, just like every secret military power throughout the history of mankind, they'd been trained to fight one specific enemy: those who were genetically different. People who couldn't be controlled as easily as the rest of society.

Telepaths.

Anamtaigh had made an easy target. A mostly rural planet with no military, precious little in the way of defense, and a society that, on the whole, was openly accepting of everyone. Mind reading had never been taboo here; everyone had simply adapted to the concept of people with a new skill set by setting up common sense rules of privacy. In fact, Laura and a few fellow graduates had been instrumental in drafting the first official policy dealing with telepaths to be adopted into the Anamtaigh civil charter some fifteen years ago. It had met no opposition anywhere on Anamtaigh.

Until the Shadows descended.

And while they'd been blasting Hadran City into the dust, killing people—children under her care—Laura had stood by, wishing for her best friend. The boy who'd used to race her to the lake and tease her about her pigtails before he'd turned his back on her and put on one of their uniforms.

The weight of his betrayal hadn't hit her until she'd woken up in the hospital, covered in bandages, with four of her friends and six children dead and eight more injured. And it had crushed the last secret bit of her soul that had childishly continued holding on to the hope of seeing him come back one day.

"What if—"

"No, there is no 'what if' here, William. Finn is a Shadow. Nothing can ever excuse that."

In the face of her ire, William became an icon of patience. "Is he in uniform? Is he armed? Is he hurting or threatening any of us?"

His continued defense of the villain pissed her off to no end. She refused to dignify it with an answer.

"Then you don't have enough evidence to assume he is a Shadow at all, much less convict him of any Shadow crimes. But, given your particular gift for judging one's character on sight, whether you're trying or not, your reaction would appear to weigh heavily in favor of his innocence. Relatively speaking."

"Relatively speaking."

"Well, he did leave with the Shadows. I suppose that does make him complicit in some way."

Naturally. "Have you lost your mind? Why are you being so calm about this?"

He wove his fingers together in his lap. "How would you like me to react?"

"Be angry! Be scared—hell, at this point, I'd take any emotional response at all. If nothing else, you might try summoning at least a pretense of jealousy. If he's not a Shadow, as you seem so eager to believe, he's the boy I used to love."

"I suppose I could. But to be perfectly honest, I'm rather relieved."

Had her jaw not been connected to her skull, it would have hit the ground.

"I think I'd better do this myself," William said, picking up the razor.

Laura was too shocked to argue, watching her husband carefully apply the blade to his face. He didn't need a mirror. Muscle memory kept his hands steady as he scraped away stubble with adroit sweeps. When he finished, he wiped away the excess soap, applied aftershave, and arranged everything neatly back into its place on the tray for her to put back onto the dresser.

She should say something. What he'd said to her required some kind of response. If he'd said it with malice, she wouldn't have hesitated to lay into him. But William didn't have a mean bone in his withering body, and he was honest above all else, which left Laura at a loss. She put away the shaving kit without a word, still struggling to make sense of what was happening.

"I think, in light of this new development, perhaps it's time to discuss our arrangement."

Laura tensed. "Don't."

William paused, as he always did when he felt he had to take care with his words. "We had an agreement, darling, and I'm afraid I haven't kept up my side of it."

"That's hardly your fault!"

William raised his hand a little in a gesture for peace. "I don't want to talk about how we got here. We need to discuss which way we go onward."

Laura shook her head, turning toward the door. "I can't listen to this. Not today."

"Laura."

She stopped with her hand on the doorknob.

"Finn is back," he told her.

"Not for long," she snapped. Whatever had brought him back into her life wouldn't keep him there once Laura made it clear he wasn't welcome. "And it changes nothing."

"It changes *everything*, darling. Whether you admit it or not. Whether he stays or not, he's already changed everything just by showing up. And you can spend the rest of your days hiding behind me and my soon-to-be corpse, or you can look ahead and forge a new path with—"

"Don't you dare presume to tell me how to live my life without you," she grated, throat raw and eyes burning with tears she refused to shed. "In case you've forgotten, we don't exactly consult each other when making important life decisions for ourselves. You dying doesn't entitle you to appointing my next partner. And even if I did want your opinion—which I don't—Finnegan Rowe disqualified himself the day he turned his back on me." And became a monster.

William absorbed her outburst without flinching. "And yet you still refer to him as the boy you used to love."

"*Used to.* Twenty years ago, when I was a stupid teenager with a hopeless crush. Believe me, I'm over it."

"Nevertheless, it appears to me that life has brought you both to this same crossroads for a reason. All I can say is think carefully before you decide which path to take. Second chances come by very rarely in this life. You're not likely to get a third."

Dusk fell too quickly for a planet that had the longest rotation of any inhabited world. One moment, Finn was holding a corner column, averting his face as Darax welded it into position, and the next he couldn't see the pile of bolts on the ground beside him anymore.

Quinn dropped a heavy hand on his shoulder. "You do good work. I didn't expect that."

Finn accepted the praise with a nod. He was used to physical strain and exhaustion, but this felt different. Instead of being weighed down, his body felt light in its weakness, as if he would float away any second.

Looking around, he noticed that most of the others had already disappeared into the compound. A young girl everyone called Rusty chased a pair of little kids in a large circle, then herded them indoors to get ready for supper. Only Finn, Darax, and Quinn were left to put away all the tools.

Finn stood back to take a good look at the structure they'd erected. Four walls and a roof sealed and finished. All they had left to do was put in the windows and doors. An impressive feat, considering the untrained labor force and archaic tools. Darax had said it was a storage house. It looked more like a panic room to Finn, a place to hole up for safety in case of an attack. He'd been meaning to ask about it, but it hadn't been the right time. Maybe now that he'd proven himself to be useful, the folks around here would be more open with him. He'd give it a try tomo—

"Are you coming, or what?" Darax called from the compound doorway. He and Quinn were both standing there, waiting.

Finn looked around, but no one else was left outdoors. "Me?"

Darax chuckled to Quinn, who grinned. "You put in a hard day's work, friend of Laura's. The least we can do is feed you."

Finn's heart thumped against his ribs at the mention of Laura's name. He dragged his feet toward them, palms sweating and mouth dry. They were inviting him into their home—into *her* home. Had they told her he'd be joining them for supper? Had she given her approval?

Stepping across the threshold felt like he was sneaking in where he didn't belong. A wide-open space of a dining hall dominated the main floor of the compound. It felt crowded with the many people who milled about, setting a long table with plates, cutlery, and serving dishes heaped with meager-looking fare. Jugs of cold tea were placed at equal intervals, within easy reach of anyone needing a refill. Everyone talked at the same time, carrying on multiple conversations with one another, exchanging smiles and casual touches. One big, loud family.

I could have been one of them.

Darax shouldered him along to an empty seat.

No one said a word about his presence. They didn't pay attention to him at all, except the minimum required to hand him dishes to serve himself and pass them on again. It wasn't a cold shoulder treatment. More like they were allowing him time to get used to them and find his way into their rhythm of interaction.

When they were all seated, Finn began to match names to faces. Sisa was the cook, he recalled. Short, stout, with a no-nonsense mouth and a pale scar marring her dark face across her blind eye. Darax was their mechanic, Quinn the strong man of all labors, with a smile that transformed his face from a formidable beast to a teddy bear. Down the long table, a tall, lanky man with tan skin and a solid black tattoo from his lower lip down under his chin was called Eskel. They hadn't officially met, but Finn had overheard enough to conclude that Eskel was their medic.

The children were all a blur. He couldn't name a single one of them, except Rusty, and only because she seemed to be everywhere, chiming into every conversation as if she'd been part of it from the beginning.

When Laura made an entrance, everyone cheered and raised their glasses. She'd changed into a gauzy brown dress with a braided belt to cinch it at her waist. Her face glowed in the dim light, eyes bright, but Finn noticed her spine was tense, and her shoulders were pulled back. The casual tilt of her head might fool the others, but Finn could tell she was uncomfortable. Her warm smile couldn't hide the clutch of her hands at the edge of the table.

She wrinkled her nose at their carrying-on, took her seat at the far end of the table from him, and fell into conversation with those around her. If she noticed Finn at all, she gave no sign of it.

How easily she put him from her mind, as if he didn't exist.

Meanwhile, Finn was painfully aware of every last detail of her presence. He saw her even when he wasn't looking. The way her hair draped over her shoulder, the way her fingers splayed when she rested her chin on the back of her wrist. He could smell the softest hint of her perfume, and it did something to his brain. The usual clear-headed alertness Finn had honed with the Shadows was gone. Instead of sitting back to observe and learn about these people, their chaotic group dynamic became background noise, and all he perceived was Laura.

A small hand tugged on his sleeve. "Pass a cawes, pwease?"

Finn looked down into the chubby-cheeked face of a child who'd most definitely been introduced to him before. He couldn't remember her name. "I'm sorry?"

The little girl pointed, straining across the table toward a plate of steamed vegetables.

"Oh, carrots." He picked up the plate and brought it down to her level, watching bemused as she stuffed two carrot ends into her mouth and palmed two more in each hand.

"Don't be greedy, Harley," said the adult version of the child. Finn identified her as Alexis. She'd been at the wall raising with her husband, Miguel, who was refilling a couple of tea jugs in the kitchen. Alexis had a square jaw, uneven on one side, and a crooked nose, but her eyes were all kindness and warmth. She had the elusive quality of being so comfortable around people it made them feel comfortable around her. "Chew your food," she ordered Harley, then grinned at Finn. "Carrots are her favorite."

"Dey shweet," Harley confirmed around a mouthful before she stuffed in one more piece to fill out her cheek.

"Harley," her mother warned.

The little girl quickly fisted her tiny hand around as many carrots as she could hold and ran, leaving Finn holding the almost empty plate.

"You can set that down now."

Finn stared at Harley's mother. "Shouldn't someone go after her to make sure she doesn't choke?"

Alexis, holding her tea glass by the top rim, raised a crooked index finger. "First rule of child-rearing: The more you chase them, the faster they run."

"Noted." As was the splint on her other wrist. Given the state of her face and hands, Finn assumed she was either a fighter or had met with some kind of serious accident in the last few months. She didn't have the timid nature of a victim of abuse. But she did move with a delicacy that suggested she wasn't fully healed from her injuries.

"So where are you from?" she asked with casual interest.

"Here, actually. I grew up in Karsengale."

He didn't volunteer more details, but Alexis seemed to read between the lines. "Like what they've done with the place?"

"They?"

"The Shadows," she said dramatically. "They're real, you know. Real sonsabitches, too. This place used to be so…" She shrugged away the rest of the sentence. "Well, you lived here, you know."

Yeah, he knew. Karsengale Valley had never been more than a picturesque hole in the wall, with a population of about five thousand residents per village, give or take. Karsengale Village had had roadways, a post depot, an Anything You Need store with an "If we don't have it, we'll get it" tagline, and a handful of restaurants. People had used to come here to treat Electronic Malaise Disorder, or EMD, by leaving behind their gadgets and getting in touch with nature to reset their internal clocks.

The road from Avencore to Karsengale led up and over Galant Hill. The first time Finn had crested the top, he'd looked down at the remnants of his home village, and something in him had shattered. Gone were the grasslands that should have been dotted with wildflowers this time of year. Gone was the blue-gray road painting a solid line between the checkerboard fields and the picturesque houses of Main Street. Instead of a crystal blue lake to grace the vista in the east, a brown swamp burped up plumes of steam and smoke.

He'd thought Avencore was bad with its weathered houses and empty streets. It had gotten off easy compared to Karsengale. Laura's compound was the only habitable structure for several miles. The few others still dotting the landscape were little more than ruins, abandoned, scavenged, and demolished. Many of them were already so overgrown they had become part of the scenery.

And the sum total of Karsengale's surviving inhabitants was currently contained within these walls.

Finn shook his head, still trying to come to grips with it all despite having had a week and a half to process. Ms. Thane, who still refused to give him her first name, had told him some of the story, but Finn still heard himself ask, "What happened?"

"The Shadows needed someplace to hide where there weren't a whole lot of guns to rout them out again. We put up a fight, don't think we didn't. But in the end…" She sighed. "Didn't make a damn bit of difference."

"Now they got us all by the short and curlies," Miguel said as he tipped the jug over his wife's glass to refill it. His hand shook so hard that he almost knocked it over.

Alexis caught the glass and steadied him. "Want me to do it?" She was already reaching for the jug with her splinted hand.

Her husband shook his head and gently brushed off her efforts as he pulled back and straightened. He rolled his shoulders and waited for the shakes to stop before he tried again. "Goddamn jitters keep getting worse," he muttered.

Finn clocked the worry on Alexis' face as she watched him pour. It was there for a second but gone when her husband winked at her. She smiled back, not in relief but in commiseration.

When Alexis' glass was full, Miguel set down the jug and kissed his wife's head as he dropped into his seat next to her. "What are you gonna do?" he said with a shrug. "Life goes on, right? You live it as best you can until you can't."

Finn was about to ask more questions, but Harley came back, stealing her parents' attention away. He contented himself with picking at his food, watching Laura ignore him, and listening to the conversations ebb and flow around his side of the table.

He'd almost managed to tear his gaze away from Laura for a full five minutes when a hush fell over the room.

Finn followed the direction of their stares to a painfully thin man dressed in an old button-down shirt. "I heard there was a party going on," he said with a crisp accent, his voice clear as a bell. Deep shadows around his eyes belied his proud stance, and for all that his clothes were immaculate, they hung on his bony frame. He stood close to the wall as if for support, but his hands were behind his back as if to prove he didn't need it.

Laura was on her feet instantly. "It's so good to have you with us," she said, her voice laced with anxiety. She played it off cool, but she was clearly worried for this man.

Others rose to greet him, welcoming him among them. They treated him with a great deal more gentleness than they'd shown one another. The man took time to return every greeting but kept the flow moving toward the table and a waiting chair.

When Laura, holding onto his arm, pulled the chair out for him to sit, he gently tugged free. "Is it true we have a guest with us tonight?"

Finn tried and failed not to see Laura's expression shutter. In deference to the man who seemed to have trouble standing for so long, he got to his feet and closed the distance so the newcomer wouldn't have to. "Finnegan Rowe," he said, extending his hand in greeting.

The man's smile never faltered. "William Belden," he replied, clasping Finn's hand in his bony one. "I was told you saved us from disaster this morning. We are all most grateful for your assistance." He spoke in earnest, with no nasty subtext, and shook Finn's hand firmly without trying to prove anything. But his eyes were watchful and far too knowing. "Sit, please," he invited. From the quiver Finn felt in William's grip, he was the one who needed a chair, but he seemed determined not to let it show. "I didn't mean to interrupt everyone's supper."

"You are welcome to interrupt us anytime," Laura assured him, retaking his arm.

William didn't sit until Finn had reclaimed his place down the table. Not a power move—he wasn't even looking, busily exchanging idle chitchat with the man seated on his right. It felt more like a gesture of respect. Finn didn't know what to make of it.

So, this was Laura's husband. Not at all what Finn had expected. As down to earth as Laura was, he would have thought she'd find herself someone practical, like Quinn or Darax. The elegant creature with impeccable manners seated by her side was as out of place as a swan among pheasants. William must have come from money, Finn decided. Everything about him screamed money, from the neatly pressed and buttoned shirt to the way he sat up perfectly straight, refusing to lean back, even though he was starting to sweat with the strain of it.

That shirt, like everything else around here, had seen better days. Whatever money William might have had in the past, he didn't anymore. And whatever ailment plagued him, Finn guessed he wouldn't be long for this world. Everyone around him seemed to know it, too. Their smiles were open, but their eyes were sad. They laughed easily but quietly. Everyone hung on to William's words and presence, the way loved ones clung to every aspect of their dying relative, committing details to memory to sustain them when they had nothing else.

William was clearly well respected. But he was also well-loved.

And he had Laura.

Son of a bitch.

"Mr. Rowe," William said, dragging him out of his brood. "As you can imagine, we don't get many visitors around here."

Eight people were seated between them on either side of the table, meaning everyone was privy to their conversation. They all hushed so William wouldn't have to strain himself shouting.

"I'm sure everyone is curious about how the rest of the worlds are faring. Have you seen what the situation is like outside of Anamtaigh?"

Everyone turned eager gazes on him, except for Laura, who busied herself nudging a piece of food around her plate with her fork.

Finn took a sip of his tea to give himself a few seconds to regroup. "Some. But to be honest, I've spent the last three years keeping to myself."

"But surely you must have seen what's been happening," William pressed.

"It's…not good," he replied, hyperconscious of the children around the table. "Not a lot of places got hit as bad as Anamtaigh, but the ones that were basically got obliterated."

Strategic targets taken out with psychopathic expedience. With two, the Shadows had hobbled the spread of information across the inhabited worlds. Three strikes against vulnerable banking centers had brought the galactic economy to its knees. The resulting chaos had created a smoke screen for the Shadows to start exterminating target communities with impunity.

To date, nothing Finn had seen suggested the general public had caught on to who the real targets were. Those who were aware kept it quiet to prevent potential witch hunts.

"Is the fighting still going on?" Eskel asked. He had the look of someone who'd seen some shit and hadn't slept a night since. Even his voice sounded tired.

Finn cleared his throat to strengthen his own. "Oh, yes. Not on the same scale, though. Mostly, the news these days is about relief and reconstruction efforts."

The officials who'd survived the initial purge to take over the Interplanetary Council of Governance wanted the channels saturated with positive propaganda. It wasn't good for their reelection campaigns to have constituents questioning their effectiveness in the fight against Shadows. They didn't know how much dirt the Special Unit had collected on them over the years. If they chose to release it, every politician in Shadow pockets would become a target, and there would be riots in the streets again.

Reemy perked up. "That's good news, right? It means the war's almost over."

William tipped his head in Finn's direction. "I suspect the most important part is what Mr. Rowe *isn't* saying." The man was perceptive. "How long, do you think, before the relief efforts come our way and Anamtaigh starts recovering?"

A carefully worded question, coupled with a direct, unblinking gaze. William was fishing. But he did it so casually that it intrigued Finn. How much did William know about Finn and his history with Laura?

He chose his words with care. "I think right now recovery efforts are focusing on high-priority hubs. They need to rebuild infrastructure before they can address anything else. It may be a while before they get to smaller worlds like Anamtaigh."

"Smaller or less important?" Laura asked.

"Both," he answered honestly. These people deserved to know what they were in for. "Anamtaigh may be twice the size of Earth, but it has one-tenth the population size. It's essentially a nature preserve. If I had to guess, I'd say you won't see any recovery efforts for decades." If ever. The ICG had much bigger fires to put out, and the Special Unit was busy holding back the Shadows, still waging their war while the rest of the worlds were looking elsewhere.

The mood around the table darkened. Finn could feel their hopes dying.

"Perhaps we should talk about pleasanter things, eh?" William said. "Where have they put you up for the night, Mr. Rowe?"

"I'm staying at the Thane & Owens Inn in Avencore."

"Oh, no, you can't go back tonight. Hasn't anyone told you?"

Laura flushed and ducked her head next to him.

"Told me what?"

Eskel answered, "It's not safe to drive in the night. The Shadows have stationary satellites over the valley, and their signals disrupt nav systems. During the day, sunlight radiation interferes enough to keep things working, but at night, you're driving blind in every sense of the word."

Finn had noticed that on his previous recon trips. It wasn't just nav systems—which his rental didn't have, anyway. It was the whole operating system. The electromagnetic levitators glitched, dropping the vehicle from its hover height, then shooting it upward again; the propulsion engine sped up and slowed down at random; steering became questionable at best. Anyone who didn't know how to handle themselves in a transport would panic, overcompensate, and crash within minutes.

Finn wasn't anyone.

He shrugged. "I'll be fine."

"No, that simply won't do," William insisted. "Alexis, would you be so kind as to make up a bed for Mr. Rowe?"

"Of course," she said. "We still have a couple of beds free on the third floor. It might get a little warm, but if you open the windows, the night breezes tend to cool things down nicely." Before Finn could protest, she left the table.

Finn noticed Miguel watching her go, and, for a moment, bitter envy gave him pause. Miguel and Alexis seemed to have the kind of relationship most people only got to dream about. Not a passion-swept romance but a deeply satisfying connection that made every touch and smile feel like coming home.

The kind of relationship William and Laura didn't seem to have.

"Thank you," Finn told William, who nodded in return. He was holding Laura's hand, an affectionate gesture, for sure, but not quite the same as when Miguel had kissed his wife. Laura didn't lean into William the way Alexis had lounged against her husband. Although, he supposed that was in deference to William's frailty.

Or maybe he was reading far too much into something he had no business reading into. Laura appeared content in the marriage. William looked like a decent sort who would treat his wife with the same kindness and consideration he seemed to show everyone.

William was the man Laura had chosen. End of story.

The conversation had moved on without him, and a good thing, too, since he was too busy wondering what the hell he was doing there to participate. If anyone noticed, they didn't say a word.

Eventually, the children went off to bed, and the group shrank to a more intimate size. Voices hushed and the serving dishes were cleared away. Everyone around the table pretended not to be watching William and the growing strain creasing his brow. He blotted sweat from his face three times, and on the fourth, his hand shook. Something was seriously wrong with the guy.

Finally, William had had enough. "Ladies, gentlemen, I thank you for a beautiful evening, but I think it's time for me to turn in now." He couldn't quite stifle a wince as he pushed to his feet, and he didn't object when Laura ducked under his arm and braced him on their slow way back to their room.

The rest of the company busied themselves cleaning up so as not to watch them go. With the stars of the show retreated from the stage, the pleasant evening get-together was officially over.

Sisa picked up William's plate with a sad shake of her head. It was still full. William hadn't eaten more than a couple of bites.

"Are you happy now?" Laura had to unclench her teeth to speak the words. She'd gotten William to bed in time for his legs to give out. He was pale, sweating, shaking, and undoubtedly in pain. But when she reached for the opium drops to mix in with his night tea, he waved it away. "Did you get what you needed out of your little show back there?"

At least he didn't try to deny it. "So that is the infamous Finnegan Rowe," he mused, wincing as Laura tugged and yanked the covers from under him to tuck him in. "I must say, from your description, I expected him to look a lot more…diabolical."

Laura scoffed.

"No horns, no tail. I wonder what happened to his hand."

"He probably cut the pinky off on a dare," she muttered.

William chuckled. "How long before you stop bristling, do you think? As much as I enjoy your tender ministrations, they aren't for the faint of heart."

Laura released the pillow she'd been pummeling to death while William leaned forward. Murmuring an apology, she settled him back more gently. "Was it necessary for you to strain yourself like that?"

"Yes," he said in all seriousness. "I am still your husband, feeble as I am. If the man poses a threat to you in any way, I need to know."

She rolled her eyes. "And what you saw eased your mind enough to invite him to stay the night."

"I invited him to stay because it was the right thing to do. And also, because I haven't seen nearly enough of the legendary Mr. Rowe to form a proper opinion. I should like to have a longer chat with our Mr. Rowe, I think. Man to man."

"No. Absolutely not." Laura checked the levels of each of his medications. A couple were running low.

William raised an eyebrow. "Are you afraid he'll do me harm?"

"Please. Why would he bother when you're doing such a fine job of it all on your own? Take the digestive, at least."

William closed his eyes briefly, his throat working on a swallow as he shook his head. "I'm all right. Just tired."

Between weeks of bed rest and hardly eating, Laura was shocked he'd managed to walk out of this room at all, much less all the way to the table. It hadn't escaped her notice that he'd left most of his supper untouched again.

Laura pulled his drapes closed. He wouldn't like it, but too bad. "Tell me why."

"Why what?"

She took a seat by his bed, forcing down her temper to hear him out. "Why are you dragging the man into our lives?" William always had his reasons for doing the things he did. As much as it sometimes infuriated her, he didn't always deign to share them with her. But his fascination with Finn was putting her into the middle—by design. He owed it to her to explain.

William sighed with what might have been exhaustion, defeat, or both. "Because when your judgment is clouded, it's my job to act in the best interest of our community. Your personal hurt won't let you see him as anything other than a villain. I see the potential for something better. I don't think you realize how much he could help us."

Laura snorted.

"He knows the Shadows," William insisted. "If nothing else, he can provide invaluable insight into the way they think and operate. That alone is an advantage we can't afford to pass up."

Laura deflated. "Fair. But what he knows and what he decides to share could be two very different things." Which he'd already proven during dinner. She could well believe everything Finn had told them about the situation outside of Anamtaigh, but even William had noticed Finn holding things back. In a situation as precarious as theirs, omitting a single piece of information could be as harmful as lying about ten others.

He gave her the Look. The one he'd used to give his students when they did something naughty and thought he hadn't seen. "He's also connected with the outside worlds in a way we simply can't be and has access to resources we can't even dream of."

"And again, that doesn't mean he'll share." And even if he did, the Shadows would shut him down the same way they'd shut down everyone else.

Ignoring her counterargument, he tiredly concluded, "The very things that make Mr. Rowe a threat can be used to our advantage. It is a risk, but I don't think we can afford not to take it. I know you don't like to do it, but if he does prove to be hesitant or obstinate, you do have the ability to make him more amenable, darling. Although I doubt you'll need to."

Laura rolled her eyes. "You're putting an awful lot of stock into a man you've known for a whopping three hours."

He harrumphed a weak chuckle, eyelids drooping, but he moved himself to speak again despite his words starting to slur. "Not at all. I am putting my faith in my wife of sixteen years, who's proven herself to be a formidable force time and time again. I couldn't resist you. What chance does he have?"

"The same one he had twenty years ago. He had no trouble walking away then." And she'd been a much less complicated person back then.

William's head was dipping lower. He closed his eyes, sinking deeper into the pillows. "Forgive me, darling. I think we'll need to pick up this circular song and dance another time."

"Sleep. I'll be close by if you need anything."

What he needed was a nutritional IV drip and a proper surgeon to address his ulcers and tumors. Eskel did what he could, but he didn't have the equipment, supplies, or training for any procedure more invasive than stitching up a wound.

William hummed. "Laura?"

"Yes?"

"He still loves you, you know."

He was asleep before Laura could tell him how much bullshit that was. Finn, love her? What a joke. She closed the door with care. In her room, she washed up, brushed out her hair, and put on her pajamas. The fabric had worn down to almost nothing, one strong tug away from coming apart, but it was still the most comfortable thing to sleep in on a night like this.

Too bad she couldn't sleep.

The house was completely quiet. Laura had nothing to distract her from her thoughts, and those kept bouncing back and forth between the missing supply shipment and the man sleeping two floors above her.

She turned to her side, facing the open window. A moment later, she rolled over toward the door. The blanket was too heavy. She kicked it off, hoping the cool breeze on her exposed legs would soothe her.

No dice.

She kept thinking about what William had said. As *persuasive* as Laura could be, her ability was not an easy burden to bear. Changing someone's intentions went so much deeper than surface thoughts. If she wasn't careful, she could change who they were as people. It was intrusive, insidious, and for lack of a better word, evil.

Even so, Laura would happily have taken a stab at the Shadows, but Noemi had been right back in Hadran City. Her persuasion might have been powerful, but it was limited. Humans were complicated. They didn't think or plan in a linear fashion. Often, one intent was tied to several others, to circumstances, to environmental factors—all of which played a part in their actions. The chain reaction of changing one could have several other unintended side effects.

Telling people to run could make them run straight to their deaths.

In order to successfully manipulate one person's intent in one isolated instance, she had to focus on them for several minutes. It might be doable with a civilian, but Shadows never acted alone, and they were trained to spot telepathic manipulation and put an immediate end to it by any means necessary.

And the Shadows holding her valley hostage had a cruel streak. If Laura got caught, they would sacrifice whomever she'd tried to manipulate without hesitation to protect the integrity of their unit. Then they would kill her on the spot. And then they would swoop down on the compound and kill everyone inside, just to make a point.

They'd done it before. It was how they'd taken over the valley in the first place. Any sign of dissent, insubordination, or direct attack had been met with deadly force on a terrifying scale. They'd leveled the village of Karsengale because the mayor had dared to call for military assistance. The military had never responded, but the Shadows hadn't cared. They'd only wanted to ensure no one else would ever risk trying it again.

Noemi's last instruction to Laura had been to hide. Physically and telepathically. That's what Laura had been doing ever since. Staying quiet. Staying under the radar. Keeping her family out of Shadow crosshairs.

She'd grown comfortable in her inert state.

And now William wanted her to throw caution to the wind and put her persuasion to use again.

On Finn.

Laura got up and climbed out the window, heading for the fields. Across the battered road, the corn had grown taller than her. Barring some disaster, it'd be ready to harvest in a week or two. She walked into the thick of it, curling her toes into the soft earth. No stars above. The clouds that had blown in from the east sat heavy in the air, turning the entire valley into a hothouse with the promise of rain that wouldn't come for days or weeks. But here and there, a speck of light flashed through. Shadow satellites reminding all and sundry that the battle might have ended, but the war was far from over.

"Can't sleep?"

Years of self-control practice alone stopped her from screaming her head off. How the hell had Finn managed to sneak up on her without making a sound? How long had he been walking beside her without her noticing?

And why was she almost glad to see him?

Not *glad*. She wasn't happy, more like eager to get a few things off her chest without witnesses. Oh, if only she could. Then maybe this whole heavy history between them would lie down and die already and let her get on with her life. Laura had a whole compound full of problems and complications; she didn't need this on top of everything else.

"What are you doing here, Finn?"

She couldn't make out his features in the dark of night, but she felt his gaze on her. How like a Shadow to become a pitch stain against the night. The rank fit him. He felt dark to her now. All of his former sunshine was gone, leaving nothing but shadows and ghosts. "Just out for a walk," he said. His voice was deeper, now with a slight rasp to it. So different from the clear tenor of his youth.

Laura shivered and stepped back to put some distance between them. "No, what are you *doing here?*" In the place he'd abandoned, along with her.

He didn't stalk her retreat, allowing her to take her space. How considerate. "I needed to see you. To make sure you were safe."

Her laugh was short and lacked any humor whatsoever. "You gotta be shitting me."

"Laura, I'm sorry."

"For what?"

"Everything."

Too easy. "Tell me," she prompted. "Confess your sins, and I'll decide if you deserve to be forgiven."

He sighed, giving her his profile. Avoiding the question.

"Let me start you off. We kissed." It might have been on stage as part of a play, but she hadn't imagined his pause or the look in his eyes right after. He'd felt something, too. "And afterward, you asked me to meet you the next day so we could talk. You remember that?" She did. The Shadows had cut in and led him away before she could say yes. "And when I came over, you treated me like shit. You turned your back on me, on your family, on everyone else, and you disappeared for *two decades!*"

His head dipped forward.

"Did you know your parents died in '28? I didn't see you at their funeral."

Had he flinched?

"No big deal? Okay, let's talk about something else. How about… You joining an army that ended up razing the civilized world back to a third dark age?"

"I thought I would be doing the right thing—"

"Bullshit, you did." There was no way he could have. One look at those soldiers had been enough to give Laura nightmares for a week, and Finn had just packed up and left with them in less than a day.

They must have told him one hell of a story for him to turn into a stranger overnight.

"I didn't—"

"*You broke my heart!*"

Thank heavens the corn swallowed her voice before it could carry to the compound. She was shaking, her shields hanging on by a thread. Faint pulses of a glowing aura outlined Finn's shape in the darkness. Not enough to guess at his thoughts. She shut it out.

"You volunteered to become a monster."

How *dare* he stand there and make excuses for running off with the people who'd destroyed her home world and so many others? What possible reason could ever be good enough to justify that much death?

"Go ahead, tell me some more lies. Tell me about all the great and wonderful things you did while your brothers-in-arms razed our home to dust. Or were you with them when they came for us?"

He might have been among them. The burning of Anamtaigh hadn't been the work of one shuttle but dozens, and no matter what William said, there was every possibility that Finn had been on board one of them. One of the hundreds of nameless, faceless soldiers who'd flown in trailing fire and smoke and dropped bombs on simple people going about their lives.

"Did you watch Karsengale burn?" Had he skygazed at the rainbow miasma of fallout that had hung over the valley for two weeks after? Had he enjoyed its beauty as it'd poisoned and killed the few of them still left standing? It made Laura sick with grief to think he'd been part of it. If not here, then elsewhere.

That was what it meant to be a Shadow.

Another faint flare of white—a desire to be believed strong enough to filter through her shields. "You have to know I would never be part of something like that."

"But you were!"

"No," he insisted, and the white flare brightened with the purity of truth. "I have done some nasty shit in my day, not gonna pretend I didn't. But wholesale destruction of cities and worlds is not one of them. I defected before the Shadows mobilized for attack. I didn't even know about it until—"

"Don't you get it?" How could he not? "Every day you spent wearing their uniform, you were helping them lay the grounds for this. You defected before the war? Whoop-dee-doo, good on ya, pal. We'll just forget about everything that came before, shall we?"

He offered no response, but his white aura faded to almost nothing with an intention that flowed opposite to action. It indicated a desire to hide. She'd struck a nerve.

"Do you feel accomplished now? You certainly did something that mattered, just like you wanted to. So tell me, what was the thought process behind coming back? Battle's done, fighting's over, for the most part. What exactly are you looking for? Because, in case you haven't noticed, there is literally nothing left. And if you're waiting for me to go weak in the knees and thank my lucky stars that you decided to come back, all I got is, 'Fuck you, Finn.' Fuck you and the nag you rode in on."

"I deserved that."

"Oh, you deserve a hell of a lot more," she grated.

"Go ahead." Finn opened his arms in invitation. "Lay it on me."

Don't mind if I do. Laura hauled off and punched him as hard as she could across the jaw.

Finn staggered. "Someone taught you how to fight." Was he laughing at her? "I'm glad. Show me some more."

Furious as she was, Laura didn't think to hold back. She launched at him with a quick combination of punches and kicks, and he let her land them without putting up any kind of resistance.

Someone had, indeed, taught Laura how to fight—several some-ones, who'd known trouble was brewing before any of the rest of them had caught on. Three had given their lives to protect her students when the Shadows first fell on Anamtaigh. Four more had risked everything evacuating many of the youngest and most vulnerable to safety off-world. A great many had fought, bled, and died so that she and hers could live, and Laura wasn't about to shame them by pulling a single punch.

But Finn wasn't fighting back. All he did was move enough here and there to protect himself from serious damage. Laura became single-mindedly absorbed with hitting him, to somehow avenge all the lives the Shadows had taken and destroyed—as if it would do any good. She put all of her rage and hurt into every strike, and somehow, it only made everything worse because he didn't fight back.

She didn't notice when Finn stopped taking a beating. But at some point, she brought her knee up toward his groin, and he caught it. When she followed up with a punch to his throat, he twisted out of the way, then blocked her next elbow strike with his forearm.

All of a sudden, they weren't fighting anymore. They were dancing, with Laura setting the pace and Finn flowing with her movements like so much water streaming over rocks. He didn't avoid her touch completely. The opposite—he seemed to be going out of his way to maintain contact. His hold lingered. When he shifted to avoid or deflect, he did it so she would brush across him. With Finn sticking so close she felt his body heat against her, launching any kind of effective assault was next to impossible.

And then he started giving her pointers.

"Twist your hips into the punch," he said, and though she couldn't see him behind her, she felt the hum of his intent against her entire back. It purred a need to keep going, to transfer his knowledge onto her and make it stick.

The momentary distraction cost her. Her bare foot slipped on a leaf, but she didn't fall—Finn's hold on her was too tight to let her.

"Make sure your foot is secure before you kick," he instructed.

Laura paused long enough to strengthen her shields. They kept fading and slipping, letting more of his intentions seep into her mind. It made her clumsy and gave him the upper hand. But instead of responding with anger, Laura accepted his notes and made the adjustments he suggested.

"No, don't bend. It throws off your center of gravity. If you can't twist, move."

She twisted, and he moved with her, staying at her back. His left hand briefly wrapped around the arm she'd poised to punch with her next turn. He corrected the angle of her elbow without slowing her pace one iota and turned with her, matching her move, kicking her foot into a position that felt much more stable. "There you go. Beautiful."

Laura pulled her next punch.

The cornfield was a steam box with tall stems and big leaves insulating them from any potential breeze. It mucked with her brain, making her thoughts go sluggish. Her anger began to fade, leaving behind hurt and loneliness. Twenty years of it.

Weak in the knees, she was not. But, despite everything she knew, the heartbroken young girl in Laura wanted to believe *her* Finn had come back to her. Despite everything she'd seen, the way he handled her now made her almost desperate to find some shred of redeeming goodness in him.

He'd said he hadn't been part of the Shadow attacks, and she believed him—she would have known if he was lying. He'd said he'd defected from the Shadows—also not a lie. His timing sucked, but he had come back home, which couldn't have been easy. He'd helped the others raise the storage house walls, and now he was basically picking up her combat instructions where her teachers had left off.

If she wanted to, Laura could come up with any number of ulterior motives for every one of those actions.

The problem was, she didn't want to.

Now that she'd gotten the worst of her anger out of her system, the familiarity and comfort of their young friendship was coming back to her. It felt like having her best friend back, and as much as she wanted to keep hating him for everything he'd done, Laura had missed him too much to completely turn her back on him.

It was stupid.

And yet, she was still there, going through the motions, soaking in the heady excitement of a dangerous dance beneath the night sky.

Finn caught her by the waist from behind, his big hands burning through the worn material of her top, and her belly quivered. "Your core's gone soft," he said at her ear, and suddenly her pajamas felt much too abrasive on her skin. "You're not getting tired, are you?"

Just for that, Laura jabbed back as hard as she could with her elbow. He groaned, and she gritted her teeth against a whimper. Now her arm was numb from the elbow down. She spun away and faced him, fists raised in readiness, but her heart wasn't in it anymore. From the sound of his chuckle, Finn was enjoying the hell out of this little exercise.

Saints forgive her, so was she.

Laura knew how to fight.

She'd been trained well, and she was good at it.

When he'd offered himself up as a punching bag, he'd expected a flurry of ineffectual slaps or a kick to his shin as she raged herself out. He'd expected her to quickly run out of steam, maybe burst into tears, which would have given him an opportunity to comfort her and get a word in edgewise to explain himself.

Instead, she had roundly kicked his ass.

Finn didn't know why, but it made him happier than he'd been in a long time.

Laura had grown into a force of nature. She'd gone through hell and come out on the other side strong enough to face the Devil himself. But not the Shadows. Finn couldn't undo their past. But he could make a difference in Laura's present—if she let him.

"That could have been better," he said. "Your arm's numb, isn't it?"

Laura launched herself at him. He caught her up, pinned her arms to her sides, and lifted her off the ground. Goddamn, she smelled so good, he forgot where he was and what he was doing.

Then she reared back.

"*Don't* headbutt. I move my head an inch in any direction, you'll knock yourself out."

She did it, anyway.

Luckily, he saw it coming and leaned his head to the side, out of the way so she wouldn't hurt herself. "If you get pinned like this, you don't have the leverage to strike out. Fight dirty. Bite something off. Get your feet on the ground any way you can."

And, because he didn't feel like losing half his nose, he loosened his hold enough to let her slide down his front. The fight went out of her as soon as her feet met the ground, and she froze.

Finn should have let her go. He tried to. His arms wouldn't obey.

Instead, he did the stupidest thing he could. He leaned down and pressed his mouth to hers.

Laura gasped and, for a second, turned rigid in his hold.

But then, she shivered and parted her lips. Finn couldn't have resisted if he'd wanted to. He delved his tongue into her mouth, stealing what might be the only taste of her he'd ever get. Laura's fingers curled into his shirt at his sides. She gave a little moan when he tunneled his hand underneath the fall of her long hair to anchor her nape.

Fuck, but it felt good. Like holding on to a living flame.

It felt like coming home.

All too quickly, she tore herself away, shoving free of his hold.

It took every ounce of Finn's self-control to let her go.

Laura stumbled in her retreat, catching herself a few steps away. He couldn't see her expression, but her silhouette was poised on the verge of fight or flight. Her quick breaths muffled as she raised a hand to her lips.

Finn would have given his left nut to know what she was thinking right now. But she didn't say a word, leaving him in limbo once again.

"I'm not sorry I did that," he said, breathless, cold without her in his arms.

"I'm married," Laura replied in a strange, vulnerable tone that cut him to the quick.

"I know."

Silence. She didn't move, and Finn didn't trust himself to say a word. This was different than her outburst earlier. The moment felt so fragile he didn't dare breathe too deep or loud.

"I prayed you were dead," she said after a while.

Finn flinched.

"When the Shadows came for us, and I saw what they did… I prayed you had died before they made you like them. It was the only way I could live with the memory of watching you get into their transport."

"I wish to hell I'd never left."

"Do you?"

"More than anything."

Rowe, Rowe, row your boat gently down the stream...

It was there, at the farthest edge of his consciousness, a wordless melody on the lightest down feather caress as her telepathic presence skimmed his mind. He went rigid, waiting, wanting to feel her mental touch, and he didn't care what it commanded him to do.

But it didn't come.

Laura sighed, her shoulders slumping in the darkness as all awareness of her pulled back, leaving him bereft. "Go home, Finn," she said. "Wherever the hell that is these days." She reached up to gather her hair into a twist. "Just go home and leave us be."

Finn didn't follow when she edged around him to return to the compound. He stayed right where he was, booted feet rooted to the soft earth, hands fisted at his sides. He stood there until his heart rate slowed and his chest stopped hurting.

And then he marched back across the street to the threadbare bed two floors above Laura's with only one thought in his head.

Like hell I will.

8

June 34, 3039

The first lesson Finn had learned as a Shadow Hawk was not to hesitate. The smallest opening was an opportunity. Hesitation and lack of action were the best ways to ensure failure.

Finn wasn't in the habit of failing his missions.

Convincing Laura that he wasn't one of the monsters she feared was the most important mission of his life, and he couldn't afford to make a single mistake. Which meant he couldn't afford to leave. He needed to stay close to Laura for as long as possible to make his case.

His every word and action would be scrutinized. He would have no privacy. Laura, and everyone living with her, would pry into every aspect of his life to vet his worth. They would leave no stone unturned, and he would have to maintain a dangerous balance between how much he revealed to satisfy their curiosity and how much he kept to himself for their own good.

As fate would have it, his Hawk training had prepared him for precisely this type of high-stakes situation.

The long night gave him a lot of hours to plan out his strategy. He thought it through from every angle to the minutest detail, with intricate steps and counter steps to overcome opposition in all forms. He made plans B, C, D, and E to be safe.

But going down each branch of the decision tree, he realized all his plans ultimately headed toward one unexpected, unintended end game: winning Laura for himself.

And each time he got there, Finn slammed into the one roadblock he couldn't overcome: William Belden.

His Shadow training whispered inside his mind, *Kill him. He's sick and frail. You'll be doing him a favor.*

Maybe he was the monster Laura feared.

The thought forced him out of bed before anyone else had begun to stir in the compound. These people didn't deserve the shit Finn carried on his army boots. He didn't belong here any more than with the Shadows. If he really cared about Laura, he would involve himself as little as possible. Get her community stable, get them safe, then leave and never darken their doorways again.

Finn went down the stairs barefoot, carrying his boots to avoid making noise. He didn't even notice Eskel at the tea cupboard until the lanky medic in a wrinkled T-shirt and pants nodded to him in greeting. He did a double-take, frowning at Finn, and set down the pot of boiling water. "Ran into the doorknob in the night, did you?"

Finn rubbed a hand over his bruised cheek. Laura's punch had spared him a swollen eye, but his lip was split, and he'd have bruises all over his torso and thighs. "Something like that."

Eskel shook his head and wriggled his fingers for him to come along, leaving his cup of tea unfinished.

Finn put on his boots. "Why are you up so early?"

"Can't sleep more than two hours at a time," the medic said. "So I work twenty-six-hour shifts to keep myself occupied. It's just how the fallout fucked me up." He shrugged, his gaze flicking to the back of the space where a short, dark hallway led to a set of doors. "I got off easy. Others weren't so lucky."

"Fallout?" Finn trailed Eskel out to the infirmary. This was a variable he hadn't known to account for.

"Yeah, didn't anyone tell you? We all got hit with it, everyone who's still here. Everyone messed up in a different way. Thousands of people died from it, too. Most of them in a lot of pain." He opened the door for Finn to precede him. The lights came on, illuminating a room more gray than white. Two threadbare beds on each side formed a central path toward the exam chair in the back. Seeing the chair, Finn flinched on his next step. It looked exactly like the one Dr. Wen had used. The last time Finn had come anywhere near it had been three years ago. He'd been sent to watch his oldest friend die at the hands of the doctor they'd trusted to take care of them. And then he'd watched the man get brought back to life by one of the people who were supposed to be their enemy.

"Take a seat," Eskel invited, turning to the sink to wash his hands. He had a box of gloves on the counter but didn't bother with them as he picked up a small flashlight and waited.

Finn broke out in a fine sweat. His jaw clenched at the memory of a delicate white band settling over his head and searing electricity frying his brain cells. Every time he'd sat in that chair, it'd turned him into a drooling mess for an hour after. But he'd sat in it every time they'd asked him to.

"Here," Eskel said, hooking the toe of his ragged boot around a wheeled chair and propelling it toward him.

Finn caught it and sat, cursing himself for having shown an obvious weakness.

Eskel's approach to medicine was matter-of-fact. He checked Finn's pupils, felt around his cheekbone, then had him pull up his shirt to listen to his lungs. The sight of mottled bruises over Finn's ribs and abdomen didn't get so much as a twitch. "Pissed any blood?" he asked.

"Not yet."

Eskel hummed his acknowledgment and put away his tools. "No serious injuries, that's good. I'd give you something for the pain, but we're too low on supplies as it is. Besides, something tells me a guy like you doesn't need painkillers much."

Finn pulled his shirt back down. "I can handle it."

"You got it out of your system now?"

Not even close. "Tell me about this fallout. Is everyone here sick?" Even Laura?

"Everyone I know about. You'll understand if I don't share my patients' personal health details. But yes."

"That's why William looks so weak," Finn guessed. And why Miguel shook the way he did and why his wife looked like she'd been shattered and put back together by an amateur puzzle maker.

"William got the worst of it. He ran right into the blast, trying to shield a trio of kids." Eskel ducked his head and returned his flashlight to its place. "The kids didn't make it."

Fuck.

"I did everything I could for the survivors. My clinic in Hadran City got a shipment of chem-treatments right before it happened. Everyone got a double dose."

Ever since the fallout of 2829, the government mandated every person alive to receive a chem-treatment injection directly after birth. It was supposed to stabilize a person's DNA to ensure they lived a normal life and were able to conceive again. It had been the only way to restore population growth back in the day.

In recent decades, though, secretly—*illegally*—gathered data started tracking more and more people showing resistance to those treatments, and somewhere around seventy-eight percent of them showed a great deal more. Some developed ailments that couldn't be treated and defects that ruined their lives. Others never knew they were different until something happened to cut their lives drastically short. But there were those, like his old friend John Wayland, everyone in the Special Unit, and Laura herself, who developed gifts and abilities the rest of humanity could only dream about.

That was what had driven Senator Matthew Griffith to create the Shadows in the first place. And for such a violent action, an equal and opposite reaction had formed among the chem-resistants, giving rise to a group who'd called themselves the Evolutionaries. Unlike the Special Unit telepaths who stayed under the radar and wanted nothing more than to live quiet, productive lives, the Evolutionaries had wanted one thing: to stir the pot and make it boil over.

"But, as it turns out," Eskel continued, "those of us who weren't chem-resistant before are now. And there's not a goddamn thing anyone can do about it."

"I need to talk to Laura." Finn had resources at his disposal, contacts among the Special Unit and their extended network who specialized in this sort of thing. They must have come across this already and probably had their best people working on all kinds of solutions. If he could get them here, or Laura's people there—

"She's not here," Eskel said.

"What do you mean? Where is she?"

Eskel shook his head. "You really have no idea, do you? Wow, I didn't see that coming."

"I don't like games, Eskel."

"The neighborhood Shadows have the whole region locked down tight. They put embargoes on banks, the post, everything. Any shipment that comes heading our way, they intercept. We might see ten percent of it if we're lucky. The last three were completely derailed. We're going on fumes here, and we are out of options."

Finn didn't like where this was going. "Where—is—Laura?"

"Last time one of our shipments went missing, Laura went to the Shadows and got a few things from them. Urgent necessities. Food and such. We were supposed to get another shipment this week. The way Laura stomped out of here, my guess is she gave up on delivery and went straight to the Shadows to—wait, you don't even know where they are!"

Finn was already out the door, racing for the transport he'd left three miles down the beat-up road.

~

Seventy-two miles from Karsengale

Going on a whole lot of adrenalin and no sleep was not the best condition in which to approach a gang of mass murderers. Laura briefly acknowledged this, if only to herself, as she climbed down from the levpad. Her conveyance was a flat platform that hovered off the ground to make it easier for people to move heavy loads from one place to another. In the absence of better options, they'd added an engine and a seat and repurposed it to serve a number of other needs, transportation being one of them.

The Shadow base was a former emergency supply vault bored into the side of a mountain without a name. They called it The Roost. Only a narrow footpath led up to the hover pad in front of the cave-like entrance in the saddle, but the Shadows still felt it necessary to post four sentry guards at the mountain base to screen traffic.

They were waiting for her, weapons in hand, before Laura's feet touched the ground. "What do you want?"

As tempting as it was to make them turn those weapons on each other, she kept her persuasion firmly in check and stopped a respectable distance away. Shadows always had multiple security measures in place. These guys were just for show. There'd be more of them watching everything from deep inside the vault.

Laura took down her shields enough to see angry red sparks floating around the Shadow soldiers. Trigger-happy animals. They were ready to shoot first and ask questions later if she so much as twitched wrong. She focused on those sparks, slowed their mad flight, and mellowed their color from maroon to red, telling the soldiers, "I'm here to see a man about a horse."

One of them almost smirked. The others waited for her to explain.

"You have our supply shipment. I want it back." She pushed ever so lightly with those words, fading the red sparks a bit more. It wasn't enough to make them lower their weapons, but it blunted their thirst for carnage enough so they wouldn't "accidentally" shoot her on the spot.

The two soldiers closest to her lowered their weapons. The two behind them retreated a few more steps and turned their backs to have a conversation with the black metal flame pins on their collars. Com units. One of them nodded to the front guard, and they let her through, but all four of them kept their weapons in hand just in case.

Laura was used to being on her feet most days, but the trek up to the hover pad had an elevation difference of five hundred feet and left her winded. When she reached the saddle, she paused to compose herself and get her shit together.

She couldn't see soldiers in the entrance, but the sparks of their intent hovered there, tracing lazy shapes in the darkness. Blue—they were bored and wanted to sneak away for a nap. Laura slowed those fireflies even more, making the soldiers sleepy as she crossed the hover pad toward them.

But several yards from the entrance, she slowed. Static electricity buzzed inside her mind, making the sparks waver like a mirage. She focused on them harder and the electric charge bit. Laura had enough presence of mind to keep going, covering her flinch with a sneeze. She hurriedly pulled her persuasion back behind her shields and walked past the guards at the entrance as if nothing was wrong.

Something was very, very wrong.

Walking into the cave felt like stepping into a hive filled with pissed-off bees. The sound wasn't in her ears but in her mind, pounding at her temples until her eyes watered and her nose ran. She faked another sneeze so she could wipe both and kept going across a wide-open space stacked with crates, some of which she was sure belonged to her. With every step, Laura pulled deeper into herself, thickening her mental shields to make sure they were secure.

The hum didn't hurt per se, but if she tried persuading anyone to her will, Laura had a feeling the shock she'd felt outside would be strong enough in here to fry her brain.

The Shadows had put in a telepath security system since her last visit.

Which meant this entire trip had just become a dangerous charade with no possible payoff. All around her, Shadow soldiers watched her walk past, each one armed to the teeth and alert to the smallest sign of distress. Laura kept her chin up and her gait steady, but her spine tingled with the sense of imminent pain. She'd come too far. Turning back now would only tip them off to her ability to sense their security measures. She'd be dead before she reached the hover pad outside.

The Shadow leader was verifiably unhinged, as evidenced by the burning wing tattoos along the sides of his head and the black flame insignia on the shoulders of his crimson-and-gray camo uniform. He had a broken beak of a nose, and Laura could never decide whether he'd smashed it himself or had it smashed by someone else. Either way, he seemed to be proud of it.

He'd built himself a platform six steps above the main vault floor and put a deep red couch at its center to serve as his throne. A faithful group of bodyguards were allowed to lounge on the stairs, but everyone else needed permission to approach, and Laura hadn't seen anyone up on the couch with him since the first time she'd been here, interrupting a party.

"Well, well, well, look what the rat dragged in," he drawled, grinning through a short, dirty blond beard that made him look older than he sounded. "To what do I owe this rare pleasure, Lady Belden of the Last Hope."

Laura ignored the insult. "A shipment of supplies was supposed to arrive at my compound this week." The Shadow commander, who called himself Talon, didn't respond to emotional appeals. They tended to rile him into a murderous frenzy. The safest and most efficient way to communicate with him was directly, with as few words as possible. "I haven't seen a trace of it, which leads me to believe it's now with you. I want it back."

He inspected his nails and addressed one of his bodyguards. "Vega, have we taken in any of Lady Belden's shipments this week?"

The woman seated highest on the stairs had long black hair braided in the same style as Laura's. But that was where all similarities ended. There was no softness to Vega. Her face was never anything but blank. Laura knew she was aware of everything going on around her, but she kept her thoughts to herself unless addressed directly. She wore her dog tags on a chain looped around her wrist and had a habit of idly fiddling with them—when she wasn't sharpening her knives or cleaning her guns.

Having been addressed by name, Vega glanced at her commanding officer and shook her head. "Haven't seen anything on the manifests."

Talon shrugged. "Looks like I can't help you, Lady Belden. We don't have anything here that belongs to you."

"Right. Fourteen crates of food, tools, and medical supplies just disappeared into thin air, like all the others."

"Are you calling Vega a liar?"

Vega's clinking dog tags got silenced in a clutch of her fist.

Laura bit the inside of her cheek. Without her persuasion, there was nothing else she could accomplish here. "We're done." Whirling on her heels, she headed back out. She'd have to find another way to provide for her people. The sooner she was free of this place, the better.

"Wait," Talon ordered, and eighteen Shadows stirred.

Laura stopped.

"You came all this way. What kind of host would I be if I didn't offer you a little something for your trouble?"

That was her cue to go back to the foot of his platform. From the tone of his voice, Laura had a sick feeling about what was about to come, but it wasn't as if she had a lot of other options at the moment. She turned and walked back, keeping her spine straight and her expression neutral. Her eyes still watered, and she was too close to Talon to do anything about it without signaling her discomfort. Better for them to think she was crying.

"What was most important to you in your missing shipment?"

"A crate full of medicines. ID number 1876-24." She'd had her source tag all of the crates, and she'd memorized their IDs.

Talon waved an imperial hand. "Do you happen to have a packing slip? A list of items in that crate?"

Laura rattled off every item in there. Each one meant life or death for one of her people, William among them. Of course she knew them all by heart.

"Those are all basics we have in heaps," Talon said. "You're telling me *that's* your emergency? Not food? Not tools? You mentioned both of those."

He knew damned well she needed all of it. "The medicines are what I need most right now," she told him, furious with herself. Now he knew how bad their situation really was.

"Incoming," someone said without alarm.

Talon nodded to one of his other bodyguards, a short man with bulging shoulder muscles that almost bridged the entire distance up to his chin, making his thick neck nonexistent. The man got up to confer with the speaker, then both of them left.

Laura didn't pay them any mind, waiting for Talon to play out his hand.

He made her wait a count of ninety-nine, then leaned forward on his throne, bracing his elbows on his knees. "You caught me in a generous mood today, Lady, so I'll tell you what. If you ask me really, really nicely, I might be persuaded to give you what you need."

"Please," she grated.

Talon grinned. "You'll have to ask nicer than that."

Swallowing her pride, Laura dipped her chin and dropped her gaze. "Please, will you help me?"

The bastard Shadow commander clucked his tongue above her. "I want to believe you, I really do but… Maybe if you got down on your knees."

Soldiers chuckled all around her, enjoying the show.

Laura's insides burned, her shields quivering with repressed rage. She couldn't risk doing anything rash. Hands curled into fists, bruised knuckles aching, she lowered to one knee. "I beg your mercy for my people, if not myself. Please, help us."

"Now isn't that something," Talon crowed. "Wonder what else I could make you do. For the sake of your people."

Her breath hitched as her entire body shuddered. She didn't dare look up too early, but her mental shields were a thought away from collapsing. She'd rather get her brain fried than endure whatever the hell the twisted son of a bitch had in mind for her.

When he sucked in a sharp breath, she flinched. "Vega, take Lady Belden back to her…conveyance, and make sure she gets her medicines."

It took Laura a second to fortify her knees and stand up again. When she did, Vega got up to lead the way out.

Strange, for a second there, as Vega had glanced in her direction, Laura could have sworn she'd glimpsed a hint of sympathy in the soldier's cold, dark eyes.

"Farewell, Lady," Talon called after her. "And thank you for your help."

Laura stopped. "My help?"

She was too far away already to see his expression, but his voice strained with repressed laughter when he said, "Testing our newest telepathic countermeasures. Now I know they'll work against a mindfucker even as strong as the infamous Laura McNally. Consider your crate a payment for services rendered. I trust I won't see you back here again without an invitation."

Her head swam as they laughed her out of the cave. Weak in the knees, she tripped four times on the way back down the switchback trail, once so badly only Vega's hard grip on her arm kept her from tumbling down to the base of the mountain.

But Talon was as good as his word. By the time she got to her levpad, fighting for breath and gritting her teeth to hold back a break-down, a sealed crate was loaded behind the seat. She climbed up and drove off as quickly as she could, shaking so hard the makeshift vehicle veered wildly left and right.

Only when she was safely out of sight did she stop and burst into sobs. She allowed herself fifteen full minutes but not a second more. Wiping her face clean of tears and snot, she twisted around to inspect the crate. The seal over its latch had a grid code stamped on it. Underneath, the ID number 1876-24 stood out in bright, laser-etched red.

Laura slumped in her seat. That son of a bitch. The Shadows had her entire shipment again, and Talon wouldn't release it—at least not without a higher price than Laura could pay. The medicines would help, but without all the other things, they were still dead in the water.

What else could she do? What else was there *to* do?

Now that the Shadows knew about Laura's abilities—had they always known?—she wouldn't be able to get anywhere near enough to strike against them. It would take an actual army to take out the Shadows, and all Laura had was a handful of people whose lives depended on a schedule of pills and injections that wouldn't last through another month.

She doubted the Ulster brothers would do business with her again. No scan on delivery meant no supplies for Laura and no payment for them. It would all stay with the middlemen she'd had to use to place her order, and they wouldn't deal with her anymore. She'd officially exhausted all off-world options. So where did that leave her?

With Finn as her last resort.

No. Not yet. She still had one more straw to grasp.

Dunn Rowan was a hundred and fifty miles away outside the region's border. It could be far enough to have escaped the worst of the Shadows' terror. They might still have some supplies left to share.

Laura looked up at the clouds gathering in the sky. They'd been threatening a righteous storm for days, and she didn't have a rain shield on the levpad. But if she could score even a handful of necessities in Dunn Rowan, it'd be worth the drive and the soak.

Either way, Laura couldn't go back to the compound with so little to show for her folly. She had to at least try. And who knew? She might even get lucky this time.

Technically speaking, any vehicle that could hover above the roadway had flight capability. Manufacturers programmed in a fifty-foot rise limitation to keep their vehicles from accidentally shooting into the sky if something glitched, but it could be disabled. If, for example, a former Shadow Hawk with fifteen years of mechanical training and expertise had too much time on his hands and enough curiosity to dick around with a transport rental agreement one restless night.

It never hurt to have full capabilities enabled where possible. And it stood Finn in good stead as he punched in a series of commands to push the rental transport a hundred miles an hour above its documented limit so he could fly a straight line to the Shadows' outpost he'd identified a week ago.

They saw him coming, too. But no one opened fire. Big weapons, capable of bringing down entire shuttles, traced his flight path, but he was allowed to land directly in front of the cave entrance without incident. There weren't too many people outside the Shadows with the technical know-how to do what Finn had done to the transport. It as good as announced his identity ten miles before he touched down. As a fellow Shadow, they'd take his measure before they engaged.

Six soldiers in red-and-gray fatigues he'd never seen before came out to meet him, weapons at the ready. None of them said a word.

Finn raised his hands and let them pat him down. He had a stun grenade disc stashed in his boot. Another Hawk would have known to look for it. These soldiers weren't Hawks. He couldn't tell what they were. Their uniforms were radically different from proper Shadow gear, ostentatious and bright, with black flame insignia on the shoulder. Whatever that meant.

"Identify yourself," one of the men barked.

Finn pinned him with a withering stare. "You first." Hawks didn't take orders from Hounds.

The soldier tilted his head, listening to whoever spoke in his com piece. When he'd received his orders, he jerked his weapon to the side and stepped out of the way so Finn could precede him into the cave.

Finn took quick stock of his surroundings, eyes peeled for any sign of Laura. The cave vault had been built out with meticulous care, with hermetic seals on every drawer and cabinet that now hung open behind haphazard stacks of crates and boxes. It was messy and disorganized, with too many people and not enough room to maneuver. They'd gotten complacent in their high-ground fortress. He couldn't wait to meet the man in charge.

With no visible offshoot hallways or tunnels on either side, the only path led straight back to a raised platform. At its top, a dark blond soldier with the same red-black camo pants as the rest but a sleek, all-red jacket stood at ease, watching Finn approach.

Finn's first impression of the man was of a grenade with the pin pulled out. From his boots up to his waist, he was a foot soldier. From waist to neck, he was an officer. And from the neck up, he looked like a common thug hopped up on so many stimulants his head was on fire. Oh, wait, those were just tattoos.

"Finnegan Rowe, as I live and breathe."

Finn stopped five feet from the bottommost stair. He knew that voice. But no, it couldn't possibly be… "Latham?"

The former Hound grinned wide. "It's Talon now."

The last time he'd had any interaction with Latham Bigellow, Finn had called him the living, breathing reason why no Hound would ever be a Hawk—right before John Wayland had wiped the floor with the guy. It seemed nothing had changed. Not Latham's aspirations to go Hawk or his total inability to do so. "Shit, man, I thought you were dead." But, of course, a weasel like him would have found some way off a sinking ship.

Latham—Finn couldn't bring himself to accept a name as ridiculous as Talon—descended the stairs, hand outstretched in welcome. "Nah, I was the first one out of Green 24." He said it with so much pride, too.

"Soon as they brought back that crazy redhead bitch, I took myself a shuttle, grabbed a few buddies along the way, and got the fuck outta dodge." Noticing that Finn wasn't about to shake his offered hand, he clapped him on the shoulder instead and asked, "How did you get out? I heard those mindfuckers leveled the outpost in, like, two hours or something."

"I got lucky," Finn said. He'd had Michael, the Evolutionaries' strategist and prognosticator, to vouch for him as they'd hauled John Wayland's half-dead weight out of the compound and into the waiting shuttle. It'd been the last thing Michael had done before he'd dropped to the ground and died out of the blue. Hadn't even made it all the way through the door.

He'd used to think Michael had held on long enough to make sure Finn survived. It would have meant Finn wasn't a waste of flesh. That, despite everything he'd done, he was worth keeping; he had a purpose and a future.

"What—that's it?" Latham prodded. "That's all we get? The opening skirmish of a three-year-long war leaves all of, what, ten Shadows standing, and we don't even get a story out of it?"

Finn gave him a tight-lipped smile.

Latham's bloodshot eyes twitched with an impending eruption of his volatile temper, and Finn braced himself for an attack. But just as quickly, Latham laughed it off. "Fucking Hawks, am I right?"

The men closest to him chuckled along, but their hearts weren't in it. They shifted from foot to foot, looked at each other, or dropped their gazes to avoid eye contact.

They were afraid of the man.

"So, what brings you to my doorstep?"

Tread lightly. Latham appeared wildly unstable. Managing him would require finesse and a silver tongue. "I'm looking for someone."

"Are you now?"

"Uppity bitch called Laura Belden. You heard of her?"

"May have, may have. The one with all the sick freaks down in the valley, right? Yeah, I know that one. What do you want with her?"

Finn turned his face a little to better show off his bruised cheek. "What do you think?"

"Oh-ho-ho-ho, don't tell me that little pacifist got the drop on a Hawk. How fucking drunk were you?"

"Very," Finn said darkly, imagining Latham with his tongue ripped out and shoved up his crazy ass.

Latham shook his head. "Never thought I'd see the day. *Never.*" He pointed to Finn as he addressed his people. "You see this? The big bad Hawk got a shiner from a girl. My respect for Miz Belden just went up a notch. Maybe I shouldn'ta been so quick to send her packing, eh boys?"

"She was here?" Finn kept his tone even while his pulse raised enough to thump out a quick rhythm in the side of his neck.

"Hmm," Latham hummed in the affirmative. "About an hour ago. Crazy bitch was going on about some shipment we stole or some shit. I gave her a little treat to shut her up and sent her on her way."

Finn took a second to breathe down a wave of ill-advised fury. "I'm surprised."

"Why'zat?"

He shrugged with casual disinterest. "Hear tell she's the kind who can make you break your back trying to suck your own balls."

"Oh yeah? Who told you?"

That was a trap. "Didn't. I hear things. I don't converse."

"Hmph." Latham circled Finn, sizing him up. He'd been a disgrace as a Shadow and was fit to be put down now. Nothing but a stray dog sniffing at his legs. A rabid stray dog. "Guess we wouldn't know, would we? Not with our defenses up and working like a charm."

"What, the guns out front?"

"Nah, man, check it out." His men jumped out of the way as Latham shot across the open space to a metal framework tower about twelve feet tall with a small white gizmo attached to the top. "See this? Anti-'path tech adapted from the helmets they gave us. Remember? Not a single mindfucker could touch us in those. Well, this takes it to a whole new level. 'Path comes in, tries to mindfuck us"—he clapped his hands together—"*Bam!* The signal rebounds back on them and fries their little mindfucker brains right out through their ears." He laughed, a mad, feverish gleam in his eyes. "It's genius."

Finn raised his eyebrows. "Impressive." He looked around the space, counting an even dozen towers in plain sight, and he'd lay odds Latham had more tucked away for backup. "You still got any of those helmets left? I could use one. And I can pay you for it. Name your price."

With one of those, he could try to reverse engineer its function to protect the wearer from whatever the hell those white gizmos did. It probably wouldn't hold up for more than a few seconds, but for the right telepath, seconds were more than enough to take someone out.

Latham left the tower slowly, watching his own feet on his way back to Finn. He came close enough to practically breathe into Finn's nose when he looked up and said, "Tell you what. I'll make you a sweet ass deal right here and now."

Not about to give an inch of ground, Finn twitched his chin in encouragement. "I'm listening."

"I'll give you your very own helmet to do with whatever you want. All you have to do is put on a uniform again." Eyes rabid, he flashed his teeth in a feral snarl. "And bring me John Wayland's head."

About to clench his hands into fists, Finn stopped himself and stared the psycho down, waiting for another bout of laughter at his own joke.

But Latham just stared back at him, breathing hard, like he was barely restraining himself from tearing into Finn's throat. Rabid fuck-ing dog.

From the corner of his eye, Finn clocked movement up on the stairs. He didn't dare look away, but the clink of dog tags sparked a memory. The blurred figure was female, with a rope of black hair hanging over one shoulder. And he'd bet his last credit she had at least one throwing knife in her hands right now. Vega Ortiz.

She could wait. Right now, Finn had a bigger problem. He tilted his head to the side. "How crazy are you right now?"

The mad dog grinned wider, and all the rest of them waited, frozen. "Latham—"

"It's *Talon* now," he snarled.

Sore point. Good to know. Instead of correcting himself, Finn continued. "John Wayland is dead. And if he isn't, he wishes he was."

Latham bounced on his feet with glee. "Oh, you're gonna play coy, how cute!"

Finn gritted his teeth. "First of all, either get a breath mint or back up a step."

Latham laughed and danced a little circle away from him, then faced Finn again. "This is gonna be so good, I can tell. Go on, keep going."

"I was there when Dr. Wen strapped Wayland to the chair and fried his brain. He flat-lined in front of me."

"And yet *my* sources say the mindfuckers dragged a Hawk off-world before they leveled the place." His mouth twisted. "Burying our brothers like so much trash."

So now they were brothers. What had they been when he'd gone AWOL and left them for dead to save his own ass? "I don't know what to tell you, man. I saw what I saw. If John Wayland's still alive somehow, he's a vegetable, at best."

Latham thought this over for a second, the few rusty wheels in his head turning with an almost audible creak. "Well, I guess if his head's as fried as you say, he won't miss it, will he?"

Fuck.

"Now come on, let me show you what you're buying into."

When he rounded the raised platform, Vega pushed to her feet to follow, a throwing knife in her hand and her signature blank mask firmly in place. She inclined her head for Finn to precede her after Latham.

It was true. No Hound would ever be a Hawk. But Vega had come damned close to breaking that stereotype. She'd been disqualified on a technicality, and rather than wash her out of the Shadows completely, they'd put her in with the Hounds. Finn wasn't surprised to see she'd made it through the war. Finding her here, shadowing Latham, of all people—that was a shock. He'd have expected better from her.

"Walk," she prompted to get him moving.

Finn walked but made a mental note to find a way to talk to Vega in private later.

Beyond the central vault chamber, a hallway wide enough to fit two hovers side by side led deeper into the mountain. On one side, big glass doorways opened into labs that had already been trashed and cryo units that had been shut off. Hanks of animal pelts and old bones littered the floor in there.

On the other side, plain doors had been blown off their hinges to reveal utility closets and empty storage shelves. Latham turned into the last plain doorway on the right. Lights turned on in there as he crossed the threshold.

A few yards behind, Finn and Vega were now out of sight of him and everyone else who'd stayed back in the central chamber. He took a chance. "The fuck you doing here, Vega?"

He didn't expect an answer, but a few steps later, she gave him one. "Surviving."

It told Finn everything he needed to know. Whatever Vega had gone through to get here, joining Latham's band of thugs hadn't been a choice; it'd been a last resort. It also told him that people who joined, whatever the circumstances, weren't allowed to change their minds and walk out later.

Figured the one aspect of Shadow structure Latham would keep alive and well was their brutality.

"You ready to live instead?"

They were at the door. Just before they turned into it, Vega murmured, "You suicidal?"

The room Latham had led them to was decked out like an army barracks. Bunk beds filled the space, some made with the same militaristic precision their owners had learned in basic training, others not so much. No privacy, no personal storage for any of the bunks.

No windows, either. Someone obviously cleaned in here. The floors were gleaming, and any clutter was confined to the bunks, but laundry didn't smell to be a priority.

"Eh?" Latham prompted. "Impressive, right?"

Sixty-eight beds, total, around fifty-seven of them confirmed occupied. Eight were bare mattresses, and the rest were too neatly made. Could have had occupants or not. No way to tell until all of the Shadows actually filed in there and claimed their bunks.

Time to gauge Latham's intel. "Looks like the whispers were true."

"Whispers? What whispers?"

Finn shrugged. "Word among the Shadows off-world is that someone's pulling us all back together. Someone who's established a new outpost on a quiet, backwoods world where we can rebuild again without anyone giving enough of a shit to try and stop us."

Latham preened, taking Finn at his word. He had to be completely cut off from the Shadows—which made sense, considering he'd deserted his unit and left them all to die. His ego would be his downfall. Finn didn't have a word for what Latham had accomplished here, but a thriving, cohesive Shadow unit it was not. They were well-provisioned, but their lack of discipline made them weak. Not to mention the fact that they were led by a certifiable madman.

But madmen were dangerous.

"So, you ready to sign on the dotted line, or what? You get your own bunk, your own uniform—your own helmet, as promised. You'll have your brothers at your back and first pick of whatever supplies we bring in." He shrugged humbly. "Call it a gesture of respect for your former rank."

"Former?"

"We're all equal here, brother. Shadows first and last."

Finn made a show of walking around to inspect the space. He went past Latham to the doorless opening behind him and found communal bathrooms, clean enough but littered with personal effects all along the sinks and shower stalls. Finn had seen prison blocks more inviting than this place. "It's impressive, but I dunno, man."

"What, your back already get used to that soft bed you pay for in Avencore?"

Finn played it ignorant, raising an eyebrow at Latham. "You know where I'm staying?"

Latham scoffed. "Bitch, please. That's nothing. We got the whole region under surveillance. No one comes onto my turf that I don't know about. We clocked you two weeks ago."

Again, with the pride. Finn knew every one of Latham's Avencore men by sight. They weren't exactly subtle. He could take them all out in two hours if he wanted to.

Latham bounced on the balls of his feet like he was expecting another compliment.

Finn didn't give him one. There was only so far he could pretend to have sunk before he lost all credibility as a Hawk.

"So, what now?" he finally asked.

"What you did before you got here, that's your business. All I care about is what you do next." Latham offered his hand. "Are you a Shadow, or do I make you a stain?"

Had there been only Latham to consider, the threat would have been laughable. But he had sixty-some-odd other soldiers standing between him and the way out. As good as Finn was, he wasn't that good.

And then there was Vega.

She'd made herself comfortable by the barracks door, playing with her knife. She showed no interest in the discussion, but Finn wasn't fooled. If he remembered correctly, Vega had an eidetic memory. She would remember every word and gesture and form her own opinions on the matter later. Of all the soldiers he'd seen so far, including Latham, Vega would be the most formidable threat. He needed a better read on where her alliances were.

"I'll think about it," he said.

Latham didn't take kindly to having his hand go unshaken twice. "You'll *think* about it?"

Finn gave the man a tell. He twitched his eyes a little to look like he'd just stopped himself from rolling them in the face of Latham's ire. "I came here on business," he explained, lying with the truth. "It's not finished yet. Unlike some, I don't bail before the mission's done."

"How interesting." Latham circled him again, putting on more of his tiresome airs. "You still think you're better than the rest of us. Your intel must be old, Rowe. Around here, if you don't fall in line, your *business* becomes mine. And I can make your *mission* go bust real quick."

Arms loose at his sides, feet stepped wide at ease, Finn calmly met Latham's challenging stare. "You do that, and we're gonna have a problem."

Latham's mouth twitched. He held his ground for a decent while, but when Finn didn't back down from the staring contest, something in him shifted. Latham backed off a slow step and looked Finn up and down. "One month," he decided. "Don't ever let it be said that ole Talon ain't a fair kind of guy. Finish your *business*. Get your affairs in order. Then we'll talk again."

Fin turned on the balls of his feet to head out.

"Rowe," Latham called, and Vega casually pushed away from the wall, ready to step into Finn's path if he didn't stop. Her expression never changed, but the tilt of her head and the subtle flicker of her gaze communicated a clear warning. "The next time you come here—because you will—I'll expect you to have Wayland's head for me."

Finn gritted his teeth and marched out. Only one set of footsteps followed him, creating a window of a few seconds between Latham and the rest of his soldiers. "What the fuck is this?" he asked Vega softly without turning around or moving his lips too much.

"What you see is what you get," she replied, low and neutral.

A shirtless soldier strolled across the end of the corridor, glancing in their direction. They were out of time. Finn pushed his luck, anyway. "Not good enough. Give me something."

"I'll give you some advice. Leave while you can."

The shirtless soldier stopped to wait for them, grinning and flexing his pecs. "Yo, Vega, what's happening, baby? You ready to take me up on this?"

"No," she said. Without looking at her, he knew her expression hadn't changed in the slightest.

Having witnessed her deal with this sort of thing back in the day, Finn hoped the guy would keep pushing so he could watch Vega break his face. But he appeared to have at least a handful of brain cells left. He walked off with a good-natured laugh.

One last chance as they rounded Latham's platform. "Push comes to shove, where do you stand?"

She didn't answer.

Back in the thick of things, Finn glanced over his shoulder. Vega had reclaimed her seat on the steps, leaving him to find his way out on his own.

The men had returned to their usual tasks, ignoring Finn altogether. He took the long way around to the exit, passing the com station to see what he could pick up. The screens showed aerial maps of the region and sound waves of chatter he couldn't hear. Latham hadn't been lying. Based on the maps, he had eyes and ears over the whole valley and then some. But it fell short of Avencore, which would explain why he'd put boots on the ground there.

Finn didn't linger but paid close attention to every word they spoke.

Dunn Rowan was mentioned more than once, immediately making it a place of interest.

The two soldiers who'd guarded his rental stepped aside when he climbed back in. They didn't return to their posts until Finn got the vehicle up above the hover they had sitting on the pad. The same guns that had brought him in followed him back out, tracing his flight path until Finn couldn't make them out anymore.

He set a roundabout path toward Dunn Rowan, stopping briefly in several places he remembered from his youth. They were all ghost towns, shattered and overgrown, without a soul in sight. The thriving network of villages that had made Karsengale Valley such an adventure to explore twenty years ago was gone.

It was about midday when he reached Dunn Rowan. Much like Avencore on a smaller scale, the village looked haggard, with half of the houses damaged or destroyed, but at least it still supported a small community. Finn cruised down the main street to see what might have caught the Shadows' attention, but nothing stood out.

Until he spotted a familiar figure turning the corner out of sight a few yards ahead.

Not wanting to draw attention to either of them, he passed the intersection without turning into it, but he pulled over at the charging station on the next block.

Laura was okay. She was unharmed and looked like she was busy going about her business as usual, none the worse for wear.

Throttle down.

He took a deep breath and shook out his arms, but the tremor in his hands lingered.

She might have dodged one bullet, but the volley wouldn't stop coming. This situation with Latham was going to be a problem. He couldn't even approach Laura now without making things worse for her. Latham might decide to mess with her just to see if it got a rise out of Finn. He couldn't risk it.

But he couldn't leave, either. The thought of Laura in Latham's crosshairs switched his brain into combat mode. He needed to regroup and figure out what to do. Without his usual gear or backup, he was flying blind with one hand tied behind his back, and the stakes had never been higher. Had it been only Finn, he wouldn't have hesitated to go after Latham head-on.

With Laura in the middle, the smallest mistake could jeopardize her life and the lives of her people. Which meant he now needed to come up with some reason for being in Dunn Rowan in the first place.

One more deep breath and Finn got out of the rental to use the charging station facilities.

Something occurred to him when he splashed cold water on his face in the tiny but clean bathroom. Why had Laura set herself up in Karsengale with Dunn Rowan close enough to relocate? She had some means of transportation available to her, and the Shadows hadn't stopped her from using it to come here. What was stopping her from moving all of her people into the village?

The answer literally glared him in the face when he stepped out again. A haggard old man Finn assumed to be the station owner waited for him with his arms crossed and his feet stepped apart. "We don't like strangers hanging around here," he said.

"I won't be staying," Finn assured him.

"We don't like strangers passing through, either."

Tough shit. "I'm getting the sense that you don't like strangers here."

The old man's glare deepened. "What do you want?"

"Just picking up a few essentials in the store while I recharge. Then I'll be on my way."

The old man narrowed his eyes. "You one of them red soldiers?"

What was that, the new official greeting on Anamtaigh? "Definitely not a soldier. Got two left feet and a missing pinky." He held up his left hand to prove it.

Mr. Friendly didn't look convinced.

Their conversation had attracted more guards in the form of two younger men who now flanked Mr. Friendly. They had the look of farmers about them.

Finn sighed. "How do I get out of this in one piece?"

"Quickly," one of the farmers said.

Finn nodded. "Fair. You going to follow me to the store and back?"

"What're you buying?"

"What do you have to sell?"

The young farmers exchanged a look.

Mr. Friendly answered, "Not much for the likes of you."

"Really? I've got money. Cash," he added to sweeten the pot.

They didn't go for it.

"Money's only as good as what you can do with it," Mr. Friendly informed him. "We do business in trade here."

Finn took a good look around. The village main street only had one open storefront, and the two people he'd seen walking through the doors had carried in as much as they'd carried out. It would make sense for a community so dependent on what they could produce themselves to guard their resources closely. Dunn Rowan looked as isolated as Karsengale, only with more people. They didn't have enough to share with outsiders. And, if no supplies were coming in, money, even cash, would be useless.

Even if they could be persuaded to welcome twenty more hungry mouths among them, Laura and her people wouldn't be any better off here. Limited resources could only stretch so far, no matter how willing people were to work for their rations.

Finn turned back to the conversation. "Well, all I have is the rental, and I can't trade that."

"Guess it's time you moved on, then."

"Guess so."

They let him get back into the rental and glared at him until he drove off. Not the friendliest place he'd ever been, Dunn Rowan.

Back at the edge of the village, Finn pulled over by a dried-out grove of fruit trees to get his bearings. In the few minutes he'd spent interacting with the welcoming committee, he'd lost sight of Laura, and now the weather was starting to turn. He couldn't linger without attracting more local attention, and he couldn't go back to Laura's compound without alerting the Shadows.

His best course of action was to take his chances in Avencore. As the rain began to fall in earnest, Finn raised the transport high off the ground and made a straight line back to town.

10

Rain was pouring down in heavy sheets when Laura returned to the compound with a full levpad and a passenger. She pulled up by the new storage house, happy to see the windows and doors had been put in and closed against the rain. There were still a few hours of sunlight left, but not many. An important thing to keep an eye on for the sake of her passenger.

Her people must have been watching out for her. Quinn came running out into the rain when the levpad stopped and helped them unload the sealed crate of medicines and two open boxes covered by rain sheets.

Laura's passenger checked everything to ensure it hadn't been damaged, then nodded to Laura. "All set, then?"

Laura offered her hand so he would know there were no hard feelings. "All set."

He shook it but quickly let go and returned to the levpad, driving off with it back to Dunn Rowan as fast as the vehicle would move. He had time to get there before dark, but it'd be a race before he started losing maneuverability.

"You traded our levpad for supplies," Quinn guessed.

Laura couldn't look at him. "I didn't have a choice."

Catching a hank of her hair between his fingers, he gave it a light pull. "And this?"

She rubbed the back of her neck, which was fully exposed and cold now that her hair had been shorn to below her ears. "What? I just wanted a change." And the trader in Dunn Rowan had thrown in something infinitely more precious than hair in exchange for her braid—good deal in Laura's book.

Quinn didn't say anything, but the look on his face was enough.

"We'll make do," she promised him. "You know I wouldn't let anything happen to any of you if I could help it, right? We needed these things more than a levpad."

"Because you have a strong man on hand to carry the load. No, yeah, I get it. It was a good call."

"Oh yeah, that's totally why I did it," she snarked. "We only keep people around as long as they're useful, right? And it's not like you've been pulling your weight."

He had the good sense to flush.

"You want to know why I gave it away? Look around. The storage house is done. There's nothing else we can do around here that we can't do on our own." They couldn't afford to make any more big improvements if they wanted to. "One problem solved. Now I have to solve the next one—the fact that we're all starving."

"And what happens if we need to get out of here in a hurry? The levpad wasn't only a tool. It was our exit out of the valley."

He wasn't wrong. The closest thing they now had to transportation was an antique wooden wagon out back. It could barely be considered decoration. Without a propulsion system, and with all the roads as damaged as they were, the wagon wasn't good for any form of travel.

"I'll walk to Avencore and steal us a proper transport tomorrow, okay?" She was only half joking. "Can I just handle one emergency at a time, please? Maybe get some sleep before tackling the next one?"

Quinn flushed. "You're right. I'm sorry."

She hated seeing him so dejected. Putting her hand on his arm, she made him meet her gaze. "You have no idea how much it means to me that you care."

"We all care, Laura. Maybe if you let us in on the decision-making process every once in a while, we might be able to contribute something more than muscle around here."

She flinched and dropped her hand. "I didn't know you all felt this way." Another blow to her heart. How many more could she take before nightfall? It seemed like all she ever did lately was take a beating. Life was kicking her ass so hard she couldn't get her bearings anymore, and Laura didn't know how much longer she could keep going this way.

Quinn shrugged. "All this stays here?"

Laura unsealed the crate and loaded his big hands with a few small medicine vials. "These go in for William, Reemy, and Miguel. Eskel will need to sort through the rest in the morning and restock the infirmary." She took a basket of vegetables and a light linen pouch wrapped in plastic from one of the covered boxes. "I think I'm about ready to call it a day. How about you?"

Grunting in agreement, Quinn headed back into the compound, hunching over to protect the medicines from rain. Laura took an extra second to breathe back the feeling of an unnamable bad nipping at her heels before she closed the door securely behind her and splashed across rain puddles into the compound.

She was immediately assaulted by people cheering to see the vegetables and exclaiming over her short hair. She received hugs and kisses left and right, which was almost enough to convince her she'd made the right decision in Dunn Rowan, not just the only one available. They would need a vehicle of some kind eventually. But they needed food now.

Sisa took the basket in hand, her good eye glowing to see such bounty. "The things I'll do with you," she crooned to the radishes on her way to the kitchen.

"All right, all right, everyone take two steps back," Eskel told them. "Let the woman breathe, will you?"

Someone threw a towel over Laura's head before they all retreated. Eskel came up to her to check her over.

"I'm not made of sugar," she told him. "Can't melt in the rain."

"I know," Eskel assured her, in no way dissuaded from a thorough inspection. He picked up her hands and lifted them to the light, exposing the bruises and swelling on her knuckles. "Just wanted to be sure." Lowering his voice for her ears only, he asked, "Are you okay?"

Laura scoffed. "Please. You should see the other guy."

"I did. That's why I'm asking."

Laura freed her hands to hug him and kiss his cheek. "And I love you for it. But I'm perfectly fine. Actually, I want to have a word with Finn. Where is he?"

Everything she'd seen with the Shadows and in Dunn Rowan today had hammered home how right William had been about involving Finn in their plans.

Her people needed help.

Finn had the means to help them.

It was Laura's responsibility to ensure he did.

And, while she was prepared to use any means necessary, a small part of her still hoped she could talk him around without using persuasion. After all, she didn't need him to play the altruistic hero. They technically had the means to pay him whatever his mercenary heart demanded—once they recovered access.

And, as much as she hated admitting it to herself, it'd be a lie to pretend she wasn't looking forward to their negotiations.

Last night had been eye-opening. Once she'd gotten all the fight out of her system, she'd enjoyed sparring with Finn. Laura was used to people touching her constantly—couldn't avoid it in a household as crowded as this—but it'd felt different with Finn. The whole time they'd fought, every brush of his skin against hers had felt like it should have been accompanied by an appreciative purr. Laura couldn't explain it, but never before had fighting felt so much like foreplay.

"Well, if he's not with you, I don't think he'll be coming back."

Laura went cold. "What?"

Eskel had his doctor's face on. It was a no-nonsense expression he always wore when examining a patient who wasn't doing so well. She hated when he used it on her. She could never hide anything from him when he studied her so closely. "He chased out after you this morning. Hasn't come back since. I can guess at the reason why, but I'd rather not."

"He didn't go after me to the Shadows. I would have crossed paths with him."

Eskel shrugged. "Like I said, I'd rather not guess."

Finn was gone. All her big speech planning had been for nothing. All her mental preparations to ignore everything that'd happened between them last night and pretend it han't affected her in the least—wasted.

He'd kissed her as if he'd been waiting to do it for twenty years. He'd clutched her to him as if an entire army couldn't pry her from him until she'd pried herself away on her own.

I'm not sorry I did that.

God, neither was she. Twenty years of could-have-beens and might-have-beens. His kiss had swept her up so thoroughly she'd almost been willing to forgive it all.

But, once again, Finnegan Rowe had fucked off into the sunrise and left her holding the emotional baggage.

Eskel was still watching her.

Her face felt numb. "I need to go check on William."

Eskel squeezed her shoulder in passing. She barely felt it.

William was still up when she'd composed herself enough to enter his room. No doubt waiting for her. For his sake, she plastered a smile on her face. "I brought you something."

"Did you now?"

Laura knelt by his bedside, so she wouldn't get rainwater on his sheets, then pulled out the linen pouch and unwrapped it from its plastic cover.

William brought it straight to his nose and breathed in deeply. "Oh, darling, how you spoil me," he said on a long, appreciative exhale.

Laura grinned. "I thought you might like it. Yorkshire Gold, or so they said. We should have enough there to brew up at least ten pots of proper English tea."

"Is it my birthday, and no one told me?"

"I just wanted to do something nice for my husband," Laura said with a shrug. "You've been so down lately. I hate seeing you like that."

William cupped her cheek, then ran his fingers through her short hair. "And what's this?"

"Something nice for myself. What do you think?" She turned her head left and right to show off her new haircut. It wasn't a total lie. The idea of selling her hair had been at the back of her mind for years. Dunn Rowan had a master wig maker, and real hair carried a premium. Not as much these days, but still. Laura hadn't been growing hers out for vanity. Long hair was a nuisance most of the time. A liability in a fight.

"You always look beautiful to me," William said. He sounded exhausted.

"Have you been waiting up for me all day? You didn't have to."

"I worry when you go to the Shadows. There's always the chance you won't come back. Like our new friend, Mr. Rowe."

"Good riddance," she muttered.

"You don't mean that."

She tugged at a loose thread in her sleeve. "Don't I?"

"You'd be a fool to pass up an opportunity for help, no matter the source. And if there is one thing you haven't been for a single moment in all your life, it's a fool."

As a matter of fact, she could think of a few.

"Well, it's all moot now. I told you he wouldn't be around for long."

Although, even by her expectations, a surprise appearance and immediate exit felt out of character.

It was petty and childish to be so torn about the whole thing. Laura was glad Finn was gone. But she also regretted it. And somewhere in the back of her mind, she worried about what might have happened to him. He'd said he'd defected. How would Talon react to a traitor encroaching on his territory?

What if Finn was hurt?

What if he'd decided to sign back on with the Shadows?

Laura rubbed her face to hide. She was too raw and worn out to hold on to her neutral expression for much longer. One day. One goddamned day of Finnegan Rowe back in her life, and she was a basket case.

"Did something happen between you two?" William asked.

Laura waved that away. "Nothing important. But the Shadows have become an even bigger problem, and I don't know where to go from here."

She told him about the stolen shipment and Talon's little mind game, omitting the humiliation he'd put her through and focusing on how royally screwed they were now that the Shadows were shielded against her persuasion. And then she told him about her day in Dunn Rowan and the deal she'd made in exchange for the levpad. Scott Gully, the farmer she'd given it to, had promised her five months' worth of produce delivered on the vehicle on a weekly basis.

Laura had made sure he'd be well motivated to make the long, dangerous trip, but she'd seen the state of his farm for herself. Mr. Gully didn't have much to spare, and Laura hadn't had it in her to rob him blind. If his yields didn't cover what he and his close ones needed, the delivery would not come.

"Perhaps the time has come to reevaluate our position, darling."

Laura picked herself up and sat properly in the chair by his window. "Not this again."

"You must realize we're not going to win this fight. We are stranded here, with no way to sustain ourselves. It's time to leave."

"And go where? And how do you propose we get there? Without access to funds, we can't even get *to* a shuttle, much less *on* one."

"The old Islingtons' ranch is only a four hours' walk. If they still have a horse or two, perhaps they could be persuaded—"

"I am not leaving you behind," she declared, knowing where his little speech was headed. Four hours of walking would mean closer to eight or nine with a group their size, lugging all their belongings. It'd be a struggle for most of them and something William couldn't manage on his best day.

William closed his mouth and waited for her to calm down.

"Besides," Laura continued in what she hoped was a more logical direction. "If the Shadows catch wind that we're evacuating en masse, they might decide to get nasty."

William nodded, dipping his head to hide his face, but not fast enough. She caught the disappointed droop of his mouth and the sadness in his eyes. "One day soon, you won't have me to use as an excuse to bury your head in the sand."

She flinched. William was too polite to ever snap at someone, much less her, which made any reproach from him as cutting as it was unexpected. Another thing Laura had let herself forget: her husband might have been physically frail, but he was far from a pushover.

"You brought back enough supplies for two weeks of proper, hearty meals. My advice, if it means anything at all, is this: Don't ration. Get everyone fed and strong, and *leave*, however you can, whilst you still can."

She shoved to her feet. "This conversation is over."

"Are you really going to sacrifice everyone inside this house because of me? Everything we've worked for, fought for, bled for, you're going to let me die with that much guilt on my soul, knowing they all suffer, because you won't let me go?"

"*No one* gets left behind," she snapped back. "Isn't that what we agreed when we started all this? We save as many as we can, and no one gets left behind. We're supposed to be a family, William. Don't you dare ask me to trade one life for another. I already have enough misery in my heart. I am not going to add to the count."

She slammed the door shut between them before he could say anything else, but his words kept ringing their accusing chorus over and over in her mind. Laura was cornered. She had nowhere else to turn; no one else she could appeal to for help.

William wasn't wrong. The logical way out was through the Islingtons to Avencore.

But she wasn't wrong, either. That kind of trek, on foot, would leave them far too exposed for far too long, and there was still no guarantee that the grass would be any greener in Avencore. Farther from Talon, maybe, but Laura suspected that nothing short of leaving Anamtaigh altogether would free them from his reign of terror.

Which left her exactly where she was now: at the end of her rope, with no way out.

I wish Finn hadn't left.

Wait.

It wasn't as if anyone had seen him board a shuttle this time around. He might not have actually left.

What was it he'd said last night?

He was staying in Avencore at the Thane & Owens Inn.

Laura sat at her little table in the corner and turned on her com screen. She only used it when necessary—the model was old and damaged, and she never knew which call would end up being the last one before it died. As it was, the screen glitched and wouldn't respond to her touch. She had to stab at it hard with her finger to pull up the local directory and find the inn.

When the call connected, the resolution was so bad she couldn't make out the person on the other end. The warbled voice belonged to a woman. "Hello? Who is that? What do you want?"

Not a greeting she would have expected from a business establishment. It caught Laura off guard, and for a second, she thought she'd made a mistake.

"Something's wrong with your com," the woman said. "I can't see you, and if you're talking, I can't hear you. Did you want to make a reservation or not?"

Sounded like the right type of business, at least. "Uh, I'm looking for a guest who's—"

"Hello!"

Laura adjusted the com in its holder. "Hi, can you hear me?"

"Yeah, what do you want?"

She leaned closer and shouted at the device, enunciating as best as she could to make herself understood. "I'm looking for a guest who's staying with you. Finnegan Rowe?"

The connection froze for a second, and Laura held her breath. "…ver heard of him. You got…ong place, lady. No…name here."

"Are you sure? He's tall, with brown hair, and a missing—"

The device shut down.

"—pinky."

Laura's hands shook when she took the com screen off its holder and gently placed it into her desk drawer with all the other gadgets that had died over the last three years.

It marked the severance of her last link to the outside world.

The beginning of the end for all of them.

~

Avencore

Finn had learned an extra trick or two since severing ties with the Shadows. Being cut off from his established network of contacts didn't mean he couldn't create new ones. Better, with the Special Unit's seal of approval, his options had expanded tenfold. He didn't like leaning into the SU's resources—it made him feel beholden to them. But this wasn't about him; it was about Laura.

As soon as Finn returned to town, his Shadow tails latched on and followed him from the grocery store to the post depot to the barebones community center. The empty rooms with entertainment screens and consoles built into the walls put every visitor on display. The Shadows couldn't blend into a nonexistent crowd, so they were forced to either fall back or come up and introduce themselves.

They fell back.

With a little more breathing room, Finn took over one of the entertainment room consoles and hacked it to make a call.

"Pizza Palace, how can I help you?"

"I need an extra-large thin-crust galaxy supreme." It was code for a secure, long-distance one-way relay transmission. The connection would pass through a number of different relay pods, just like the Pizza Palace, and each one would scramble the signal in a different pattern along the way to become untraceable and, best of all, completely private.

The sweet-faced young girl on the screen nodded and gave him her profile while she put in his order. "Delivery to your current location?"

"Yes."

"Got it. May I ask how you heard about our restaurant?"

She was asking for the message recipient. "Gal named Bree the Pizza Queen sent me your way." It was one of several code names for his get-anything black-market dealer. This particular one communicated the need for urgent delivery. "She said the pizza was out of the world." A coded message to let the girl on screen know that Bree was located at the only relay pod not on the ground—it was a space station in orbit around Mars 2.

"Oh, we love Bree! She gets us so many repeat customers. Okay, so that's one extra-large thin-crust galaxy supreme coming up! Scan your chip for payment."

He did.

"Excellent. Your pizza will arrive in thirty minutes. Thank you, and have a wonderful day!"

The video cut off, but a virtual keyboard took its place. He typed in two short messages and sent them off. Bree would get them in a couple of hours. One would result in Finn receiving a package addressed to Bree at the Avencore post depot tomorrow. It would accept his fake identity—which he'd just provided by scanning his chip—as an approved proxy for pickup and include every item on his short but specific list.

The other message would be delivered to the one person Finn counted on to respond with the required urgency.

When it came to telepathy, Emma Calen was a unique specimen in an already small group of individuals. She'd been born with her abilities, whereas most telepaths didn't develop theirs until puberty or later. As a result, her brain didn't follow any comprehensible rules—a fact the Shadows had grossly underestimated back when they'd captured her before the war. Instead of breaking down and falling in line, she'd gone feral and leveled their outpost without mercy. All while still recovering from the damage they'd done to her mind during her imprisonment.

Three years later, she was not only in charge of the entire Special Unit network but also collecting strays from the other two sides of the conflict. With the organized strength of the SU, the chaotic guerilla tactics and underground connections of the Evolutionaries, and the strategic competencies and intel from deserted Shadows, Emma now had an army at her command the likes of which could change the face of civilization. And she was putting it to work to do exactly that—in her own loopy and incomprehensible way.

As unhinged as Latham was, he still didn't hold a candle to Emma for one simple reason: he was still fairly predictable.

The only thing Finn could predict about how Emma would react when she got his message was that it would be swift and involve extreme prejudice against Latham and his Shadows. For her, this war was personal. The Shadows had made it so when they'd scrambled her brain and, for all intents and purposes, crossed her boyfriend off the local census. As soon as she learned the Shadows were harassing a local telepath and had put out a bounty on her comatose man's head, Emma would take matters into her own hands and probably forget Finn was even in play.

Not that he planned to let her bench him. Finn still had too much at stake to let Hurricane Emma sweep through Karsengale unchecked. But he'd done all he could for today. The battle would resume once he was fully equipped and had a solid backup squad in place on the ground.

For now, he just needed to maintain the illusion and wait for his pizza to arrive.

Finn restored the screen to its original function and selected a movie for some background noise while he planned out his next course of action.

11

June 35, 3039

Breakfast started as a cheerful affair with a bounty of foods they hadn't seen for months. There was so much to choose from that Sisa set the hall table. The meal turned into a party, with the whole family laughing together, sharing a rare moment of carefree joy.

It all died when Laura told them the news.

The hall plunged into silence. Even the kids who weren't yet old enough to understand the significance of a broken com picked up on the adults' change in mood. Most of them huddled close to their caretakers. Some started crying. No one touched another thing on their plate.

Then, out of nowhere, Quinn slammed his big hand on the table and pushed his chair away so hard it screeched across the floor. "I'm going out," he said before stomping outside into the pouring rain.

He didn't come back again.

By noon, Laura began to worry.

Two hours later, she started losing her mind.

Quinn's heart could give out at any time. With Eskel nearby, they had a chance to revive him, but out there, on his own, he could already be lying dead in a ditch somewhere.

She endured another hour before she got her raincoat and headed out the door.

Eskel met her there and took hold of her arm. "Ready to go," he said, immediately changing her trajectory toward the infirmary. They both got soaked along the way, and Eskel slammed the door shut as soon as they got inside. "What the hell are you doing?"

"I'm going to look for Quinn. Someone has to."

"Brilliant plan. Let's go. Where do you want to start?"

Laura deflated. Quinn wasn't one to wander. If he needed space, he usually went out to the cornfield and returned an hour or two later. This time he hadn't stuck around within sight of the compound, which gave them three hundred and sixty degrees of options for where he might have gone. And with the rain and mist clouding the valley, visibility would be a problem. They could walk right past him lying in a puddle and not notice.

The Shadows, Finn, William, the com, and now Quinn…

It was too much.

Laura's knees buckled. "I can't do this."

Eskel caught her and helped her sit on one of the beds. "Breathe, Laura. No one is asking you to do anything."

"Oh? Who's going to do it, then? Will you go talk to the Shadows next month when our food runs out? Should I send Alexis to Dunn Rowan for supplies? Maybe William can help with the corn harvest!"

The infirmary door slammed open, admitting a pale, shivering Quinn drenched through and through. "Or Quinn can go talk to the Islingtons," he said, teeth chattering with cold.

Laura and Eskel sprang into action at the same time. Eskel guided Quinn to a bed, yanking his sopping shirt off him along the way. Laura grabbed a heated blanket and threw it over Quinn's shoulders, then ran to the back cabinet for Eskel's Quinn bag. It was an emergency kit for the worst-case scenario, with everything the medic needed to treat Quinn's heart condition in any situation short of an actual arrest.

"What the hell were you thinking, man?" Eskel berated the big guy, piling more blankets over him as Quinn stretched out on the bed. His booted feet hung off the edge.

Laura handed over the kit and got to work on Quinn's boot laces.

"Closest settlement," Quinn said quickly between shivers. "Went for help."

So much for her not needing to do everything. Laura checked a glare at Eskel. This wasn't the time. She wrestled Quinn's boots off. He wasn't wearing socks, and his toes were white, starting to turn blue. "Eskel?"

He glanced at Quinn's feet but, at the moment, he was too busy to address them. The heart monitor was in about as good a shape as Laura's com. He had to take great care when applying it to Quinn's chest and taking it off again. If it broke, Quinn's lifespan could be shortened drastically.

Laura took hold of Quinn's feet and started chafing them to restore blood flow.

"Stop," Eskel said. "We need to warm his core first, or the cold will kill him."

She stepped away at once and turned her back on them so they wouldn't see her wrestle down the immediate stab of panic.

"Heart's still thumping," Eskel said. "Don't think I need to stab you today. But you're here until I say you can leave."

It was a stay of execution at best. Without surgery, Quinn was living on borrowed time. Eskel's treatments managed his condition, but nothing short of a heart transplant would cure him.

Once Laura got herself under control, she returned to Quinn's bedside and brushed his wet hair away from his face. "How far did you get?"

"All the way," he said before a hard shudder caused his jaw to clench.

"How are they doing over there?"

To say there was bad blood between Laura and the Islingtons might be a stretch too far. But they definitely weren't friends. Back when Laura and her group had first started setting up the compound, she'd gone to the Islingtons to see if they might want to pool resources and work together to get through the war. They'd chased her off before she could get a word in edgewise and threatened to shoot any other trespassers on sight.

"Gone," Quinn said. "No one th-ere."

"What?"

Quinn tried to turn on his side and curl up, but Eskel stopped him. "I need you to lie flat, buddy. That's our last monitor you're wearing."

The big guy made a small sound in protest, but he did follow the medic's orders.

"Talk to me," Laura prompted to distract him. "What did you see?"

Quinn shook his head. "Nothing. House empty. Animals gone.

Bugged out."

"Recently?"

"Month, maybe." He shifted around in his blanket cocoon. "Pocket."

Eskel reached under the blankets to root around in Quinn's pockets and pulled out a small device. It almost looked like a beat-up old personal com, but much bulkier. The wrist strap was gone, and the flexible screen, thicker than it should have been, was half torn from the scuffed black brace that housed all the electrical components.

"This look like a normal com to you?" Eskel asked.

Laura shook her head. "Not that I've seen."

The device had definitely taken a beating, but it didn't look like Quinn had dug it out of the mud. It was wet from his trek, but there was no dirt or dust—it would have been stored indoors, away from the elements. The brace had jagged grooves along the seams, like someone had tried to pry it open, and the screen had holes in it on the torn side. Someone had worked on the device, possibly to attempt repairs, but without proper tools.

Quinn voiced what they were all thinking. "Sh-shadows."

The Islingtons had somehow gotten their hands on a piece of Shadow technology. And now they were gone.

"Did you see anything we could salvage? Tools, supplies, anything?"

Quinn shook his head.

"If they left, they would have taken anything useful with them," Eskel said. "And if they didn't…"

"The Shadows would have taken it for themselves," Laura finished. Either way, it didn't affect their situation at the compound. "Do you think this could still be repaired?"

Eskel made a face. "I fix people, not electronics."

"Maybe Darax could take a look at it." If he could use components from their dead com, he might be able to fix this one.

"To what end?"

"What, you don't think we could use a functioning com?"

The medic raised an eyebrow. "And if it ends up being synced with the Shadows?"

"Then all the better." They could tap into their communications, learn what the soldiers were planning, and maybe get a step ahead of them for once. At this point, Laura would take any leg-up she could get.

Eskel stepped away and turned his back. His shoulders rose and fell with big, deep breaths. When he faced her again, he looked furious. "You, of all people, know what those sons of bitches are capable of. The second that thing turns on—if it even can—they will know."

"S'a ch-chance," Quinn said.

"I can't just do nothing, Eskel. I can't sit here and wait for the end."

"You want to fight," the medic said in a dry tone that made it a mockery and an accusation at the same time. "Your back is to the wall, and you want to strike out any way you can."

"Yes!"

"Then do it on your own," he snapped. "You want to orchestrate your own death your way, that's your prerogative, but you don't get to make that choice for the rest of us."

Laura flinched.

"I don't have the answers here, Laura, but I'll tell you this much. You start messing with that thing, and I'm out."

Laura looked at Quinn, but the big guy didn't have any more to say.

The gadget in her hand felt too heavy for its size. She didn't want to give up on the hope it represented. But Eskel was right. It was just another straw, one too small to make a difference. All it did was present her with a faster way to die.

"Finn would have known what to do with it."

She had no business thinking about him, much less in any heroic capacity. But a part of her still wished for him the same way she had since the first time he'd left. Laura would pay any price to have him on their side right now.

Eskel sighed, his ire deflated. "Finn's not here."

No, he wasn't. He hadn't shown himself since the cornfield, and he was no longer at the Avencore inn—if he'd ever stayed there at all. Which meant that, even if they managed to get the com working, Laura had no one left to call.

"This isn't the end for us, Laura," Eskel said. "We're a smart bunch of people. We'll put our heads together and figure something out."

"Always do," Quinn added.

Laura nodded, trying her best to give them a brave smile.

If all else failed, she still had one last card to play. She could give herself over to the Shadows in exchange for the safe extraction of everyone else off-world. It had always been a last resort at the back of her mind. Now, it looked like it would become her only option—sooner rather than later.

"We'll be fine," she agreed, giving Quinn's hand a reassuring squeeze. Then she dropped the com into the nearest trash bin.

July 1, 3039

Latham had put more watchers on Finn. Three had already been set up in the house across the street, but now there were two extra at the end of the block and more in downtown Avencore. All of them were dressed in civvies and pretended to blend in with the crowd, but they stood out like red flags everywhere he went. Stiff, blank-faced, rough-voiced. Finn doubted they fooled anyone.

It stuck in his craw that Latham thought so little of Finn and so much of his men.

It also severely limited where he could go and what he could do without telegraphing his every move to Latham. So, when the sun came up, Finn decided to go for a jog. Some exercise might help him get a better perspective.

He set out from the inn, heading toward downtown. Avencore looked slightly better in the light of day. The residents made an effort to create an inviting town center, with touristy businesses and quaint restaurants ready to take a credit from anyone who still had some. But there was a bleakness in their eyes and an edge of hunger in their smiles that they couldn't disguise all the way. The people here were less desperate than those in the valley, but not by much.

Finn's path took him past the Daily Grind Café with its lovely outdoor seating area. At the moment, one lonesome customer sat at the table with his stiff back to Finn. The Shadow didn't need to see Finn coming; he had four lookouts around the square covering every entrance and exit. Finn knew the second they informed him he had company. If possible, the man stiffened even more, almost sitting at attention as he leisurely picked up his coffee cup to take a sip.

He set it back down, far away from him as Finn ran up. Good. He didn't like causing property damage. Pretending to stumble, he rammed into the Shadow and smoothly slammed his head against the table's metal rim to knock him out.

"Shit, sorry, man." He righted the now unconscious soldier, giving him a more natural pose than he ever could have achieved while awake, and in the same motion, slipped his fingers into the inside of his collar. They came away with a flat metallic disc of a com unit between them. "You good?" A soft snore answered him. "Yeah, you're good. Have a nice day."

Finn jogged down to the intersection and stopped. Pressing the com unit to the side of his neck, he looked at the brand new cuff on his other wrist as he spoke. "Northeast corner shop window." Out of the corner of his eye, he saw the Shadow there back up deeper into the store. "Westside, red transport." That one hunched down in his seat as if it would make him invisible. "South end sidewalk." The jogger heading toward Finn along the sidewalk across the street took a hard left into an alley and disappeared. "And southwest rooftop." Finn looked right at the Shadow up there to get his point across. The sniper held steady for an impressive three seconds before pulling back and out of sight.

"One warning," he told all of them. Then he dropped the com on the pavement and ground his heel into it before continuing on his way. He nodded to the grocery clerk in passing.

Nice old man, with a facial expression perpetually on the verge of tears, but he greeted every customer with a smile. "Looks like rain again," he said, as usual.

Finn grinned at him and responded, "Doesn't it always?"

The clerk chuckled and waved him off.

Finn ran one more block to the post depot, where he turned left in the direction of the local high school. He'd established this route weeks ago to make the Shadows feel in control. If they thought they knew his routine, they wouldn't expect a deviation.

Coming up on the alley behind a restaurant, Finn braced himself.

As soon as he cleared the corner, the Shadow hiding there grabbed him and used his momentum to spin him toward the waste disposal chute. Finn was ready. He took the running start, kicked himself off the chute, and rebounded back in full fight mode.

The Shadow managed to twist away from a punch, which made him cocky enough to grin. "Didn't see me coming, did you, asshole?"

Finn straightened from his fighter's crouch and clasped his hands behind his back. He quirked an eyebrow at the Shadow in silent invitation to do his worst. This one seemed to be in marginally better shape than the others, so Finn didn't expect him to attack foolishly.

He also didn't expect the son of a bitch to pull a gun on him, either. Finn ducked, rushing the Shadow. The gun went off over his head, scorching a black mark on the decorative brick wall at the end of the alley. Lethal setting, then, which meant the Shadow was fair game.

Finn relieved him of the weapon in three deft moves. The Shadow put up a decent fight, but he was out of practice, and his anger made him sloppy. When he pulled a knife next, Finn stopped playing nice. The Shadow charged. Finn side-stepped, taking hold of the man's knife wrist. A twist here, a little force there, a shoulder positioned just so. A split second and the blade slid into the Shadow's throat, still securely in his own grip.

"One warning," Finn said as the Shadow choked and gagged.

He was still somewhat alive when Finn threw him down the chute and waited. At exactly eight o'clock, the bottom of the chute opened, releasing its contents onto an underground conveyor belt for transport to the municipal incinerator. Not a drop of blood on the ground. Aside from the scorch mark, there was no evidence a fight had ever taken place in the alley.

Finn picked up the Shadow's discarded weapon, tucked it into the back of his waistband, and turned his back on the chute—

—to find a young kid at the mouth of the alley, staring at him slack-jawed.

Fuck.

The kid looked no older than sixteen, a classic rebel with spiky hair dyed dark green and an old leather jacket four sizes too big. And by the look on his face, he'd seen enough to implicate Finn in murder. If he ran off to tell the police—

"Dude, that was *awesome!*"

What?

"That was a soldier, right? I knew it! What are you, like some sort of superhero? I've never seen anyone move so fast before. Can you teach me?" The kid was bouncing on the balls of his feet, his eyes bright and excited.

This was not good. "I don't know what you're talking about." Finn stretched his arms up and leaned to one side, then the other. A runner pausing for a workout. Nothing more.

"Oh, right." The kid winked. "I didn't see nothing. But seriously, can you teach me?"

Finn dropped the act. "No."

"Aw, come on!" He followed Finn out of the alley at a jog, but already out of breath. "There are more of them in town, you know. I could help you find them. I got eyes everywhere. I know when someone doesn't belong."

So do I.

"And no one ever has to know about—"

Finn grasped the kid by the throat and shoved him into the next alley, pinning him against the wall. "One warning," he said, the same way he'd said it to the Shadows.

It was an empty threat, but the kid didn't know that. His eyes went buggy, and he closed his mouth with a snap. Terrified. But he didn't cry, or scream, or beg for mercy. More spine than a lot of adults Finn had come across in his day. He didn't want to hurt him.

When he was certain he'd gotten his message across, Finn slowly released the boy.

"You don't belong, either," the kid said in defiance, a bitter twist to his mouth. "But you just cleaned a pile of trash off the street. That makes you one of us."

"Stop. Talking."

"They hang around our school. That's why half of us don't go anymore. One of 'em tried something with my friend Sadie, and the teacher stepped in to help, so the soldier stabbed him and left him for dead."

Finn didn't want to hear this. He had his own problems to deal with.

"And last month, Ms. Alder from the community center went missing. She had a husband and newborn twins."

Finn turned to go on his way again. "Not my problem."

The kid jumped into his path. "I don't care!" Now there were tears in his eyes. Desperate, frustrated. He was so ready to fight but didn't have a snowball's chance in hell of making any kind of difference. "Far as I can tell, you're the only one badass enough to take them on. That means you *have to*."

"I'm not a hero." He tried to get around the kid again, and again the kid stepped into his path.

"No, you're a killer. And right now, that's what we need."

He was not going to let this go. The look on his face said he was halfway to a vigilante suicide quest already. Finn had just shown him a Shadow *could* be taken out, and now the kid was ready to go off and die trying. And if he managed to convince his little rebel buddies to join him…

Fuck.

"You want to be useful?"

The kid's eyes went wide as saucers and fiercer than a lion cub about to pounce on his father's tail. "Hell yeah!"

"*Shh!*"

"Right. Sorry."

Finn made a show of looking around for potential eavesdroppers, then pulled the kid deeper into the alley. "If I give you a mission, can I count on you to stick to it and not go off script?"

An eager nod.

Finn gave him a measuring once-over. "All right, here it is. Go back to school."

The kid deflated, "What ev—"

"I can't go there without making a lot of people nervous. You can."

Understanding dawned. "What's the mission?"

The kid was driven and desperate. The worst possible combination. Finn needed to give him something to keep him occupied, but not enough to get himself into trouble. "For now, I want you to watch and learn. I need intel. How many soldiers in and around the school? Whom are they talking to? Who is friendly with them?" He pointed a stern finger at the kid's nose. "Do—*not*—engage. If you blow my cover, I will kill you."

"Can I have the gun?"

"No. But you can have this." Finn pulled a small throwing knife out of his boot. In his hand, it looked tiny. In the kid's, it suddenly grew to deadly proportions. "Not a toy," he warned. "Last resort only. You pull this, you better be prepared to die using it. One of those soldiers sees you with it, you're a corpse."

Wide-eyed, the kid nodded and slipped the knife into his pocket. "Do I meet you here again tomorrow for a debrief?"

"First rule of spying, kid. Never become predictable." Finn pulled a small roll of credits out of his pocket. "When you have something to report, go to the grocery store. Buy a bread roll for every soldier you counted that day, an apple for every person who fraternized with them, and a juice bottle for every kid you believe to be in imminent danger." The kid looked half-starved. At least this way he'd get a little something to eat. "Do not say a word to anyone about me. If you see me around, you don't know me. Mind your own business."

"But what if I need to talk to you?"

"Don't."

"But what if it's an emergency?"

Pitbull with a bone. "Buy a bottle of hard liquor."

"They won't sell it to me. I'm a minor."

"Exactly. Now get out of here before I lose my patience."

The kid firmed his mouth. "I won't let you down."

Finn shrugged. "You do, you die."

The kid had the temerity to grin, then extended his hand. "I'm—"

"No names. From now on, you're Moss." It fit with the color of his hair.

His chest puffed out. He liked the codename. Or, more likely, the idea of having one. "Got it." He looked like he would say more but then just nodded and murmured a quick, "Thanks," before running off.

Finn hoped to hell the boy didn't get himself killed before week's end.

He waited until he was sure Moss was gone before he emerged from the alley, making a mental note to talk to the grocery store clerk later today.

"That was kind of sweet."

Finn reacted on instinct, pulling his newly acquired gun on the woman who'd snuck up behind him.

Vega knocked the barrel aside, and the shot scorched a black line along the wall. Then she stepped back and held up her hands. Her no-nonsense expression never changed, and her hands were free of any knives. "Not like I could have knocked."

Funny, in her own way, that was exactly what she'd done.

Finn lowered the gun but kept his finger on the trigger. It was as much of a truce as he could allow. If Vega wanted to talk, he'd let her. But he wasn't about to let down his guard around her.

Seeing he'd stood down, Vega lowered her hands to her collar and flipped it outward to show him there were no coms on her. "The others have pulled back to base camp."

"You'll forgive me if I don't believe you."

"Wouldn't expect you to." She pulled up her sleeve to reveal a flexible screen wrapped around her wrist. Activating it with a few taps, she showed him a map of the area with red dots to indicate where the Shadows were. "Confirmation. Talon's got us all chipped like dogs, so he can always know where we are."

The map showed only one red dot within a mile: Vega.

The gesture could have been a declaration of intent or a carefully orchestrated manipulation. If she was genuine, Vega risked a hell of a lot by approaching Finn out in the open and revealing sensitive information about the Shadows. It would mean her situation was desperate enough for her to take Finn up on his subtle offer of help. If she wasn't, then her visit was part of some larger strategy on Latham's behalf after his full-court press at the vault had failed to bring Finn to heel on the spot.

Plans within plans, subterfuge, and manipulation were all on par with Hawk training and well within Vega's wheelhouse. But that level of sophisticated scheming felt beyond Latham's mental abilities. Vega's boss was a true Hound with an ingrained mindset of shoot first and sort through the wreckage later. Finn couldn't imagine him utilizing Vega's skills like this.

Either way, it meant Vega was currently at the helm, and Finn was curious enough to play along—for now. He tucked the gun back into his waistband. "You have my attention."

"What are you doing here?"

"Consider it a homecoming."

Vega nodded. "Planning to stay a while, then?"

Finn half-shrugged his non-verbal answer.

"Talon doesn't like rogue Shadows interfering with his business." A warning to tread lightly.

"Yeah, *Latham* made his stance on that pretty clear already." Warning noted and dismissed.

Unlike her psychotic boss, Vega seemed to understand and respect Finn's aversion to joining up with him. She even twitched the corner of her mouth at Finn's utter lack of respect for their institution.

"What's he got on you?" he asked.

Vega's jaw tightened. "A leash." Her physical reaction spoke volumes more than her words.

Finn took a calculated risk and matched her transparency with a little bit of his own. "What's he want with Laura Belden?" With the direct mention of her name, he'd just claimed her under his protection.

Vega quirked an eyebrow. It confirmed Finn's worst fears. Latham wouldn't have driven Laura and her people into such a desperate corner unless he had plans for them. The siege was textbook Shadow recruitment strategy at play. Torture at a distance: break the subject in such a way that the Shadows became their only hope of relief. By the time they agreed to whatever the Shadows wanted, they'd be grateful for the opportunity.

And now that Finn had declared himself, it put him in clear and direct opposition to Latham.

The conversation had reached an impasse. Vega had gone as far out of line as she could and having drawn a line in the sand, Finn had no other moves to play.

Vega could report it all to Latham, but Finn doubted she would. She'd likely stand back and watch the game until she had no other option but to get involved. The way the board was laid out in his mind's eye, Finn figured Vega would likely end up being the deciding factor in the outcome of any conflict.

"I guess that's it, then," he said, bringing their meeting to an end.

Vega nodded. "Seems to me you're short a knife." She pulled one of her infamous blades from its sheath on her upper arm. Vega didn't skimp on her weaponry. All her knives were custom-made from a unique metal alloy that reacted to friction by becoming harder. Every time she sharpened one, she made its edge stronger. The one she offered, perfectly balanced on her index finger, gleamed. It would fly true and cut bone like butter.

Finn had seen other Shadows fight and die, trying to steal one from her. He accepted the gift with the same gravity she showed by offering it. "See you around."

As another show of truce, Vega nodded and turned her back first. Finn watched her casually walk down the block and turn the corner before he tucked the knife into his boot sheath and continued on his way.

Exercise. Always an excellent way to gain perspective.

July 3, 3039

Anamtaigh's weather patterns had a halting rhythm to them. The rain continued pouring for two whole days, with sporadic breaks in the deluge. The entire valley was covered in water, the lowest elevations flooded out completely.

Laura's compound was high enough that most of their rainwater drained down the road. They also had huge storage tanks underground that captured some of it, which left semi-solid ground around most of the area, and only about an inch of water where it tended to pool.

Darax was on flood duty, making rounds twice daily to check for roof leaks and ensure windows and doors weren't left open. He performed the task with all the grace of a sullen teenager, sulking, muttering to himself, and stomping around the place, but he did as he was told. It was important. Rusty's skin had become even more sensitive to water exposure. She was now breaking out in hives when air humidity was too high, and direct contact with the smallest droplets caused her painful welts and blisters, almost as if she'd been burned with acid. To be extra safe, Rusty usually parked her butt in the second floor hallway on rainy days. With rooms on either side and a whole level above, it was the driest place in the compound. The younger kids kept her company up there, drawing pictures and telling wild stories until the hallway echoed with their giggles.

Everyone else busied themselves with whatever they could, doing small chores around the house, playing games, napping, and in general, trying not to go crazy in the confined space. With so many people living under one roof, they'd been forced to master the art of staying out of each other's hair as much as possible. It worked, for the most part. But when the weather kept them all indoors for days in a row, everyone's temper got a little shorter.

Since no one would bother crossing the wet courtyard to see him in the infirmary, Eskel stayed inside the main house on bad weather days. He chafed in the close quarters probably more than any of the others, used to the solitude of a mostly empty infirmary. Today, Eskel had decided to sit with William, relieving Laura for a spell of privacy.

She and William hadn't spoken much since their fight. When she was with him, Laura kept herself busy straightening up or reading to him, and when the silence got long enough for a conversation to start, she excused herself and left back to her room.

It wasn't much better in there. With nothing to distract her, Laura's thoughts drifted back to Finn and how badly she'd messed up by chasing him off after their kiss in the cornfield. The more she thought about it, the more she came to accept the true reason why Finn had left: she'd told him to.

And, as much as she regretted losing a potential lifeline they all desperately needed, the bulk of her remorse stemmed from something far more personal and selfish. Those minutes in the cornfield had felt like surfacing for a breath of air before the tides pulled her under again. While they'd fought, she'd thought of nothing but herself. When Finn had kissed her, the shock of it had yanked her out of her troubles and slammed her back into her body, into the present moment, where nothing else mattered except the feel of his arms around her and the taste of him on her tongue.

One moment of pure, unadulterated feeling.

Laura couldn't let it go. Such a small, brief thing but to her, it had felt monumental.

Just like it had twenty years ago on a high school theater stage. The only difference was her level of maturity and how her mind took the tiny seed of passion he'd given her and grew it into a verdant garden of fantasies she had no business cultivating.

Laura considered herself to be firmly grounded in reality. She had to be, with so many people depending on her. But the things her mind had been conjuring recently, and with such frequency, made her uneasy. She could be reading to William and not register a single word she said while thinking about Finn's hands touching her, stripping her down as his mouth traced a hot, moist path across her flesh. She dreamed about him nightly and woke up winded, sweaty, and tangled in her covers.

It couldn't be healthy. Laura was going on a decade without sex, and it had never been an issue before now. She had work and her charges to keep her too busy for such nonsense. By the time she made it to bed at night, Laura was usually too exhausted to think about sex at all. Besides, it wasn't as if opportunities for romance had been falling out of the sky to distract her.

Maybe that was the problem. Finn had made her remember she had a body capable of much more than hard work. It could feel pleasure and give it. He'd reminded her of what it used to feel like to not think about anything but the present moment and revel in the seamless harmony of a sensory overload.

It hadn't been gentle, but Laura wouldn't have wanted it to be. Life was hard, and whatever pleasures it had in store didn't come easy.

And yet, when Finn had presented himself to her for the taking, she'd chosen to walk away instead. In hindsight, she recognized the fear in her decision, not of Finn, but of what it would mean if she gave in to him. Laura hated how deeply the man was rooted in her life. But she couldn't imagine her childhood any other way except with him in it.

What kept dragging her back into her brooding mood was that Finn had to feel something similar. Otherwise, he never would have come back in the first place. Which made his second departure so much worse than the first. This time, Laura had no one to blame but herself.

She was getting worked up again. Tossing aside the book she hadn't been reading for the last half hour, Laura paced around her bedroom prison and glared at the rain.

Finn was gone, and he wasn't coming back unless she invited him—which she couldn't without a working com or any form of conveyance. Therefore, she had no reason to keep thinking about it anymore. So why couldn't she stop?

When someone knocked on her door, it startled Laura so badly that she jumped.

"Hey, Laura?"

She pressed her hands to her burning cheeks to cool them. "Yeah?"

"There's a taxi here for you," Rusty said from out in the hall.

Laura waited for the punchline.

"Are you coming?"

What the hell? She opened the door, ready to tell the girl to go prank someone else, but there was no telltale grin on Rusty's face. She looked confused and ready to bolt. "What are you talking about? What taxi?"

Rusty shrugged a bony shoulder. "It just showed up at the front door. The message says it's got a round trip for one under the name Laura McNally. Eskel said that's you."

It was pathetic how quickly her mind decided Finn must have sent the taxi. There was no logical reason why he would send a taxi for her when driving up in his own transport would have been much easier and cheaper. But who else would have used her maiden name for the reservation? She hadn't been Laura McNally for sixteen years; few people still remembered she'd ever been anyone other than Laura Belden.

"Are you leaving us?"

Laura rolled her eyes. "Round trip, sweetie. Means I'm coming back." *Eventually.* She was so desperate to get out of the compound she had her feet stuffed into her boots in seconds. Then she frowned, bending over to tie the laces. "Does it say where I'm going?"

"Map's got a marker in Olendra? That's out by Hadran City, isn't it?"

"Thereabouts," Laura confirmed. What would Finn be doing out in Olendra? It was way outside their region, hours beyond Avencore, where he'd said he was staying.

Which would mean it might be far enough out of Talon's territory. Olendra was a good-sized metropolis, nothing like the valley. They would have much better infrastructure and possibly even reestablished supply routes. Whoever had ordered the taxi had just thrown Laura a priceless lifeline. Out in Olendra, she might be able to access some funds. She could secure some much-needed resources for the compound, maybe even a functioning com and a conveyance.

It had to be Finn's doing.

"You should take Quinn with you. Or don't go. Yeah, I think you should send it back empty. I don't like it when you go away!"

A selfish, desperate thought occurred to Laura before she could squash it. Olendra was a short, half-hour drive to the Britannia shuttleport. What if she *didn't* come back?

She hated herself for thinking it, but God, there was only so much a body could take. Laura had given everything she had to this place and its people, and as much as she loved them all, a small part of her wanted to take the easy way out, run, and never look back.

She grabbed her raincoat from the hook by William's door and considered knocking. Should she tell him she was leaving? Despite his ridiculous notions lately, William could be a font of wisdom in times of uncertainty. It wouldn't hurt to get a more level-headed opinion before Laura climbed into an unknown vehicle to be whisked far away for who knew how long.

She looked at the bruised knuckles poised to knock and lowered her hand. If Laura told William she suspected Finn had sent the taxi, he might decide to do something drastic in her absence. Like take himself out of the equation, thinking Laura now had someone else to lean on.

"Rusty, can you ask Alexis to keep an eye on William while I'm gone?" Alexis was supposed to be on bed rest after Harley jumped on her and broke her clavicle. But despite the frailty of her bones and the constant risk of injury, the woman wouldn't stay down if Eskel tied her in place. At least this way, she would be out of harm's way, and her naturally positive outlook on life might do William some good. "And let Eskel know that the medicines are all prepped for tonight in case I don't make it back on time."

Rusty's eyes went round and wet. "You're really leaving?"

"I'll be back before you know it." Laura kissed the top of Rusty's head and gently ushered her out. "Keep the kids out of trouble, will you?"

Miguel and a few others had gathered by the front windows to stare at the bright orange transport hovering beyond the glass.

Laura shrugged into her coat. "Trip for one Laura McNally? I don't suppose any of you had anything to do with it."

The joke wasn't well received.

Quinn shook his head. "I don't like the look of this." He'd recovered from his hypothermia fairly well but was still pale. Eskel checked on him as often as William, which was a sure sign the medic still had concerns.

"Come on, big guy, what's the worst that could happen?"

"You disappear, and we all die with no one to persuade the good folk of Anamtaigh to lend us a hand or two."

No pressure. "I'll be fine. I promise."

She shouldn't have said that. Quinn could be right. What if it was the Shadows? Talon knew about her abilities. What if he'd decided to make her use them for his benefit? Or he might have a fancy new weapon he wanted to test on a telepath. Laura could end up in a dark cellar somewhere with her brains leaking out of her ears.

But what was the alternative?

Sitting on her hands and waiting for their supplies to run out.

"Hold down the fort until I return."

She got into the taxi before they could say anything to change her mind. The doors closed automatically, and a screen in front of her blinked with a request for identification. Laura scanned the chip implanted under the skin of her left wrist. With a light blooping noise for confirmation, the transport raised two more feet off the ground and took off much faster than the old levpad or any other vehicle Laura had ridden in years.

After a while, the exhilarating tickle mellowed out, and she sat back to watch the scenery rush by for the next—she checked the console readout—five hours and eleven minutes.

Anamtaigh had used to be a beautiful place, with snow-capped mountains, vast green valleys, and lakes the size of oceans on other planets. As she gazed out the window, Laura realized the world she'd once loved so much was gone. She'd know the war had caused incredible damage, but knowing it and seeing it were two different things. With every shuttle wreck and scorched crater she passed, Laura felt as if the scars on the land were hers. Even if the rest of Anamtaigh had gone untouched—it hadn't—seeing her home region reduced to this hurt.

I don't want to be here anymore.

William had been right. It was time to leave.

Olendra had once been the second most populous metropolis after Hadran City. Much of it had escaped destruction, but a big chunk of its northeast corner was now gone beneath a blanket of ash and soot.

The taxi was programmed to skirt around the damaged area and take a winding path through narrow side streets until it turned right onto a main road and right again, pulling over in front of a house with planters full of yellow flowers hanging from light posts on either side of the front staircase.

Laura's door opened automatically to let her out. When she stepped onto the sidewalk, the taxi idled down to wait for her return trip back to the compound.

This was it. If it was a trap, it was cleverly disguised as something out of a travel brochure. The neighborhood around her consisted of lovely little cottages with green lawns and tidy porches. At one end of the block was a park with paved paths, wooden benches, little drinking fountains, and bird baths scattered among the trees. On the opposite end, an intersection cut off the road, and the space on the other side was open to foot traffic, with storefronts and outdoor restaurants.

It would have been the perfect place for families to settle down and live a nice, quiet life.

A shame it was empty.

The cities on Anamtaigh had a responsibility to maintain any and all unoccupied properties to uphold the image of a picturesque travel destination. But if Laura looked beyond the trimmed lawns and colorful flowers, she saw nothing. No transports in driveways, no bikes or toys littering the porches. All the windows were closed, all the curtains drawn. Yes, there were beautiful outdoor restaurants down the block. But they had chairs propped against the bare tables and the oversized umbrellas closed and secured against the wind.

And it was so quiet.

The rain was a soft drizzle, hardly worth the effort of pulling up her hood, so Laura left it flat against her back and walked up the stairs to the front door. She lowered her telepathic shields to be safe, ready to defend herself. She sensed people inside—two, maybe three. Most of the house was empty.

Now would have been a great time to have proper telepathy that could tell her whom she was about to meet. All Laura got was a sense of sparkling excitement from someone impatient for something to do. It left a fizzy taste in her mind.

Definitely not Finn. His presence felt a lot heavier.

The taxi must have been programmed to send a message upon arrival because the door opened without her needing to knock. There was no one on the other side.

"Hello?" she called, stepping across the threshold onto polished wooden floors.

A small, cozy nook opened outward on her left, tucked behind a staircase sloping toward the other end of the hallway. The nook was set up like a waiting room with two plush armchairs and a small table. To her right, closed doors created a solid wall going back to a corner where the space opened up again, out of sight.

"Anybody home?"

"Sorry!" a woman called from somewhere up above. "We're coming!"

Laura waited, drumming her fingers on her thighs. Those armchairs looked so comfortable, but in her old, drab clothes, Laura didn't feel fit to sit in one of them.

Luckily, she didn't have to wait long. Two sets of footsteps came down the staircase. Laura gently pushed out with her power to get a sense of them. A rainbow of sparks fluttered around one of the people coming to greet her. The other was a blank. No one alive walked around without any intentions whatsoever. It simply wasn't how the human mind operated.

The footsteps stopped just short of the main floor, and after a few seconds and a mad dash of flashing sparks, a tall man stepped down and rounded the banister to approach Laura.

All of the wild, colorful sparks stayed on the stairs. This was the blank. "Shadow," she guessed bitterly, backing up a step. He was a good fifteen feet away, and the door was at her back. She could make a run for it, but could she get into the taxi, activate it, and drive away before he caught her? Unlikely.

He stopped at her retreat and held up his hands, offering a casual smile as if to put her at ease. "Former," he corrected.

"Aren't they all?"

The man shook his head. "No, but the dark ones are easy to shine."

"Huh?"

The man flushed a little and scratched his head. "Sorry, I talk funny sometimes. My name is John. And you're the Orderer."

"The what?" Was he using some code she didn't know about? Nothing he said made sense.

He huffed a breath. "You can order people. Yes?"

He had to be one of Talon's men. Which meant there would be others hiding throughout the house. And if they were like this one, she'd never feel them coming. Laura pushed at his mind with an urgent need to turn around and go back upstairs, but her persuasion slid across the top of his head as if it was made of glass.

"Yeah, you can't work me," he said with an apologetic shrug. "I'm a wall."

The colorful sparks flared bright through the staircase underside as the woman from earlier growled and stomped her foot. "*The* Wall," she said, coming down to join him. Waif-thin, with a wild mane of bright red hair, the spitfire glared up at the man and thumped him lightly on the temple. "*The* Wall. We talked about this."

"What's the difference?" he demanded with a dark scowl that made Laura want to be anywhere else but in his vicinity.

The redhead met it with pure, unadulterated sarcasm. "One holds up the roof, the other's your number." Then she turned a sunny smile on Laura, and the rainbow around her head coalesced to mellow shades of green, yellow, and light pink. Their crazy flight patterns were likely due to her hyperexcited state, but the colors were all inviting. She posed no danger to Laura—the opposite, actually. Whoever she was, she wanted Laura to feel safe and welcome.

Which meant nothing when she had a Shadow at her back whom Laura couldn't even read, much less persuade.

"I'm Emma," the redhead said, then rushed forward and threw her arms around Laura. "It's so good to finally meet you!"

Laura was used to physical affection, but not from total strangers. "Umm… Hi. Let go, please." She was too weirded out to make it a command, but the woman did step back.

"Come in! Come in. There's so much to talk about." Taking Laura's hand, she tugged her along into the house.

The Shadow stood aside to let them through but hooked his finger on the back of Laura's coat collar, tugging it down. She managed to get one arm free but then had to pull Emma to a stop to get the coat off completely. Emma released Laura's left hand without missing a beat, took her right, and kept going. Laura's coat stayed with the Shadow, who folded it neatly over the staircase banister.

Around the blind corner, the space opened onto a kitchen with a table and three chairs by the window. A pot of tea and a plate of cookies had been set out on it, with three cups lined up at the edge, ready to serve.

"What the hell is this?"

Emma pulled back her shoulders and declared, "Cookies!"

Laura blinked at her.

Emma's shoulders drooped. "No?" She looked at her Shadow, who pointed at her ass. "Oh, fine." Reaching back there, the young woman pulled out some papers, folded over several times. She smoothed them out, then smiled at Laura and started to read. "Hello. My name is Emma Wayland of Torrey. I am the dir…" She frowned at the paper. "The dir…" With a frustrated huff, she slapped the papers against her thighs and complained, "I told her not to make it permanent."

"You approved this," the Shadow said.

Emma made a face, then raised the papers again. "I am the *acting* director of the Special Unit, an organization whose mission is to locate, train, support, and protect telepaths." She read ahead a bit, then looked up at Laura. "And other weirdos now. She left that out."

"She?"

Emma nodded but didn't elaborate.

The Shadow shrugged as if this was normal for the redhead.

"I am reading this from a script written by my secretary to make it easier for us to communicate," Emma continued from said script. "If I've already said something strange, I apologize." The papers went down again. "I don't think I want the Brain talking for me anymore."

"Emma, babe. Keep going."

Laura held up her finger. "Just… May I?" She cautiously reached for the papers and pulled them out of Emma's hands. With a bear-with-me smile, she read on her own.

…If I've already said something strange, I apologize. My commu-

nication ability was severely damaged by my imprisonment with the Shadows three years ago. I sometimes mix up my words, and they don't always make sense to others, but I assure you I am sound of mind and mean you no harm.

"The Shadows did this to you?"

Emma nodded soberly.

Laura turned to the Shadow who'd called Emma "babe."

Understanding Laura's obvious confusion, her hostess stepped up to the man and put her arm right around his waist. He reciprocated by pulling her into his side and ever so slightly hunching over her shorter frame. It wasn't just an affectionate gesture. It was a protective one. "He's my seashell," Emma explained, and John grinned.

"Right." Laura went back to reading.

What I want to say is that I am happy and honored to finally meet you. Word of your charity has spread far and wide. I know it doesn't seem that way now, but there are a lot of people watching over you, and they are very invested in the outcome of this conflict.

On the table before you, you will find a pot of tea and a plate of fresh-baked cookies. This is our way of welcoming new telepaths into the fold, a tradition started by our founder, John MacMurphy, who is sadly no longer with us. There's something homey and comforting about cookies, don't you think?

There was a page and a half more, but Laura had run out of patience. "What's this all about?"

Emma started to say something, then gingerly reached out to reclaim her papers. She scanned through the first one, then set it aside to read the second. "We are aware of your situation with the Shadows and want to help."

Laura's heart skipped a beat. She probed hard at the colors swarming around Emma to get to the truth of her intent. The sparks took on a shade of teal for the kind of sorrow that made people want to shelter a wounded animal, even if it ended up biting them. It also included a silvery shimmer of awareness. Emma knew what Laura was doing; she could shut herself down at any moment, but she didn't. She wanted Laura to see what she was feeling.

Laura flushed and pulled back to passive observation. Emma's patient tolerance of having her privacy invaded shamed her.

"Due to other circumstances at play," Emma read, "we can't be seen in direct contact with you yet. But we have made some arrangements that should alleviate some of the pressures on you and your people." Emma frowned at John. "*Alleviate*? And I'm the loopy one?"

John took the paper from her and read through the rest quickly. "When you leave, your taxi will be loaded with enough cash credits to get you through the next two weeks and a box of medications formulated by us to treat specific ailments caused by the Shadow weapons' fallout. You can leave anytime, but we hope you will stay for a rest and a cup of tea. Even the strongest among us need to set down our burdens every once in a while."

Laura couldn't breathe. Did she dare believe them? Risking herself was one thing, but if the medications they offered made her loved ones worse… "Why are you doing this?" Her voice didn't get far above a whisper.

"We take care of our own," John said.

"Why now? Why not sooner?" *Where were you the last three years?*

Emma answered, her cheerful firecracker sparks drooping into a halo of pale blue around her head. She was struggling not to cry. "Our people are hurting as much as yours. We lost many in the first two suns. Our letters are smaller, harder to write."

Laura felt Emma's mental touch, politely asking for entry. Hesitant, Laura gave the appropriate response. Her mind filled with a barrage of images as scrambled as Emma's speech. But the picture they put together was horrifying.

She saw green fields littered with dead bodies; morgues with black body bags stacked around the walls because there were no more cooling drawers left to hold them; infirmaries filled to bursting with the sick, injured, and dying while medics and children in white lab coats fluttered from one to the next, too tired to hide their haunted expressions behind a caring smile.

She saw groups of telepaths joining hands, their powers building on one another until their will and direction were inescapable. She saw war shuttles stopping mid-assault and turning around, sometimes dropping out of the sky, and soldiers surrendering their weapons.

She saw halls filled with a loud circus of important people suddenly fall silent as a pair of telepaths walked to the front of the assembly to lay down the law.

And, between flashes of blinding white, Laura saw those same telepaths walk to the edge of a cliff and off it.

She whimpered.

Rumor had it, telepaths had the ability to make themselves so strong they could command entire communities, even cities. But the price for such a move was a complete and total mental merge. Once they connected so thoroughly, they could never again disconnect to return to their individual selves. The resulting hive mind was more destructive to telepaths than any weapon or prison ever devised by Shadows.

The ones who had already died fighting the war—and there'd been many—had done it willingly, choosing to end their lives rather than remain trapped in such a state. They'd sacrificed themselves so humanity could survive the worst, most destructive conflict they'd had in hundreds of years.

But the war wasn't over yet. The sacrifices might have slowed, but they have not stopped, and they could not until the societal rift was healed. As the SU director, Emma carried the weight of those sacrifices on her conscience. She didn't want anyone to die. By refusing to order any telepath to take part in the conflict, she gave the responsibility of choice to her people, but that didn't make it any easier to live with.

Laura had a compound of people who depended on her to keep them alive. Emma's flock numbered in the millions and stretched across every inhabited world. Each loss was equally as personal to Emma as the death of a family member would be to Laura. And she'd had to endure hundreds of them every year since the war began.

Laura's knees went weak. She sat in the chair closest to her.

Emma poured her a cup of hot tea and pushed the plate of cookies toward her. "Chocolate chip," she said. "There's brownies, too."

Laura nodded her thanks, meeting Emma's gaze so she would know it was in earnest. In between the messages Emma had wanted to convey, she'd inadvertently included some she might not have intended. Images of bright white with nothing in it, cutting her off from the world, from other human beings. The total isolation had pressed on

Laura's mind making her want to scream the same way Emma had screamed, cried, and begged.

But she hadn't given in.

The Shadows had cracked something in Emma but hadn't broken her. All they'd done was give her an edge so sharp it had ultimately gutted them. Her altered speech was the battle scar that would never completely heal. It was a testament to her strength, and Laura was humbled to sit in her presence.

Emma poured herself a cup of tea and offered some to John, but he declined. He kissed Emma on the top of her head, nodded his farewell to Laura, and left them to it.

When he was gone, Laura expected Emma to launch into more nonsensical babbles, but she didn't. Instead, she sipped her tea, watched the rain fall on the garden outside, and let Laura catch her breath and process everything.

Starting with Emma's secretary, the Brain, a young girl barely older than Rusty. As the SU's head medic, she had personally formulated all the serums they were giving Laura.

And then John Wayland, the Shadow who'd captured Emma, rescued her and sacrificed himself to help bring down an entire Shadow outpost. As far as the Shadows knew, John was still where they'd put him—in a coma. The moment he was seen, he'd become a target. Yet here he was, right beside Emma, putting himself in harm's way for her because he was her seashell, and she was his pixie girl.

Somehow, these living legends were on Laura's side, willing, able, and ready to step in and make her life easier.

There had to be a price—there always was.

Whatever they asked of her, if it brought this endless nightmare to a close, Laura would do it with a smile and a spring in her step.

"Can you get us off-world?"

The mellow green sparks around Emma turned a determined purple. Purple had a component of red, which stood for violence. "In time," she promised. "But first, we need to put down a dog."

14

Avencore

Something was wrong. Finn hadn't received a response from the Special Unit. They'd been plenty eager to keep in touch with him when he'd had no interest in joining their cause. For them to go radio silent now that he actually needed them, felt like trouble. At the very least, he would have expected Emma to write back and acknowledge his message.

Contacting them again would establish a pattern. He couldn't risk it.

Luckily, Bree's package arrived on time and without issue. Finn now had a rudimentary Shadow Hawk starter kit, equivalent to a portable arsenal. The items he'd ordered included a standard issue multi-functional defense wrist unit, two side arms, a set of knives, and a secure personal com, among other things.

The issue arose when he tried using the com to contact Laura.

The Shadow device didn't work like the civilian version by linking with a local registry to find someone. Instead, it scanned the area for other devices capable of receiving a call and let the caller pinpoint them on a three-dimensional map.

Except when Finn tried it, the com didn't find any devices fitting the description in all of Karsengale Valley. The Shadow satellites might have had something to do with it, but, considering his com was also Shadow-made, it should have been able to patch through their interference.

Conclusion: he had no way of contacting Laura short of showing up on her doorstep again. And, as much as it drove him up the wall not knowing if she was okay, Latham had made it clear he wouldn't tolerate Finn trespassing into his territory a second time. Going in on a whim, unprepared and without a plan of defense, would put Laura and her people on the receiving end of a lot of firepower. Their new bunker storage house would crumble under Latham's brand of full-force assault.

Finn would need to figure out another way to get in touch with her so it couldn't be traced back to him.

To that end, he shifted his attention to Avencore to gauge the extent of Latham's reach. He changed his daily run to make circuits past the post depot to the local school, looping back around through the nearby residential neighborhoods.

He found signs of Shadow occupation in the apartment building across the street from the school and three different neighborhoods. They were established enough for the window blinds to be permanently warped and a tricked-out transport to be parked in front of each location, in full view of the public.

Combined with their glaring lack of a presence downtown, they might as well have pointed a bright red arrow at their intended targets: the students.

Moss was as good as his word. He left Finn daily reports by way of shopping sprees for items they'd agreed on and then some.

Good.

Finn had deliberately given Moss much more cash than he would need, hoping the kid would use it well, and he did. The tally of items he bought in the afternoons was also added to Finn's shopping bill the next morning. The old store clerk got paid twice for the service of passing on Moss' coded message, and no one was the wiser.

According to the teen, five Shadows were in play at the local school. They had at least two informants among the teachers and staff and appeared to have singled out two targets among the kids. There'd been no attempts to buy alcohol, which meant Moss didn't think his schoolmates were in danger yet, but Shadows didn't take an interest in someone unless they had plans for them. The targets would be telepaths, potential recruits, or both.

If Latham was recruiting young blood, his plans extended beyond regrouping the surviving Shadows. He was laying grounds for an expansion, and that was something Finn couldn't allow to happen.

But, on his own, with only his wrist unit, a couple of guns, and his swinging dick, it'd be a suicide mission, and others would end up paying interest.

Collateral damage was something he would have deemed acceptable three years ago. The thought still lingered in the back of his mind: *In the pursuit of a greater good, sacrifices have to be made.* Latham posed a real and immediate threat. In the galactic scope of reality, a few lives would be well worth Latham's downfall.

He didn't want to think that way anymore.

To distract himself, Finn returned to the subject of Laura. More specifically, her husband, William Belden. He searched through local databases and synced up with the one working orbit satellite to query public records on the closest worlds. He found nothing beyond a one-line entry in the Karsengale registry for the date of his wedding to Laura four years after Finn had left.

It was human nature to want to be seen and acknowledged. People went to a lot of trouble to make sure their names and faces were known as far and wide as possible. William Belden appeared to have gone in a totally opposite direction, which meant he had something to hide, which could make him a potential threat to Laura.

Naturally, the suspicion had nothing to do with the fact that Finn hated the man on principle. He was merely looking out for Laura. She didn't love William—a woman in love with one man didn't kiss another the way she'd kissed him in the cornfield.

Laura had been achingly close to falling back into their old connection that night. Finn had felt her mental touch brush against his mind, and it'd been a promise of home waiting just out of reach. He had no way of knowing how much time Laura had spent in his mind when they'd been children, but it had been enough for him to feel bereft without it. For her to tease him with a taste of it again and then pull back had hurt worse than a kick to the balls. She hadn't even cared enough to command him to leave.

At sunset, the movie he'd had playing for background noise cut off, and the screen flashed a SIGNAL LOST message.

As soon as it went quiet, Finn picked up on the white noise of another heavy downpour outside.

He rubbed his tired eyes and stretched up from his hunch at the small writing desk. Where had the day gone? He could have sworn it'd been noon a few minutes ago. He pushed to his feet, wincing at the pins and needles shooting down his legs. Hours of sitting on his ass always made him feel like he was in hibernation. His whole body felt stiff and heavy, and his head throbbed with a dull ache.

Maybe he should go for a run. The cold rain and fresh air might help clear his mind.

Finn put on his boots and headed out.

Soft-slippered footsteps drummed down the main staircase, and by the time Finn reached the front desk, Ms. Thane was already at the front door turning locks and sliding bolts to get it open.

She didn't like being crowded, so he hung back to give her space. "Your big party of guests finally here?" he teased.

"Not 'til the sixth," she returned, deadpan.

Just like she had done when he'd first arrived, the innkeeper only opened the door enough to look out. Her foot was braced against the panel from the inside as if it could stop an intruder from coming in if he really wanted to.

From the other side of the threshold, a soft voice said something Finn was too far to hear. He came a little closer. The inn didn't get many visitors. Ms. Thane's routine was to lock and bolt the door as soon as the sun set and keep it locked until morning.

"No, I already told you on the com. There's no one by that name here."

Finn was at her side in two strides, moving Ms. Thane away as gently as possible so he could pull the visitor inside and close the door behind her.

Laura blinked in the sudden light and then broke into a bright smile. "You're here."

Ms. Thane looked from her to Finn, then shook her head. "I don't want to know." She closed and locked the door, then headed back up the staircase, her robe billowing behind her. "Your problem, not mine."

Laura was soaked through and through, bone pale and shivering.

"What are you doing here? How did you even get here?"

"Tax-si. Shut down two blocks aw-way when the s-sun went down."

She was freezing. "Come on, let's get you warmed up."

What were the odds that his Shadow watchers across the street hadn't noticed her coming through the rain?

Inside his room, he pulled Laura straight to the bathroom and turned on the shower as hot as it would go. "Towels are clean. I'll get you something to wear when you're done."

Laura managed a nod and started undressing before he'd fully cleared the door. He closed it in a hurry and went to double-check his privacy shield. The small gizmo was something he carried with him everywhere he went. It created interference within the confines of a walled-in space to prevent spying equipment from picking up on any sounds or conversation. Finn kept it on at all times to thumb his nose at the Shadows.

Then he picked up his com and scanned the area for Laura's taxi. The only one within Avencore was parked two blocks away, as Laura had said. The com automatically spoofed an admin code and gave him access to the taxi's ride history for the last two days. He found the most recent order originating in Olendra with two round-trips: the first to pick up Laura in Karsengale and deliver her to Olendra, and the second to drop her off and return to the depot.

The name on the order was Sue Torrey. Also known as SU, planet Torrey.

Finn shook his head and turned off the device. All this time, he'd been waiting for a response from Emma, and the crazy bitch had sent him Laura.

Emma, are you there? he thought, picturing her in his mind. Finn wasn't quite sure of her telepathic range, but he figured it was at least a couple thousand miles. If, as he suspected, she was in Olendra right now, all he had to do for her to hear him was think with some volume and, for lack of a better word, direction. *Emma, answer me.*

She didn't.

She thought she could ignore him? *Emma. Emma. Emma. Emma! Emma! EMMA!*

—*Enough!*—

He sat on the edge of his bed and rubbed his face. She really was on Anamtaigh.

What the fuck, woman?

—You called. You tell me.—

Yeah, he had contacted her for help. But he'd never expected her to personally leave town, much less her home planet. Unlike Finn, who couldn't stomach watching his friend float lifelessly inside an oversized fish bowl, Emma had been devoted to him to the exclusion of everything and everyone else. She wouldn't have left John's side unless she'd had no more reason to stay.

Had something happened to him?

Would she break down if he asked?

She could probably pick up on his thoughts already. He waited for her to address it.

She didn't.

Safe to conclude, the topic wasn't up for discussion. It hit Finn harder than he expected, and he hung his head for a moment in mental silence. John Wayland had been the closest thing he'd had to family among the Shadows.

Where are you? he asked Emma.

—In the loop.—

Do you understand what's going on?

—Define 'understand.'—

Finn groaned. *Please tell me you brought reinforcements.*

—I'm confused. Isn't she there yet?—

He swallowed back a few choice thoughts but couldn't rein in his frustration. *Laura is not a player in this.*

—I'm confused. What game are we playing?—

Grasping for patience, Finn tried again. *Focus, Emma. Laura cannot be here. She's a target for Latham. If she's seen with me, they'll hurt her. Why would you send her here?*

—I have every secret that you are fully equipped to handle the situation. Byeee!—

Emma?

Nothing.

Emma!

Did she just hang up on him?

Son of a bi—

The bathroom door opened. Laura came out with a towel wrapped around her.

Finn shoved to his feet, trying not to stare. The heat of the shower had restored her color, and a fine sheen of moisture still glistened over her skin. His mouth went dry.

Clothes. He'd promised her clothes.

He pulled a clean T-shirt and a pair of jogging pants out of the dresser drawer and handed them over. "Here. You hungry? I have some leftover pizza in the mini-fridge." It really was out of the world and as good as fresh even days later.

She pulled the T-shirt over the towel, and when her head cleared the neckline, his attention stuck to the short crop of her hair. When had that happened? "Thank you, but no," she said, shaking the wet strands out of her face. "I kind of stuffed myself with cookies earlier."

Finn nodded. "Chocolate chip, right?"

"How did you know?"

"I'm guessing they were served by a loopy redhead?"

Laura paused with the sweatpants halfway up her legs. "I didn't realize you and Emma knew each other."

"We used to have a friend in common." Punch in the gut. "How do you feel?"

Fully dressed, Laura removed the towel from under the T-shirt without flashing an inch of skin and folded it neatly over the chair. "Better. Thank you for that. Hot showers are kind of a luxury in my neck of the woods." She was still barefoot.

"Any time."

The room only had a large bed, a dresser, and a tiny desk and chair. The logical action was for Laura to get in the bed and keep warm under the covers. But Finn didn't trust himself going in that direction. Just being with Laura in such a confined space made coherent thought an exercise in futility. Knowing she was two very loose garments away from nakedness didn't help, either.

Laura broke their awkward staring contest, rubbing one bare foot over the other. "I can tell you want to kiss me again."

And then some. "Am I that obvious, or are you reading me?"

"You've never been obvious," she retorted. Which meant she was reading him.

The admission should have angered him or at least put him on guard. Instead, he felt something akin to relief. He crossed half the distance between them before he stopped himself. "What does it feel like to know what people around you are thinking?"

Her gaze traced invisible things around his head and shoulders before settling on his face. "I don't know what you're thinking. Only what you want to do. Intent."

Finn's hands curled at his sides. "And?"

15

The heat of her shower had almost dissipated. Now it all came rushing back. Laura couldn't lie if she wanted to, not with Finn watching her with such unblinking focus. The bright pink sparks of his intentions had coalesced into an aura glowing around him. His entire body was tense from the effort of holding back.

She licked her lips.

He clocked the gesture, and his next exhale was a little stronger, a puff of breath accompanied by a small shiver that drew the same from her.

"It feels…" She searched for the right word. "Intense. It has a visual component, in a sense. But mostly it's like a physical knowing. I *see* you want to do something, but I *feel* what it is. If it's strong enough, sometimes it feels like it's me wanting it, not the other person."

Finn blinked and leaned back. Or rather, straightened away from leaning in. He'd read the subtext and was making an effort to give her mental space. He didn't want her to feel what he felt because of some glitch of her abilities. "Can you block it out?"

She nodded. "Most of the time, I do."

"And when you don't?"

Laura closed her eyes, but it didn't help. Finn's closeness alone seemed to make her shields not want to stay put. It was as if her mind had decided it belonged in his head. Staying out felt wrong. "Sometimes it zings through me. Other times…"

Her head felt woozy. In the mental realm of wants, physical desire was in a league of its own. And when directed at Laura, sometimes it created an echo chamber, rebounding back and forth, sweeping her up until she couldn't tell how much of what she felt was hers and how much the other person's. "Other times, I feel like I'm holding on to a live wire, but I don't want to let go."

She felt his fingers brushing along her jawline, gently nudging her to look at him. When Laura opened her eyes, Finn was right there, the aura of his desire encompassing them both. "I do want to kiss you," he said, and Laura's heels left the ground as she raised up on tiptoe to close the distance between them.

Instead of touching lips, Finn angled his head down and rested his forehead against hers. "But you're still married. And I'm not that guy."

Truth.

Laura stayed with him for a few seconds more, shoring up her inner strength to rebuild her shields. They only came up as a veil to make the bright pink less blinding. The desire was still there. He simply refused to act on it.

"William would be the first to push me off on you," she said, pretending it didn't hurt. Her marriage was nothing like what Finn probably imagined, but it had been a solid partnership until the war. Now, every time she looked at her husband, all she saw was his resignation. He'd given up—not just on her, but on everything, including life itself.

Finn threaded his fingers through her hair. "Then he doesn't deserve you." The touch was almost involuntary; he hadn't thought about doing it. He'd just done it. But when Laura thought he would take it further, Finn released her and stepped away, shoving his hands into his pockets. "But he's still your husband, and I can't see you petitioning a dying man for divorce."

It wasn't as if William's condition was hard to notice, but hearing Finn bring it up so readily cooled the effects of his desire a great deal. Laura got chilled standing barefoot on the smooth, wooden floor.

"Um, I should probably explain something."

Finn raised an eyebrow for her to proceed.

This wasn't a conversation she wanted to have standing in what was essentially his bedroom, but it wasn't as if she had another choice.

Laura sat on the edge of his bed and pulled her feet up onto the mattress, hugging her knees to her chest. "My marriage to William is purely a business arrangement," she confessed. "He's one of the Jericho Beldens."

The name traced a thousand years back to Earth and came with courtesy titles passed down through the sons. The family was one of the richest in existence, owning and operating a slew of businesses on fifteen worlds. And they maintained their wealth by sharing none of it. The Belden enterprise had a long history of profiteering from misery, making record profits in the hardest times.

"But he's nothing like them," she rushed to assure Finn.

He sighed, sitting down beside her. "Lady Laura Belden."

"I really hate that title." Along with everything it stood for. "I met William at a charity auction. He bid two million credits on an antique record player worth about two hundred. We got to talking, and it turned out he has a humanitarian streak. But his family finances are locked down with about a thousand caveats and addendums. No Belden heir is allowed to donate more than a miserly amount to charity annually."

"I'm assuming those rules don't apply to spouses."

Laura clicked her tongue. "Exactly. As his wife, I am entitled to twelve million credits a year as my stipend, with an additional five earmarked for household upkeep."

"And that means, as long as you and William live *at* the charity, you can spend all of it *on* the charity, and the accountants can't cut you off."

"Yep."

"And you get all this money in return for what?"

Laura winced. She didn't want to talk about William's personal affairs. "For the most part, William's satisfaction of sticking it to his family. Our personal relationship isn't romantic." They had tried. But after the total of three times they'd slept together, the glaring lack of any sort of chemistry had made further attempts pointless. "We're friends and partners." To be fair, there was slightly more to it than that, but Finn didn't need those details.

He lay back across the bed where he sat. She didn't get a clear read on his intentions, but some of his physical tension had eased. His posture and expression said, *What a fucking mess,* and she couldn't help but agree.

Laura turned sideways to face him better, leaning against the headboard. It put the tips of her toes a couple of inches away from his waist.

"What's the family marriage contract have to say about infidelity?"

She scoffed. "You're kidding, right?" The decorative pillow at her back had a big wooden button digging into her hip. "It doesn't say anything at all. Families like the Beldens don't put stock in fidelity. According to William, affairs are perfectly acceptable, even encouraged, as long as there are no children." She pulled out the pillow and set it aside. "The problem is, the Shadows cut off our access to everything. It's all sitting there in our bank accounts. Each one has a fortune in it that could solve all of our problems a hundred times over. And the stipends are still coming in, so the money pile keeps growing. But we can't touch a credit of it."

"And, let me guess. Because William's spent his whole life thumbing his nose at his family, they won't lift a finger to get him out of this mess, am I right?"

"They cut him off in every way except financial," Laura confirmed. "He's had no contact with them since our wedding. They still send the stipends because they can't figure out how to get those pesky contracts undone. They did manage to keep the bulk of his inheritance, though. It got redistributed it to his siblings and cousins. And they paid a fortune to have our names *distanced* from the rest of the family."

"They buried you both."

"How do you mean?"

Finn shrugged and tunneled his arm behind her ankles, tugging her legs to straighten across his torso. Another reflexive action, like breathing. "No public records, no news coverage, local or off-world. After your marriage license was recorded, you both just disappeared."

"You looked for me?"

Finn's hand was on her calf, his thumb rubbing her skin back and forth in a slow, subconscious rhythm. "Took me two years of looking everywhere else to find out you never left Anamtaigh in the first place," he told the ceiling.

He'd looked for her for two years. That was almost as long as the war'd been going on.

Laura took a chance and let go of her partial shields. Flickers of pink still floated lazily around him, and the brightness from before was dulled with white for the kind of truth that just was and didn't need to be proven. But there were also streaks of gray and a feeling of holding back more than he revealed.

"My taxi didn't shut down in this neighborhood by accident," she admitted. "I rerouted the path to take me this way. I wanted to see you." She'd told herself it was because she still needed his help. But, with Emma and her people on her side now, it wasn't entirely true. "There are things I need to know. And I need you to answer without holding back." She didn't mean to, but a light thread of an order laced the words to encourage his compliance.

Finn sat up and faced Laura with an eagerness that shocked her. "Ask me. Anything." He meant it.

"Truth." This time, she tried to stop the persuasion, but the smallest bit leaked out anyway. Barely enough to make someone think about something they might not want to do.

Finn crossed his legs and rearranged hers so her knees bent over his and her calves bracketed his hips. "The whole truth, and nothing but."

He felt her manipulation; Laura could tell. But instead of fighting it or taking offense, he was waiting for more, and his desire ramped up her persuasion in response. It sneaked out with a desire of her own, and Finn reacted…unexpectedly.

His eyelids drooped as he straightened his legs to either side of her and pulled her closer so he could weave his fingers together at her back. It brought them almost nose to nose again in a loose embrace that trapped a great deal of heat between them and gave Finn no place to hide.

But he didn't seem to want to. His heavy-lidded gaze met hers head-on. His posture was comfortably settled in place. No resistance at all. If he were a cat, he'd be purring.

Laura flushed, realizing he *liked* being persuaded. And not just in the sense of back rubs or compliments. He was getting physically aroused. His body reacted to her commands as if she'd stroked him. With his decision not to engage with her still forefront in his mind, he had no intention of doing anything about it, but his enjoyment was palpable.

It wouldn't last.

"Why didn't you come back before now?"

His eyes blinked open a little wider, a little more alert. "Did you want me to?"

"I never wanted you to leave in the first place." He couldn't possibly have forgotten the scene she'd made out by the Shadow transport, crying and begging him not to go.

"But I did," he countered. "And I broke your heart doing it. That's what you said." There was a query lurking beneath the words, and Laura got a sense of him studying every minute aspect of her person for her response. He noticed the way her gaze strayed from his and the way her breathing changed. He picked up on the smallest tension in her limbs as if she had shouted, and his intentions shifted accordingly.

Laura flushed, her heart stuttering on an eager, painful beat. The things he wanted couldn't even be organized into a coherent thought or word, but they were intense enough to rob her of breath.

She swallowed hard. The current of his intentions was so strong it threatened to sweep her far off course. But this was too important for her to let it go. "Answer the question, Finn." A conscious order to get him back on track.

His aura flared pink again. He leaned forward an inch more, and his arms tightened, pulling her hips an inch closer. "I'm ever at your command."

16

He was in heaven.

Better. He was home. He had Laura in his bed, in his arms, and in his mind, soaking into every thought and desire. Her command wasn't even the strongly-worded suggestion he'd imagined it to be. She made him *want* to obey as if it had always been his intention. Rather than set her will against his, she danced around it and swayed him to her rhythm.

And Finn loved the hell out of it. The pleasure of her persuasion was as sharp as it was unexpected, and he didn't want to lose it by giving in too quickly. Did it have the same effect on everyone, or was it just his particular brand of perversion?

"I'm waiting."

Finn almost purred. He closed his eyes for a moment, basking in her presence until it became a shield against the ugliness he was about to share. "The Shadows are extremely selective when it comes to recruiting. They have a very specific list of requirements, but when they find someone who fits, it comes down to any means necessary. I've only ever heard of two or three people getting out of the draft. They have ways of persuading you to their side of things."

Sometimes, recruits were chosen because their ideology and aggression made them a perfect fit. But more often than not, candidates had to be forcefully brought to heel.

He didn't want to go into those details.

Laura wasn't about to let him omit a single one. "How did they convince you to sign on?"

Her will was a phantom caress along his jaw, commanding it to unclench. His lips parted as if for a kiss, and his tongue unstuck from the roof of his mouth to speak the truth he knew would break her heart all over again. "They told me about you," he confessed. "Not you specifically. Your gift of persuasion."

She tensed. "I never—"

"I know," he said quickly, hating the anger in her voice too much to let her finish the sentence. "*Now*. Back then, all I heard was the betrayal."

"How did they even know about me?" The lightest of tremors moved through her limbs.

Her vulnerability cut him to the bone. He let go of her to pull back the covers so they could get under them and hide. Finn spooned Laura, tucking her tightly into him when she shrank in on herself. He could shield her from anything except the truth—because she wouldn't let him.

"To be honest, I don't know that they did. They never used names. They talked around the persuasion like it could be anyone in my life. Read me like a book and pushed every button to drive the point home." Straight into his heart. He'd broken Laura's by leaving with them. They'd shattered his by making him think she'd betrayed him first.

"So they made you hate me so much the whole planet wasn't enough space to put between us," she said bitterly.

He squeezed her tighter, eliminating any remaining distance. "Something like that."

"And it took you twenty years to realize they'd lied?"

"I was young and naïve, not an idiot. I thought myself out of that nonsense as soon as I calmed down—about an hour into the shuttle flight off-world. But…"

"But what?" A harder push. This was too important for her to allow him to leave anything else unsaid. She was still tense, and now she wasn't even breathing.

Finn's throat ached with the need to speak—his, not hers. "Once you're in, there is no way out. Except in a body bag."

Laura sighed, unclenching the slightest bit on a shiver.

Her original command still had hold of him. Now that he'd said the worst part—for her—the rest came out easier. "Their basic training is brutal. They work you until you drop, and then they prop you up and make you work some more. Roughly twenty percent of my unit washed out from there." Half of them in body bags.

"And then the real work begins. There are tests you have to go through, so they can sort you into the proper ranks. Obstacle courses with live weapons in play, strategy games where one wrong step can get you maimed or killed, and when your body's exhausted and your head's spinning from constantly being on alert and in fear for your life, they sit you down in a sterile room, and make you take a written exam. Another half of us gone."

Finn had watched one guy break into tears and shove his arm into a vat of acid up to his elbow to make the terror stop. The Sergeant Major had put a bullet in his head rather than waste time and medical resources trying to treat him.

He buried his nose in Laura's hair and breathed deeply for a few seconds.

She raised his left hand, inspecting the scar left over where a pinky should have been. "Sparring injury," he told her. "Shadows get pitted against each other to toughen up. It's one thing to fight against a civilian or even a regular soldier. But when you're facing another Shadow, that's someone who's been trained alongside you and who's been ordered to use deadly force. It's not the same."

"They made you fight against your friends."

Finn laced his fingers with hers and brought her hand to his mouth. She had the softest skin. "I got off easy. The guy I was sparring with didn't like inflicting pain. He was about to wash out—the hard way. But numbers is numbers, right? So the Sergeant Major decided to force him to toughen up. Threw him into the rink and ordered him to kill me. My arm was broken. I was holding it against my chest when he stabbed me. The blade took my finger and stuck in my dog tags underneath."

"That's horrible!"

Finn absorbed her outrage like a balm that fell short of soothing the pain. "John could have speared a fly at ten paces with that blade. He could have aimed an inch to the side, punctured a lung, and we wouldn't be here, having this discussion right now. The Sergeant Major chalked it up to bad aim but, really, what John did was defy a direct order. And no one noticed but me."

And they'd never talked about it, even to each other, until the day John got his brains fried for the last time. They'd saved each other's asses dozens of times in training and on assignments, but that one act of mercy had hung over Finn's head ever since. He'd owed John his life, and when the time had come to repay his debt, Finn had stood back and watched his friend die.

And now he would never get the chance to make it right.

"Is that all?"

How he wished it was. "You already know the Shadow's primary targets are telepaths."

"How could I forget?"

"Well, you can't send soldiers with guns against people whose minds are weapons. They told us we'd be undergoing treatments to make us less susceptible to telepathic manipulation. Once a week for six months, and then every other month after that, we had to report to the infirmary. The doctor sat us down, strapped us in, put a thin little band on our heads, and fried the fuck out of our brains."

Laura went stiff as a board in his arms, twisting to look at him, but he held her in place, facing forward. He couldn't talk about this shit to her face. It was bad enough to say it out loud at all.

"You can probably guess, it didn't do jack shit against telepaths. But it was never meant to. It was EMC. Targeted electromagnetic pulses, coupled with an extra special blend of chemicals injected straight into the brain. One fried neural pathways, the other made it harder for them to reform."

"What do you—"

"Mind control. Stress-induced conditioning wasn't enough. They needed to make sure their troops would never step out of line, no matter what they were ordered to do. A brainwashed soldier doesn't ask questions. He doesn't have a conscience. He doesn't feel the need to get out."

Laura whimpered.

Finn hunched a little tighter around her.

"How did you get out?" she asked.

Her fingers were still entwined with his. He rubbed his thumb over her knuckles to make her unclench. She was squeezing his hand so hard her nails would draw blood soon. "I got lucky. I was sent to betray my only true friend, and he reminded me of something they'd tried really hard to make me forget." Another mercy and one more debt weighing down his soul. He'd carry it to hell with him, and it would burn him for all of eternity. "He said I used to call out your name in my sleep."

His words fell on Laura like physical blows. She hurt for him, and she felt ashamed of ever thinking badly of him. For so long, she'd wallowed in her own misery, hating him for leaving her, and the whole time, he'd been stuck in hell, calling out for her.

They'd cut him off from everyone he'd ever loved, anyone who could have stepped in and helped him, and messed with his mind in the cruelest, most sadistic way possible to make him into something he would never have become otherwise.

They'd taken away his free will.

How was she any different? Sure, her way was less painful, but the end result was the same. And she was doing it even now!

As he'd talked, Laura's hold on Finn's mind had already frayed to almost nothing. She released him completely and began to draw her shields back up.

He sucked in a sharp breath, and a desperate stab of panic pierced through her. "Stop! Don't leave, please."

"But you just said—"

Non-starter. His need for connection overrode everything else. "I said they tried to fry you out of my head. They knew as long as I had you, I was a potential liability."

"You got your free will back when you deserted. I can't take it away from you again."

Another shot of fear. He needed to convince her otherwise—as the Shadows had taught him, by any means necessary. In this case, the only leverage left to him was desire.

He pressed his mouth to her shoulder, "Sweet, sweet Laura, you still don't understand." Finn trailed kisses up the side of her neck to the sensitive hollow at her ear. She couldn't concentrate. Her partial shields threatened to disintegrate. "Your persuasion is the only reason I survived with my brain intact. My memories of you singing to me kept me from turning into a brainless psychopath."

"I can't…"

A flare of needle-sharp orange sparks exploded from Finn, passing through her to encompass them both. They jittered anxiously, their elongated spikes pointing outward. "What they wanted was control," he said, palming her breast with one hand and slipping the other down her belly, under the waistband of her loose pants, to cup her between her legs. "What we have is trust. I need that. I need you."

Echo chamber.

Everywhere Laura turned, all she felt was desperate need. His, hers—it didn't matter anymore.

Her legs twitched apart to give him better access, her body arching into his touch. "Oh, my God…" Too long without intimacy.

Had it been anyone else, Laura would have fought it. But this was Finn. He was as much part of her as she was of him. Their bond had survived twenty years of separation, torment, and hardship. That made it more than just unbreakable. It was inevitable.

The meager shields she'd managed to build up crumbled. Without them, the orange sparks of Finn's panic flared to a blinding brightness, sending her heart rate through the roof.

Laura caught his hands, her desire-hazed mind sluggish to form words. "Wait, Finn, wait."

His clever fingers stroked down her clit, teasing at her slick entrance, making her moan. It would take so little to send her over the edge.

"Trust me," he said against her jaw. "Let me do this. Let me make you feel good."

But this was wrong. Finn wasn't that guy. It wasn't true desire that drove him. It was fear. She's made him relive his worst memories and left him in them. He wasn't even hard anymore.

Laura curled her fingers around his and turned her will on the orange sparks, dulling them enough to make him loosen his hold. He was in no way dissuaded, but it gave Laura enough room to turn around in his arms and press her mouth to his.

Finn yanked her leg over his hip and clamped his arms around her to hold her in place as he thrust his tongue into her mouth with desperate force.

Laura couldn't form a proper command. His mind was elsewhere, hidden beneath an impenetrable cloud of nightmares. The only recourse she had was to try dulling his fear.

The visual component of her persuasion wasn't much more than a directional marker, but when emotions ran high enough to interfere with conscious decision-making, sometimes the lights and sparks worked like anchors. Laura caught the spikes of his fear hovering far outside of him and his control. She became a vortex, swirling through them, dulling them into points of light, drawing them closer, all the while stroking her hands across his shoulders and back in what she hoped was a soothing rhythm.

He was shivering, his fingers digging hard into her hips with the force of his panic.

Even lessened in their intensity, the orange sparks fought her efforts to pull them back. They might have lost their sharpness, but they still stung, returning back through her to cling to Finn's skin. Already, his shivers eased, and his breathing evened out. His desperate kiss softened as he registered her in his mind and began to regain control of his thoughts and actions.

The sparks flickered wildly between orange and pink as his hands unclenched and his knee drew up, pressing his thigh snuggly between her legs. Laura cocooned his mind in calm and "breathed" safety through it, infusing his fear with blue roots of lethargy. The orange faded to white, then took on a pale blue.

Finn shuddered and ended their kiss on a sigh, pressing his forehead against hers. "I'm sorry. I didn't mean… This wasn't supposed to—"

"Shh," she soothed. "It's okay."

She began to pull back into herself, but a stray orange spark flared out from him like an ember. "Stay with me," he pleaded.

"I'm not going anywhere."

Finn's desperate hold on her relaxed a little. He brushed her short hair away from her face. His heavy-lidded gaze traced the path of his fingers as he feathered them across her brow, down her nose. His thumb caressed her cheek, down to her jaw, and across to the center of her chin as if he was trying to memorize her face. "Are you real?"

Her heart broke for the uncertainty in his voice. "Yes. I'm real. You're safe now."

He smiled a little, but her command was already making it hard for him to keep his eyes open.

"Rowe, Rowe, row your boat, gently down the stream," she whisper-sang, deepening his need for sleep. "If Miss Laura should command, life is but a dream."

Finn's eyes closed, and his limbs turned heavy as he sank into a deep sleep. With his breath puffing a gentle rhythm against her forehead, Laura closed her eyes and drifted off as well.

She dreamed of dark hallways and bright white rooms and chasing a shadow of something always just out of sight.

~

The Roost

Talon was in a mood again.

Vega pulled out a knife and honing stick to keep herself busy and out of the way. Her jaw muscles ached. If she wasn't careful, she'd pull one again. Down three steps on the main floor of the vault, Talon's men had built a rink out of old, empty crates. And inside of it, Talon was getting his rocks off pummeling a guy who was too scared to put up a real fight. The last guy who'd tried had earned himself a hearty handshake and a shot to the head. Their psychotic leader didn't like being shown up.

It was late. Everyone was too damned tired for Talon's theatrics, but they all still gathered to give him at least a half-hearted cheer when he landed a solid blow. He didn't notice, too busy venting his vitriol on the poor schmuck in the rink with him.

They all knew what had Talon fit to be tied. The recon teams he'd put on Rowe weren't giving him shit. Rowe spent most of his time in his room. If he went out, he didn't do anything except jog, eat, stop by the grocery store for a six-pack of beer, and then go back to his room. They hadn't seen any sign of him making inquiries about John Wayland. He hadn't used his inn console to initiate off-world calls or search any off-world databases. He hadn't even gone back to the charity house in the valley.

Another thing Talon didn't like: lack of intel.

Which was why he was now shirtless, sweating like a pig, and all but frothing at the mouth as he beat the shit out of Matt Kerrigan, one of the first Hounds outside of their original unit to be inducted into Talon's little enterprise.

An extra loud cheer went up.

Vega glanced over. Matt was on the ground and not getting up again. Talon had won the bout but didn't look satisfied. *Fuck.* It was going to be a long, bloody night. She ducked her head and applied herself to sharpening her blade. As long as she stayed under his radar, Talon wouldn't summon her into the rink. She was the closest thing he'd ever have to a Hawk under his command. He wouldn't waste her needlessly. Although the device he'd injected at the base of her skull for insurance wasn't exactly reassuring her of her value to him.

The crates scraped across concrete as someone shoved them out of the way to yank Kerrigan free of the rink. His face was fucked up, and he had blood coming out of his ears. Vega would be surprised if he made it through the night.

Talon, meanwhile, had a snarl hooked into his mouth as he surveyed the gathering with bloodshot eyes. He pointed a bloodied finger at someone else, and Vega almost swore out loud. The guy was new and hadn't learned the ropes yet. He might actually give Talon a fight. And then die for it.

Whatever. She wasn't about to get involved. As the only woman in Talon's growing army, she had learned not to stand out. It only made her a target. Being singled out as one of Talon's seconds in command was bad enough. Vega went out of her way not to make waves unless she was ready to kill someone—because that's what it usually came down to. You didn't leave a Hound defeated and humiliated and expect to see the sun rise again.

And the sick part was, Talon encouraged them all to settle disagreements cleanly. In his mind, defeat meant weakness, and he wouldn't have it among his ranks. That his ranks were made up of rabid, disorganized dogs ever at each other's throats as a result didn't seem to bother him.

The newbie entered the rink; the crates enclosed him. He squared off with Talon, grinning because he didn't know any better, probably itching for what he thought would be a decent spar.

Meanwhile, Talon spat blood on the floor and hopped around like a championship fighter, still full of his boundless manic energy. Vega had never seen Talon tired. Lazy, yes. Asleep, sure. But never tired.

Out of nowhere, Talon stopped, shook his head hard, then clutched at his temples and roared.

In the next second, he was shaking out his arms and wiping his nose, back to hopping around as if nothing had happened.

Vega shifted an inch farther along her stair. Not much farther she could go; she was almost at the corner.

The sounds of fighting resumed, and Vega ducked her head lower, turning a degree more into the stair. She couldn't look away completely—Talon would notice—but she'd become pretty adept at tuning out unsavory sights and sounds without losing all awareness of what was happening around her. Knowing they were about to be two men down gave Vega a lot of food for thought.

There'd been six Hawks total in Vega's original unit and close to three hundred Hounds. By her measure, those proportions had been roughly equal across all Shadow units. Hawks weren't like Hounds. They were made different, trained to think and fight differently. Talon would give anything to get one, but Finnegan Rowe?

Most people who'd gotten drafted into the Shadows had either washed out or fallen in line. No middle ground. But there'd always been something the slightest bit off about Rowe. He'd never stepped out of line like Wayland had, but Vega had seen his brow quirk down for a split second once when he'd received an order he hadn't liked. She'd heard him hesitate a breath before answering a question—and dammit, why couldn't she remember what the question had been?

Rowe was smart, skilled, and resourceful. More importantly, he could think for himself and was good at it.

He also didn't seem to think much of Talon or what he'd managed to accomplish here. Talon would never get Rowe to heel on command. And if it came right down to it, she believed Rowe might actually have a fighting chance at bringing Talon down.

The idea was worth explor—

A glint of something metallic sailed across her vision and clinked off the stair two above the one she occupied. "Are we boring you?"

Vega loosened her white-knuckled hold on her knife and covertly worked her jaw unlocked before she turned to face Talon. She didn't dignify his remark with a comment. A trick she'd learned during her short stint of Hawk training before they failed her was that people didn't like silence and non-answers. Keeping one's own counsel was the best way to get an enemy riled enough to make a mistake.

In Talon's case, it could mean risking life and limb, but Vega kept forgetting why she should exercise caution. She could take him in a fight if need be; she could outshoot him any day. The only thing keeping her in line where Talon was concerned was that motherfucking little device attached to her spine and the controls for it he'd programmed into a chip in the side of his own neck.

The new guy was bent over, throwing up into one of the empty crates, but still alive. Someone must have clued him in. Or maybe he just wasn't as good as Talon. Noted.

"You keep sharpening those knives, there won't be much left of them." Talon snarled a grin, showing off his bloodied teeth. "What say you and I go a round, eh?"

Vega slid her knife into its sheath, holding his challenging gaze. Then she took out another one to sharpen.

"No," he said, accurately interpreting her wordless response. "How about I give you an advantage? I'll let you tie an arm behind my back."

She ignored him, running the honing stick slowly down the blade from hilt to tip.

Electric fire erupted at the base of her skull, searing her brain and racing down her spine. Her implements dropped from her hands as her body convulsed for several seconds. When it stopped, Vega was leaning against the stairs above, shaking.

"How 'bout you look at me when I'm fucking talking to you?" Talon growled down below.

Caution.

She kept forgetting the why.

"Got your attention now? Huh?"

A side effect of the zap was that the muscles in her fingers and toes kept cramping for an hour after. It hurt like a sonofabitch, but she couldn't make a sound. Any show of weakness would make her a target. Rolling her shoulders straight again, Vega swiveled around in her seat to face Talon. "Waiting"—she took a breath—"for you to show me. Something worth looking at."

"The fuck did you just say to me?" He still had a hand on his neck. The smallest tap would initiate another merciless zap.

"You're toying with him," she said. "It's beneath you."

Raising an eyebrow at the challenge, Talon crossed the rink to the newbie. He maintained eye contact with Vega as he grabbed the guy by his hair to yank his head back.

The newbie made a weak attempt at defending himself, but now there was a knife in Talon's hand, and he pressed the blade to the newbie's throat, waiting for Vega's reaction.

No one else moved a muscle. The half-hearted cheers had stopped, and everyone present was watching the interplay, waiting for someone to tip their hand.

Better him than me.

That was really all it came down to. Someone was going to die tonight, and Vega still had things to live for. So she didn't say anything as Talon watched her, didn't give him any response at all, putting it all on him.

And she didn't blink when he pulled the blade across the newbie's neck with enough force to cut almost halfway through it.

Talon shoved the corpse aside and tossed away the knife like so much garbage, still staring her down. Didn't look like this would be one of the times when he burst out laughing at his own joke and moved on to something else. Tonight, Talon was out for blood and might be crazy enough to ask for Vega's next.

Funny how it didn't upset her much. She was tired of dealing with his particular brand of unhinged. She might take him out herself, save Rowe the trouble.

"We got a transmission!"

Talon broke their staring contest as casually as someone in his state of mind could. "From where?"

"Avencore."

Vega breathed a covert sigh and picked up her knife and honing stick again. Her hands cramped too much to use them, but at least they gave her something solid to hold onto while she listened to the Mars 2 Hound mutter at the controls.

Their satellites were a handy disruption, but they made even Shadow communications more complicated. Instead of video calls, they had to rely on one-directional transmissions. When the frequency was tuned correctly, the transmission was instantaneous. When it was off by the smallest fraction, the message had to be hunted down and reconstructed, and sometimes they didn't catch all the pieces to make a whole. The people in charge of communications played a merry game with the weather always shifting the bands out of sync. And Talon had no patience for mistakes.

The two at the controls scrambled to retrieve the message while Talon, still dripping with the newbie's blood, stalked over to them. No one wanted a rabid animal at their backs.

Finally, something came through, and Talon leaned closer to the screen to watch it twice over. From her perch, Vega could see over his shoulder. The video was short: a figure in a long coat coming down the sidewalk in the rain to enter the inn. It had been shot from across the street, so they didn't get a clear view of who it was. Vega recognized the walk, though, which meant Talon would, too.

"Is there audio?"

The Hound shook his head. "Not in this transmission. It may be coming separately."

And they couldn't do much other than wait for it to arrive. If they tried to respond, it might disrupt anything else coming their way.

Vega couldn't quite contain her snort. "Send a Houd after a Hawk."

She didn't realize she'd said it out loud until another zap clenched her teeth close to cracking. Pain in her jaw—strained TMJ, exactly what she'd been trying to avoid. She'd be eating her meals through a straw for the next week.

"What was that? Didn't quite catch it."

Vega couldn't speak. Her brain felt fried, words floating like autumn leaves between her ears, and she couldn't catch any of them. Only a pained moan would come out if she tried to open her mouth. Better to keep it shut.

Then Talon was standing over her, bloodshot eyes wide with a feral kind of craze. He plucked the knife out of her hand and pressed the tip of it to her cheek under her left eye. She felt it break the skin but couldn't do a damned thing about it, cramped from head to toe, seconds away from sliding down the stairs.

"I own you," he told her, pulling the knife across her cheek and down to her jaw, leaving a bloody, inverted C in its tracks. "You continue to live only as long as it pleases me to keep you around. Don't ever forget that."

When he was finished, he held up the blade, turning it into the light. "This is an exemplary tool. Now I get why you keep it in such good shape." He sounded almost sincere. "Better put it somewhere safe," he advised and stabbed it into her thigh.

Vega, holding her breath to keep from making a sound, almost passed out, but she refused to leave herself vulnerable. The others left her alone, bleeding on the stairs, while Talon handed out orders. Now that he finally had something to go on, the rabid energy from before was all gone, replaced with the militaristic drive of a professional killer. It was almost a welcome change of pace.

"I want five more men on Rowe," Talon was saying. "Six on Laura Belden's charity. And someone find out how the fuck she got all the way to Avencore!"

He didn't believe in coincidence any more than Vega did. If Laura Belden was making house calls to the Hawk, there would be a reason, and Talon would follow that clue to its bitter end on the off chance it would bring Finnegan Rowe to heel.

Glancing back at Vega still huddled on the stairs, he gave her an indulgent smile, far more sinister than any other expression she'd ever seen on his face. "Even a Hawk has tells. You just gotta know where to look."

That might be true, but Vega would still lay odds on Rowe over Talon any day.

Regardless, Laura Belden didn't deserve to get caught in the middle of their turf war. Talon was mean enough to torture her in all kinds of creative ways if it made Rowe squirm. Or just for the hell of it.

Vega would feel sorry for the woman later. First, she had to work the cramps out of her hand long enough to remove her own goddamn knife from her thigh.

There'd be time enough to think about the other players and plot her revenge after she'd stopped the bleeding.

17

July 4, 3039

The room was set to gradually brighten at dawn. Beams of artificial lights whispered across Finn's eyelids, dragging him from the deep, dark pit of dreamless sleep. With his front pressed to the mattress, Finn felt as if he'd dropped onto the bed last night and hadn't moved until morning.

It took him longer than it should have to register another presence in the room with him. He turned his head.

Laura was right there, watching him. The imitation of sunbeams filtering through swaying tree branches played across her skin, adorning her in a golden glow. "You're here." He hadn't dreamed it.

Which meant…

Finn groaned and buried his face in the pillows.

"How do you feel?" she asked, all solicitous concern. He imagined it was the voice she used on her charges or wild animals that needed to be soothed.

Meanwhile, Finn's memory of the night before made him wish he could sink through the mattress and keep sinking until he'd made it all the way through the core of the planet and out the other side. All this time he'd thought he could be her knight in shining armor, and at the first test of inner strength, he'd not only failed, he'd practically attacked her.

The line he'd crossed was unforgivable. She should have run from the room straight back to Karsengale.

Laura's fingers sifted into his hair, her nails scraping lightly across his scalp. "Hey, you okay?"

Finn knew she was being kind, and it made him feel worse. He pushed himself up to sit on the edge of the bed, facing away from her. Christ, how did everything get turned on its head so quickly? "I shouldn't have told you what I did last night."

"I'm glad you did." There was that fucking tone again.

"I shouldn't have done what I did, either."

"You weren't yourself."

Finn scoffed. "Wasn't I?" *Live among monsters long enough, guess what you become.*

A pillow hit him in the back of the head.

Finn twisted around to find Laura glaring at him.

"Are you done kicking yourself? Let me answer that: You are. *I—can—feel—intent.* And I'm not some helpless, blushing maiden, either. Big bad Shadow or not, if I sensed you meant me harm, you better believe you wouldn't have lived long enough to act on it." He opened his mouth to argue, and she held up her hand. "Period. End of story. You need me to kick your ass again to prove it?"

Finn scowled. "I let you win that time."

"I let you let me win."

A tickle of laughter tightened muscles over his still-bruised ribs, underscoring her point. Sort of. "Okay, okay, I give up. Peace." Despite all her training and proficiency, Finn still maintained there was no way Laura could match him in a physical fight. But, as she'd proven last night, she didn't need to.

It didn't excuse his actions but there was a small sense of relief in knowing he didn't have to walk on eggshells around Laura. She'd seen his demons, and she wasn't running away. And that made them—and Finn—hers.

As if sensing his change of mood, Laura became serious. "So… where do we go from here?"

It sobered him, as well. "You need to go back to Karsengale." There was a house full of Shadows across the street who'd seen her spend the night with him at the inn. Finn had to make sure the information didn't go any farther, and he needed Laura far away and out of the line of fire when he went knocking at their door.

She didn't look happy with his answer. "Will I see you again?"

"I'm not going anywhere."

"Even though I'm still married, and you're *not that guy*?"

She was being flip, trying to make light of the situation. Finn should have played along. But, when it came to Laura, every moment felt too important not to grasp. So he met her gaze and held it until her cheeks flushed and her lips parted a little. "I'm trying not to be that guy, Laura. But I'm still only human." With twenty years of regret and longing under his belt. "Remember that next time you come knocking on my door."

And, because she could read intent, he made sure she picked up on every nuance of his. Finn wanted Laura enough to fight and kill for her. He wouldn't trespass where he wasn't invited, but if she came to him again, he wouldn't be stopped by a marriage certificate, her family obligations, or even his conscience. If she chose him back, whatever happened would be inevitable. But it would be by her choice.

He knew they had an understanding when she got shy and changed the subject. "What about the Shadows?"

The Shadows were a problem, but a significantly smaller one now that Emma was in play.

Still, none of them could afford to underestimate Latham.

Finn crossed to his dresser to retrieve a clean set of clothes. "Assume they already know everything about everyone. They'll have all your escape routes mapped before you decide which way to go. They'll know what you can do and take measures to protect themselves from your persuasion. If they want to kill you, you'll never see them coming."

Laura gulped. "At ease, man. Damn."

Finn rounded the bed and pulled her out from under the covers to stand up with him. "There's no such thing as 'at ease' with the Shadows."

She tucked her hair behind her ear. "So, what are you saying? There's no way to escape them?"

"Depends on how badly you want to escape and what you're willing to leave behind to do it."

She paled. "What?"

Fuck, this was impossible. They needed weapons, transportation, and a clear path from Karsengale to Hadran City. If Finn could get them all there, he could get them off-world and someplace safe within the SU network.

The getting there was where his plans fell apart.

"We have to operate under the assumption that whatever plan we come up with will fail. Someone's going to get caught."

Laura was already shaking her head. "No. Unacceptable. No one gets left behind." It wasn't an order, just Laura putting her foot down.

"Did I say we were leaving someone behind? You wanted to know what you're in for. I'm telling you. No matter what we do, how well we prepare, how hard we try, we will fail at some point. Knowing it is an advantage. It gives us a chance to prepare in a way they might not see coming. Who else in your group can fight like you?"

Finn kept saying 'we.' And he didn't only mean himself and Laura. He was including all of her people by default. It meant everything to her.

Laura gave it some serious thought before she answered. "Miguel, Gigi—Georgiana—Henley, and Beau."

"What about Quinn?"

Laura shook her head. "He could throw things around if he had to, but he's not a trained fighter." And she didn't want him to use himself as a living shield, either. "He'd be more useful getting everyone and their belongings to safety.

Finn absorbed the information without comment. "Who are your most vulnerable, aside from William?"

"The kids, of course. We have eight under the age of ten and Rusty." Rusty would want to fight. It'd be a battle just to get her out of the line of fire. "You should know none of the adults are in what you'd call fighting form."

"I'll need a list of their ailments and weaknesses."

Laura bristled.

Finn held up his hands for peace. "No one gets left behind, right? So we get the weakest out first and fastest. Your rear guard should only be made up of people who can take a stand to hold off the enemy and then haul ass out of there as soon as everyone else is clear."

It made sense, strategically speaking. "I'll be the rear guard," she decided. She could tell he didn't like the idea. "I can fight, and if you have a spare weapon, I'm a pretty good shot, too."

Finn crossed his arms over his chest and sized her up like a soldier trainee he wasn't quite sure was up to snuff. "Shooting at people is a lot different than shooting at painted targets."

"I am, actually, aware of that."

"Can you shoot someone down, knowing they'll never get back up again?"

"Well, it's not like I'm looking forward to it. But it's my job to keep my family safe. If I have to kill a Shadow or two to give them a fighting chance, I'll find a way to live with it."

Finn stared her down as if expecting her to flinch. Laura would have thought by now he'd understand how hard her back was pressed against the wall. She had no path of retreat, no other course of action available to her except to fight her way out.

Emma understood. She was counting on Laura to do her part, and Laura planned to be ready. The redhead could explain it to Finn when she brought him up to speed.

Finn's shoulders drooped a little on a sigh. "You should get going. Your family will be anxious to have you back."

"What about you?"

"Checkout's tomorrow at nine," he said with a smirk. A shower of angry red sparks flashed out from him, threatening violence aimed away from Laura. "Guess I'll have to go find another place to stay." He reached underneath the mattress and pulled out a handgun. "In case you run into trouble."

Laura accepted the weapon. It was pretty standard as far as handguns went. Lightweight, with only a battery cartridge and a barrel that ended in a lens. It fired concentrated plasma pulses that could be programmed to stun or burn a hole through a person's head, depending on the set level of intensity and the charge left in the battery. She checked the side. "Figured you wouldn't be the warning shot type." The gun was set to full blast.

Finn cupped her chin and made her look him in the eye. "I need you to understand the second you leave here, you're at war."

"Finn, I've been at war for the last three years."

18

Despite the brave face she put on, Laura was nervous stepping out of the inn. Early morning heat had kicked up a thick mist after last night's rain. Everything beyond ten feet in front of her was a wall of white with who knew what hiding there. Finn's speech had made her paranoid. She flinched at the smallest rustle of leaves or the patter of unseen footsteps. She imagined Shadows circled around her, waiting to shoot her down at any second.

Laura had never been so glad to get into a taxi and close the door. It activated, rising off the ground and displaying the unfinished route on the screen with an option to resume or cancel. She canceled the pre-programmed navigation. The screen asked her to confirm an extra charge, which she did, hoping Emma would understand. The taxi's service changed to a day rental. It would let her drive wherever she wanted until eight in the evening, at which point it would stop wherever it was to let her out and then return to its depot. Laura planned to be done with it long before then.

Luckily, the miserable weather kept the roadways clear and the stores empty as she made the rounds. She got what she could from the half-empty shelves, splurging on hearty, good-quality foods with meats and plant proteins for energy. With plenty of cash still left, she stopped at a clothing store to get a few items for herself and those at the compound who needed them most. The kids always grew out of their wardrobes in a couple of months, and there were only so many times seams could be let out.

The parking lot for the clothing store was across the road from a doctor's office. Laura stared at the big red cross, glowing in the misty soup for a whole five minutes, wheels turning in her head. Finn had said they had to get the most vulnerable among them out first and fastest. She checked the time, then closed the taxi and ran across the road into the doctor's office.

Two hours later, Laura made her way back to the taxi much slower than she'd left it.

Focus on the good, she told herself.

She'd made appointments for William, all the kids, and Rusty for tomorrow. They'd get checked out with proper equipment and get proper diagnoses for what the fallout had damaged and how to fix it. Same as Laura had just done.

Focus on the good, dammit!

All of her most vulnerable people would be leaving the compound first thing in the morning, and none of them would go back if she had anything to say about it. With William so sick and the others in need of extensive care, it made sense to move everyone into town rather than ferry them back and forth between doctors' offices and the compound.

Laura hoped the Shadows ran themselves ragged trying to trace her new source of funds. Maybe it would keep them too busy to notice their gradual evacuation.

She almost took a turn back toward the inn to tell Finn about her plan, maybe take strength from him before heading out to Karsengale. Her brain kicked in and made her swerve the taxi back onto the road out of town instead. Finn had told her they couldn't be seen together.

Still, it left her feeling hollow and strangely fragile as she drove out of Avencore and over the mountains back to Karsengale Valley.

Does it really matter?

It didn't.

In the grand scheme of things, her ailment was a small price to pay compared to some. Eskel slept less and less these days. Miguel got tremors so bad he couldn't stand upright. Rusty had to use a sonic cleaner wand to wash herself and couldn't take the smallest sip of water. Alexis' bones were now so brittle that the lightest bump fractured them.

What was a relatively healthy future without her own biological children compared to that? She had plenty of other kids to take care of; she didn't need any more.

At least the weather in the valley had cleared up. The sun shone bright, and the ground was almost dry again when Laura returned to the compound.

Rusty was the first to run out and greet her with a suffocating hug. "We thought you'd never come back! Where have you been?"

Laura hugged her back just as fiercely, nodding to the rest of them who'd come out, all grim-faced and wary. "I'll tell you all about it over lunch. But first, can you help me unpack?"

Rusty's eyes lit up, and she squealed as Laura opened the taxi's storage compartment. Naturally, the rest of the kids flocked in right after to see what the fuss was all about. Before Laura could say anything, they started pulling out the clothes and running off with them like little squirrels.

Eskel, of all people, sidled up to crane his neck for a peak. "What's all this?"

"Laura," Quinn piped in, holding up a twelve-pack of frozen beef patties. There were three more underneath that one. "This is insane. Where did it all come from?"

Darax shouldered him aside and pulled out a big basket of breads to carry inside. "Gift horse. Not looking." He inhaled deeply and shuddered. "Smells almost too good to be true."

While they unloaded, Laura ducked back to the console and programmed a new trip for the morning. The cabin could hold five adults, but if they squeezed in really tight, she could probably fit in all the kids and William. Possibly Alexis, too. They'd need a second babysitter to look after the kids while Laura tended to William.

Eskel was waiting for her when she climbed back out of the cabin. That always meant bad news. "How is he?" she asked softly.

"Same, for the most part."

She wasn't sure whether to be relieved or disappointed. "Has he asked about me?"

Eskel shook his head.

"Oh."

"Laura, we should talk about…" he trailed off as the noise inside the compound raised to deafening levels.

Laura managed a crooked smile. "I think they found the ice cream."

Eskel raised an eyebrow. "Yeah, that would do it."

"I have something for you, too." From the passenger seat, she retrieved a black bag with a flat bottom and a secured rack of glass bottles inside. "I thought you could take a look at these and tell me what they are. The people who gave them to me don't seem like the type to hurt folk for the hell of it, but even so. I'd feel much safer if you confirmed the contents."

Eskel nodded, rubbing his chin.

"And let's hold off on our discussion for a bit, okay? I'd like to get all the adults together after lunch. I think…" She looked around to make sure no one was within hearing, then motioned Eskel closer to whisper directly in his ear. "I think I may have found a way out."

He pulled back to search her gaze. "Are you serious?"

"After lunch, okay? We don't make a move unless everyone agrees."

Making sure the taxi was idled down and wouldn't be going anywhere until she was good and ready, Laura took Eskel's arm, and they headed inside. They were swarmed immediately by excited children and wide-eyed adults. Rusty hugged her around the waist again and wouldn't let go for a full five minutes while Laura answered questions left and right.

"Okay, okay," she finally said. "The rest can wait for later. I need to go check on William."

Rusty reluctantly let her go. "Don't leave us like that again, okay?"

Laura kissed her forehead. "Not if I can help it," she promised. "Now go help Sisa with lunch."

Rusty ran off.

Laura took a few minutes to change her clothes and brush out her hair in her room before heading into William's. "I have some really good news and some great news. Which do you want to…" the words trailed off into silence.

An unfamiliar, round-cheeked face smiled at her. "Hello, Mrs. Belden."

Fury rose like hot magma up her spine, making her quiver.

"Laura, don't," William cautioned.

The Shadow lounging so casually in her chair pushed to his feet.

He was about as tall as Laura but outweighed her once over with pure muscle, stretching his red-gray uniform to its limits. "Before you start throwing your weight around," he said, inching closer to William, "you should know I'm not here on my own. I got six buddies out there, listening. They will raze this place to the ground if I'm compromised."

"It's all right," William tried to assure her. He looked remarkably calm in the presence of a murderer. How long had the Shadow been there? What the hell had he said to William?

"Do you want to sit and talk like reasonable adults, or do I tell my men to open fire?"

Laura's blood boiled. He was telling the truth. Attacking him in any way would just get her and everyone else in the compound killed.

"I should also mention that my men have protection," the Shadow added, tapping his right temple.

"But you don't."

He was wide open, a halo of green with hints of yellow glowing around his head. "Show of good faith," he said. Bullshit. He was playing with her because he knew he couldn't lose.

"What do you want?"

"I want to know who your new friends are." Three stray sparks of bright red flared out into the halo. "You took a hell of a ride, Mrs. Belden." He said her name with an inflection that made color rise in her cheeks. "And you came back today with a whole taxi full of goodies. Last I checked, Christmas isn't for another five months." He sat on the bed beside William and put an arm across the headboard. Two more red sparks joined the first three, and Laura's hands curled into fists. He'd hurt William to get answers out of her.

William, for his part, remained utterly composed and unafraid. Laura should have taken strength from his confidence, but all it did was make her want to scream. There was no fight in him. He wouldn't lift a finger against the Shadow unless he thought it would somehow help Laura escape. She quickly nudged him away from that plan. No one was getting hurt today because of her.

"Talon wants answers, and I figure the fastest way to get them is straight from the source. So. If it wasn't Santa Claus gifting you taxi rides and presents for all the good little boys and girls, then who?"

"The Easter Bunny."

The Shadow chuckled, and his green halo flared red. "You know, I like you," he lied. "Talon thinks you might pose a threat, but me? Nah. I think of you more as a...*challenge*." Pink snaked through the red. "I think there's a part of you that secretly wants to be dominated. But you won't give in easily, will you? You like a bit of fight."

"That's enough," William snapped.

"Oh, I'm just getting started."

"No, you're done," Laura said, pushing at the red halo to shrink it into a deep orange. It was enough to scare him off the topic but not change his attitude, so she gave him a verbal push from another angle guaranteed to make him squirm. "You don't want to keep Talon waiting, do you?"

His ugly smirk faded as his mouth pressed into a tight, nervous line. "No, we wouldn't want that," he agreed. "So why don't you tell me what I want to know? Then I can get out of your hair, and you can get on with whatever it is you think you're going to accomplish here."

"I have nothing to tell you. Talon can go fuck himself."

Of course, Rusty would have to choose that exact moment to let herself in without permission. "Hey Laura, Sisa wants to know if—" She stopped dead, eyes huge.

"Get out of here," Laura snapped.

"No, stay," the Shadow countered. "There's always room for pretty girls like you."

"Rusty!"

The girl fled. In five seconds flat, everyone would know the compound had been infiltrated. Laura hoped to God they followed protocol and didn't do something reckless like try to attack.

"Last chance, Mrs. Belden." The Shadow now had a knife in his hand, scraping the tip of it up and down William's cheek. He had a very specific plan for it. If she pushed him to reconsider, he'd definitely notice, and he'd sic his buddies on the compound. She couldn't risk it.

She couldn't let him cut out William's eye, either.

And she definitely couldn't tell him the truth about her benefactors.

"Tick-tock..." The blade pushed in a little more.

William sucked in a deeper breath and froze on a flash of fear.

"I don't know!"

The knife stopped half an inch from William's eye. The Shadow waited.

"I don't know where the taxi came from, okay? It showed up on its own yesterday morning."

"She's telling the truth," William added. He sounded so calm.

"Where did you go?"

"Avencore."

William winced, and a droplet of blood appeared at the tip of the knife.

"Don't lie to me. We know you left the region."

"Okay, fine." Laura pushed him to ease off on the knife. She didn't say another word until he'd complied. "Olendra. It took me to Olendra. There was a house with a stack of cash and a note." Not a complete lie. Just not the whole truth.

"Where is the note?"

"I left it there."

"What did it say?"

"'Use as needed.' I stopped in Avencore to buy supplies and make appointments for the kids at the doctor's office in town." Still part of the truth. He wouldn't mark the lie in any physical tell if it was at least a partial truth.

The halo around his head turned a cruel shade between green and red. "Where did you spend the night?"

"At the only place I could," she grated.

"With…?"

"A hot shower and a warm bed. I told you what I know. Now I want you to get out." Harder push to make him lower the knife away from William's face.

The Shadow contemplated William, who now stared straight ahead, with his jaw tight and his hands curled into fists around the covers. A drop of blood had painted a straight line down his cheek and underneath his chin. The Shadow sighed and put away the knife. "Talon won't like what I'll have to tell him."

"Then tell him this: The next asshole in a uniform who comes into *my house* without permission will not be walking back out." She underscored it by snaking a deep desire through the Shadow to get himself and his buddies out of there as quickly as possible and never come back.

A fine sheen of sweat broke out on the soldier's forehead. He kept his composure, but the halo around his head fractured into sparks of yellow and white. He couldn't wait to leave, but he'd still make a production of it—for his buddies' benefit.

And, because she didn't want her home to turn into a massive, scorched crater, Laura let him stalk up to her until his nose was inches from hers. She endured his rancid breath on her face when he spoke his final, "I'll be seeing you again."

He hadn't entered through the front door, but he did leave through it, trailing mud across the floor the whole way.

Laura waited for something big to happen after the door closed behind the Shadow. She wouldn't have put it past them to blow up the taxi, just to show they could. But when the soldier's marching footsteps faded into silence, it stayed silent for a long time, with only her ragged breathing to mark the passing minutes.

Finally, William sighed. "Laura—"

"Pack a bag. We're leaving. Right fucking now."

19

Finn had done his best to stick to his usual routine after Laura left, giving the Shadows no reason to think he was in any way concerned about her. He'd gone for a jog, checked in at the grocery store to get the kid's receipt from the clerk, and stopped at the Café for a casual breakfast, where he'd covertly watched Laura's taxi as it'd passed by on the way out to Karsengale. He'd made himself sit there for another hour before returning to the inn.

That was as far as his patience would stretch.

It occurred to Finn he had two problems to solve. One: No other lodgings were available in Avencore or any of its closest townships for a hundred miles. Two: The Shadows assigned to watch him had a record of his night with Laura, which they might or might not have already relayed to Latham.

Two birds, one stone.

Finn checked his wrist unit and left lens to make sure they were linked and functioning, then set his gun to seventy-eight percent—enough to kill without the mess of blood spatter to clean up afterward. With a rapid rhythm of blinks, the vision in his left eye changed to pick up heat signatures. He saw a prone figure through the ceiling at the back of the inn. That would be Ms. Thane, still sound asleep.

Finn hoped she wouldn't mind that he left the door unlocked when he let himself out. It wouldn't be for long. The fog was thick enough to cut with a knife, but the lens, controlled by his wrist unit, automatically popped up a holographic grid of the street layout around him. The roadway was heated from underneath, but the mechanism had broken down a while ago, from the looks of things. It caused hotspots in his vision where the heating worked overtime while leaving the rest of the path cold.

The dilapidated house across the street registered three heat signatures, all clustered in a room upstairs. How disappointing.

Finn crossed the street, jogged up the stairs, and knocked on the front door, putting his hands casually behind his back. Good manners were the hallmark of a proper Hawk. He didn't hear the occupants rouse, but their heat signatures moved fast. Two of them armed up while the third stayed by the window facing the inn.

Finn hummed to himself as he waited for the two to make their way downstairs. Through the doorway, he saw one heat signature fall back behind a corner as the other approached the door sideways, a weapon in his hand. Adorable. Futile but adorable.

The door opened onto a very confused former soldier doing his best impression of a normal person. Finn gave him a sunny smile. "Hi there, neighbor!" Then he raised his gun and fired.

The Hound fell back before his brain had registered he was dead. Finn pushed his way inside and closed the door as he dived sideways to avoid a shot from the backup. It scorched a hole in the reinforced door where his head had been a second ago. Good aim. Slow reflexes.

"So, which unit were you with?"

Unimaginative curses floated his way, and Finn grinned, twisting the dial on the side of his wrist unit to remove a small pin. He tossed it down the hallway toward the soldier and covered his eyes.

The flash was silent but blinding. He heard the soldier yelp as he fumbled around, tripping over his own feet. Finn counted to ten, making sure the flash had burned itself out, then came into the hallway to find the former Hound writhing on the ground, sweeping his weapon left and right. Finn shot him in passing, mostly to make sure he didn't accidentally land a hit somewhere important.

The third occupant of the house was on the floor above. He would have heard some subtle commotion but nothing to indicate an all-out fight. Still, he should have been there to cover his buddies, especially when he knew they were surveilling a Hawk.

"Anybody else home?" Finn called in advance of his reaching the second-floor landing. The heat signature was still in the same room a few yards ahead, except it had moved from the window to the door.

Finn didn't relish the idea of a prolonged shootout. He had the house down the block to hit after this one, and he wanted to get it done quickly in case one of them decided tailing Laura around town was anything less than a suicidal idea.

The heat signature hadn't moved. Finn cocked his head, then twisted the top of his wrist unit just short of activating a percussion pulse.

Sounds behind him registered a split second before the blow to the backs of his knees. Finn dropped and rolled away, coming up in a twist to catch a booted foot aimed at his head. He shoved away the Shadow shimmering with a heat shield. Clever. Finally, someone with a few braincells still in semi-working order. Very few.

Finn winked three times to clear the heat sensor from his vision and surged up to meet the idiot who'd decided hand-to-hand combat was the best way to bring down a Hawk. "You know," he said as he broke the guy's elbow, "a Hawk would have put a bullet in my head when he had the chance."

The soldier, following combat protocol, pulled a knife.

Finn deflected with his gun, then raised it to fire one shot through the underside of the Shadow's jaw. Blood sprayed from his mouth as his teeth slammed together and shattered. Finn winced, wiping some of it off his face. He quickly swept the rest of the house, but only the Shadows' equipment remained. Most of it was outdated or damaged in some way. None was worth taking. Not even their weapons, which all had a battery pack so depleted they weren't good for more than a shot or two. At least that explained why only the backup downstairs had fired at him.

Their surveillance equipment was set to record, not stream. Finn checked it, and confirmed they had more than enough to deduce Finn and Laura were an item. He erased it, then smashed everything for good measure. It wouldn't do shit if the Shadows had already sent the recording in a batch transmission, but it made him feel a little better.

He retrieved his light flare pin on the ground floor and closed the door behind him when he left the house, heading for the next one.

Someone must have called in an attack. A knife flew out of the mist and whooshed past his ear as he approached the second house. Finn had barely enough time to reactivate the heat sensor in his lens before the soldiers attacked at once.

Eight heat signatures—he fired twice and got the gun kicked out of his grasp—six heat signatures hid in the mist. More than three times the number he'd anticipated. Latham must have sent reinforcements in the night, which meant this wasn't the full assault team.

A blow to his jaw sent him spinning straight into a kick to his midsection. Finn dropped and raised his wrist in preparation for setting off a percussion pulse that would drop all of them, but someone in the gang still remembered what a wrist unit was. He leaped forward and tore the gadget from Finn's wrist, which also deactivated the lens.

The percussion pulse went off high above them as he tossed it into the air. Then three men laid into him, pummeling him without mercy.

Finn pulled Vega's knife out of his boot and slashed the first leg he saw coming at him. Worn-out boot leather was a meager barrier against the tough, sharp edge of the blade. The Shadow's Achilles' tendon was severed. The soldier fell back, giving Finn a brief two feet of space to get his legs under him before hands grabbed him to yank him back. He cut one wrist and stabbed another, leaving the blade behind as he was shoved onto the ground.

A knee pressed into the center of his chest to keep him in his place as the soldier it belonged to drew back for a punch. Too slow. Finn brought his legs up, hooking his ankle around the guy's head to tip him off balance. Sloppy—he'd been aiming for the throat. They rolled and broke apart, but before Finn could find his feet again, someone else knocked him over.

That someone then dropped to the ground next to him, glassy eyes staring into the sky.

Finn braced for more. By his count, three were now dead, two incapacitated, and one more injured but functional. Three were still unaccounted for. Without his wrist unit, he couldn't track them by heat. He was blind in the mist, and although sounds carried well, he couldn't pinpoint their origin. He drew two more knives and pushed to stand.

His knee buckled, keeping him down.

Quick footsteps to his left.

Finn turned and threw his knife at the oncoming threat.

Nothing but a killer reflex saved the man's life. He knocked the blade off course the way a normal person would swat a fly. Then the ghost of John Wayland stepped out of the mist, grinning as he came up to Finn and hauled him to his feet. "Hello."

"What—"

"You dropped this," John said, slapping Finn's wrist unit back onto his arm.

Right on his heels, Emma greeted Finn with a sunny smile and a wave. "That was fun! You got any more?"

Finn must have taken a blow to the head at some point. This couldn't be real. "This isn't real. You can't be here."

John-motherfucking-Wayland.

Not in a coma. Not dead. Not on Torrey.

His hair was longer, and he was sporting a short beard like some kind of savage. If he'd been trying for a disguise, he'd failed. And he was smiling as if nothing was wrong in his world when he and Emma knew John had a bounty on his head.

"Tell me you're not here right now!"

Emma made her expression as sober as someone like her could. "We're not here right now."

"But we are," John said.

"Sweet Jesus, are you both insane? You trying to get your ticket punched?"

John scowled. "I'm not retired."

"What?"

Emma rolled her eyes. "What he means is, he's not *retired.*"

"Thanks for the clarification. You can let go now."

John released him, and Finn's knee promptly buckled. "Fuck."

"You're getting old, brother." John hauled him to his feet again and shoved a shoulder into his side, forcing Finn to lean on him as they led him back toward the inn.

"Hey, this is a nice feather," Emma said, sliding Vega's blade back into Finn's boot sheath. "You shouldn't leave your gifts lying around. Someone might betray them."

John pumped his fist in the air. "Viva la Vega."

Finn stared at him. "You sound like Emma. The fuck is wrong with you?"

"Prose conflicted," John said with an easy grin. "But muse fully operational."

Finn shook his head. One clusterfuck at a time. "We need to clear the bodies off the—"

"Taken care of," Emma told him, holding the door open for them. She closed it behind them and turned every lock and bolt exactly the way Ms. Thane always did. "Let's sit."

Finn's ass had just made contact with an armchair when Ms. Thane came rushing down the stairs. "Who let you in?" she demanded of John.

"The door was open."

"No, it wasn't."

"Then how did we get in?"

The ornery innkeeper didn't have an answer. "I'm booked up starting tomorrow."

"We know," the three of them chorused.

Then John produced a stack of cash. "Reservation under Sue Torrey. We're early."

At the sight of money, Ms. Thane's eyes lit up, but she covered admirably with a scowl in Finn's direction. "I'm one room short until tomorrow. And there'll be an extra fee for checking in ahead of schedule."

Good God, the woman was mercenary right down to her cash register of a soul.

"He's keeping his room," Emma declared. "Part of the booking."

"John," Finn waited until his crazy-ass friend met his gaze, then told him in no uncertain terms, "*No.* You need to disappear."

John grinned. "Motherfucker, who you think you're talking to?"

Someone knocked on the front door. The bell was still broken.

"That would be our friends," Emma told Ms. Thane. "It's safe to let them in."

Not about to be ordered around, Ms. Thane made a show of putting away her cash first and bringing out the big ledger behind her check-in desk to write something down. They all waited for her to finish, including whoever was on the other side of the door. They didn't knock a second time.

When Ms. Thane finally moved herself to unlock and open the door, a group of people walked in whom Finn vaguely recognized.

"Street's clear," said a man roughly in his twenties, with the lanky build of someone not yet fully matured into his frame. If memory served, it was Sorry, so named because it'd been the one and only word he'd spoken for the first two weeks after being taken in from the gutter.

Behind him was a young girl with wild hair pulled back in a lopsided bun. The Brain. She didn't waste time on greetings. Bag of medical tools in hand, she came directly over to Finn. "Look straight ahead," she ordered, shining a light into his eyes.

Two more members of Emma's branch of the SU and a third Finn didn't recognize hauled in a big suitcase and a duffel bag each and kept Ms. Thane busy with room assignments while the Brain tortured Finn with her inspection.

He brushed her away when she reached for the waistband of his pants to pull up his shirt. "Enough already."

"As your primary care physician—"

"I'm gonna stop you right there. You're not."

She was in no way dissuaded. "—it is my duty to make sure you stay in one piece."

Finn raised his arms wide. "Still in one piece."

"He can't walk," John tattled.

Finn could have happily murdered him.

The Brain sat on the floor and cut through Finn's pant legs to mid-thigh. She propped his foot on the little coffee table and then twisted to inspect the underside of his knee.

"This is embarrassing." The Brain might have been a genius, but she was still all of sixteen years old if she was a day. She looked more like a kid playing pretend than an honest-to-God medical professional.

John snorted. "Wait 'til she asks you to turn your head and cough."

Emma frowned at the window. "What did we do with the inkblot?"

"Scattered," John told her. "Is something wrong?"

Emma shook her head slowly, her gaze growing unfocused.

Finn sat up, a cold knot tightening in his gut. He didn't like the look on her face. "What's going on? What do you see?"

Emma flapped her hand to shut him up and crossed to the window, pulling back the drapes to look out onto the street. She wouldn't see much through the mist, but she wasn't trying to.

The Brain finally emerged upright. "Bruised tendons. You'll be fine."

"Like I told you," Finn retorted, but his attention was on the redhead gazing out into nothing, her head tilted as if she was trying to hear the ceiling talk. Every muscle in his body tensed in readiness. Whatever she was picking up meant trouble. He quickly thought through the layout of the inn, the fastest route out of town, and any place along the way they could use for cover. If the Shadows were coming, it wouldn't be on foot.

"Finn, you have a horse, right?" Emma asked without breaking her stare.

"I have a rental if that's what you mean." Could never be sure of anything with her.

Emma let the drapes fall back into place as she headed for the door. "Sorry, get ready to ride," she said, swinging the door open wide to admit—

Finn shot to his feet, bruised tendons notwithstanding. "*Laura?*" He was halfway to the check-in desk before his knee gave out, forcing him to stop where he could use a wooden pillar for support.

She came through, supporting her husband on one side, with the young girl, Rusty, holding him up on the other. William looked ready to call it, shaky, sweaty, his face pinched with obvious pain. Still, he tried his hardest to stay on his own two feet.

Behind them, a gaggle of kids rushed in and swarmed throughout the place, buzzing in awe at everything and everyone.

As soon as the kids were out of the way, the Brain and another telepath relieved Laura and Rusty of William's weight. "We'll take him."

Laura nodded and let them. "Thank you."

"What happened?" Finn demanded.

Laura started for him, then stopped herself, looking uncertain. "Talon sent one of his Shadows to pay us a visit. I thought we'd be safer here. I have all the kids, but I couldn't fit any more into the taxi.

Finn, I need to get the rest of my people out of there."

"I'll drive."

"No, you won't," John said. "Shit hits the fan, you don't even have an umbrella. I'll go."

"The hell you will, man! They'll shoot you on sight."

"Then I'll have to stay quiet, won't I?" He dismissed Finn and turned his attention to Laura and Sorry. "You lead, we follow."

Laura shot Finn a quick glance, then nodded. "Let's go."

Emma had the grace to wait until Laura was out of sight before she ducked under his arm to help him back to his room. Like a fucking invalid.

Like William.

"They won't be seen," Emma assured him. "I won't let them."

Finn winced when she sat him on the bed. The tendons would be fine in a few hours if he could get the Brain to score him some ointment to keep down the swelling. But until then, he was about as useful as a doorstop. "It's not enough. I need to—"

"Rest," Emma told him. "Just rest. You have an army at your back. You don't have to fight the war alone."

"Tell me she's going to be okay," he said quietly, searching Emma's gaze.

Her eyes went unfocused. "As safe as any of us."

He gritted his teeth. "That's not an answer." He needed to be there to watch Laura's back, to make sure she got out safely and that no one followed her out of Karsengale.

Emma gave him a sad smile. "It's all I have without Michael."

20

Three transports were a lot better than one. Still, the whole way back to Karsengale, Laura worried that she'd arrive to find the compound reduced to a pile of rubble. The drive took almost two hours and left her nothing to do on the way but chew her lip bloody.

As soon as the three vehicles came to a stop outside the compound, people started pouring out the door. Darax and Eskel coordinated the distribution, neither one wasting time on questions. Quinn and Miguel were in charge of stuffing their meager belongings into the storage spaces. They'd had plenty of time to pack but, thank goodness for their resourceful hearts, they hadn't packed more than the barest necessities.

With everyone and their belongings onboard, and space left over in the taxi, Laura sent the other two transports on their way. She and Quinn raided the storage house for anything that would travel and keep. "Waste not," Quinn said, picking up a crate of produce like it was made of paper and air.

"I only wish we could take all of it." What a waste to leave even a morsel of something so precious behind. But the taxi could only hold so much.

"Don't even think about coming back a third time."

It physically hurt Laura to turn away from a box of raw potatoes and radishes. But she did—she had to. "I can't, anyway. It'll be dark by the time we get to Avencore."

The storage box had to be forced shut, and the taxi wavered in its hover as she started it up again. A warning message flashed on the screen, saying the weight limit had been exceeded, and then another one saying the passenger count was over capacity. Laura cleared both, accepting the additional charge in case the vehicle was damaged, then took off as fast as the taxi would allow.

No sign of Shadows yet.

Reemy wheezed in the back seat. She was sitting on Kolbi's lap, squished all the way to the window to give Alexis on Gale's lap more room so she wouldn't get bumped and hurt accidentally. With Vex all but crushing Ollie underneath him, it was an uncomfortably tight squeeze for all of them.

Laura opened the window on her side so the air would flow back to Reemy.

"Do we have a plan?" Ollie asked. He tried to shift into a better position and bumped Vex's head against the ceiling in the process. "Sorry."

Vex winced. "All good." He was too busy squinting out the window. Poor thing probably couldn't see more than blobs of color. He'd be blind in a few months if he didn't get proper treatment.

"The plan is to get to Avencore," Laura said.

"And then what?" This from Quinn.

She hadn't had time to explain anything to anyone earlier. As soon as the Shadow had left, she'd packed up William and the kids and hit the road, promising to be right back to get the rest of them. But "right back" had still taken a round trip of several hours, even without delays. It was a long time to go on very little information. They had to be scared out of their minds.

"I was contacted by an organization that wants to help us," she explained. "I don't know all the details, but they sent the taxi, they gave me the money to buy more supplies, and they're offering to get off-world."

"Off-world to where?" Alexis asked.

Laura shrugged. "Anywhere." She had the funds for anything they might need. No more scraping for bare necessities; no more raising walls by hand. They could have a mansion each and plenty left over to live in the lap of luxury—just not on Anamtaigh. "We can figure out the details later. Right now, I need to get everyone someplace safe."

"And you're sure this organization is *safe*?" Ollie pushed.

"Yeah," Reemy chimed in. "What if they end up worse than the Shadows?"

"Do you trust me?"

Seven different voices sounded their yes.

"Then *trust me*."

Laura had no doubt she'd get a hundred more questions from the others once they reached Avencore. She'd have to be ready to give them at least some answers, but she'd need Emma and John to help her.

After a moment of silence, Quinn shifted in his seat, not quite relaxing, but close enough. "Do we at least have a place to sleep in Avencore?"

~

When they finally arrived at the inn, its entry hall was quiet. Ms. Thane met Laura at the front desk and told her their reservation—of which Laura knew nothing—was for a whole month, paid in full. She handed Laura a touchpad to program room keys to each person's wrist chip, then told them where to find their rooms and where to get food if they were hungry.

Laura made the rounds first, checking to make sure everyone was settled in and comfortable. She didn't get the questions she'd been expecting. It appeared the SU delegation had done most of the explaining for her. Laura was grateful but couldn't escape a nagging suspicion that there was more going on, telepathically speaking.

The whole group had been divided five people to every room, with at least one adult in the room to keep an eye on the kids. It was still a tight squeeze, but compared to the conditions in the compound, the inn was a plush mansion. Not to mention, every room had a bathtub, for which every woman thanked her profusely.

By the time she'd assured herself that everyone was settled, it was late into the night, and Laura was exhausted. She was dragging her feet to the room she'd be sharing with William when she came up on Emma sitting on the staircase with her head resting against the railing and her eyes closed. "Ts dotted and Is crossed," she said without moving.

Laura nodded and took a seat on the same stair. "I can't thank you enough for this."

Emma sighed. "Nothing in this world is free." She sounded tired, saying it as if she was speaking from a dream. "There will be a price to pay."

"Of course. I'll make sure you and the SU are repaid in full for every expense—with interest."

"'Fraid this is going to cost a lot more than money."

Laura was prepared for that, too. "Whatever you need."

"Do you trust me?" Emma asked, echoing Laura's words from the taxi earlier. She even said it in the exact same inflection, pitching her voice to match Laura's.

But they'd been at least a hundred miles away when she'd said it. How could Emma have picked up on it from so far away?

You're exhausted. It was nothing more than her weary mind playing tricks. She was on edge and reading too much into nothing. "I think so," she replied.

Emma slit open one eye to look at her. "Terrible idea, really."

Laura chuckled. "I figured as much." Then she sobered. "But beggars can't be choosers, right? We don't get to be picky about who pulls us out of hell."

Emma hummed in agreement, a small smile playing on her lips. "Maybe not. But we do have other choices. Like what we do with the hand holding ours once we're out." The way her chin tilted ever so slightly, it was almost as if she was hinting at something in particular.

An image of Finn popped into her head, standing tall yet still unsure in a slant of sunlight and shadow right after he'd helped them raise the first storage house wall. Laura couldn't tell whether it was her own doing or Emma's, and that worried her. Shouldn't she feel when she was being manipulated?

"How come you're so coherent all of a sudden?"

Emma groaned and tapped a finger against her temple. "Brain's here. Therapy time. Never does anything calendarly, but makes her feel like she's swimming."

"I'm told your medic is encouraging my people to keep their doctor's appointments." There was a question and maybe a bit of accusation behind the statement. Laura had made the appointments out of practicality, but part of her had expected the treatments to come from

Emma's SU. With the Brain in the house, she would have thought the young medic would take over the care of her people and collaborate with Eskel to get them the treatments they needed. To have them all referred back to the Avencore clinic was a bit of a slap-down. It was a not-so-subtle message that they were in different lanes and that Laura should stay in hers until she was told otherwise. Until she'd paid off her debt?

"Waste not," Emma said as she pushed to her feet. Another echo of Laura's earlier conversations from even farther away. "The Shadows will come, you know. If we're weakened, they'll swallow us."

In other words, the SU medic needed to save her energy and supplies for when the fighting started. She wouldn't be wasting it on things others were fully capable of doing. It was triage, pure and simple. And, although it stung, Laura understood.

"You should get some sleep," Emma advised, dragging her feet upstairs to the room she shared with her former Shadow husband. "Heavy day tomorrow."

"Heavy day?"

But Emma was already too far to bother clarifying.

Laura rubbed her brow. She was tired, but the thought of sleep made her anxious. Nevertheless, she descended the rest of the way to the main floor and to room number one, where William would probably be fast asleep. She passed number three along the way and paused for a second.

The moment they'd crossed city limits into Avencore, Laura had realized she'd be spending the night under the same roof as Finn again. She'd dreaded facing him with all her people there to scrutinize every look and word passing between them. She'd worried she'd start blushing every time they crossed paths and give herself away.

She needn't have bothered.

Finn hadn't been there to meet Laura when she came back. He hadn't come out of his room a single time to say hello or ask her how it went.

I'm still only human. He was leaving the choice up to her.

Laura kept going to room number one.

William had propped himself up against the headboard to wait for her. The bedside lamp was on, but, as she'd thought, he was fast asleep, chin to chest. The taxi ride had taken a lot out of him. Eskel had left a note next to the meds to let her know William had had his nightly dose and should sleep soundly through the night.

Laura gently tugged her husband into a more comfortable position and tucked the covers around him. She was too tired to do much more than take a quick shower and brush her teeth, but when she climbed into bed next to William and turned off the lights, sleep wouldn't come.

She stared at the ceiling, counting William's deep breaths for what felt like hours, and still, her eyes refused to close for longer than a blink.

The clock beside her read 12:26.

Maybe she was hungry. Laura hadn't eaten anything since that morning except an apple on the last trip back from Karsengale.

Her stomach clenched at the thought of food. Nope. Not hungry.

Something felt off. The covers didn't sit right. The mattress was the slightest bit dented in the middle. The curtains were drawn, and it was too dark.

Something too much and missing at the same time. Just like her shoes.

The room didn't fit.

Laura turned her head to check on William, then quietly slipped out of bed. She didn't bother with shoes, but she did pull her sweater on over her worn pajamas. Closing the door softly behind her, she padded a few feet down the hall to the room opposite hers and knocked as softly as she could, with almost no sound at all. No way anyone would have heard it, including—

The door opened.

Laura gulped, looking up into Finn's face. He'd acquired new bruises today, but they must have been treated because they'd already faded to almost nothing, along with the ones she'd given him. He was glowing pink all over, residual firefly sparks filling the room behind him. His gaze snared hers with a silent knowing. It warmed and burned and pushed and pulled and mirrored everything she was feeling, too.

Neither of them spoke—there was nothing to say.

Finn had left the choice to her, and she'd chosen to knock.

He pushed the door open wider, quietly admitting her inside.

21

The inn was finally filled to the rafters, as Ms. Thane had threatened it would be. Between Laura's people and Emma's team, every room was filled to capacity and then some. At least ten of the residents were telepaths, trained to keep their thoughts to themselves, but Finn knew they'd be picking up more than a few surface thoughts, especially if they were loud enough.

They would have been getting a mindful from Finn all day.

He hadn't been able to stop thinking about Laura. The way she'd felt in his arms last night, in his mind. Finn wanted a do-over. He needed Laura by his side, in his bed, to know she was safe. To be able to touch her the way he craved. Not a mindset he was itching to advertise to all and sundry. So he'd hidden in his room as soon as Laura had left and hadn't come out since.

And now she was there as if he'd summoned her out of a dream.

He closed the door and softly latched it, locking them in the heady darkness. The blackout blinds were drawn; the privacy shield engaged on the off chance a stray Shadow still lurked somewhere nearby. It was just him and Laura and a bed.

She shouldn't be there. But he couldn't bring himself to send her away.

Only human. A flawed, selfish one who'd been pushed far beyond the limits of his endurance today. Finn's attack on the Shadows and their visit to Laura were both declarations of war. As of this morning, there was no predicting how it would all turn out, and every moment was too precious to waste.

Finn had no intention of asking questions. He was too busy cataloging his blessings, starting with every cropped strand of hair on top of her head down to every frayed thread of her worn-out pajamas.

Laura turned to him, her hands whispering at his waist, not quite touching. Her bare feet aligned with his, and her loose sweater brushed his stomach, making his abs clench in anticipation. He could feel her body heat teasing along his skin and smell the barest hint of her perfume underneath the clean unremarkable scent of soap.

But what little was left of the sane, logical part of his mind held him still, insisting she might have come to him for another reason. So Finn waited. The first move would have to be hers.

And then it came, the softest brush of her mind against his, all silk and warmth, nudging his hand up to her cheek. She nuzzled into his palm and let him tilt her face up for his kiss. None of the rough, sloppy desperation from before. Finn took his time and savored every taste. He thrilled at the hitch in her breath, the little sound she made as she leaned into him.

She would feel his need, but it was her desire guiding him, and Finn was eager to obey, catching her up in his arms, squeezing her securely to him as her legs wrapped around his hips.

She wanted safety, to be hidden from the world and all its troubles. So Finn yanked up the covers and bore her down underneath them as they billowed back into place. He pulled up her sweater and pajama top enough to bare her breasts, and she let him go so he could make a feast of them.

Laura slapped a hand over her mouth to smother a moan. She might as well have screamed an aria into his ear. Finn ground his hard-on into the mattress, already on the brink of coming, just from this.

But he wanted more.

He slipped his hand into the waist of her pajama pants, cupped her ass cheek, and squeezed in appreciation. He never released her nipple from the light scrape of his teeth, but she felt his pleasured groan reverberate against her flesh as she tilted her hips up to his. She wanted to feel more of him, the hard length of his erection against her, inside her.

He obliged her with one hard, deliberate thrust, and then he was gone again, pulling her pants all the way off. *Yes!* No more barriers.

But too much space. Her silent command willed him back. He

couldn't tell anymore what he did of his own accord and what he did because she wanted him to. Her need and his danced around in his head, complimenting each other, *agreeing* until there was no more distinction between them, and Finn felt Laura as if their minds were one.

Self-control was a garment Laura had left behind when she'd walked out of room number one. There was nothing left in her but need. Bright magenta blazed in her vision. Finn's desire—hers. A sea of it drowning out everything else.

And then she felt his mouth on her stomach. Her abdomen. He licked across the crease between her right thigh and her torso and followed the line to her pussy. She felt his breath against her clit; felt his shoulders shudder between her thighs. A blinding flare of pink, and then his mouth was on her, and Laura bit down on her wrist to hold back a scream.

Sucking, licking, nipping, the thrust of his tongue against her, inside her. He clutched her thighs to keep her still as he ravished her with a hunger she wouldn't have expected. Not enough brain power to even think of stopping him. He wouldn't even if she tried. Finn had one goal in mind, and he wouldn't be denied by anything or anyone.

His desire throbbed a steady rhythm in her mind, mirroring the movement of his tongue: *Come. Come. Come.* He built her up so high all she could do was shatter. And he lapped up her pleasure, all but purring against her as she shivered with the aftershocks.

Finn climbed up over her, tenting the covers, pulling them up over their heads. He kissed her hard, letting her taste herself on his tongue. Snaking an arm around her waist, he tilted up her hips, and her knees fell outward to receive him.

But there, with the hard length of him sliding up and down over her slick folds, he released her lips to say, "Still not too late."

Still trying not to be that guy, despite how much he wanted this. He would not take what wasn't given not just freely but with vibrant enthusiasm.

So Laura reached down between them to grasp him at the base. His breath left him in a soft "*Ha!*" that fanned across her chin. She couldn't see his face clearly, but she saw the way his pink aura deepened with the strength of his need. She stroked him once, twice, loving the way his back bowed and his hips curled into her touch.

Then she brought the tip of him exactly where she wanted it to go, wriggled her hips lower to take it in, and gave him free rein.

Finn shuddered over her, resisting for a heartbeat before he lowered his weight onto her, pressing her deeper into the soft mattress. He brought his knee up, pushing her leg farther out, and then he moved, and, *Oh, sweet Jesus and all the saints.* Laura's head fell against the pillows, her eyes rolling back at the sheer beauty of it.

He pushed in slow, and thank God for that. His girth stretched her almost to her limits, a soft burn accompanying the heavenly fullness invading her. She moaned at the loss when he pulled back, arched into him when he thrust forward, deeper each time. Harder.

Laura felt him watching her. Finn wanted to see, hear, feel, and taste—everything. Every minute detail of their joining. He wanted to remember.

It sent her over the edge a second time, and her nails bit into his shoulders. She couldn't tell if she'd drawn blood. He wouldn't have cared if she had. The smile he hid against the crook of her neck as he slowly rocked into her orgasm, savoring each spasm and shiver, was almost more than she could bear.

Come with me, she commanded. Goose bumps raised over his skin where her hands could reach. He tensed all over, pounded into her, huffing against her shoulder, clutching her so tight it almost hurt. Laura gave herself up to it, welcomed the ferocity of his lovemaking with everything she had and everything she was.

When she felt him come, it was almost a relief. The final piece of a vexing puzzle snapped into place at last. *This* was what she'd been missing all those years.

This finally felt *right.*

She let him roll them onto their sides but hooked her leg around him to keep them joined. His arm lay heavy over her waist, but he kept twitching it to pull/keep/hold her close. The beat of his heart raced in tandem with hers, and Laura savored it, sighed her contentment against his chest, and pressed a kiss to his clavicle. They were both exhausted, and she felt how hard he fought to stay awake, to not lose the smallest fraction of this moment. "You should sleep," she whispered, making it a command.

Finn tucked himself tighter around her and, with a soft whisper against her hair, fell asleep.

And for a long time afterward, Laura stayed awake, trying to wrap her mind around those three little words he'd just given her like a bedtime prayer.

22

It was still dark, and Finn was still fast asleep when Laura slipped out of his bed and quietly let herself out of the room. Not a single soul stirred through the hallways. No one was around to see her slip back into William's room and softly close the door behind her.

The light came on, making her jump.

"Are you ready to have that talk now, darling?"

Laura's stomach clenched, her entire body heating with a flush of shame she firmly told herself she had no reason to feel. Still, it took a great deal of effort to turn around and face her husband, however platonic, after having spent the night in another man's bed.

"You can't avoid me forever, you know. Only until I run out of time."

"William I—"

"If you don't mind, I should like to do the talking this time. And I very much need you to *listen*, for once."

Laura ducked her head. "You're angry."

He sighed. "I am tired, darling. I can't keep fighting my body *and* you at the same time anymore. Will you let me say my piece?"

He wouldn't be put off any longer.

When he held out his hand, Laura crossed to the bed, sat, and put her palm to his.

He had the hands of someone much older than his real age, bony, with loose skin and muscles that sometimes clutched too hard. His nails were immaculate but a hair longer than they should have been, making his fingers look skeletal. He'd been wasting away for so long Laura had stopped marking each change.

The sum total of them was now inescapable. William was a fraction of the man he'd used to be.

Husband or friend, they'd been in each other's lives for so long, she couldn't bear the thought of a world without him in it.

"I am dying." It was a statement of fact and nothing more. "And, were it only you and I, perhaps I might have accepted my lot with a little more grace, but it's not."

"Finn has nothing to do with this."

"I wasn't talking about our Mr. Rowe, but it is telling that his name was the first to come to your mind."

Laura flushed harder. Her jaw clenched against helpless tears. She kept doing everything wrong, saying all the wrong things. Maybe he was right; she needed to shut up and let him speak.

"You have a house full of people who are depending on you to keep them safe. Time was, I would have been right there by your side, making sure they were taken care of. That was our agreement. I was supposed to be your partner. As it turns out, I've rather become a hindrance."

"You are no such thing!"

He squeezed her hand and held up his other one for silence. "I don't need you to defend me, Laura. I need you to understand. I—am—finished. I have done everything I set out to do, and it's time for me to move on."

"*Now?* Just when we finally made some progress? We get out of a hole, and you want to call it quits before you even know what's possible?"

"What do you imagine to be possible for me? A decade or more of lying in bed with tubes shoved down my throat and into my veins? Days spent staring out the window at a world I can't ever walk again? Nights writhing in pain when the medicines wear off because I can't handle another dose? I know I haven't been the partner you deserved, but that seems like far too harsh a penance for my sins, don't you think?"

"The people who are helping us have a lot more resources at their disposal. They could have you on your feet in a month, for all we know."

Her words had no effect other than eliciting a look of pity from William. "A waste of time better spent on the others. They still have something to live for."

"And you don't?"

He raised an eyebrow. "Such as a wife and children, perhaps?"

Laura went cold all over. "That's not fair."

"But it is true," he insisted. "We have both made choices that led us here. There is no point in one blaming the other for them. *Choices*, Laura. Yours and mine. I have one choice left, and I have made it. For your sake, more than anything, I've put it off for as long as I could, but it's time. Now, I know you could stop me. But for my sake, I beg you not to."

Disarmed. He'd left her no ground to fight for. And still, she couldn't let it—him—go. "Will you at least see the doctor at the local clinic tomorrow before you do anything drastic? One day, that's all. Let them do some tests and give you a proper diagnosis, and after that, if you still want to… I won't stop you."

He looked away from her, almost as if he couldn't bear the sight anymore. She saw the muscles in his jaw twitch wildly as he closed his eyes for a while.

Thinking it over, or just bearing down against more pain?

Neither possibility eased Laura's conscience.

He made her wait for so long she thought he would ultimately refuse. But then his chin dipped in a nod. "One day," he agreed and released her. Discussion over.

"I was expecting you to rail at me about…something else."

Something that might have been the beginnings of a smile briefly tipped up one side of his mouth. "You've given me as much comfort as our respective positions allowed. How could I deny you the same?"

Laura buried her face in her hands. "I don't know what I'm doing anymore."

"That's not necessarily a bad thing," he retorted. "You always act like you have all the answers to solve all the problems. To have one's composure rattled is a necessary thing. It keeps us humble. As long as it's done with the right intentions, of course."

"You think Finn has the right intentions?"

She already knew he did. Finn might have been the boy who'd turned his back on her, but he'd returned a man who would put himself in harm's way without a moment's hesitation to keep her safe.

That protective instinct had been inside him from the moment he'd shown up, saving them all from a wall collapse, and it had only grown stronger since. It was ingrained in everything he did, down to the smallest, most unremarkable actions, like which side of the bed he took—the window side so he could shield her from it while keeping his eye on the door at her back.

The promise of safety in his arms and in his heart reached out to her every time he came near. It was so insistent it had become a part of his overall makeup, and it pulled her in so hard Laura couldn't resist anymore.

Three small words.

Would Finn even remember he'd said them out loud?

Had he meant them, or was it just something people said in the afterglow of amazing sex?

She hadn't said them back.

Finn was here—*now*. But what about a week from now? A year from now? What would happen once she got everyone to safety and didn't need Finn to protect them anymore? Would he stick around or call it mission accomplished and move on?

Would she want him to?

"Life is not about having all the answers," William said. "It's about the thrill of trying to figure them out."

~

July 5, 3039

Finn woke up to noises in the hall, holding a pillow instead of an armful of warm, soft Laura. He rubbed sleep from his eyes, listening to the commotion outside. It sounded like an invasion, laced through with children's voices squealing and laughing.

He'd slept through worse in his Shadow days. But this was the first time he thought a crowd of people outside his door might not be such a bad thing. Yes, they were loud. But in a way, the noise they made was almost comforting.

Laura must have left early to avoid being seen. He could understand that. Still, he wished she'd woken him up to say goodbye. The bed felt too big and empty without her.

Which meant he had no reason to stay in it.

He got up and worked out the stiffness from his joints. The Brain had come through, not just for his bruised tendons but the rest of his injuries, too. Aside from a little tension here and there, he was good as new. He'd have to ask her for more of that ointment before she left again.

A hot shower and a quick workout put him back to rights physically, but something still felt off. He wanted to see Laura, make sure she was okay.

Hand on the latch, Finn thumped his forehead against the door. *I'm not that guy.*

Nope, not true anymore.

So what now? Did Laura want him to act like everything was normal? Her sneaking away as she had would indicate so. But what if she'd been seen? Finn didn't want her to face the consequences on her own. Plus, it didn't sit right to leave William in the dark. He was a decent person who deserved the truth, and Finn was man enough to accept whatever came of it. But if William didn't know, and Finn told him, he might take out his anger on Laura.

"*Fuck.*" Finn was *not* this guy, goddammit.

But he didn't regret a single second of last night, either. And he had no intention of backing off as if nothing had happened. Laura had chosen to come to him, and that meant… Something.

Only she hadn't told him what.

And Finn…

He swore a long string of creative curses, banging his head against the door. He remembered thinking something right before nodding off. Couldn't recall if he'd actually said it out loud or not. Fucking Christ, he hoped not. That was the last thing any of them needed. Emotional entanglements complicated everything, especially in the heat of battle.

He needed intel. Couldn't form any kind of strategy if he didn't have the first idea of what the lay of the land was. He'd talk to Laura, get his head on straight, and go from there. Easy enough.

Finn opened the door and let himself out.

"Ah, Mr. Rowe. Just the man I was hoping to see."

Finn reacted like a Shadow trainee caught mid-fuckup. He pulled his shoulders back and turned at attention. A Hawk never showed weakness.

William was dressed in the same clothes he'd worn the night of the dinner, but they seemed to be even looser on him now than before. His illness was obvious in every line on his face and the slight hunch of his body as he made his way forward with one hand on the wall for support. The eight steps required to bring him within arm's length cost him dearly. He was winded by the time he stopped in front of Finn, his pallid face burning with two bright spots of color on his cheeks and a sheen of sweat across his brow.

Finn's first question slipped off his tongue before he could think it through. "Should you be out of bed?"

William waved away the idea as unimportant. "I thought we might have a chat, you and I. Man to, well, walking corpse, as it were. If you're amenable, of course."

Consequences. Finn nodded. "Do you want to come in?"

William didn't look any more comfortable with it than Finn. "I'd rather take a ride if you wouldn't mind." He pulled a flask out of his pocket. "You drive. I provide the spirits."

Finn held out his hand, indicating for William to lead the way. His rental transport was parked right outside, but it took five minutes to get to it, with William's slow, shuffling gait. Finn would have offered to help, but something told him the man was hanging on to his dignity by a thread. He didn't need his efforts undermined.

Finally, they were both seated, and Finn raised the vehicle off the ground. "Where to?"

"There used to be a lovely little hilltop above Old River. Do you know it?"

Oh, he knew it. "As I recall, it had a beautiful thousand-foot drop down into the gorge."

William smiled. "Shall we?"

Finn was getting a bad feeling about this. "Does Laura know what you're up to?"

"Happily, Laura is occupied with other matters at the moment and unavailable to tell me I'm too weak for a friendly outing."

"Is it? Friendly, I mean."

William looked him dead in the eye, and for the life of him, Finn could not find a hint of animosity in the man's steady blue gaze. "Is there any reason it shouldn't be?"

Finn pulled away from the curb and set course toward Old River. They didn't speak along the way, something that didn't seem to bother William nearly as much as it bothered Finn. Silence was always the best way to throw an opponent off balance. He knew this. It was a tactic he used often because it was so effective. Now he was gaining a new, deeper understanding of why.

The drive wasn't long, half an hour, maybe. When they got to the drop-off, Finn made sure to set down a safe distance back from the edge.

It truly was a beautiful site.

Serene, one might say.

The grass was still green here. The mountains on either side of them were a patchwork of brown and gray rock. The river itself wasn't visible except from the very edge of the drop-off, but the valley stretching out from the mountain's base was breathtaking. Late morning shined every color to its most vibrant. Puffy white clouds meandered across a cerulean sky. Now that the rains had finally moved on, everything burst with fresh life, and the air was scented with clean, wet earth and flowers.

William lowered himself to an even patch of grass and breathed a sigh so deep it almost doubled the circumference of his emaciated chest on the inhale. "Stunning," he said on the exhale. "Please, sit."

Finn did.

William offered him the flask he'd brought. "Whiskey? I've been saving this for a special occasion."

Finn accepted and took a swig. The alcohol ran down his throat, smooth as melted butter. He handed it back with a nod of appreciation. "Good stuff."

William took a drink. "Do you have any siblings, Mr. Rowe?"

"Only child." One whose parents had been about as loving as they could manage. They hadn't batted an eye when Finn had informed them he was going to be a soldier—his mother had helped him pack so he wouldn't be late for take-off. Their obituary, which he'd found months after the fact, had said they'd drowned in a riptide during a casual nighttime swim. He'd mourned them as he would have next-door neighbors.

"Do you know, I have five brothers and eight sisters. I know all their names, their spouses, and children. I know their hobbies, likes, and dislikes. I even know their favorite games. And yet I can't remember ever playing with them."

"Fourteen kids? My sympathies to your mother."

"Perish the thought, Mr. Rowe. My mother spent too much money maintaining the perfect body to ruin it with something so pedestrian as giving birth to her own children. That's something poor people do. Those who are able, anyway."

The last was almost too low to hear and carried a subtext Finn didn't want to read too closely.

A quiet pause settled over them, not as uncomfortable now as it had been in the transport. The open air absorbed any tension the alcohol had left behind.

"Our Laura is a one-of-a-kind specimen," William said. "I think we can both agree on that."

Here it comes. "Agreed."

"I presume she told you at least part of the nature of our relation-ship?"

"She did."

William nodded. "I'm afraid she got the short end of the bargain."

Finn didn't respond. There was no need. William addressed himself to Finn, but it was almost as if he was talking to himself now.

"And I'm sure she's left things out, too. Such as the fact that I was already ill long before this whole mess of a war ever began."

Finn couldn't stop a quicksilver frown.

William noticed. "That's Laura. All her sins on her sleeve, but never a bad word to say about anyone else." He saluted Finn with the flask. "Except you. But I think that's understandable under the circumstances."

Fair.

After taking a swig, William offered the flask again, but Finn shook his head. Something told him he'd better keep his wits about him for now. "It wasn't supposed to be this way, you know." Emotion too strong to contain made the man's eyes gleam, but he swallowed it back. "The deal was that I would fund Laura's school in exchange for her companionship"—he swung his head around to look at Finn—"Read: *friendship*"—and back to gazing out across the land—"until my illness forced me to seek full-time care. I won't lie and say I never hoped for more. I'm not a eunuch or a saint. But it simply wasn't meant to be." He cast a self-deprecating smile Finn's way. "Despite whatever she might have made herself believe, I don't think she ever truly gave up on you."

Finn's jaw clenched.

But William didn't dwell on it a moment longer, moving on with his tale. "Once my condition reached the point of no return, Laura was supposed to take me to Jericho and leave me to live out the rest of my days there whilst she moved on with her life. And, upon my death, she would have inherited what remained of my estate for her trouble."

Another pause, then a bitter chuckle. "Life is a bitch, is it not? The day I decided to seek treatment, the Shadows fell upon the land." Another sip. "And I was the idiot. I thought I could spare everyone the trouble and save a few lives in the process. Only…"

"Only they died, and you didn't."

A miserable twist of his mouth couldn't quite be called a smile. "Laura told you."

"Eskel."

"Even better. Yes, my good deed came to bite me in the end. All of us, really. The truth is, I *should have* died. But Laura wouldn't let me. She takes her responsibilities very seriously, our Laura." He was starting to slur. "She used a great deal of money to get me through the worst of it, and then the Shadows cut us off from everything, and we were left stranded. All of us. Nowhere to go, no one to call. And all that money just sitting there, the solution to everything completely out of our reach."

And Laura had stayed to take care of all of them, to keep all the promises she'd probably made when money had been plentiful.

"She's still doing it, you know. Refusing to let go. It's not something that comes easily to someone so determined to hold on."

Finn's mind flashed twenty years into the past, to the day he'd stood outside a transport with three Shadows at his back, waiting for him to get in, and Laura crying and begging him not to.

No, she wasn't someone who ever let go. It wasn't in her nature to be accepting of fate, even when there was no other choice.

"Is that why we're here?"

William sighed, turning his gaze up to the sky. "Do you love her?"

Taken aback, Finn didn't answer right away.

"Forgive the impertinent question, but, you see, I have a vested interest in this. A lifelong debt to repay, if you will. Laura deserves someone who can take care of her. I couldn't do it. I don't want her to get stuck with someone else who can't. Or worse, won't. She deserves better."

"I didn't come back to hurt her."

"Why did you come back, then?" William shifted to face Finn as if the answer was the most important thing he'd ever hear.

Why had he come back?

Because he couldn't not.

The moment John had reminded him of Laura, she'd become a ghost haunting his every move. Even when he'd been on the run, lying low, covering his tracks to stay ahead of the Shadows, he'd risked everything time and again, using their networks to search for her. He'd spent three years telling himself she was better off without him, all the while making plans to find her.

What he felt for Laura went far beyond anything as simple as love. She'd been a part of him since they'd been children, jumping cannonballs into the lake. The Shadows might have stolen Finn's memories of her for a while, but she'd never truly left him. Not during training, not after countless EMC treatments—not for a moment in all the twenty years he'd spent away.

You broke my heart, she'd told him, and it might as well have been a bullet through his. Finn would spend the rest of his days groveling for forgiveness if that's what it took, and he'd consider it a privilege.

Whatever William read in Finn's expression, he appeared to deem it acceptable. "You have very interesting friends, Mr. Rowe. When they carried me to the room they so graciously provided, one of them left these two little bottles for me on the nightstand."

Finn took the small vials and read the labels: IN CASE YOU CHANGE YOUR MIND and IN CASE YOU DON'T.

He handed them back without comment.

"I know I'm putting you in a difficult position, but it's the only way I can bring myself to drink this—if Laura isn't here to have to clean up afterward. You strike me as a capable man. Someone who can be trusted to take care of matters with the required efficiency. The authorities will need to be tipped off—anonymously, of course. Otherwise, Laura won't be able to collect on her due. They will need positive identification." He held up his left hand to show Finn the inside of his wrist. The identification chip was implanted a couple of inches up from his wrist joint, marked by a faint scar. But above it, William had a royal blue tattoo of what looked like a family crest. If it was as unique as Finn expected it to be, the coroner would only need to scan it to confirm William's identity. No need for Laura to be involved at all.

William never wanted her to have to see him again. It was the last act of kindness he could perform for her, but Finn didn't think she'd see it that way. She'd hate them both—William for leaving without a proper goodbye and Finn for helping him do it.

"What do you want me to tell her?"

Something in the way William drooped, almost with relief, indicated he'd expected Finn to refuse. The thought had crossed his mind, but only briefly. As much as he hated the thought of causing Laura pain, he'd seen too many men suffer too long to deny William the relief he sought.

William smiled, and in that moment, Finn believed the man held a depth of feeling for Laura he might not even have been aware of. "Tell her... *Adieu.*"

He struggled to stand but brushed off Finn's attempts to help. With another of those deep, appreciative breaths, Laura's husband walked to the edge of the drop-off and sat with his legs dangling in thin air. For a long moment, he simply gazed out across the land, taking in the beauty of a world he probably hadn't seen in years. Then he toasted the sun and upended one of the bottles down his throat.

It didn't take long. Thirty seconds, maybe less. William's body listed to the side, slipping from wakefulness to sleep, from life to the after, as he slid off the edge and disappeared below.

Finn stayed there for a while longer, waiting for something, some sign to tell him it was okay to leave. He imagined William's soul, or spirit, or whatever rising from the river like mist and streaking across the valley, finally freed of the heavy shell of his corporeal prison. He wasn't in pain anymore. At least Finn could tell Laura that. Maybe it would even be enough.

The flask was still beside him in the grass. Finn raised it in a wordless eulogy, then downed the rest of its contents and returned to the transport.

23

Vega kept time by the pulsing pain in her face. She'd managed to find a last bit of healing tincture in their pilfered crates with enough left to cover the cut on her face, so her scarring should be minimal. Her leg, she'd had to suture the old way, with needle and thread.

For all his grand plans, Talon had yet to recruit anyone with any medical training. His people were effectively left to their own devices to waste supplies for as long as they lasted. And once they were gone… Vega didn't let herself think about that.

Right now, they had bigger problems. The recon team in Avencore never sent a second transmission and hadn't checked in at all since the first. That included the additional men Talon had sent to cover Rowe's movements.

And now the team from the valley had returned with news that Laura Belden and her entire flock had evacuated the building. Completely. In a matter of hours. And none of them had lifted a finger to stop it.

Talon was furious—way beyond what he'd been last night. He wasn't lashing out mindlessly anymore but holding it all in, fuming so hard his entire head was red, and she could almost see smoke puffing out of his ears. He hadn't moved from his couch for hours, just staring off into space.

This was when he was at his most dangerous, and all of them knew it. Four dozen hardened soldiers pussyfooted around the vault, taking care not to bump anything or make any kind of noise that might distract Talon from his thoughts and bring his wrath down upon them. Given the state he was in, anyone was fair game, including Vega.

She'd tucked her dog tags into her sleeve so they wouldn't clink and hadn't pulled a single blade to work on. With no busy work to keep her occupied, all she could do was sit there and wait for Talon to snap the fuck out of it. And she dreaded it with every fiber of her being.

"Where did they go?" Talon asked softly, his tone even and every syllable carefully measured.

The coms officer gulped. "Due west."

"Avencore," Talon clarified. It wasn't a question. His fingers curled into the armrest, denting it down, and Vega heard his nails scratch along the fabric's surface. It was too tough to tear, but there would be marks left behind.

Laura Belden, a telepath who could control people's actions, had spent the night with the Shadow Hawk, and now she'd taken her whole congregation straight to him, and none of their men were responding.

Vega could have called that play in her sleep. The coms officer was wasting his time requesting status reports over and over. He'd never get a response. Finnegan Rowe had called Talon's bluff and played him for a fool. Good for him. Vega would toast him at his funeral.

Sucking in a harsh breath, Talon surged to his feet to pace.

Vega barely stifled a flinch.

"What did we get from Olendra?"

He'd sent scouts there, too, thinning their ranks even more to trace the taxi's path and find out who was behind it. Vega had seen the coms officer receive a transmission from them while Talon had been checked out. He hadn't said a word. That meant bad news. They had a full accounting of Rowe's movements on the day Laura Belden had embarked on her little adventure. He hadn't stepped foot outside of Avencore. Whomever she'd met in Olendra, it hadn't been Finn.

The coms officer was sweating. His hands shook as he retrieved the transmission. Instead of trying to relay the message, he cast it up in a holographic projection in front of Talon's seat. It lit up the air above Vega's head. She couldn't get a good look at it from her angle. Tilting her head up pulled on the still-healing wound on her face, limiting her range of motion. But the accompanying audio was more than enough.

"Hello, Shadow people!" The cheerful greeting came from one of their men in a tone she'd never heard from him before. "Sorry we missed you. Please leave a message with the troll in the dungeon, and we'll get back to you just as fast as we fly. See you soon!" The projection then folded in on itself as if the soldier it represented crumpled into a ball. It shimmered with subtle movement, like a full-body shake, and then came the scream. Raw, wretched, almost animalistic. A sound of pure terror that sent a chill of dread down Vega's spine.

She hadn't been there when it'd happened, but she'd heard the report of Emma Calen's escape from her holding cell. At the exact same time, every last soldier on a base sprawling over twenty-seven acres had dropped where they'd been standing, thrust into some kind of nightmare that had taken over their minds and flooded them with sheer terror for several hours. Two had suffered heart failure before the attack wore off. Three more had never recovered and had to be put down. The rest had been recalibrated and returned to the duty roster within days. Back to business as usual.

Talon would have felt it in person. They would have wiped his immediate memory of it but left the residual effects as a mental warning system and more fuel to drive his hatred of telepaths. Vega figured it must have worked a little too well in his case. Why else would he have run when they'd recaptured Emma Calen and brought her to Green 24?

Vega risked a glance in his direction. His face had gone deathly pale. Fear rolled off him in waves she could almost smell, and she half expected him to start pissing himself.

If Emma Calen was involved and working with Laura Belden and the Hawk, Talon was in deep, *deep* shit. He knew it, too, from the look on his face. And if Vega could see it, others would, too. Not to mention, anyone left over from Green 24 would want to head for deep space right about now, which meant Talon would have a hell of a time keeping his troops in line.

Time for him to step up and remind them why they all jumped when he whistled. Running like a bitch only worked when you didn't have a whole vault full of soldiers watching your every move, expecting you to lead them into the battle you promised them they'd win.

"Arm up," Talon said, almost to himself. In the total silence around them, it rang out like a shot. "Full mobilization. Alpha Team with me. Vega takes point with Bravo Team." He speared her with a venomous glare. "Do not disappoint me."

A Hound does what a Hound does—make noise. Talon only had

one strategy in his bag of tricks. He would take a hostage and bring the storm down on the battlefield of his choosing. He thought home ground would give him an advantage, but that only worked against other Hounds. A Hawk would already have the lay of the land, and he wouldn't bother with a frontal assault. He would swoop down from an angle none of them saw coming and tear Talon limb from limb.

And if it was personal, as Vega suspected it to be, he would make it hurt.

Refusal was not an option. Retreat would get her killed. Vega would need to play a very careful game to get out of this with her skin intact. Not about to make Talon wait long enough to zap her again, she pushed to her feet, careful of her injured thigh. "Bravo Team! Scatter!"

Talon stepped into her path as she headed toward the armory stack. "Take a helm," he ordered. "And bring me back that Belden bitch. Whatever it takes, understand?"

Meaning if she had to sacrifice the team to get what he wanted, she had the green light. Every one of them was expendable, including Vega.

"Roger," she said and limped off to arm up.

~

Avencore

With John and Emma's telepaths on guard at the inn, Finn wasn't in a hurry to get back. They'd keep everyone safe for a while longer, and as long as he stayed within range, Emma could let him know if trouble came their way. He took the scenic way back, circling around Avencore to establish a wider perimeter. He told himself it was a patrol run to make sure the Shadows weren't mobilizing in his blind spot. The truth was, Finn needed time to think.

He didn't look forward to his next conversation with Laura. As soon as he told her what happened, she'd blame Finn for his complicity in William's death, and he wouldn't be able to deny it. He couldn't say he regretted it, either, and it had nothing to do with William being Laura's husband. Finn would have done the same for anyone suffering as much as William had.

You're a killer, the kid had told him, and he hadn't been wrong.

Once a villain, always a villain, Finn supposed. He had no delusions of being any kind of hero in anyone's scenario, and he'd made his peace with that a long time ago. But trying to reconcile it with the idea of sticking around Laura and her makeshift extended family for any length of time was enough to give him heartburn.

Having circled around to the north side, Finn turned onto Mt. Alder Street toward downtown. Might as well stop by the grocery store before heading back to the inn. He'd heard some of Laura's people mention they'd left a lot of freshly-bought supplies back at the compound. He could pick up a few things and get in an order for dinner with the catering counter. Laura's people had hosted him, after all, it was only fair to repay the kindness.

Despite the day and hour, downtown Avencore was almost completely deserted. Finn parked the rental right in front of the store and checked everything twice over before getting out.

"Listen, kid," the clerk snapped loud enough for his voice to carry clear out onto the street. "You need to go play your games somewhere else. Now are you going to buy the rest of that or what?"

Finn cocked his head. In the two weeks he'd been around, he'd never heard the clerk so upset. He walked in, expecting to see some punk trying to get something past the man without paying, but the spiky green hair and leather jacket said otherwise.

Finn stepped up. "Is there a problem?"

The kid whirled around, and Finn was shocked to see tear tracks down his dusty cheeks. He left his shopping—more than a dozen bread rolls and a bottle of vodka—on the counter and came straight at Finn. "You got a transport."

"Uh…" Finn looked up at the clerk, who shrugged.

The kid grabbed him by the sleeve and yanked hard. "Let's go." Four other transports were parked out front, but the kid made a beeline straight for Finn's. He didn't seem to need Finn to unlock it, either, hunching over the passenger-side door pad to do some rapid tapping. One loud honk echoed down the empty street as Finn reached the driver's side door. It was already unlocked.

Both of them got in at the same time.

"Talk," Finn ordered, starting up the engine.

"Soldiers came for my friends. They were just talking when I left, but I heard one of them tell Mika to pack her bag."

Finn turned the transport around, heading back toward the school but, "I just drove past the school. There's no one there."

"Yeah, 'cuz it's summer break. We were all at Lake Camp."

Finn turned right at the next intersection and gunned the engine, raising the transport twenty feet off the ground and above any on-coming traffic.

The sharp acceleration slammed the kid back against his seat, and he gasped, gripping the dashboard. "Holy shit."

"Tell me about your friends," Finn ordered.

Another gasp as the transport leaned almost forty-five degrees going into a turn. "Uh, Mika is my classmate. Sixteen years old. Five-four, ninety pounds soaking wet. She speaks like six languages and has a pet weasel. *Gah!*"

The transport dived into a tunnel and shot back up toward the sky on the other side.

"Kaleb is a year lower. H-he's a big kid. Chubby, you know? Umm, I think Therese is in his class. Her mom is a big deal somewhere on the Isle of Pree down south. And Bale and Marcus are twins who just graduated. Football jocks. A whole bunch of us were gonna go swimming when the soldiers showed up. They came straight for my friends. And the camp counselor just stood back and let them do whatever. How could he do that?"

"Focus."

Moss wiped his nose on his sleeve. "I stole his transport and drove it into town, but it's a piece of shit and won't start up again. And then the old bastard clerk wouldn't tell me where to find you*uuuuu!*"

Finn turned up the side of Mt. Wether, ignoring the switchback and flying the transport straight up and over the saddle. Lake Camp was about twenty miles away, down in the valley on the other side. "Any of them have any special abilities or quirks?"

"L-like what?"

"Anything. Anything unusual the soldiers might want to use."

"I don't know. Mika talks to that weasel like it can talk back, and she actually understands it. Kaleb's like fifty pounds overweight, but he runs faster than anyone in his class. Therese has to take special remote math classes by herself. She said they got some genius scientist college professor on Mars 2 to teach her."

"And the twins?" Straight down the mountain into the valley, Finn slightly underestimated the terrain. Treetops scraped along the transport's underside before he leveled off above them.

"Jesus fuck, you drive like a maniac!"

"*Kid!*"

"I don't know! They like football and VR games, and they fight each other all the time. Normal teenager stuff."

"Muscle recruits." Latham would put them through the same wringer as all the rest of them to start a new generation of Shadows.

As they neared the lake, Finn descended to road level and slowed down a little. The camp was maybe five miles away, out of sight among the trees, but Finn was looking up for the telltale shimmer of a hover's camo shield. The Shadows would want the most expedient way in and out of the area, and although they could have used a repurposed transport like Finn, Hound-strategy was to make an impression, not stay under the radar. They'd want to intimidate on sight, make it clear that to resist meant putting one's life on the line.

"How long since they got there?"

"An hour, maybe?"

"All right, listen up. When I get out of this transport, I want you to take the controls and drive straight back to Avencore the same way we came. You saw what this thing can do, so use it. Go to the Thane & Owens Inn and ask for John Wayland. Tell him everything you told me, and do whatever he tells you to do."

"What if he's not there?"

"He'll be there." They were coming up on the camp's main cabin, a two-story log monstrosity with a little yellow flag sticking out from the roof. "You ready?"

The kid nodded.

Finn pulled over and got out, beckoning for Moss to switch seats before he slammed the door shut. He didn't have his lens on him, but his wrist unit was in place on his left wrist. He prepped a percussion pulse and marched up to the camp entrance.

The two Shadows guarding it aimed their weapons at him. He didn't give them a chance to fire. Dropping to one knee, he ducked his head and raised his right fist high. The percussion pulse flared out, slamming the soldiers against the wall and giving the retreating transport a bit of a nudge.

Finn jumped up and ran forward as soon as it was safe. One of the Shadows was out cold. Finn snapped his neck for good measure and relieved him of his helmet and weapon. The other one had only been stunned by the blast. A shot to the head remedied that and disabled the helmet at the same time.

He heard three sets of footsteps coming before they cleared the corner. Finn shot one dead, but the battery charge wasn't sufficient for the other two. He ducked behind a column and twisted the dial off his wrist unit, turning it into a heat-seeking throwing star. He let it fly, barely avoiding a plasma shot that splintered and scorched the column by his shoulder. A grunt signaled one of the soldiers was down, but the second fired three more shots before the dial returned to his wrist unit.

Finn twisted it securely back into place and stepped out from behind the column. He made it as far as the corner where they'd come from. Flattening himself against it, he peeked out to gauge the situation. Five Shadows with helmets and weapons knelt in a row across the wide porch, with Latham, six more Shadows, and his newest proteges standing several feet behind them. The kids looked scared out of their minds. Finn noted a weasel wrapped around the smaller girl's neck before the Shadows opened fire, forcing him back into hiding.

There would be more coming around from the other side. If he didn't want to get pinned, Finn had to move. He pushed a sequence of small buttons to activate a riot shield and pulled Vega's knife out of his boot. Then, armed like a knight of olde, he ran full tilt at the front line. Plasma charges flared off the shield, blinding Finn to everything beyond it. He was estimating the distance to the shooters, counting on them to try to overload the shield rather than shoot at his unprotected feet to bring him down.

The kids screamed.

Someone shouted in alarm, and then a whoosh of hot air stopped Finn in his track as an out-of-control transport rammed through the porch railing and into the building, leveling the five shooters and scattering the rest.

The resulting explosion flared outward, catching Finns' sleeve on fire. He cursed and deactivated his shield to beat it out.

"I can't believe that worked."

Moss stood halfway between the log house and the lakeshore, hands fisted in his green hair as he stared at the destruction.

Finn's gut went ice cold. "*Run!*" he roared, already on the move.

The sound of his voice startled the kid. Instead of running, he froze.

Finn was twenty feet away when a plasma charge blasted into the kid's chest, scorching a four-inch hole where his heart should have been. He was dead before he hit the ground.

Finn skidded to a stop. A split second. That was all.

Enough time for Latham to fire off a second shot and for Finn to feel it slam into the back of his head before the lights went out.

24

With Miguel and Alexis in the waiting room, keeping the kids corralled, Laura sat down with the doctor to get their test results. "Give it to me straight. How bad is it?" After hours spent at the clinic, ushering child after child through a maze of testing rooms, she was wrung out to the point of numbness. All she wanted now were answers.

The head doctor, a competent-looking woman named Gina Kostas, adjusted her glasses. Laura would bet she hadn't had a day this packed in years. "The good news is, a lot of the maladies we've seen are easily treatable. I have put together a recommended treatment plan for them that I will make available to you as soon as we finish here. But I do have concerns about a few of the children."

She tapped on her glass desk, and a set of 3D holograms popped up above it: detailed scans of four of the children, slowly spinning in the air with red lights indicating problem areas in their bodies.

Laura swallowed hard.

"Penelope's brain tumor might be operable, but you should know it's an extremely high-risk operation. If it's successful, she's looking at months of rehabilitation, possibly relearning how to walk and talk. Any complications could result in permanent damage or death."

"D-do you have recommendations for someone who can do the procedure?"

Dr. Kostas nodded. "I'll include a list in the packet." She made a note for herself. "I understand that most of these kids are orphans?"

Laura nodded.

"I can refer you to financial aid resources and put you in touch with adoption services—"

"No," Laura said at once. "I don't need money. And I'm not splitting them up." The odds of someone wanting to adopt a child who would need lifelong medical care were slim to none, and Laura was not about to put any of her kids through any more trauma if she could help it.

"Understood." No further questions. The doctor moved on to the next case. "Freddie's skin tumors are treatable. Unfortunately, he's begun to develop them internally…"

Laura listened, nodded in the appropriate places, and answered the right things, but all she could think about was that one day soon, she'd have to sit with these kids and watch them die. She had the means to cover any treatments for as long as they were needed, but no amount of money could buy her a miracle, let alone four of them.

"…you said there will be more patients for me to see?"

Laura blinked herself back to the present. "Yes. One more urgent case today. My husband, William Belden."

Dr. Kostas swiped through the records she'd received to find William's. She scanned through it quickly. "These notes are from your in-house medic?"

"Eskel, yes. He's been treating all of us since the fallout."

"Hmm."

Laura didn't like the sound of that. "What?"

"According to this, your husband is in the end stage of a degenerative genetic disease. Even if we could treat the additional complications caused by the fallout, I'm afraid we won't be able to do much to extend his natural life. At this point, my recommendation would be to seek palliative care. Would you like me to provide some options?"

"You won't even see him?"

Dr. Kostas closed the file, shut down the holographic projection, and folded her hands on top of her desk. "Mrs. Belden, I would be more than happy to examine your husband if it'll give you some peace of mind. But I don't want you to get your hopes up. Has your husband shared his wishes with you regarding assisted cessation?"

Laura struggled to make sense of her words. "What are you talking about?"

"I pulled Mr. Belden's medical file from the central database. Your husband has a detailed plan laid out for his treatment and end-of-life care. Obviously, the war prevented it from being put into action, but it looks like he's thought of everything, including a signed and notarized Do Not Resuscitate order. Were you not aware of this?"

"I… N-no," she admitted, her mind buzzing. "He wanted to go to Blue Skies on Jericho once he got to the point of needing 'round the clock care, but that's it. He never said anything about… Oh, God." She couldn't breathe.

Dr. Kostas came around the desk and took Laura's cold hands in hers. "Conversations about death are never easy. I can see you love your husband very much. You should know that everything he laid out in his plans was as much for you as it was for him. He made it so you wouldn't have to worry about anything where his care and arrangements are concerned."

Laura pulled her hands free. "I have to get the children back." Away from here and Dr. Death. "Now that they're taken care of, the others can schedule their own appointments." *Keep things moving forward.* She had a laundry list of tasks that had been neglected for far too long. "Please keep all the billing under my name." She could fall apart later. Right now, her family needed her.

Out in the waiting room, Miguel and Alexis took one look at her and sprang into action, herding all the kids out into the waiting transport. They spoke to her and asked her things, but their voices blended in with the buzzing in her ears. Not that she could have answered them, anyway, with her tongue stuck to the roof of her mouth and her mind a million miles away.

William wanted to die. He'd made provisions for it in his living will—ones he hadn't deigned to share with her. He'd known it would come to this, had prepared everything ahead of time, and hadn't told her.

He tried to.

Laura hadn't wanted to hear it. She'd shut him down and kept him struggling without the care he'd wanted and needed for three years because she couldn't stand losing one more person.

As soon as they got to the inn, Laura hopped out of the transport, heading for William's room. She needed to talk to him, to apologize, and let him tell her exactly what he wanted. He was dying, and it no longer mattered what Laura wished for or hoped for. Her job was to take care of William and make sure he was comfortable in his final days. That was what she'd signed up for when she'd married him.

She opened the door, his name on her lips. Her voice bounced around an empty room. Bed made, shades pulled open, a bag set by the door. Laura's heart dropped. She listed backward, and a strong, bony hand caught her elbow, lending some much-needed support.

"You ran past me before I could tell you," Eskel said. "William left this morning. I saw him get into a transport with Finn. They haven't come back yet."

Laura bit the inside of her cheek, but a small sound still slipped out of her before she hugged the rest of them back down to her middle. Eskel helped her to sit on the bed, and then Emma was there, putting a hand on her knee to get her attention.

—*Don't blame him,*— she told Laura in her mind. She already knew what'd happened. She would have known the second the thought had sprung to life in William's mind. And she hadn't alerted Laura to the fact that her husband had been so desperate to die he'd resorted to asking Finn to help him do it.

A heavy day, Emma had predicted the night before. Had it been just a loopy turn of phrase, or had she known even then what would happen?

Come to think of it, Eskel didn't look all that shocked, either. Sympathetic, yes, but not angry or surprised. He'd already accepted the inevitable. It seemed everyone had, except Laura. The one who was supposed to be able to read intentions and turn them to her liking.

The truth was, William's intentions had started turning dark a long time ago, right around the time Laura had started to shut down her abilities around him and keep her mind to herself unless absolutely necessary. She'd chosen not to know. Feigned ignorance had been easier to bear than the truth.

She had no one to blame but herself.

All of a sudden, Emma surged to her feet and ran out the door, yelling, "Seashell!"

"You know, I still don't get what that's supposed to mean," Eskel said with a wry smile.

Laura knew. She'd caught it in the memories Emma had shared with her. But as she was about to tell him, the window at her back exploded inward.

The force of it thrust her off the bed and onto Eskel. They dropped to the ground in a tangle of limbs as bright lights flashed in Laura's vision. She heard screaming, the sounds of gunfire. Disentangling herself from Eskel, she dropped her shields, and her vision flooded with red.

Too many to count. They were everywhere, climbing through the window, swarming overhead, and in the hallways. Shadows in red-gray uniforms, ready to hurt and kill anyone who got in their way.

Fear from her people. They wanted to run, but everywhere they turned, the path was blocked. A few tried to fight, but in an instant, the flares of their intentions winked out.

Laura screamed at the darkness left behind, struggling to disentangle herself from Eskel so she could do something. As soon as she was free, she pushed out hard, dropping the three Shadows who'd come through the window for her. They'd lie there and hold their breath until they died.

Laura hauled Eskel to his feet and shoved him out the door. They got as far as the kitchen, where a gaggle of terrified, crying kids rushed them, forcing them behind the counter. Laura couldn't see past their need to flee. The mini suns blinded her to anything else, and she couldn't push them away.

Eskel shushed them all, hugging as many as his arms could encompass while at the same time dragging them down low to the floor for cover. "Can you tell how many there are?" he asked her.

Laura's head pounded. "Too many." Too many, too angry—too intent on doing harm. That hadn't been their directive, but they were just pissed enough to want some payback along the way. People, both hers and Emma's, dropped left and right, and there was no telling whether or not they'd ever get back up again.

She heard a shout somewhere in the entry hall. Emma's Shadow husband. He was a blank wave snuffing out red starbursts one after the other, but he was far outnumbered.

And then his void was gone as the red sea closed over it.

A high-pitched scream—Emma's.

A good portion of red winked out in Laura's vision, but there was more to fill the gaps.

Now, at least, she could distinguish between the individuals.

Laura left the kids in Eskel's care and stepped into the entry hall. Bodies on the floor. She didn't let herself look at them too closely. She targeted the Shadow who had her in his sights from behind the staircase, and pushed. The soldier raised his gun to his own head and pulled the trigger.

The last time the Shadows had invaded her world, Laura had frozen. She couldn't afford to make the same mistake twice. Dropping the last of her shields, she targeted every red flare inside the inn and forced them to unlock their knees and drop. Hopefully, it gave Emma's people enough of an advantage to turn the tide.

Laura couldn't stay to see it through. There were more soldiers outside, far at the periphery of her range. The hover was high above and three blocks down, but its pilot was attuned to everything going on below. He was waiting for a specific word of command, ready to swoop in, scoop up the Shadows, and haul ass out of there.

She focused on him—hard. He would not be swooping anywhere. She gave him a firm directive to fly east to the mountain range and drop out of the sky. It was different than stopping a reflexive action like breathing for a few minutes. The duration of the flight meant the pilot had to stick to Laura's specific set of instructions for a good half-hour without her supervision, all the while knowing he was on his way to die.

His natural sense of self-preservation fought her command before he'd fully changed course, instilling doubt, fear, and hesitation. Laura didn't have time to convince him the slow way. She pushed harder, stripping him of his free will. Almost there. Almost—

Someone tapped on her shoulder.

She turned right into the path of an injection gun aimed for her neck. Laura felt its sting and then the burn of the injection flooding through her veins. Her vision doubled and redoubled until identical, shiny white globes of a helmet floated in front of her.

Then her knees gave out, and everything went dark.

25

Talmadge was at the hover controls. Graye and Catton, the only other Shadows on her team with helmets, were guarding the unconscious telepaths, and the rest were on the guns, which left Vega to guard the three civilians who stared her down as if they'd love nothing better than to kill her.

Yeah, she didn't blame them. Her troops had left a hell of a mess back at the inn. But at least they hadn't taken any of the children like Wight had wanted to. He'd have a lovely scar to remember their discussion on the topic.

"How many did you leave alive?" the big one asked. They had files on everyone whom Laura Belden had sheltered in her compound. This one's name was Quinn VanWarren, a disowned heir to a massive fortune who happened to have a serious heart condition. But their intel had fallen short when it came to the full extent of his abilities. It'd taken four stun shots to put him down, and he'd only stayed unconscious for a few minutes. They'd had to truss him up like livestock to keep him from destroying the hover in flight.

"How many did you?" she countered. Eighteen Shadows had left the Roost assigned to her team. A total of five of them were coming back, including her. They had the telepaths to thank for most of those deaths, but the juggernaut got a couple before the rest took him down.

He struggled against his binds but didn't have enough leverage anymore to snap them the way he'd done with the first set. "We didn't kill children!"

"Neither did we." This time.

"But you did." This from the thin guy with a facial tattoo. The medic, Eskel Andersson, had nothing and no one outside of the company he kept. "Every one of those kids is sick and needs medications administered several times a day. If there's no one left to do that for them, they'll die."

The third one swore and started rambling a long tirade from which Vega only understood that Miguel Santos thought looking like him meant she talked like him, too.

"You're wasting your breath."

He yanked on his restraints in twitchy jerks that didn't seem altogether voluntary. "Please," he said when he got himself under control. "I have to get back to my wife and daughter."

Wife Alexis had acute brittle bone syndrome, and daughter Harley Esmeralda suffered from debilitating migraines that paralyzed her for days.

Vega gritted her teeth as she pulled out a knife to clean. She ran through the numbers in her head. She'd given her men orders to incapacitate, not kill, but Talon had conditioned an army of simple-minded murderers, some of whom didn't take orders from a woman. Some of those civilians back at the inn would definitely have died, but there had to be some still left alive.

It wasn't as if she could have paused to take a census. Snatch and grab. Them, or her. Simple math in her book.

"You have to let Eskel go!" the juggernaut shouted.

Vega tried her best to ignore him. Her hands were as tied as his on this matter. One thing she'd learned in her time on Anamtaigh: Talon required a tribute to appease his temper. As rattled as he was now, the tribute needed to be equally impressive. If she didn't bring him every single prisoner in the hover, he'd kill her and the rest of her team and then go back to reap everyone left at the inn. And, unlike Vega, he wouldn't have a single pang of conscience about wasting kids.

They were coming up on the Roost. In true Talon fashion, they had cells prepped to hold the telepaths but nothing for the civilians. Their continued breathing would depend on Talon's current mood. If the last few days were any indication, her non-telepath prisoners would be dying shortly unless Vega could convince Talon of their value.

Given his medical training, she could make an easy case for Eskel. Quinn might live long enough to demonstrate his unique strength, but unless he fell in line, Talon wouldn't suffer his continued existence for very long. Miguel was a good fighter, but compared to the other two, his skills were a dime a dozen. He'd probably die in the next hour. Unless, of course, Talon's mission had gone as swimmingly as hers and he was desperate enough to recoup their losses to keep Miguel in reserve.

She put away the cleaning rag but kept her knife on hand as she got up to prep her civilians for disembarking. Her thigh seized as she put her weight on it. She took hold of an overhead handle to keep her balance but cursed inwardly when the medic and juggernaut exchanged a look. Two steps brought her close enough without betraying a limp, but she crouched with difficulty, already cursing the pain of standing back up again.

Her knife had been cleaned to a shine. Vega pressed the tip underneath the juggernaut's jaw to tilt his face up to look at her. "You want to live long enough to see your people again?"

"Do you?" he grated back.

Vega smiled, then stifled a wince when the motion pulled at her cheek wound.

The juggernaut noticed. His eyebrows quirked in a quicksilver frown. "Who did that to your face?"

"The man who won't tolerate any of your bullshit. You want to live? You keep your mouth shut and blend in with the walls."

The hover touched down.

Vega held the juggernaut's gaze a second longer, then used her knife to cut through his ankle binds. "Time to go."

She was getting ready to stand when the juggernaut kicked off the wall behind him to turn himself and slammed his massive feet into her chest.

Vega flew back into the opposite wall, the air knocked out of her lungs, knife sliding across the floor and down a break in the grate into a utility shaft. She pulled her gun and shot blindly, then dropped to her hands and knees, fighting for breath while the other prisoners struggled to get free. They wouldn't. Vega had personally secured them to the wall.

As soon as she was able, Vega shoved to her feet, ignoring the searing pain in her thigh that meant she'd just ripped her stitches. Gun pointed squarely at the medic's head, she ordered, "Stop."

Both of them froze.

"His heart," the medic said urgently. "You shot him in the chest."

Tit for tat, as far as she was concerned. Her ribs still wailed with every breath, and her spine was on fire from where she'd struck the wall. The stun shot wouldn't have packed a stronger punch than that.

Then she picked up on the wheezing sounds the juggernaut was making.

His heart. The damaged one that could fail at any time.

She holstered her weapon and turned the man onto his back.

"How's his pulse?" the medic demanded.

Vega pressed her fingers against the side of Quinn's neck. "I can't tell." But his lips were starting to turn blue.

"He needs a shot of adrenalin—*now!*"

A med kit was by the door, but it would be at least three years old. She limped over to retrieve it. Bandages and patches spilled over the floor as she rooted through the contents for anything that looked like an injection gun. There were three. She held them up for the medic to see. "Which one?"

"The middle."

Vega dropped the other two and brought the needle to Quinn's neck.

"No! It needs to go straight into his heart."

Vega cursed and ripped through Quinn's shirt to expose his chest.

"Two inches lower and one to the right. Make sure you're aiming between his ribs."

She felt for the gap, aimed the injector gun, and pressed the trigger.

Quinn grunted as the needle shot down into his heart, then coughed until his face turned red.

Vega pressed her fingers to his pulse again.

"Are there any monitoring patches in there?"

She looked through what remained in the box, then rifled through the mess on the floor until she found one.

"Put it on his jugular. It'll turn green if his blood flow is restored. If it goes red, it means his heart has stopped."

She did as the medic instructed, telling Quinn, "You need a new heart."

"Yeah," he groaned out. "I'll get right on that."

He wasn't nearly as fearsome when he wasn't scowling. Sure, he had a face that looked like it had been carved out of stone, but—

The door opened, admitting two more Shadows. "The hell happened here?"

Vega grabbed an adhesive wound sealant for her thigh and got up to hobble out past them. "Nothing I couldn't handle."

One of the Shadows snorted. She made a point to slam into him on her way out. "Get them inside—in the same condition they are now. I'll report to Talon."

Their unstable leader was sitting on the stairs of his platform, still in full combat gear, appearing deep in thought as he twirled a knife.

"Mission accomplished," she told him, stopping at the base of the stairs. Talon liked to have the high ground.

"Is it, now?"

"And then some. I—"

The knife stopped twirling. Talon raised it up for better light, reflecting it off the blade into Vega's eyes. "Do you know where I found this?"

It probably hadn't been in the hover's utility shaft.

"Care to explain to me how Finnegan Rowe managed to get his hands on one of your knives?"

"I missed a throw," she said, keeping it simple. The more complicated a lie got, the harder it became to validate. "Didn't stick around to retrieve it."

"That sounds very unlike you."

Vega didn't respond. Talon tended to get hung up on the smallest inconsistencies; she wasn't about to feed him any, especially when she was at such a critical disadvantage. She could feel blood trickling down her leg beneath the fabric of her pants. "Did you hear what I said?"

"Yes, you accomplished your mission."

"Oh, I did a lot better than that."

"And when I get my hands on some gold stars and pats on the back, I'll be sure to save you one. But right now, I'm wondering what else you might have done that would make *this* end up in the hands of Finnegan—*fucking*—Rowe when he showed up out of nowhere to interfere with *my mission!*"

Don't react. "Who cares? You killed him, didn't you?"

Talon launched down the stairs and bowled her over so hard the back of her head cracked against the stone floor of the vault. Her vision went dark for a second, and when she came to, Talon's furious face was an inch above hers, and his hand was squeezing her throat. He looked absolutely rabid, but his voice was measured when he spoke, and his words were enunciated with crisp precision. "Give me one good reason why I shouldn't kill you right here and now. Hmm? Did you bring me John Wayland's severed head along with the Belden bitch?"

"Brought Wayland," she mouthed, her face throbbing with heat as the pressure behind her eyeballs increased. "You can. Take his head. Yourself."

Talon's grip loosened, and she coughed, clearing her airways to suck in a desperate breath. "You brought me Wayland?"

"And the redhead bitch he stole from us. Now get the fuck off me."

He did, staring at her in what might have been shock as she struggled back to her feet in feeble-bodied stages. Now her head was bleeding, too, and getting all the way upright caused her stomach to roil with vertigo. *Don't react.* She could throw up and pass out later. Right now, she needed Talon off her case.

"Where are they?"

Vega rubbed her throat and jerked her chin toward the entrance, where her team was rolling in two stacks of three sealed body cases each. The first stack would hold Laura Belden, formerly McNally, Emma Calen, and John Wayland, respectively. The rest were more of the telepaths they'd brought into Talon's territory. All of them safely unconscious until they could be processed.

Behind them, four more Shadows escorted the three civilians, still conscious and walking on their own, although Quinn was hunched and looked ready to collapse at any moment.

Talon's attention was immediately diverted and Vega allowed herself a small sigh. She felt the civilians glaring at her, and she glared right back, shaking her head a little, a signal she hoped they'd interpret as, *Shut up and stay invisible.* Not that there was anything else they could do with thirty-plus armed Shadows surrounding them other than get themselves killed.

Talon motioned to the crew bringing in the cases, and they set the stacks down in front of him. He put his hands on the top one, caressing its smooth edges from one end to the other. Then he stuck his face close to the clear window and huffed against it as if he was trying to sniff out the person inside. It was weird.

"Sir, where do you want them?"

He took a minute longer to get himself together while everyone stared at him, waiting for the next crazy outburst. "Catacombs. Double them up. Two to a cell."

"And the civilians?"

Still fully focused on the stacks, Talon prompted, "Vega?"

That was her cue to explain why she'd bothered to drag them all the way to the Roost. "Two fighters and a trained medic," she said. Short and simple.

"Bring the medic," Talon said. "Hang the others on the ledge. I'll deal with them later. He watched the men carry out his orders until they disappeared out of sight. Then he sighed and came back to Vega, her knife still in his hand. "You, my pretty bird, are skating on such thin ice." Twirling the knife over his knuckles, he caught it by the blade and offered it back to her hilt-first. "But you do it with style. That's rare these days. I'd hate to have to cut your performance short."

Vega took her knife back and waited.

He made her wait for three minutes, staring, watching her sway on her feet, before turning away and saying, "Dismissed."

Vega limped off to get herself cleaned up. She didn't dare ask what he'd done with Rowe. Unless she heard otherwise from one of the others, Vega had to assume he was dead, which meant her escape strategy was now shot to shit.

Thin as her ice was, she couldn't risk approaching the telepaths, who would be under constant armed guard. And the civilians were, for all intents and purposes, out of commission. The ledge was a semi-sheer drop-off on the northern side of the mountain with only a foot-wide shelf as a makeshift trail leading to sets of manacles that had been drilled into the rockface. Talon hung people there when he didn't have the time or patience to deal with them. More often than not, he forgot about them until weeks later and then sent the newest vagabonds to dispose of the weathered, rotting corpses to make room for the next batch.

The good news was, Talon was prepared to forget about them. As long as he had the telepaths and John Wayland to keep him occupied, he wouldn't be bothering to keep two worthless POWs under active guard.

The bad news: in her current state and position, setting them free would mean risking her own life in more ways than one.

Such thin ice.

Vega hoped the swim was worth it.

26

Finn came to slowly, aching from head to toe, but especially in his head. Saliva flooded his mouth in an instant, and he just managed to turn on his side before the contents of his stomach were forcefully expelled.

He couldn't see it. The world around him was total darkness.

Either that, or he'd gone blind.

Finn wiped his mouth and struggled to sit up, to somehow orient himself in his surroundings and take stock of the situation.

It was cold. The air smelled damp, and his breaths echoed. Some sort of cave or tunnel?

Memories were hazy and came back to him in fragments of blood spray and flashing lights. But he remembered the heat of an explosion and patted down his left arm, checking for burns.

That concern became secondary when the rest of his memories returned.

Moss.

I can't believe that worked!

A fist-sized hole through his chest. Dead before he'd had a chance to really live.

Finn didn't even know his real name. Seemed like something he should have found out before sending a kid to spy on the fucking Shadows for him.

But he'd never expected—

His stomach cramped again, doing its best to expel itself, his guts, and his spine along with it. A bout of dry heaves left him exhausted and hollow with burning guilt. He'd been careless to have left a witness. He'd been reckless to involve the kid. He'd been an idiot, assuming a sixteen-year-old with that much fight in him would tuck tail and run like Finn had told him to, as if he was another soldier trained to follow orders.

And now he was dead, and it was Finn's fault.

He'd failed his mission.

He'd failed everyone.

A door opened some three feet away, flooding the darkness with blinding light. "Looky, looky who's awakey."

Finn's vision was slow to adjust, but he'd recognize that voice anywhere. He lurched to his feet and charged Latham. A percussion blow to his chest laid him back out. The world swam, his ribs screamed, and his freshly bruised heart ached with every frantic beat.

"Get him up."

Strong hands hauled him up from the floor. He didn't have the strength to fight them. Head lolling forward, Finn was at their mercy as they dragged him out of the room into a too-bright hallway with solid concrete floors. Some part of his rattled brain recognized he was back in the mountain vault. Not ideal.

But at least he could die easy, knowing Laura and her people were safe at the inn with the SU standing guard. They might not be able to talk straight, but John and Emma had their shit together, and they had back-up. Hell, when he didn't show up soon, they might even storm the vault to save his sorry ass.

The soldiers dropped him on his face in another room. This one smelled of formaldehyde and old death. He pulled in his arms and legs to push himself up to all fours. The floor pitched and tilted under him as bright sparks flashed across his vision. *Breathe, motherfucker.* He sucked in a pained breath and released it on a groan.

A pair of dirty boot tips appeared in front of his nose, then their owner crouched down and yanked Finn's head up by his hair. "For the record," Latham said, "I was trying to kill you, too. Wouldn't you know it? Battery ran down to stun. But, waste not, as they say."

"This the part where you torture me for intel?"

"Torture a Hawk? To what end? I already have everything you failed to get me and then some."

The gloating tone twisted Finn's guts into a cold, tight knot. His brain wouldn't work right. He was missing something—something vital.

Get it together, Hawk! You're gonna let a shit stain like Latham get the best of you?

"Wha's it you wanted again?"

Latham's grin was as ugly as the rest of him. "John Wayland's head," he replied. "And your pretty little telepath bitch."

No. No fucking way. He was bluffing. Had to be.

"Got the redhead as a bonus. See, that's what happens when you send a Hound to do a Hawk's job. It gets *done.*"

Finn's heart rate went through the roof. The sudden flood of blood made his head pound. He blinked hard to clear away the bright sparks and swung a weak fist at Latham. Missed by a mile.

Latham let him go with a shove, and Finn sprawled out on the floor, struggling to breathe through the lump in his throat.

"Get him in the chair."

"I don't think that's a good idea." Different voice. Definitely not a Shadow.

Finn sought out its source as the soldiers hauled him up again and shoved him into a stiff seat. His gut clenched before his mind fully recognized where he was sitting. The soldiers strapped down his legs and tied his forearms to the armrests so tight the binds cut off circulation to his hands. As he thrashed to get free, they shoved him hard against the backrest and lashed him in place with a strap across his neck.

Finn's body froze, his lungs working overtime as he tried to hyperventilate himself out of the situation. There was no escape. The seat, the manacles—he couldn't think himself out of the panic clouding his vision. Someone was whining-growling in desperate little bursts. It couldn't be him. He could barely breathe as it was, let alone make such pathetic noises.

A harsh light shone into his left eye, then his right. It stayed when the source swung down, and Finn couldn't blink hard enough to clear it completely. But he did catch a glimpse of a black-tattooed chin. "He's concussed," Eskel said. "You can't seriously want me to do this."

"Did I ask for your opinion?" Good to know Latham was so amused by the situation while Finn sank deeper into a brutal flashback.

The arguing voices dulled to an incomprehensible hum as the room around him wavered into something else. Now, there were sophisticated computers to his right, a white plastic curtain in front of him, a feeble barrier between the torture chair and the rest of med bay. Dr Wen, with his thick glasses and his wholly unconcerned expression, fiddled with the wires and tubes to his left where Finn couldn't see. Son of a bitch was humming to himself.

"Now, let's see if we can't help cure those pesky doubts you've been having, yes?" His voice echoed with a furious shout of, "I'm not a murderer!"

Finn struggled to comprehend the dual vision. Nothing felt real enough to grasp onto. He had no more sense of time or location. Nothing to ground him in reality. There was only fear and the anticipation of a pain worse than anything else he'd ever felt in his life. He could feel echoes of it in his memories, and his jaw clenched hard, teeth grinding against each other as if it would keep the torture at bay. He was shaking, absurdly grateful for the restraints that kept him from vibrating himself apart. They dug into his flesh, and he strained harder against them, choking himself, trying to get out, get as far away from there as he possibly could. It would never be far enough.

"Doctor," the hard, cold voice belonged to the Sergeant Major. No, it was Latham's. "You should know that backtalk is subject to corporal punishment." No difference in the end. They were one and the same.

Finn thrashed hard, rattling the entire contraption in its moorings. Skin gave way across his wrists, the burning pain a feeble distraction from the conversation happening around him. The Sergeant Major was in front of him—behind him—off to the side—as Dr. Wen explained, "The treatment intensity is directly proportional to the refraction period. If you want the subject back on his feet later today, the voltage—*will kill him!*" Eskel shouted.

He needed to do something. There was a trick, an old remedy he'd used to use to get through this before. What was it? He couldn't remember. A name… A song? If he could just remember before—

"I'm sorry, man." Finn recognized genuine regret in the voice that couldn't possibly be Dr. Wen's. Too human.

A cold, thin band settled across his forehead. Thicker nodes touched down on his temples, and Finn heard a howling wail reverberate around him. Dr. Wen's lab had never echoed before.

"No"—*gasp*—"No"—*wheeze*—"No…"

"Watch the mighty Hawk plummet." Latham this time. Definitely Latham. "Gotta love a good equalizer, eh, doc? Soon as he sits in that chair, every Shadow is in the same boat."

Rowe, Rowe, row your boat…

That was it!

Someone flipped a switch.

Searing pain ripped through Finn's brain, tensing his muscles to the point of physical damage. He tasted electricity on his tongue, felt his eyes burn, and neural pathways fry across his brain, wiping away the song, the boat, and everything they stood for.

And somehow, it kept going, burning, breaking him—but never enough to kill him.

When the torment finally ended, Finn's body went slack, his face numb.

A stranger forced open one of his eyelids to shine a light into his eye. He felt cold fingers at the side of his neck, checking his pulse. Voices hummed nonsensical sounds he couldn't comprehend. Finn floated in a sea of nothing as its gentle rocking soothed his aches and pains. He remembered to breathe and inhaled foul, smoke-scented air through his nose.

A sting of pain across his face forced his eyes open again.

Another stranger hovered in front of Finn—three different versions of him with burning wings alongside their temples, batting up puffs of dark blond smoke. He couldn't make them coalesce. "Son of a bitch," they said. "He's still alive."

Should he know that face? It looked vaguely familiar.

"Name and rank, soldier."

His tongue wouldn't work properly. "F'ngan Rowe. Shadow Hawk."

"I think you zapped him a little hard, doc. Gave him delusions of status. There are no Hawks, soldier. Your rank is Shadow. Repeat."

Finn felt a frown pull on his eyebrows. Slowly regaining feeling in his face again. "Shadow," he repeated.

"Good. We're finally getting somewhere. Take him to the barracks to clean up. I want him in uniform, armed, and ready at twenty-six hundred hours."

The restraints loosened. With restored blood flow came the pain of fresh injuries. Finn stared down at his mangled wrists. Blood dripped from jagged tears onto the dirty white armrest and lower to the concrete floor.

Hard hands gripped him by the arm.

"Hang on a minute," snapped a different voice.

The movement stopped, but the grip didn't loosen.

Someone with long, bony fingers took hold of his hands and sprayed his wounds with something that stung for a second before the tissue went numb. Finn didn't feel the gauze dragging across the open tears. The stranger pinched the wounds closed and coated them with a liquid bandage. "Look at me," he ordered, forcing Finn's face up. The man speaking to him didn't look like any soldier Finn had ever seen. His hair was wild, and his face was tattooed. He looked like he hadn't slept in a week, but there was something in his eyes that sparked... something. "Do you know what day it is?"

Finn looked to the burning wings man for guidance, but he'd already left. He shook his head in the negative.

"Do you know my name?"

He could almost feel it on the tip of his tongue, but the syllables refused to coalesce. Finn shook his head again.

"Let's go, doc. You got other patients to see." Definitely a soldier, that one. His voice straightened Finn's spine and returned a little stability to knees and ankles that felt too rubbery to stand on. He might not understand what was happening or why he felt like he'd been run over by a fritzed-out shuttle, but Finn understood soldiers.

"I said give me a minute! Or do you want me to accidentally kill someone out there?"

Non-soldier arguing with soldiers. And they listened. That didn't make sense.

"Thought you weren't a murderer."

The tattooed man made a face and shook Finn a little to force him to meet his gaze. "Repeat after me: Laura McNally."

"All right, that's enough!" The soldier yanked Finn out of his seat and hauled him upright while another one stepped in on his other side.

"Repeat, soldier!" the tattooed man shouted after them. "Laura McNall—*oof!*" A heavy weight—a body—dropped to the floor.

Finn found his feet out in the hallway, relieving his escort of some of his weight to hobble along with what dignity he still had left. They took him to a barracks he didn't recognize and communal showers he'd never seen before. They stood guard outside the stall while Finn stripped out of his filthy clothes and stepped into the stream of hot water.

His mouth tasted of electricity and vomit. He rinsed it out three times while washing the grime from his skin and hair. Done in two minutes flat, he took an extra sixty seconds to put his face into the hot stream. His jaw moved as his tongue twitched to form words, and he let them, feeling the shape of each syllable in his mouth without giving it full voice: *Laura McNally.*

27

The mountain rock had a unique chemical composition which made it freeze over with needle-like crystal formations in the night, even when the temperature was mild. It was part of the reason why Talon had put the ledge to this particular use. The frost crystals were sharp enough to cut skin, so anyone who tried to escape across them would get shredded.

It also made nighttime the best opportunity to sneak out there. No one in their right mind would risk the ledge after sunset without proper protection. And, given the state in which Talon had left her, no one would expect Vega to do it tonight.

Happily, Shadow uniforms came sealed with a weatherproofing solution which made them impervious to the shards. Vega could brush her arms across the rock to clear the way for a minute or two before they regrew. It wasn't much, but it would have to be enough.

The first half of the ledge had chains drilled into the rockface for her to hold on to, but those only reached to the sharp bend. Beyond that, it was all spiky rock and manacles, with precious few handholds. Shadows usually took a repurposed transport to provide a solid surface when hanging up their prisoners.

Luckily for her civilian prisoners, that meant there was a whole bay of repurposed transports nearby, but, unlike the prisoners themselves, it was under constant guard. Vega could get past them, but once it activated, the transport needed to haul ass out of the region, or it would be shot down, no matter who was in it. She'd have to bring Miguel and Quinn to the vehicle rather than the other way around.

Vega rounded the bend and squinted into the darkness. Quinn and Miguel had been hung up on the far side of the ledge, with three more sets of manacles between them and the bend. She adjusted her stance, grateful to be covered from chin to toe. As long as she kept her balance and didn't lean her exposed face too close to the rock, she'd be fine.

She kept reassuring herself with every successful step while hanging on to the manacles as her only anchors along the way. So far, so good.

Quinn was closest, hanging like a lifeless slab of meat in a bed of spikes that had grown around the outline of his body. With most of his weight on his arms, he was struggling to breathe and appeared to be unconscious.

Vega carefully brushed away the spikes closest to him and leaned in to tilt his head to the side. The monitoring patch on his jugular had turned yellow. She wasn't a doctor, but she figured it wasn't a good thing.

Quinn roused enough to groan. "You."

"You can see me?"

"Smell you," he mumbled. Delirious.

Still, Vega felt an uncomfortable flush warm her face. "I'm going to open the manacles. Can you stand on your own?"

"Think so."

That didn't sound promising. And it wasn't as if she could carry his heavy ass all the way back across the narrow ledge. Vega stifled a curse. She edged closer to him and took hold of his arm for a secure grip as she leaned out to see around him. "You awake?" she asked Miguel.

"Yeah. And I can walk."

"Gonna need more than that. This guy isn't getting off the ledge on his own."

She couldn't see him very well, but she heard him shift in readiness. "I can keep him steady."

Quinn cursed. "I can walk."

"Sure you can, big guy. Now hang tight." She'd need to get around Quinn to free Miguel first. The only problem was Quinn was massive, which meant she basically had to climb over him. Still holding on to his arm, Vega straddled his thigh to put her foot between his. It plastered her to him from chest to hip and pressed her crotch directly over his thigh.

Quinn sucked in a sharp breath and moved. A shower of crystal needles rained over her as he pushed his legs straight to take his weight—and hers—off his manacled wrists. It left Vega hanging from him with several inches of air between the ledge and her dangling feet.

Vega looked up into his face, barely able to make out his features in the dark, even from mere inches away. But she felt his eyes on her. He was showing off to prove his considerable strength and wasting it in the process.

"I could drop you," he said, almost as a lover's whisper.

"My death would be quick," she replied in kind. "Yours wouldn't."

She could hear the baffled frown in his voice when he said, "You really don't care, do you?"

Vega almost laughed. "There are worse things in life than death."

He stared at her for a moment, then lowered until she found the ledge with her boot toe. Climbing the rest of the way over him wasn't easy, but at least his bare chest was a spike-fee surface. Once she was fully on the other side, Vega was left to the mercy of the mountain, with no more handholds except Miguel, a few feet away. She cleared as much surface area as possible by fanning her arm across the rock face before advancing.

Miguel turned his face away to protect his eyes as she brushed off the ones right by his body.

"I'll free your far arm first," she told him. "Find your feet, grind them down until they're steady, then tap me, and I'll free your other one."

"Got it." He was breathing hard, and Vega could almost hear his rapid heart rate. Whatever he was feeling, it would make him unsteady, a recipe for disaster on the ledge.

Vega grabbed hold of his arm the way she'd done with Quinn, but it was a very different sensation. Miguel felt thinner, brittle somehow. She didn't trust his physical integrity enough to put more than the smallest amount of weight on him, which meant she had to rely on the ledge for an anchor.

One arm free. He dropped it to his side with a sigh and immediately tapped her on the shoulder. She could feel him shaking.

Vega gritted her teeth and slammed the palm of her hand against his chest. "Breathe slow. Find your feet. If you slip and pull me with you, your friend dies alone." She didn't move again until his breathing evened out, and the shivers she felt beneath her palm eased somewhat.

Shifting a careful step farther, she reached for his other manacle.

"Wait."

Vega cursed as Quinn's voice startled her almost off balance. "What?" she grated.

"Can you reach both of us at the same time?"

"Why?"

"He'll be unsteady. Hold on to me when you set him loose. If he falls, I can anchor you, and you can catch him."

Vega should have thought of it herself. Her impaired thinking was a testament to the pathetic state she'd sunk to, courtesy of Talon's tender, loving care. The saddest thing about it: the two men were still willing to trust her with their lives because her sorry ass was all they had. What a team they made.

The crystals had begun to reform between her and Quinn. Vega brushed them away and shifted a foot closer to him, grabbing his thick forearm where she could wrap her fingers around enough of it for a secure hold. It limited her reach over to Miguel. "Take hold of my arm with your free hand," she instructed.

When he did, she reached up to undo the manacle.

To his credit, Miguel seemed to grasp their precarious situation. He moved slower this time, carefully lowering his arm to his opposite shoulder. They held and waited until he signaled he was ready to go.

Vega had to let go of him to clear the crystals from the path of his head and torso again before he could move. "Stay as close as you can," she told Miguel. "Hold for my signal before you move. We do this slow, but we don't stop." If they did, the crystals would reform between them, and someone would end up regretting it. "Anything feels off, you speak up."

"Laura would like you," Miguel muttered, and Quinn coughed a weak chuckle.

"Lucky me," she retorted. "Ready?"

"Ready."

Vega pulled Miguel along one small step at a time until he could reach Quinn's arm. It plastered her between the two of them, and she had to hug herself to Quinn's side to keep her balance.

When Miguel was secure, she reversed her path and climbed over Quinn to his far side. Crystal needles crunched as she pressed herself into the rockface, carefully keeping her head a safe distance from it. "Find your feet," she told Quinn.

The giant slid up against the rocky surface at his back, dislodging another shower of crystals as he grew a foot in height. Vega winced. His shoulders and nape had to be getting cut to shit. His elbows bent, taking his weight off his wrists, and Vega saw the big shadow of him lean forward on the ledge.

She reached out immediately to grab hold of his tattered shirt for all the good it would do. His breathing was labored, and pained, and the patch on his neck faded from yellow to orange and back again. The juggernaut was not okay.

He groaned and straightened, flattening his back against the rock. "I'm good," he said.

"One arm at a time. Hold on to Miguel."

Vega freed Quinn's far wrist first. His big hand dropped directly to Miguel's shoulder for balance and support. He breathed through the change, rolled his big shoulder a few times, then said, "Good."

Vega made sure she had a firm hold on Quinn's arm before she freed it. It didn't escape her that, should he lose his balance, she and Miguel would have no chance in hell of keeping him on the ledge. He'd take both of them down with him. Nevertheless, the human chain they created still made her feel marginally more secure.

"Remember, move slow, but don't stop. Slide your foot, don't pick it up. The bend is the trickiest part, but there are chains to hold onto on the other side." If they made it there, they'd be home-free. They just had to make it there.

Step by agonizing step, they made their way across the ledge. Vega kept her mouth shut, listening for any change in breathing or unexpected shift of weight in the others. She kept them inching along, then talked them around the bend until she, Quinn, and finally Miguel got far enough to grab hold of the chain.

By the time they made it off the ledge, even Vega was ready to collapse. Quinn did, crumbling to the floor as soon as he was far enough to let Miguel get around him to safety. He clutched his chest as the patch turned a slightly darker shade of yellow.

"You really need a new heart," she reiterated.

Quinn made a sound that could have been a groan or a chuckle.

"Can you walk?"

He shook his head. "Not very far."

"Just far enough."

This elevation had been used as utility corridors during the vault's construction, decommissioned, and sealed as soon as it had been finished. Talon's first order of business when taking over the mountain had been to map out every potential entrance and exit and repurpose all accessible areas. This lower part, affectionately referred to as the catacombs, didn't get much use, but it was handy for storing things like equipment and prisoners.

The three of them were currently underneath the saddle hover pad in a short off-shoot tunnel that wasn't part of the original construction. Where it emerged into a hallway, low, artificial lights held steady, indicating no movement. Vega inched closer to take a peek.

About fifty yards or so on the right was where the vault entrance would be above. The hallway split into a T there, with one path leading to a staircase up to the vault and the other toward a set of makeshift holding cells. The telepaths were being held there, guarded by three armed soldiers with white helmets. They had strict orders not to move from their posts, but if they heard any sort of noise that didn't belong, they'd come around the blind corner to investigate.

Twenty feet in the other direction, down to her left, were two more holes bored into the mountainside. One, across the hallway, led up to the hover pad—where she'd entered coming in. The other, almost exactly opposite the first, led to the transport bay. There'd be more soldiers on guard there, but Vega wouldn't be able to assess the situation until she actually saw it.

She beckoned the two men closer. In the meager light, Quinn looked pasty and sweaty, his face drawn with pain. He leaned on the wall more than not. "Get ready to move on my signal," she whispered. "Slow and quiet. Hug the wall as much as you can."

Twenty feet. No big deal.

Holding a finger to her lips for silence, she led the way out, stepping with her toes first to make as little noise as possible. She heard Quinn breathing right behind her. Miguel brought up the rear.

Everything was going great until Vega ducked into the tunnel. Quinn, coming up behind her, didn't quite clear the lower protrusion of the wall. He stumbled, sending loose rocks clattering. Vega shoved past him to make a mad grab for Miguel. She yanked him into the tunnel, shoved him toward the floor, and hissed, "Down!" as she pulled her gun.

The two men dropped for cover, and Vega positioned herself where she could peek out into the hallway and keep an eye on the other end of their tunnel at the same time.

Movement came from the hallway first. A Shadow wearing a white helmet came out from behind the corner, gun raised and ready to fire, but he didn't advance. The telepaths had highest priority. He wouldn't move out of sight of those cells unless under direct attack.

After a few seconds, he lowered the gun and returned to his post.

Vega swung her gun around to cover the tunnel, but when nothing happened for a whole two minutes, she lowered it and sagged against the wall, taking careful deep breaths to calm herself. Such thin ice…

"Sorry," Quinn whispered.

Irrelevant. "You ready for the hard part?" She eased around them to take the lead again. The tunnel bent toward her right, away from the telepaths and their guards. Light at the end marked the transport bay. She already heard voices, loud and obnoxious. The guards probably had some asinine game or contest going on. No wonder they hadn't heard Quinn stumble.

Vega stopped her two charges at the border, where shadows cast by the tunnel wouldn't hide them anymore. Three guards in her line of sight. There'd be more in the direction where those three were busy looking. Only one transport left—a small powder blue relic. What'd happened to the others? There should have been at least six of them. At least, there had been six the last time Vega had come through this way, weeks ago.

Didn't matter. One was all they needed.

She checked the charge on her gun. Already too low for a kill shot. It never charged more than sixty percent anymore and lost about ten every hour. What she had left might hold out for five shots if she was lucky. *Better make them count.* Headshots only.

Vega signaled for Quinn and Miguel to stay put. She took a deep breath, then walked out of the tunnel, aiming for the three Shadows in front of her. One shot, one Shadow. She fired three times in rapid succession, then pivoted around to cover another guard at the other end of the bay. A thin, high-pitched voice squeaked in the cage behind him when he dropped.

Vega glanced at the first three to make sure they were out cold, then went over to the fourth and his cage. Her already strained jaw muscles went so tight they hurt. The structure was roughly six feet cubed, formerly used to transport wild animals. Crammed inside were five teenagers, huddled together as far in the back as they could get.

Talon's newest recruits. Abilities unconfirmed but already prominent enough to have caught his interest. He must have snatched them during his mission today—the one Rowe had apparently crashed.

And now she had a problem.

Vega turned her back on the kids, kicked over the Shadow, who'd been doing God knew what to them before she'd arrived, and shot him point-blank in the head. A non-lethal setting didn't blast through. But at such close range, it packed enough of a punch to flatten the soldier's head by three inches, crushing his brain.

With that, the gun went dead. She holstered it and motioned for Quinn and Miguel to come out while she dealt with the others. "Get in the transport," she ordered, disarming the soldiers and using their own weapons to stop their hearts, judging them complicit. There were lines a soldier never crossed. Even a Shadow. She couldn't touch Talon, but his rabid attack dogs were fair game, as far as she was concerned.

The kids scrambled to the front of the cage. "Take us with you!" One of the oldest ones begged.

Vega swore.

As soon as they heard that voice, Quinn and Miguel stopped halfway into the transport.

"Move," Vega snapped. "We don't have much time."

"Please!" a girl cried. "I just want to go home."

Miguel shot Vega a venomous look and sprang into action, running for the cage, rattling it to try to get it open.

Growling, Vega crossed over to him and hauled him away from his futile efforts. "Get in the fucking transport."

"We are not leaving them in there!"

"You're not taking them with you," she countered. "The transport won't fit all of you. You wanna choose who gets left behind?"

"I will."

Vega swung around to face Quinn.

"I will stay," he repeated, swaying on his feet. He lurched, lost his balance, and fell sideways against a stack of crates. "Kids go, I stay."

"The hell you will." She hadn't risked her life to get them out so they could throw it back in her face.

"Not leaving kids"—he paused to catch his breath—"in a fucking cage."

"If you stay, you'll die." Talon wouldn't hurt the kids until he'd finished dealing with the telepaths down the hall. They had time. Quinn didn't.

"Worse things 'n death, right?"

Fuck! She shoved the Shadow with his dented head onto his side to pull out the gun tucked in the back of his waistband. Not Shadow-issued. It was a civilian model, a cop gun. Non-lethal setting only. Didn't matter. Vega marched over to the cage and took aim.

Kids screamed, and Miguel shouted at her, but before his voice had stopped echoing, the shot blasted out, mangling the locking mechanism on the cage. She yanked it open and stood back as the kids stampeded straight for the transport, cramming themselves inside. Three big boys took up the entire back seat. The girls had to sit one on top of the other in the front, leaving exactly one space left for the driver. The old wreck didn't even have a cargo hold for her to stuff Quinn into.

She pointed the gun at Miguel, who appeared to be frozen in shock. "Get up."

He complied, hands in the air.

"If you crash that thing and get them all killed, you better fucking believe I will hunt you down in hell and make you regret every decision you ever made."

"It's dark," he said. "Nav doesn't work at night."

"Then I guess you better learn how to drive."

"Are you ser—"

"Five seconds. Four. Three."

Miguel jumped into the driver's seat and slammed the door shut. One last terrified look at Quinn, and he started the engine. The transport shot up from the floor, lightly thumping the top against the cave roof before he got a handle on it. It should fly high above any obstacles as long as he kept the elevation steady. Not easy, but doable. Then all he had to do was head in the general direction of safety and pray to whatever deity he worshipped that he made it there before the Shadows caught up.

As soon as the vehicle shot out from the ledge, Vega tossed the gun and turned to Quinn. He was paler than before, the patch on his neck solid orange. His eyes were half closed, but he watched her as she came to crouch down next to him.

"Keep doing things like that," he said, "I might start to think you have a heart."

"Too small for a transplant match, in case you're thinking of ripping it out of me."

He gave a small shrug. "Thought crossed my mind. Not much of a heart stealer, though."

Vega snorted. "Right." She took hold of his arm and ducked under it. "Now get up."

Quinn groaned. "Why?"

"You need to hide before someone comes by to find this place deserted." She helped him to his feet and walked him over to the barrels the Shadows had used for chairs around a makeshift table. There, she sat him down again and inspected the crate the guards had laid open. Alcohol—figured. She pulled out a bottle of beer and twisted off the top. "Drink."

Quinn shook his head.

Vega grabbed his hand and forced his fingers to curl around the bottle. "You're dehydrated. Drink. And while you're at it, take your clothes off."

"S'cuse me?"

The largest Shadow was almost Quinn's size. Just a few inches shy of tall enough, a size or two narrower. He'd have to do. She started undoing his uniform as she explained, "You'll blend in better if you don't stand out so much."

"You want me to pass for one of you? Are you insane?"

"It won't be for long." With five telepaths and John Wayland together under one roof, Vega expected an epic amount of shit to start hitting the fan as soon as their tranqs wore off. "With any luck, by sunset tomorrow, this will all be over."

One way or another.

28

The wire came loose from its mooring. Finn studied it for a moment. Without that connection, the system couldn't function properly. One tiny wire pulled loose, and a highly sophisticated piece of technology was rendered effectively useless.

Finn's wrists were burning. The numbing agent had worn off a few minutes ago, but the pain didn't affect his dexterity in the least. His hands were steady as a rock when he carefully twisted the tiny screw back into place, the wire end now hanging loose beside it.

"The fuck are you doing?"

Finn looked up at the soldier who wore his uniform jacket opened. His name was Talmadge, supposedly the Shadows' best pilot. He didn't look very reliable—unkempt, with the end tail of an unlit cigar stuck between his yellow teeth.

"I said, what the fuck are you doing, Hawk?"

They kept calling him that, but the commanding officer had said it wasn't a rank. Was it his handle? Finn frowned at the deconstructed white helmet in front of him. "I don't know." From what he'd seen so far, their unit wasn't in the best shape. They were low on supplies and equipment. It had been strategically stupid to take apart something that still looked so new, and he couldn't explain why he'd been compelled to do it, anyway. "I guess I wanted to see how it worked."

Talmadge pointed a thick, blunt finger at his nose. "You better be able to put that back together the way it was, or Talon's gonna have your head."

Talon. Name, rank, or handle?

"You got three minutes."

Finn sprang into action, replacing screws, adjusting wires, and clicking covers back into place. In two minutes and forty-three seconds, he had the white helmet rebuilt to its original state. With the exception of one little wire. The switch turned it on and off. The readouts inside streamed across the visor as before. To all appearances, it looked good as new.

"Not bad, rookie," Talmadge said.

Finn didn't tell him about the wire.

"Now get moving. Talon wants to see you."

He turned the helmet off and put it in the center of his bunk. They'd assigned him the bottom one. Not ideal, but he'd make it work. At least he was close to the exit. Quick way out if there was trouble.

Talmadge didn't put himself together before they left the barracks, sauntering down the long hallway as if there were no higher-ups to discipline him. In contrast, Finn was buttoned and tucked without a thread out of place, and he marched in Talmadge's wake with measured footsteps, eyes front and hands at his sides.

He scoped out his surroundings using his peripheral vision, but nothing he saw made sense. This place didn't look anything like an army base. It was laid out strangely, and the open rooms he passed appeared to have been ransacked by animals. No one had explained anything, and it wasn't his place to ask. But his first impression suggested this was more of a hideout than a proper military facility.

There must have been an attack of some sort. Maybe he'd gotten injured and lost his memory. His head did still ache hours after his treatment. It would explain a few other things, too. Like the cloying sense of urgency that he'd forgotten something vital, left a mission unfinished. Finn's skin crawled with the need to go somewhere. But his damaged brain refused to fill in the blanks. Hopefully, this Talon person would have some answers. Going about getting them would be tricky business, though. The Shadows didn't tolerate weakness. He couldn't let them think he was damaged or compromised in any way. Otherwise, they'd wash him out, and where would that leave him? Finn had no identity outside of his name and rank.

Finnegan Rowe—Shadow.

Finnegan "Hawk" Rowe?

Finnegan Rowe—Shadow Hawk.

None of those felt quite right.

A female soldier with long black hair was coming down the hall toward them. Finn noted her state of disarray. Her braid was a mess; she had abrasions on one side of her face, and the other had a thin, precise, reverse-C wound circling around the outer edge of her cheek. She was in full uniform, including gloves, with only the top third of the jacket undone to reveal bruising around her neck. Must have just returned from a mission.

Talmadge's walk changed when he spotted her. He became bouncier and more animated, shoulders back and arms swinging. "Yo, Ortiz, check out what Talon's team brought in."

Ortiz had to be the woman's name. She blanked her face when he addressed her directly, but when she saw Finn, she stopped dead in her tracks. "Rowe?"

"What'd I tell ya, eh? Hawks ain't got shit on us. Am I right? Gimme five."

The woman ignored him, staring at Finn. She seemed to be waiting for something.

Finn wasn't sure of her rank—or anyone's, for that matter. None of them had any distinguishing insignia. Was he supposed to salute? Was she?

A ghost of a memory flitted through his mind too quickly for him to follow it. *The fuck are you doing here, Vega?* He didn't know what it meant. The way the woman was staring at him, she had to know something Finn didn't. But she didn't seem inclined to talk.

"Aw come on," Talmadge was saying. "Even you gotta admit it's impressive. They're saying Talon brought him down with one shot."

Ortiz changed her expression the way someone might put on a mask. She rolled her eyes into a glare at Talmage. "We got five telepaths and a former Hawk." She spoke the words to Talmadge, but her tone was curiously aimed at Finn. She cast him a quick glance to gauge his reaction and, seeing none, firmed her mouth the slightest bit. "I'm supposed to be impressed by a blank?"

A blank?

"What'd Talon do, fry the shit out of his brain?"

Finn recalled standing in the shower, tasting electricity and vomit. Was his memory loss deliberate? It must have been a last resort. His brain must have malfunctioned badly enough to necessitate such drastic measures. Finn would have to thank this Talon when they met.

Talmadge shrugged. "Probably didn't wanna take any chances."

The small smile Ortiz gave him was sharp and dangerous. "Because he knew he wouldn't be able to control him otherwise."

Why would anyone need to control Finn? He was a trained soldier; he knew how to follow orders.

"Bet you anything he'll send Rowe down to the telepaths," Ortiz added.

"Why would he do that?"

"To prove a point."

Finn followed their exchange with only a vague sense of a lot of subtext, which neither of them wanted to speak out loud, but both of them understood. He didn't like being the subject of it, especially when he had no foundation on which to base a reaction. Were they being insulting or complimentary? It was one or the other, but Finn couldn't tell which.

He did know they were taking a lot of time Finn and Talmadge didn't have. The commanding officer had said he wanted Finn ready at twenty-six hundred hours. It was now two minutes to the hour, and Finn had no idea how much farther they had to go.

"Yeah, I can see that," Talmadge acknowledged. "No bet."

"Fair," Ortiz said, then tapped a gloved finger against her chin. Finn noted a set of dog tags peeking out from underneath her sleeve. "How about this? Bet you two weeks' rations that as soon as he sees Laura McNally, he'll flip his switch right back."

There went that quicksilver glance again, Ortiz measuring Finn's reaction to the name Laura McNally. He didn't have one to give her. The doctor had said the name, too. Finn had memorized it, but had no face to go with it. Laura McNally was nothing but two words imprinted on his mind with no context or direction. Yet his tongue still moved behind his clenched teeth to form them.

"All right, bet," Talmadge said, extending his big hand. He chuckled when Ortiz shook it. "Man, I'll be eating good for weeks!"

"I wouldn't be so sure in your place."

"Oh, this thing is in the bag," Talmadge crowed. "Talon gave him a helmet."

The one Finn had decommissioned a few minutes ago. A strange mixture of concern and triumph made him want to raise his chin, but he stopped himself. He didn't know enough about either of these two to be as free with them as they seemed to be with each other.

Well, Talmadge, anyway. Ortiz was a lot more stoic, her smallest facial expressions carefully curated and delivered to get a particular response.

But she did have tells. Right now, the slightest twitch at the corner of her mouth told Finn she was satisfied with the outcome of her conversation with Talmadge. She'd made him reveal something she hadn't known before and gain a false sense of confidence. The twitch might as well have been a triumphant fanfare.

Ortiz snorted. "We'll see how well that works."

Finn recognized and respected her reserved style. There was a sense of kinship in it as if she was somehow like him—something Finn didn't feel when it came to the devil-may-care Talmadge. Had he known Ortiz before his malfunction?

She moved on, but not before meeting Finn's gaze for a split second, communicating some kind of message Finn couldn't decipher. All he got was a sense of dire urgency that left him with more questions than answers.

Talmadge watched Vega depart with an appreciative grin on his face. He grunted and shook his head, then jerked his chin at Finn. "Let's go. Ain't smart to keep the boss waiting."

At the end of the hallway, the space opened up into a massive circular chamber that looked like it'd been attacked recently, but Finn couldn't see or smell any plasma residue. The walls were covered with hermetic doors that had been left open to expose safe storage boxes, now empty and hollowed out. The ceiling three stories above his head was shadowed for lack of proper lighting, but Finn noted the uneven, rocky surface. This used to be a cave of some sort.

They rounded a raised platform, and Finn realized there was no door to secure the space. He could see through the ragged opening all the way outside. It was close to midnight and full dark out there. Strong breezes hinting of high altitude carried fresh air and a curious mineral scent deep into the giant chamber. He recalled smelling that scent on Ortiz as she'd passed him. Likely not unusual if she'd just returned from assignment. Finn still filed it away for later investigation.

When he would have headed outside, Talmadge pulled him back around to face the raised platform. A red couch took up a third of the available space on top, with a familiar-looking figure standing at ease in front of it, grinning down at Finn. Flaming wings were tattooed along the sides of his shaved head. Over the top, dark blond hair stood on end, trailing all the way back. He had a beard and a broken nose, and Finn knew this was the commanding officer he'd seen when he'd come to in med bay, but there was something else about him that sparked an instant sense of dislike.

"There he is."

Finn stood at attention and saluted. Like or dislike didn't matter. He knew a commanding officer when one addressed him.

"Just keep doing what you're doing, and you'll be fine," Talmadge told Finn as he eased back to leave Finn on his own. "Talon likes to feel in charge."

Then he was gone.

The man they called Talon, the commanding officer of this unit, looked Finn over from his high perch. His expression said he was satisfied with what he saw, but there was a hint of mockery in it, too. Finn didn't understand, but it offended him on an elemental level. He gritted his teeth and kept his face carefully blank.

"At ease, soldier."

Finn brought his hands behind his back and stepped his feet apart.

The men around him chuckled. Undisciplined rabble. They were beneath him and, therefore, none of his concern.

"Report," Talon ordered.

"Sir?"

"Mission report. Now."

Finn racked his aching brain for some sort of reply that would meet with the commanding officer's satisfaction but came up with nothing. "I… Mission, sir?"

"Did you suffer a head injury?"

Finn frowned.

Talon rolled his eyes. "What do you remember."

Pain. A sense of duty and purpose but, at the same time, deep shame and regret. He must have done something wrong, but, for the life of him, Finn couldn't remember what. Nevertheless, it weighed on him. He'd failed. Honor demanded that he admit to his failure and accept his due punishment. But, looking up at the commanding officer brought only a ghost of anger and resentment. Finn had failed, but not Talon.

In the absence of anything to confess, he latched on to the last directive he remembered. "Sir! Telepaths present a clear and recognizable danger to humanity's God-given free will. They are a threat the general public is as yet unaware of. The Shadows are the vanguard in the fight to protect and ensure humanity's continued existence as a species of free-thinking individuals. Our mission is to eliminate the threat without revealing the threat. Sir!"

Talon clapped his gloved hands in short applause. "Very good, soldier."

You broke my heart!

Finn blinked away the stray memory and forced himself to breathe down the sudden heart rate spike. No context other than, finally, an anchor for his shame. It had something to do with a woman. But now was not the time to think about women. He had to focus. This was a test of some sort. Talon was watching him too closely for it to be anything else. Finn had no intention of failing it.

"Are you fit for active duty?"

"Sir, yes sir!"

"Our medic says otherwise," Talon countered. "He says you suffered a concussion and recommended four days of observation."

It wasn't a question, so Finn didn't say anything. His head did ache, and every once in a while, he did feel a slight vertigo that made his stomach roil. But those were minor inconveniences for a Shadow. Nothing that would keep him from performing his duties. That he didn't remember much from before his treatment didn't matter, either. As long as he remembered going forward.

"Still the stoic," Talon said, shaking his head. "Doesn't matter. I'm assigning you to prisoner detail. You have until oh-five-hundred to get yourself together. Then you will report to me for further instructions."

"Sir, yes sir!"

"Dismissed."

Finn saluted and marched back to the barracks. Oh-five-hundred. That gave him a solid seven and a half hours to himself. Practically unheard of unless Finn really was compromised enough to warrant extra time to recuperate. The medic would know best, no doubt, but Finn didn't feel unfit in any way. Then again, given the state of things around this place, he might as well get some sleep while he could. Who knew when the opportunity would present itself again?

He took off his boots and jacket but kept the rest of his uniform on in case he needed to move out in a hurry. Setting the helmet on the floor next to his bunk, which didn't have any storage space, Finn gingerly put the sore back of his head on the pillow and closed his eyes.

A clicking sound snapped them open again. The barracks were lit but dim, allowing for sleep without full black-out. Finn turned his head toward the source of the sound to his right. Three bunks down, a tiny light blinked silently on and off in a set pattern, repeating three times over. A signal for danger. Five other Shadows slept on the bunks behind the flashing light, but no one else between it and Finn, on his side or against the far wall.

He was the only possible intended recipient of the message.

Finn rolled onto his side, facing the light, rustling his blanket enough to make it clear he was awake and paying attention.

The light flashed again in a new pattern, spelling out a word: *Remember.*

Remember what? He didn't have a light of his own to respond, and even if he did, the others would see. Whoever was signaling him was little more than a shadowy outline with no identifying marks. Finn couldn't even tell whether the soldier saw him awake and watching.

He had half convinced himself to get up and confront them when the light flashed again.

Danger. Remember.

And then once more in the same sequence, as if the third time would be the charm.

It wasn't.

The light went dark, leaving Finn on his own with a message he had no way of deciphering. His memories were gone. Finn had nothing to go on other than his primary objective and whatever orders Talon gave him tomorrow.

And now, a paranoid weight in his gut, telling him he'd have to watch his back.

It made sleep a reluctant visitor, settling over him in slow, halting stages interspersed with sharp awakenings and questions he didn't know how to answer. Chief among them: *Who the hell is Laura Mc-Nally?*

When he did finally succumb to the weakness of his body's need for rest, Finn dreamed himself into a maze of tall corn stalks, haunted by a faint hint of perfume he could never trace to its source.

July 6, 2039

The beehive had been kicked over. In total darkness, Laura heard everything around her humming and buzzing in a multitude of different frequencies that made her head throb on the verge of exploding. Was she dreaming?

Hickory dickory dock...

Her skin crawled. She felt the insects swarming in her hair, but her limbs were too heavy to swat at them—she could barely move.

The mouse ran up the clock...

Saliva flooded her mouth, and her eyes ached. She opened them and saw nothing. Her world was pitch black, with no point of reference except the cold stone floor and the song repeating over and over again in a small, whimpering voice.

It took long moments for Laura to shake the tranquilizer's effects enough to realize the singing wasn't in her head.

"The clock struck one, the mouse ran down... Hickory dickory dock."

Laura sat up with a groan. "What time is it?"

Laughter, clipped and maniacal, somewhere in the darkness. "What time is it? What time is it? What time is it?"

Laura felt her way across the floor toward the voice. "Emma, it's okay. I'm here."

A moan. "No, you're not."

Laura's hand encountered a foot, and Emma screamed, scrambling out of reach. This was Emma's worst nightmare. It was what she'd lived with the Shadows three years ago, except, back then, the room they'd put her in had been bright white with no respite from the light. She'd made darkness her sanctuary, and now they've taken that away from her, too.

How long had they been here? The discordant humming was already playing merry havoc with Laura's brain even with her limited telepathy shut down. She couldn't imagine what the more powerful Emma had to be feeling. "Listen to my voice. I'm here. I'm real."

Emma sang louder to drown her out, but her voice was muffled.

Laura once again braved the darkness to reach her new friend. She talked along the way so as not to startle Emma. "Your name is Emma Wayland. You're married to the Shadow soldier who saved you three years ago. You're the acting director of the Special Unit, and you live on Torrey."

The song quieted a little.

Good, because it sounded like Laura was right next to Emma. She lowered her voice. "You're on Anamtaigh to help me and my people. My name is Laura Bel—" Her mind caught up in the middle of her last name, reminding her that William was dead. She couldn't finish it without her heart breaking all over again. "I'm Laura McNally. I run a refugee compound in Karsengale Valley."

Her voice seemed to be getting through. Emma had stopped singing, and her desperate moans had quieted to soft whimpers and the occasional wet sniffle.

Laura kept talking. "You helped us get to Avencore, and the Shadows attacked us there."

"What time is it?" Emma whispered.

The personal memories Emma had bestowed on Laura told her it was a question she hadn't had to ask in over two years. Laura ached for the other woman. It should never have come to this. "It's time to be strong now," she said. "We have a lot of people counting on us to get them out of this."

"S-seashell?"

"I don't know where he is. It sounds like it's just you and me in here. I'm going to put my hand on you now, okay?" She reached out and found Emma's shoulder in the darkness. Emma flinched but didn't pull away, so Laura shifted around to sit beside her so she could put both arms around Emma. Her wild hair tickled Laura's cheek and ear as Emma laid her head on her shoulder. "It's going to be okay. We will get through this."

Physical touch seemed to help. Little by little, Emma pulled herself together enough to unclench from her tight ball and straighten out her legs. Laura heard her whimper. She had to be cramped and aching from head to toe.

"What time is it?" Emma asked again, sounding marginally more lucid.

"Best I can tell you is that we're probably inside their mountain stronghold. It used to be an emergency supply vault back in the day. They bored it into the mountainside. High ground, not a lot of exits or entrances. And a whole lot of Shadows." Laura told Emma what she remembered of the layout, but she'd only ever seen the one big open space and the hover pad out front.

"Seashell?"

Laura's heart broke. "I don't know." The last she remembered was John's blank space disappearing in a sea of red. She couldn't tell Emma where he was or whether he was still alive.

Emma nodded against her shoulder. "Oceans don't go dry overnight," she declared with a sniffle. "He'll echo."

That almost made sense. Sort of. "How are you doing?"

"Buzzy. Too much noise that should be a lot brighter, but it isn't. I feel it in my bones." There was a dull thump as if she'd struck herself.

Laura felt along Emma's arms to find her hands tangled in her hair. She extricated them and clutched them tight to keep her from hurting herself. "Listen to my voice." She didn't dare make it a command, relying on her tone to carry her wishes. "You need to be strong for John, okay? He can't fight an army and coddle you, too." Harsh but necessary. She firmly kept the wince and regret out of her voice to drive her point home. "You got back at the Shadows once; you can do it again. And this time, you're not alone."

Emma breathed a shaky sigh. "Not alone."

"We will get out of this together."

"Not alone."

"Do you ever meditate? It helps me get my thoughts together sometimes. Maybe we should try that."

"Don't let go!"

Laura firmed her grip on Emma's hands. "I'm not going anywhere," she promised. "Just listen to my voice and breathe slow and calm. In… and out. Feel the air flow in through your nose, filling your lungs, and breathe out all the fear and the buzzing. In… Out… Let the darkness cushion your mind. You are safe. You are strong. And you're not alone."

Laura kept talking until her voice went hoarse. She was parched. Her stomach clenched too hard for her to think about food, but it did make her desperate to know what time it was. How long had they been here? What happened to everyone else at the inn?

What happened to Finn?

We have to operate under the assumption that whatever plan we come up with will fail. Someone's going to get caught.

He had warned her. He'd told her exactly how this conflict would turn out. And Laura had been so preoccupied she'd left the defense of her people in someone else's hands. She'd thought they'd be safe with Emma's telepaths and another former Shadow keeping watch. She'd let down her guard, and the Shadows had swooped right in. If only she'd listened to William and taken her people out sooner, none of this would have happened.

The buzzing glitched for a split second of silence, and the outside world snuck in through the gap. "Did you feel that?"

Emma pulled one of her hands free. "It skipped a verse."

"Did you get anything through it?" Laura had caught a glimpse of faded lights to her right. Ghosts of intentions left over from a brief but strong burst of them before they'd disappeared again. They weren't enough to gauge whether they belonged to one person or several, but they told her the door to the cell was that way, and it was guarded.

"Someone's coming," Emma said. "Empty. No song in him."

Laura pressed closer to Emma.

They waited, enduring the incessant buzzing without a word.

When the door opened on a flare of light, it made Laura jump, and Emma along with her.

As dim as it was, the light blinded Laura to all but vague shapes and figures. One man carried a tray, two others behind him held their weapons at the ready. All three wore shiny white helmets that obscured their faces.

The one with the tray took two robotic steps into the cell and placed the tray on the ground. Four fingers on his left hand.

Laura lurched toward him. "Finn!"

"Laura, don't!" Emma cried, grabbing for her at the same time as Finn stepped back and pulled a gun on her, finger on the trigger.

Laura froze, staring at him. "Finn? Is that you?"

His silence was ice cold. Laura didn't need her telepathy to understand his deadly intent. If she so much as twitched wrong, he'd pull the trigger without a second thought.

"What are you doing?" she tried, much more cautious this time.

No response.

"He doesn't remember," Emma whispered, tugging her backward away from him. "No more song in him. They scooped it all out of his head."

Laura's stomach twisted, recalling what he'd told her about EMC. An electromagnetic pulse to fry neural pathways, a chemical injection to make it harder for them to reform.

No. No way. She was not going to lose him, too.

But her conviction was a little difficult to stand by when the knuckles on his gun hand began to turn pale.

"They attacked the inn," she said, struggling to keep her voice steady enough to form words. "D-do you know what happened to the others?"

Finn stepped backward into the doorway, gun still aimed squarely at Laura's forehead.

"Finn, please. Please remember me."

One more step, and he was outside, and the door closed between them.

"W-what…" She couldn't catch her breath.

Emma's arms came around her, her voice crooned nonsense, and none of it made a difference. Numbness set in. The beehive buzz turned into a steady, high-pitched ringing in her ears. Lights flared and disappeared as Laura stared blindly in the direction where Finn had disappeared, leaving her in the dark.

He was gone.

Not playing a role, not deep undercover—*gone.*

Of all the ways Laura could have lost Finn, this particular one had never entered her mind as a possibility, but it was worse than any of the others.

Talon had killed *her* Finn and sent her back an empty shell filled with Shadow.

~

Finn didn't lower his weapon until one of the guards put a hand on his shoulder. "It's safe," the soldier said. "They can't get out."

It took him five more seconds to compose himself enough to holster the gun without letting on how hard his hand was shaking once he relaxed it.

Please remember me.

Finn couldn't breathe inside the helmet. He ripped it off and sucked in as much air as his lungs would hold. "Who the hell are they?" he heard himself demand as if he had any authority to ask questions.

The guards didn't seem to mind. "Mindfuckers," one of them answered, spitting on the floor as if the word left a bad taste in his mouth. "Who gives a shit? They'll be dead by tomorrow, anyway."

Then why bother feeding them? Talon had sent Finn down here with explicit orders: Go in, deliver food, and get out. Don't talk to the prisoners, and keep the helmet on at all times. The two soldiers on guard duty were there for backup in case one of the prisoners decided to try and make a break for it, but Finn would be a pathetic excuse for a soldier if he couldn't handle a couple of bedraggled women.

Please remember me.

Finn shook his head hard.

"What's the matter with you?" the second guard snapped. "Not like you haven't dealt with their kind before. Your head still scrambled, or what?"

"I'm fine." He was far from fine. "Where are the others?"

"Put your game face on for this one." The guard tapped the helmet Finn had ripped off. "You're gonna need it."

Finn breathed down the shakes, pushed the Laura woman from his mind, and put his helmet back on. It might as well have been a cell door, locking him in with her. As soon as the visor came down, all Finn saw was her pleading face, flashing back and forth between the dark cell and a bright sunny day outdoors.

Same face, same tears, same desperate look.

Different ages.

He hunched over, stomach clenching with the weight of guilt it brought him.

It'd been a clever attempt at manipulation, blending in the different time frames and scenes to build artificial history, but she'd miscalculated. There was no possible way he'd ever met the woman before in his life.

He'd never have forgotten her.

Game face on. He had another tray, and the guards flanked another cell, ready to back him up with their weapons set to non-lethal force. Mutiny would not be tolerated, but their orders were to keep the telepaths alive until Talon decided otherwise.

The door opened as Finn braced himself for more forlorn looks and desperate mind games.

An animalistic roar was all the warning Finn got before a man charged straight at him and bowled him over. His tray flew in one direction, his helmet spun off in another. The prisoner looked ready to kill, his fist poised to pummel Finn's face into the rock, but he stopped, the same shocked look on his face as the woman from the first cell. "Rowe?"

Finn exploited his moment of inattention and punched him in the throat. In two deft moves, he'd reversed their position and delivered a merciless blow to the man's jaw.

His opponent took it in stride and launched his own attack. They grappled along the hallway, so evenly matched Finn couldn't get the upper hand on him. The prisoner anticipated every move he made, and though he didn't telegraph a single one, Finn always seemed to know where the next blow would come from.

The third time he ended up on his back, it became clear Finn would not be winning this match. He'd almost resigned himself to shouting for help, something he would never have thought himself needing to do, when a gunshot toppled the prisoner off Finn.

Non-lethal setting. He was still conscious when the guards dragged him back into the cell with the other telepath they'd knocked out.

Finn shot to his feet and pulled his gun in case the son of a bitch tried something else.

The guards dropped the prisoner in the dark cell and backed away.

He sat up with a groan. "Don't let them hood you again, Hawk," he mumbled, wiping blood from his mouth. "Remember her."

What the fuck?

"Laura McNa—"

The cell door closed, cutting him off.

Finn kicked the spilled food tray against the wall.

"Told you," one of the guards said with a shrug. He didn't seem at all concerned that one of his prisoners had just attempted an escape. Then again, why would he? *He* hadn't failed to perform the simple task assigned to him.

The other guard looked Finn up and down. "You all right?"

Finn turned his back on them while he retrieved his helmet, taking a second to pull himself together. His heart was pounding, and he couldn't seem to breathe fast enough to keep up. He'd had a full night's sleep; his physical condition should not be this compromised.

Laura McNally.

Remember her.

The prisoner had called him Hawk. "That wasn't a telepath," he said.

"Nope, deserted Shadow."

"Yeah, he'll get what's coming to him."

Finn had lost track of who was speaking. In uniform, with their helmets on, both guards looked the same to him.

"How does he know me?"

Another shrug. "Heard tell you two used to be buddies back before the war."

Then why couldn't Finn remember him? Someone who knew him well enough for an even spar must have spent a great deal of time with him. Shouldn't that have left some kind of mark on him?

He clenched his left hand into a fist, then flexed it open again. The scar where his pinky should have been itched like mad. "What's a Hawk?"

The guard's mouth firmed. "Something that don't exist no more," he snapped. "You start getting an attitude again, it ain't gonna go well for you here. Now are you gonna do your job, or do I tell Talon you're unfit for duty?"

Finn glared at the man for a few seconds before putting his helmet back on. He picked up the last tray and delivered it into the third cell holding two young telepaths without incident. As soon as the door closed, he pivoted on his heels and marched back upstairs to report to Talon, as requested.

"How'd it go?"

For a commanding officer, Talon didn't treat his rank as Finn would have expected. He lounged across the red couch like an indolent king presiding over his court. Two stairs down from the top of his platform, Ortiz sat sideways with one foot propped three stairs below the other. She was rattling the dog tags hanging from around her wrist, flipping them one way, then the other. She didn't look at him, but Finn got the sense she never missed a thing, including Talon's every twitch.

Finn took off his helmet, figuring he should face his superior head-on without hiding behind a darkened visor. "Mission accomplished, sir."

"Did our guests give you any trouble?"

"Nothing I couldn't handle, sir." He recounted the fight with the former Shadow, waiting for Talon to fill in some blanks.

Instead, the commanding officer inspected a familiar-looking cuff on his wrist. "What about the telepaths?"

The name Laura McNally hovered on the tip of Finn's tongue. He swallowed it. "Child's play. The helmet really did the trick."

He's empty. No song in him. What did that mean?

Talon preened. "As well it should. You know they cost us a lot to acquire."

Not a question. Finn stayed silent.

His lack of response appeared to annoy Talon. "You're on guard duty outside for the rest of the day. Dismissed."

Finn saluted and pivoted back toward the massive hole in the wall that served as an entrance and exit to the cave chamber. In the light of day, he saw scorch marks where it had been blasted open. His gaze slid smoothly around the inside perimeter, marking tall metal towers with small white machines attached to the top. His thumb brushed across the smooth white surface of his helmet. Not much else he'd seen around here sporting the same color and sheen. It stood to reason the towers served a similar purpose. He wanted to take a closer look at them.

His post out by the hover pad gave him a view of the entire valley and the endless sky. Never before did Finn remember being so grateful to be outdoors. Aside from a couple of mechanics working on the hover, the hover pad was empty. The only other soldiers on duty were inside, bracketing the entry.

Positioning himself on the valley side, out of view, Finn leaned back against the rockface and set his breathing to a deep, slow rhythm, savoring the warmth of early morning sunlight.

Truth, he told himself as a blast of cool air hit him in the face, momentarily distracting him from noticing the word he'd thought hadn't been in his voice but a woman's.

The truth was, he was in unfamiliar territory, thrust into a situation fraught with mental and physical danger, and he had no bearings to tell him which way to go. Finn couldn't tell whether his concerns were real or just delusional paranoia, but he couldn't help feeling as if he was somehow behind enemy lines.

Please, remember me.

He was trying to! Every time he pictured the woman in the cell, Finn got another punch of guilt straight to his gut, and he didn't understand why. The redhead had called her Laura. It was a common enough name. But it would be one hell of a cosmic coincidence if she *wasn't* the Laura McNally people kept name-dropping.

Don't let them hood you again, Hawk.

Why did that sound so familiar? Finn didn't even understand what it was supposed to mean, but the words carried a weight of forgotten memory. The prisoner—a former Shadow, for fuck's sake!—had said it with such disappointment and frustration borne of repetition. As if he'd told Finn before, and Finn had failed to listen.

Fragments. That was all he had. Bits and pieces of a much larger whole. Until he could put enough of them together to get a clear picture, Finn was at a severe disadvantage. Everything felt wrong, from the faces he saw to the uniform he wore.

Instinct, or possibly something trained into him, said he had to exercise extreme caution. He couldn't trust anyone within the mountain, be they in uniform or on the wrong side of a prison cell. Which meant he was all on his own.

For some reason, that part at least felt bitterly right.

30

"What do you think?" The question was low, and addressed to Vega.

She busied herself with her dog tags until she could school her expression before answering. "I think I just lost two week's rations. And you got everything you wanted."

Talon chuckled. "I did, didn't I?" He held up his right hand, admiring the wrist unit he'd stolen from Rowe. She'd noticed Rowe checking it out, but he hadn't appeared to recognize it. Or, if he had, he was one hell of an actor. "You know, I always wanted one of these. They didn't hand them out to Hounds."

"I remember." The wrist unit was a modern soldier's utility weapon. It had multiple functions that served as one-off survival arms in a desperate situation. By nature of their rank, Hounds attacked in force and didn't need such gear. Hawks were lone agents. Or had been, anyway. Their assignments had put them behind enemy lines with little to no backup. They'd been trained in combat and all the same weapons of war as Hounds but, more often than not, their only weapons had been a wrist unit and their own wits. She'd seen Hawks use both with such efficiency it had looked like magic.

In Talon's hands, the wrist unit was just another blunt instrument to abuse until it ceased to function. What a waste.

"Shame he didn't have the lens on him."

She could imagine how the examination must have gone. Rowe was lucky he still had both of his eyes in full working order. Talon wasn't exactly subtle when he wanted to get his hands on something.

"So what now?" she dared to ask.

Talon was too distracted twisting dials and pushing buttons to get his ass hairs in a twist over her tone. "Let's give it a day."

"A lot of hours in a day."

Talon's smile was slow and oh-so-satisfied. "Anticipation is the sweetest torment, don't you think? I want to see how our newest Shadow acclimates himself in our ranks. Then I'll have one more test for him." He reached underneath the couch and spun something red and metallic across the platform to her.

Vega caught the handle of an ax. "What's this?"

"Something to keep your hands busy for a while. It's made of the same alloy as your knives. I want you to sharpen it."

She couldn't read his intent behind the task. Practically speaking, it made sense to assign it to the one person familiar with the metal's properties. But her recently acquired paranoia sent up red flags over his tone. Was he testing her?

Always assume the worst. Talon would be testing everyone in any way involved with this. That would include Vega, the medic Eskel, anyone else who might have known Rowe in another life, and all of their high-priority prisoners.

If Vega did anything other than comply, she'd be dead before she cleared the staircase off his perch. She took up the ax, testing its balance as she stood up from her seat. "I'll need time. And a few things from storage."

"You know where it is."

"Consider it done."

"By the way," he said, stopping her two stairs down. "The two weeks' rations you lost. What was the bet?"

Vega felt her mouth tighten and spoke up before he noticed. "I bet Talmadge that Rowe would flip when he saw Laura McNally." She had no qualms admitting it now that it no longer mattered. The damage was done, and it was catastrophic.

"So little faith in me, my pretty bird. I'm hurt."

She shrugged. "It's Finnegan Rowe. I figured he'd have more resistance." She'd been wrong. Whatever Talon had done to Rowe's brain had burned out every last trace of the man he'd used to be. His report earlier had all but hammered the nails into Vega's coffin. He'd not only seen Laura and come out unaffected, he'd fought with his best friend right after. Neither had rattled him enough to remember, which could only mean he had nothing left to remember. A blank slate. A highly trained living weapon for Talon to mold to any purpose he chose.

Oh, Talon would enjoy the hell out of pulling on Rowe's strings. And the shittiest part of it was, after tonight, only Vega might be left to remember how fucked up it was.

Which once again brought up the question of Talon's intentions. If he still suspected Vega of treason, then all of this was as much a test for her as it was for Rowe, and he'd draw it out until she either broke or learned not to give a shit.

Talon lowered his hand with the wrist unit and sat up to lean his elbows on his knees. "You should take care not to put too much stock in fairy tales."

"Sir, yes sir," she retorted. "Can I go now?"

"You *may*," he said. "Report back at twenty-one hundred. I want that thing sharp enough to sever a head in one swing."

Vega turned and left, clutching the ax so hard her fingers cramped. So that's what the last test would be. Ever the coward, Vega would bet her last credit Talon wasn't Shadow enough to take John Wayland's head himself. He'd make Rowe do it for him and probably turn it into a big theatrical production for his amusement.

If she knew Talon—and she did—he'd get everyone crammed in for the show, so they would see what happened when someone decided to cross him. Every last Shadow in the vault would be in attendance. Because Talon was just the type of overconfident to think himself invulnerable.

Vega made a detour to the room they'd cleared out to serve as a clinic. Their newly acquired medic was in there, taking inventory of the crates of supplies they'd carelessly dropped in the far corner. A bin off to the side was already half filled with broken bottles and soaked towels. The medic didn't seem like the wasteful type. The trashed items must have gotten damaged during transport.

Eskel was bleary-eyed, and his defiance had mellowed out into exhaustion when he looked up at her entrance. He didn't waste words on a greeting but took note of the ax in her hand before turning back to his inventory.

Vega set the ax by the door and took a seat on the edge of the exam table, undoing her pants to slide them down to her knees. "Get over here. We need to talk."

Eskel looked like he wanted to argue but didn't have the energy for it. With a sigh, he pushed to his feet and came over. He peeled the bandage off her thigh and made a face. Yeah, she hadn't come to him for tea and cookies.

"This is infected." Stating the obvious but with a hint of satisfaction.

"Then get busy," she told him, fully prepared for whatever retaliation he felt obligated to deliver. "And while you're working, you can answer some hypothetical questions for me."

He raised an eyebrow. "Hypothetical questions?"

She gave him a meaningful look. "Work while you talk."

Shaking his head, Eskel reached over to the side table for a suture kit and started cutting out Vega's torn stitches—without an anesthetic.

She breathed through the pain and kept her expression neutral. "Suppose someone with a bad heart spent a few hours hanging by his wrists out in the elements."

Eskel yanked harder on the next stitch, and her leg twitched. She grabbed her thigh above the wound to hold it steady. "Interesting thought experiment," the medic murmured.

"Suppose," Vega growled, "that someone got him inside and rehydrated, but heart function didn't improve." Quinn's patch had been golden, bordering on orange when she'd left him hiding in the storage chamber below with a bunch of blankets and more beer. But it wasn't as if she could pop by to check on him every so often.

The last stitch came out, and her wound opened, oozing blood and other, nastier fluids. Eskel probed the ugly red flesh surrounding torn tissue. "Sounds like this hypothetical individual would be in need of professional medical care." A hard push forced out more fluids and made Vega gasp.

"Suppose that's why I'm here."

The pressure eased. Eskel sat back and met her gaze. "You need to take me to him."

"Not unless you want to get all three of us killed."

Eskel looked ready to argue but, in the end, swore and shoved out of his seat to retrieve more instruments and supplies. He laid them out on the exam table by Vega's good leg. "Where is he?"

"Hiding. I can make one trip to check on him today. Make it count."

Eskel injected her thigh with something that eased some of the pain and some of the redness before he stuck a flat metal instrument into the tear to scoop out the infection. "I think I can keep the troops occupied for a while. Most of them haven't had a check-up in years, and they would have been exposed to the same fallout as the rest of us. Probably not as much, but it might still have been enough to cause some issues."

Vega couldn't turn her head without signaling weakness, so she opted to close her eyes instead. "Thanks," she grunted. His plan was subtle enough to get the Shadows chasing their own tails instead of doing more dangerous things. Like going down to the transport bay to check out the new recruits—who were no longer there. And looking for the three missing Shadow guards—who currently painted a significant amount of ravine a thousand feet below the transport bay.

"What color was the patch last time you saw it?"

"Light orange."

Eskel exchanged one instrument for another. "There's a small silver pill packet by your right thigh. Take it." He did something that made her see stars, and Vega jerked, bracing her hand on the table next to her, covertly taking possession of the packet he'd indicated. "I'm going to spray a cleaning solution into your wound. It'll be messy, and it'll hurt. When I tell you, hand me the gauze over there, and take the injection gun."

The pressure felt like it would force the liquid clean through her thigh and out the other side. Vega growled through gritted teeth, swiping up the gauze and gun in the same motion. When he took the gauze from her, Vega slipped the injection gun into her breast pocket.

"Breathe," Eskel instructed. "The worst is over." He left her to wash his hands and rummage through the supply crate and came back with his hands full of more stuff. "Where is Miguel?"

"Hypothetically, far from here, along with five local kids."

That gave him pause, and the needle he'd been about to shove into her flesh slid in smooth and slow. His stitching was a lot neater than Vega's, she'd give him that. "The white case with a blue cross on it is a heart monitor. Interesting little tool. It's used in cases where a patient can't reach a medical facility." He worked while he talked. "Fun fact: soldiers like it for triage. When placed over the patient's heart, the screen shows the organ *in vivo* without the need for a surgical incision."

"Fascinating." The heart monitor disappeared into her largest thigh cargo pocket. "What might one learn with it?"

"One might see where the heart muscle wasn't moving properly and use it to target the tissue for a regenerative serum injection, for example." The last stitch was in. "Its effects wear out in roughly a day or so. It's not intended as a long-term treatment but has been used for that purpose in the past. In poor communities where medical care is a luxury."

The venom in his tone told her this was how Eskel had been treating Quinn at their little shelter down in the valley. Not an easy task with the Shadows constantly stealing their medical supply shipments. That the big guy had survived this long was a miracle in and of itself. And now, it seemed, his life was in Vega's hands.

Eskel wiped her thigh clean and applied an adhesive bandage that stuck to the wound like second skin. "Keep this clean. Try not to stress the tissue. I recommend heat and rest. Plenty of fluids, one pill from the silver packet twice a day, and three nutrient packs to replace what was lost."

Nutrient packs? Vega frowned.

Eskel inclined his head to her right.

She swiped the gelatin packs as she pulled her pants back up. Good thing Shadow uniforms had so many versatile pockets. Her hands were empty when she hopped off the table, careful not to put too much weight on her bad leg. "Thanks, doc."

"Hypothetically speaking, heart conditions left untreated for too long become irreversible."

She nodded her understanding and picked up the ax on her way out.

Down in the catacombs, she greeted the guards on duty in front of the telepath cells before turning left into the same hallway she'd used last night. They would call in her presence and receive full authorization from Talon.

Past the tunnels leading to the ledge and the transport bay was a much wider opening for a massive storage space. The locals would have used this to store everything while they'd been working on the vault above. It still had rows of tall shelving units dusted with the remnants of building materials and outdated machinery that hadn't been worth retrieving at the end of the project. In combination with the low-luminosity lighting, they created the sense of an endless dark maze. Most of the Shadows' supplies were stored by the entrance, giving soldiers no reason to venture deeper.

Vega passed the first two aisles, then turned left into the third. It was as far as she'd managed to walk Quinn last night before he'd collapsed.

She found him curled up in a nest of blankets, his eyes closed in sleep. But when she knelt beside him, his big hand shot out to grab her by the throat. Weakened as he was, she still felt the strength in his loose grip. He could give her throat a light squeeze and crush it into mulch if he wanted to. But he only applied enough pressure for her to feel her pulse throb against the confining cage of his fingers and thumb. An instinctual response to being startled.

As soon as his glassy gaze focused enough for him to recognize her, Quinn let go and collapsed back onto his nest. "Sorry," he said, sounding anything but.

Vega's neck was still sore from Talon's choking earlier. Quinn's attack, however benign, aggravated the bruising enough to make her wince. "Almost killed yourself," she told him. "Eskel sends his regards."

That had Quinn sitting up again. "You saw him? Is he okay?"

Vega cleared her throat and rolled her head on her shoulders to make sure it was still attached. "Fine." She began pulling the things he'd given her out of her pockets and laying them out in a neat row.

When she waved her hand for him to sit back, he did and pulled apart the edges of his stolen jacket to expose his chest. Vega had seen him shirtless before, but it struck her again how impossibly big he was. With his heart condition keeping his physical activity to a minimum, Vega estimated he had to be down at least twenty-five percent in body mass, yet he was still solid muscle the likes of which normal people struggled for years to attain. What had he looked like at full health and vigor?

"Pill or injection first?" This was his routine; she figured he had to know best.

Quinn took the pill and chased it down with one of the nutrient gel packs.

Vega unpacked the heart monitor next. It was a rectangular patch about ten inches long and six inches wide. At a quarter-inch thickness, it was bigger than any other patch she'd ever seen, but the material was as flexible as fabric. It adhered to the skin to stay in place when she positioned it on his chest. As soon as full contact was established, the monitor activated, giving Vega a clear view into Quinn's chest cavity as if it was cut open.

His heart tissue was darker on the left side than the right and totally still. She didn't trust herself to meet his gaze. Instead, Vega reached into her breast pocket for the injection gun. "Talon's planning something big for tonight, and Eskel's keeping everyone distracted with medical crap. With any luck, no one will bother checking in at the transport bay for a while." But it wouldn't take them long, and Vega had no plan for how to deal with it.

Aside from a busted lock on the cage, the transport bay showed no signs of a struggle, and she'd taken extreme care not to be seen anywhere near there. But with Talon already suspicious of her, Vega didn't dare pin her hopes on him assuming the three soldiers had busted out the kids and escaped with them on their own. And, when he discovered the prisoners gone as well, he would swing around to point blame at her. Every passing hour brought her a step closer to a very ugly death. And there were a lot of them left to go before she was supposed to report back with the sharpened ax.

"Good time to make a run for it."

"With your love of leaving people behind?" Vega shook her head and brought the barrel of the injector to his skin. The heart monitor recognized it and showed her a thin red trajectory line, given the angle of the gun. A nifty little tool. She adjusted the angle as she spoke. "Much as I hate to say it, our best chance for survival is if we get everyone out together. And we might get *one* try."

Plus, it wasn't as if Vega could just walk out the front door while Talon still had a leash on her. Her only possible way out of the Shadows was to retire him—permanently. There was no scenario in which both of them lived through this. As long as he was still alive, that trigger in his neck would be a constant threat to Vega, and she'd spend the rest of her life looking over her shoulder until he tracked her down. The way the trigger worked, Talon didn't even need line of sight to use it. He only had to be within range. Vega would never see him coming.

"So what's the plan?"

She snorted and pulled the trigger on the injection gun. The syringe shot straight into the affected heart tissue. "There isn't one."

Quinn didn't react to the injection beyond a small twitch of his left pec. "How long do we have?"

Before her eyes, the darker heart tissue pinkened outward from the injection site until it matched the rest of the organ. Quinn signed as he slowly regained full heart function. Vega checked the monitoring patch on the side of his neck—it was turning green. She tore open another gel pack for him, pulled his jacket closed over the heart monitor as far as it would go, and then tugged the blankets up to cover the gap.

With the weight of Quinn's gaze on her, she retrieved her ax and sat beside him. "If someone goes by the transport bay at any point before the show, odds are you won't see me again."

He shifted in his seat. "Then you need to find a way out of here fast."

"No dice." Too many Shadows, too amped up with anticipation. They might be distracted, but not that much. No, she needed proper chaos. A full-on battle to focus all of them on each other and not on Vega. A shame she didn't have an army of her own.

That said, Vega wasn't totally without hope yet.

"Talon wants me to report back to him at twenty-one hundred, with this thing sharp enough to—quote—*sever a head in one swing*."

Quinn swore.

She twirled the ax, admiring the red handle and the twelve-inch edge. Not quite an emergency tool, and not quite a weapon of olde. "The way I see it, if I do my job right, this baby will sever at least two."

31

Reconning the Roost was surprisingly easy. For all that Finn seemed to be the primary topic of many conversations, no one actually paid attention to where he went or what he did. Most of the men had already gathered in the main area in front of Talon's red couch platform—no one lingering behind it—with a few outliers to join in shortly. They'd formed fairly static groups, indicating an inflexible social order which Finn was unlikely to penetrate.

He removed himself from one group jovially discussing an out-of-control transport killing several of their number when their laughter opened up an inexplicable aching hollow in his gut. The next triad he passed by was deep in conversation about some medical issues pertaining to a fallout. Apparently, the medic with the chin tattoo had raised some concerns the soldier had heard from another one, who'd heard it from a third. The gossip had already spread through most of their ranks and they'd been lining up to see the medic for a complete physical all day.

Finn ended his social beeline at a gathering of five Shadows talking about a recent mission that involved the deserted Shadow prisoner.

He didn't linger there. Hearing them discuss a violent attack on an inn full of civilians was making him twitch with the need to beat in their grinning faces. When he left the group, laughter followed in his wake.

No, he would not be making any friends here.

Instead, he took a stroll around the perimeter to explore the open wall storage units and, in the process, covertly study the tall towers with their white machines on top.

The storage units were benign. A total lack of residue inside suggested whatever had been kept there had been sealed and likely insulated. They were hermetic but not lockable, which meant they could have been repurposed to hold all the things currently littering the main floor. The Shadows had been at this facility at least long enough to build out a barracks, yet no one had bothered to clean the place up.

The towers were a different story. Whenever his trek brought him close to one and out of easy sight of Talon and his rowdy troops, Finn paused for a good fifteen seconds to take a closer look at it. The white machines appeared to be independent of the tower structures, using them for a high perch and nothing more. He only saw one small wire exiting the white box and snaking around one of the tower legs to the floor. Finn traced it to the next tower, where it snaked back up to the white box there, connecting the pair.

He was now at the entrance. It was coming up on sunset. This high up, the temperature was pleasant, a steady breeze freshening the air. He breathed it in, searching for hints of the mineral scent he'd detected last night, but all he got was a whiff of burning metal from the hover repairs going on down the hover pad.

Finn continued his round to the other side and the next tower. No easy cover there; he didn't pause. But from the corner of his eye, he traced a connection from the closest tower to the next one over, then encountered another gap. Pair bonds.

In between the next pair, Finn stepped on the wire, set his helmet on a crate, and knelt down as though to tie his shoelaces. Covered with a layer of dust, the wire was thin and insulated. Without cutting it open, Finn wouldn't be able to gauge its function. It definitely wasn't for power. If the boxes were as similar to his helmet as he suspected, they would have an ambient recharge—the surface would absorb static electricity from the environment.

"Having fun skulking about?"

Finn reacted before the sentence had finished, pulling a knife from his boot sheath. The blade snicked across the floor as he brought it down and back up in an underhand throw at Talon's face. The commanding officer knocked it aside, then grinned as he retrieved it from behind a shipping crate.

"Good to see you only lost your mind and not your edge."

Finn checked a frown as he pushed to his feet.

"Find anything interesting?"

Matching Talon's informal approach, he adopted a conversational tone. "Not as yet. Should I?"

Talon shrugged, toying with Finn's knife. "Depends on what you're looking for. What are you looking for?"

Answers. "Just familiarizing myself with the grounds. I don't like not knowing what's around me."

"I'd give you the grand tour—again—but it looks like you're doing well enough on your own." He hefted the throwing knife and looked it over. It didn't appear to meet with his approval. "Remind me to requisition you some better knives. Vega has a superb set. Have you seen them?"

"Vega, sir?"

"Vega Ortiz. My right hand. She has a kink for knives. Never leaves one behind." Talon paused there, and Finn wasn't sure whether or not he wanted a response. After a few seconds, he shrugged and continued. "I'd recommend not getting on her bad side unless you want to lose an appendage. You're already one finger short, as it is."

"I'll keep that in mind, sir."

The fuck are you doing here, Vega? Still no context. But at least now he had a face to match with the name.

"Now come on. It's time to get this show on the road." Talon returned Finn's knife to him in passing. "By the way, Vega wouldn't have missed."

Finn allowed himself a small smile at Talon's retreating back. *Who says I did?*

He dragged his boot a fraction of an inch along the floor, shifting the severed wire underneath it out of alignment. Focused on defense, Talon hadn't even noticed the knife's path before it had left Finn's hand. His blade might not be as impressive as Vega's, but it was plenty sharp and, when applied with proper strategy, highly effective.

Pretending to slip it back into his boot sheath, he squinted at the wire's cross-section, trying to figure out its function, but he had neither the time nor the light to do it properly. Either way, this pair of machines was now disconnected. No alarms, not telltale sparks—no way to know what he'd actually accomplished, but Finn walked away after Talon feeling marginally satisfied nonetheless.

Talon ran up the stairs to his platform with enough flare to catch the eye of every Shadow present. Going back around the slow way, Finn took advantage of the moment to sever one more wire before sheathing the knife and joining the fray.

He had willfully sabotaged equipment belonging to the Shadow unit—which included him. And he felt no remorse.

Something had to be wrong when doing the wrong thing felt like the right move.

No one inside the facility behaved the way Finn would expect. There was no discipline. It was almost like they were all on leave, but Finn knew that wasn't the case. And Talon, despite commanding full and complete attention at all times, didn't have the respect of his men. Fear, yes. But not respect.

Helmet under his arm, Finn pushed his way through toward the front of the gathering. Two rows ahead, Vega Ortiz fell into step with him, carrying a gleaming red ax. "Remember yet?"

So she was the one who'd signaled him last night. He wanted to drag her to a quiet corner to get answers out of her, but Talon couldn't be kept waiting. "Nope."

"Then you're walking into a world of pain."

One more row. "Then clue me in!"

Out of time. Talon pointed their way, and the soldiers in front of them parted to let them through. Vega twirled the ax a couple of times, producing an audible whistle as the blade sliced the air. She presented it to Talon for his inspection.

Finn caught another pointed glare from her before she took her place halfway up Talon's platform, facing the troops at ease.

You broke my heart! Could the voice have been hers?

"Everyone *shut up!*" Talon shouted.

The troops fell silent.

Finn looked over the crowd of faces. Forty strong, and at least ten more throughout the facility. The medic was standing off to the far right, with two soldiers guarding him on either side. His resentment was palpable, but he made no move to fight or escape. Did they know each other? His face looked so familiar, but Finn couldn't place him, aside from a sense of deep weariness resulting from too many sleepless nights.

On the opposite side, Finn clocked a straggler sneaking in from behind Talon's perch. Shirtless, with his jacket hanging open, he dragged his feet and hugged the wall, keeping to the shadows. Smart move. Low standards notwithstanding, if Talon saw him in such a pathetic state, Finn suspected the soldier wouldn't be long for this world.

"Did I deliver, or what?" Talon demanded and his troops roared with approval. "For three years we have fought this war. We stood strong when the mindfuckers routed us out of our bases. We have made them eat the dust of their dead. We may have been scattered, but we are *not defeated!*"

The crowd stomped their feet to sound their agreement, but Finn sensed some conflict behind it. Not everyone here agreed with Talon. Those at the forefront were fervid with a fighting spirit, but Finn noticed some faces farther back wearing looks more similar to the medic's.

"The war may be over, but our mission isn't finished." Talon speared Finn with a sharp look. "And Shadows aren't in the habit of leaving their missions unfinished."

Again, the sense of failure twisted his gut. Finn wanted to spring into action so badly his limbs tensed in readiness to move. Except he had no idea what he was supposed to be doing. How could he complete a mission when he didn't know what it was?

"We have grown double since we got here. And yes, we've had some recent setbacks. But our fallen brothers have died in the name of the greatest good there is, and we will honor them by *not giving up!*"

Another cheer went up, and the Shadows around Finn pumped their fists in the air, chanting a round of wordless noises in salute to their fallen comrades.

"Tonight, we end one chapter and start a new one. I promised you results, and the time has come to get them. Vega, be a doll and go fetch out guests."

She took a second to respond, the only indication that the order had caught her off guard. "I'll need to go get my helmet."

"Take mine," Finn offered. She wouldn't talk to him—fine. She was on her own. Finn wasn't above throwing her to the telepaths with a compromised helmet. It was past time to start drawing lines and cataloging people as either a friend or an enemy. He couldn't afford any gray areas.

Vega glared murder at him, but accepted the helmet on her way down the stairs. Her stiff-backed march forced everyone out of her way. She passed through the crowd with five feet of clearance on either side.

"Teamwork," Talon said with an oh-so-satisfied grin. "Mark of a true soldier. Beautiful thing to behold." He came down the stairs in Vega's wake. "Are you ready for your next assignment, Shadow?"

Finn straightened to attention. "Sir, yes sir!"

Those closest to him whooped and jeered, reminding him of hyenas waiting for their turn to descend on a carcass. Finn wasn't worried about them. But he did take note of the four who had put on their own helmets. Talon's was sitting on the armrest of his red couch.

"What is our primary directive?" Talon demanded.

The one question Finn didn't have to think about. "To safeguard humanity's God-given free will." The answer left a sour taste in his mouth. *Wrong.*

"Are you willing to do whatever it takes in service of that goal?"

"Sir, yes sir."

"Think it over, soldier," Talon warned. Had he noticed his hesitation? "After today, there will be no turning back. No one leaves the Shadows."

Except in a body bag. Finn remembered having said that.

Talon addressed his troops. "Tonight, we will administer justice to a traitor and a deserter."

The crowd cheered.

"We will strike a blow our enemy *will not recover from!*"

A stampede of drumming boots accompanied a deafening roar.

"Tonight, the sharpest weapon in our arsenal will strike the killing blow."

The crowd hushed as Talon held out Vega's red ax to Finn.

"This is your final test, Shadow. I have judged our prisoners guilty of treason. I task you with their execution."

With a fucking ax?

Finn tried to read Talon's expression for some clue as to the meaning of this circus. What he saw was madness. A fervid gleam lit the man's bloodshot eyes. His whole head was flushed, and his breath came hard and fast.

He put his hand on the ax handle next to Talon's white-knuckled hold, tempted to swing it at the crazed man's neck. The impulse was slow to fade, as Talon's grip was slow to loosen. He felt like he was facing off with an adversary rather than his commanding officer, and the instinct to take out such an obvious threat was so strong, it gave him tunnel vision.

A hum of noise moved through the gathering, pulling Finn's attention away from Talon.

The prisoners were being led in.

Vega motioned to two other Hounds with helmets on her way out from the assembly. Wight and Catton fell into step behind her. Catton was the stoic type, didn't talk much unless addressed directly. Wight had gotten drunk on the fervor Talon had riled up. He whooped and cheered with the rest of the crowd until they reached the staircase.

"Man, I haven't felt this good in three years," he said. "Can't wait to see those mindfuckers get theirs."

Easy way to tell which of the Shadows had had their higher thought function permanently fried out of their heads: they were so taken in with Talon and his personal war they'd adopted his catchphrases. Vega had categorized them as Avoid At All Cost.

Catton made a sound of disgust.

Wight heard it, too. "The fuck's your problem?"

"Nothing. Just wanna get this shitshow over with." Probably referring to the assembly upstairs, but his tone was more bitter than usual.

Worth looking into later—if any of them got a later. "Helmets on," she ordered as they reached the catacombs level. She stopped at the bottom of the stairs to don hers. The visor activated with readouts on her immediate environment. It seemed to be in working order. Then again, if Rowe had rendered it defunct in some way, she wouldn't know until it was too late. Vega briefly considered switching helmets with one of the others but discarded the idea. There was still a chance, albeit a small one and continuing to shrink, that Rowe really was the best actor in all the worlds, and he'd given her his helmet for a reason.

Either way, it didn't matter. Vega's options had narrowed to one: hoping the telepaths possessed more self-control than her fellow soldiers. If the helmet was compromised, and they decided to strike without testing the waters, Vega would be done for. They had to be better than that. She'd told Quinn nothing but facts earlier. Their best chance of getting through the night alive was to work together. There was no other option.

The visor readouts showed elevated heart rates for the three guards on duty in front of the telepath cells. Sound didn't carry very well through the rock, but they all had coms, and the commotion up above had already riled them up but good. They would have been briefed on what was about to happen, and Vega showing up with two backups meant it was time to start.

"Everyone, sound off."

"Check," Wight said immediately.

Catton echoed him, followed by the other three.

Vega pulled her gun and led the way forward. The guards stepped apart, one to a cell, and Vega's triad matched them. One Shadow for each prisoner.

"Anyone else coming?" asked one of the guards.

"You got a problem keeping one civilian in line?" she returned.

"Not the civilian I'm worried about."

"I'll take Wayland," Wight offered. A little too eager for Vega's peace of mind. She nodded, and he switched places with Catton.

"Look sharp. Cell one." The guard there opened the cell. He and Catton stepped inside and came out with their prisoners in tow. One was a teenage girl with glasses, and her hair frizzed all over, barely restrained with a makeshift tie. She looked smart. At least smart enough to know she couldn't overpower six guards. She didn't try to resist. The other was a lanky twenty-something man, shaking like a leaf.

"Check," Catton said. He had the girl.

Vega nodded. "Cell two."

The second guard pulled his gun, and Wight followed suit. Wight covered the guard when he opened the cell and stepped inside, then followed him in. She heard fighting immediately and raised her gun on the first pair of telepaths in case they decided to exploit the situation.

The cell was totally dark; she couldn't see deeper into it than half a foot. But her visor registered four rapid heartbeats, and the noises told her Wayland was giving the guards one hell of a fight. Good for him. She almost hoped he'd beat the shit out of Wight. The guy rubbed her the wrong way.

A gun went off. There was a grunt and then a panicked wail. Vega frowned when the guard dragged out a woman of middling height and flat features. She resisted, trying to go back into the cell after Wayland. "Stop it! Stop him!"

Inside the dark cell, Wight cursed, and then Vega heard a volley of physical blows. She shoved the guard with his prisoner aside to step into the cell. As soon as her environment got dark enough, her visor automatically switched to infrared, and she made out Wayland's form crumpled on the ground. Wight was furiously kicking at him as if he'd lost his mind.

Vega lowered the setting on her gun to minimum and shot him in the hip.

Wight fell sideways, knocked off balance but unhurt. "The fuck you do that for!"

Wayland still had a heartbeat, but he wasn't moving. *Shit.* Two potential allies out for the count.

"You got it out of your system?" Vega could have happily killed Wight on the spot. Her trigger finger itched to do it.

"Not yet," Wight snarled. He shoved to his feet, heading for Wayland again.

"You do anything other than pick him up, you're not walking out of this cell."

Her scalp itched inside the helmet. A sense of being watched. Vega raised the setting on her gun and stepped out into the hall to check the telepaths. The three under armed guard were suspiciously placid, including the woman who'd been so intent on helping Wayland.

"Who gives a shit!" Wight demanded. "He's just going up there to get dead, anyway."

"Talon will," Vega lied. "Now get him up."

Instead, Wight dragged Wayland out of the cell by his ankle, leaving him sprawled out on the ground, beaten and bloody. The insult cut deep. Wight wasn't fit to shine Wayland's shoes. He'd never have been able to take the Hawk in a fair fight but give him a helmet and a gun, and suddenly he was a tough guy.

Vega crouched down to check Wayland's pupils. Wight wasn't wrong. The former Shadow was headed to the gallows, and his best friend held the ax. But if any of them had any hope in hell of surviving the night, Vega needed him awake and lucid.

Another itch, deeper this time, on the underside of her skull.

Vega shook it off and slapped Wayland awake.

He groaned as he came to, blinking first at the ceiling, then at her. No more fight in him; he wouldn't be able to walk on his own.

Cursing, Vega called it in. "Talmadge, get down here. We need more muscle. Bring a helmet."

"Copy," he replied through her com.

Wayland mumbled something she couldn't catch. Vega leaned in closer, and four guns raised to cover her in case he tried something funny. But he didn't attack. He just kept muttering Emma's name over and over again.

"She'll be out in a minute," she promised, but it came out as more of a threat.

When Talmadge arrived, he and Wight hoisted Wayland up between them.

The telepaths didn't move, standing silent watch over it all.

"You three are being very quiet."

All of them looked at her at the same time.

Vega sucked in a breath. None of them had spoken out loud, but she still got the sense they were testing her somehow. Trying to get inside her head. She raised her gun.

"You all right, Vega?" Catton asked.

The telepaths blinked at her, all in unison. Son of a bitch Rowe had compromised the helmet.

Too long without a response. The guards aimed their weapons on the telepaths. "On my mark," Catton said.

The frizzy girl winced.

"Stand down," Vega snapped. "I'm fine."

The guards held steady, unconvinced.

"I said, stand down," she snapped, taking her finger off the trigger. "We have two more." And they were the most dangerous of the lot.

Wight grunted underneath Wayland's weight on his shoulders.

"Then why are we still standing here?"

Because Vega didn't trust her senses at the moment. Everything looked and sounded normal, but was it really?

"Vega!" Talmadge snapped.

She flinched and lowered her gun.

"Talk to me."

"I'm fine," she said. *I can't do this.* What had she been thinking? With Rowe and Wayland out of commission, she had no intermediary with the telepaths. Putting herself at their mercy on her own was like offering herself up to a pack of hungry lions because the hyenas were worse.

You need them, came a wayward thought. *Stronger together than apart.* Was it hers or theirs?

Did it matter?

"Are you?" Catton asked.

"You wanna try me and find out?"

The soldiers looked at each other, and one of the guards shrugged. No one moved.

She didn't have time to debate this. The telepaths *might* end up destroying Vega the second they didn't need her anymore, but that still gave her a window of opportunity to prove her worth. Talon *would* destroy her without a second thought the first chance he got.

Vega took a breath and ground her heels into the floor to center herself. "Back in formation," she ordered. "Cell three."

When the guard opened it, Vega raised her weapon again. Emma Calen and Laura McNally walked out on their own, their hands up in surrender. Emma took one look at Wayland, and her expression turned murderous. She picked out Wight as if she could see through his helmet to memorize his face, and Vega knew then and there that Wight would die bloody for what he'd done. She felt no sympathy.

"Where's Finn?" Laura asked.

"Move it!" Her guard shoved her down the hallway toward the stairs.

Vega took hold of Emma's arm and pulled her along after him.

—*Finn is empty,*— Emma's voice said, startling Vega into a flinch. She looked around at everyone in their procession. No one else appeared to have heard it. It should have scared the shit out of Vega, but it didn't. The statement was a eulogy rather than an accusation. Non-threatening. Something one might say to a friend. *Trust the telepaths, or die.* Was it part of the manipulation?

—*We don't change people.*—

Vega looked at Laura McNally.

—*Well, some can. Actually, I can, too. But I don't.*—

That was reassuring. *What the hell do you want from me?*

She felt something then, a physical sensation in her mind that defied description. —*Laura wants her Shadow back, but he's gone. It's just his ghost now. Echoes. Breadcrumbs.*—

She sensed sorrow in the sentiment. Emma mourned for both Rowe and the woman he'd left behind. Vega had pretty much already figured Rowe was beyond recovery, but having it confirmed felt so final. As if he really was dead.

—*We can't change you. We need you as you are,*— Emma said. —*Stronger together than apart. Remember that.*—

Together. Physical contact. Her mind took a circuitous path to the understanding, and it brought along a sense of danger and loss. Vega was pretty sure the thought process wasn't hers. It didn't even make sense, really. But there was a certainty behind it, a deep-seated faith in what "together" could accomplish, and it was enough to bring her a smidgen of hope for the first time since she'd crossed paths with Rowe after his wipe.

And then she remembered the anti-'path system Talon had installed up in the vault.

33

Dim as the stairway was already, with thirteen people shading any available light, it became pitch black. Laura made her way up one careful step at a time, her heart racing.

With the cell's sensory dampeners glitching every so often, Emma had been able to catch glimpses of the outside world here and there throughout the day. The guards had been shielded by their helmets at all times, but Vega hadn't been. Emma had sensed her coming down earlier to check on Quinn and later on her return trip with a sharpened ax. They now knew for a fact that Quinn and Eskel were still alive, and Miguel had escaped with some local kids—all thanks to Vega.

Now, as they trudged toward a whole lot of Shadows eager to see them all die, Vega's helmet appeared to be for show only. Laura read her like a book, and what she saw wasn't at all comforting. Vega's intent wavered wildly between wanting to incapacitate the telepaths and resolving to trust them. Her uncertainty was blinding, filling the stairway with rapid flares of color that disoriented Laura and made her trip on the next step.

Her guard yanked her up again. "Keep moving," he barked.

Emma was fully convinced that necessity would compel Vega to side with them when push came to shove. In fact, she was so certain, she'd declared Vega under SU protection as soon as she'd stepped out of the cell.

The others had accepted this without question.

Laura had her doubts. She, of all people, knew how danger and desperation could make a person do things they didn't plan for. Vega might be open to an alliance now, but in the heat of battle, who was to say she wouldn't turn on them to save her own neck? She was still a

Shadow, after all—one who hadn't even formed her own decision yet.

They could try to force her to their side, but if they did, Vega would lose the instincts they needed for what was to come. And that was assuming she didn't kill them herself the second she felt them try it. Her tolerance of their abilities was so fragile the smallest misstep could turn her against them before a single shot was fired. They couldn't afford to risk it. All they could do was trust in Vega's character and hope it weighed in their favor when it counted.

—Upstairs will hurt,— Emma said. She relayed a handful of images pilfered from Vega's memories: tall metal towers with white boxes on top. In Laura's mind, they linked with the painful hum and the sting of static electricity she'd felt on her last visit to the Shadows' Roost.

It'll kill us, Laura thought back to Emma. Unlike the redhead, she didn't have the ability to communicate mind-to-mind, but if she thought loudly enough, Emma picked up on it.

Emma didn't respond in words, only a sense of dark acceptance.

They'd devised a plan of sorts while waiting to be dragged to the gallows, as Vega thought of it. Someone would have to bite the bullet for the others to get out safely. That someone had to be powerful enough to cause instant chaos, and Emma and Laura were the only ones capable of that. Emma would act as the battering ram, clearing the telepathic way and boosting Laura's ability so she could issue a blanket command. It would be messy, would likely kill them in the process, and might not even work in the end.

It was all they had.

This was what Laura had signed up for when she'd accepted Emma's help. To win the war, sacrifices would need to be made. With William dead, John incapacitated, and Finn…

Laura was the last line of defense for her family. She'd die gladly if it meant they'd have a chance to live.

You'll feel the shields once we get topside, she thought to all of them. *Do not try to get through.*

All of them responded their understanding.

As soon as they cleared the stairwell, the static covered her mind with prickles of an electric charge. It wasn't as strong as Laura re-membered. She felt it like sharp needles raking across her mind, but they didn't stab her as they had the first time. It was still enough to make her eyes water.

The others felt it, too.

The Brain and Sorry balked when they emerged topside, forcing their guards to shove them into forward motion again. Esme, the other telepath in the group, whimpered, and Laura heard her weeping in the back.

"Laura!" Eskel was ten feet away, looking haggard but blessedly all in one piece. He tried to come to her, but the soldiers on either side of him yanked him back.

"Eskel! Are you okay?"

Her guard wouldn't let her anywhere near him. "Keep moving."

"I'm fine," he said as they passed him.

"Where's Finn?"

She craned her neck to keep him in sight as long as she could. Eskel struggled against his guards to no avail. "He's not who he used to be," he called to her. "Don't trust him!"

Dagger in her heart. And Laura was already hanging on by a very fine thread. She gritted her teeth to keep herself together.

The vault was filled with Shadows in uniform all gathered around Talon's perch, chanting rhythmically to whatever speech he'd just delivered. They parted before the prisoner procession, creating a tight gauntlet.

Furious faces filled Laura's vision. Vicious, foul curses assaulted her ears. Their murderous frenzy was palpable—they barely restrained themselves from falling on the telepaths like a pack of rabid hyenas.

One of them lunged at her, and Laura flinched away. The soldier was caught and dragged back by another one who looked marginally more in control of himself. There were dozens of them, but outside the prisoner procession, Laura didn't see anyone else wearing a white helmet.

Fighting back her fear, Laura made herself look around, taking note of every face with an expression more animal than human and every pair of eyes that turned away with what might or might not have been shame.

She glanced back at Emma.

The look the redhead gave her confirmed she had noticed the same thing. Not all of the Shadows were as bloodthirsty as Talon.

The gauntlet spat them out in a good-sized opening at the base of Talon's platform. Behind them, the hostile horde formed a near-solid wall of bodies blocking the exit. Finn stood at the platform's base. Her Finn, who was no longer the boy she'd loved, or the man who'd returned to be her shield.

As Talon retreated up the stairs to his perch for a better view, Finn turned toward them, a red-handled ax in his hand. The sight of him completely devoid of expression broke Laura's heart all over again.

Her guard shoved her down to her knees. Emma met the same fate next to her, and the rest followed suit, all lined up in front of Finn, who had yet to look at any of them.

The noise level had grown deafening as dozens of feet stomped out a rapid rhythm, and fervid voices joined together in a wordless chant. The front row acted as a barrier, holding the rest at a distance, but right behind them, the most violent members of the crowd strained to hurl insults at them.

"Die, mindfucker!"

"Burn in hell, bitch!"

She tried to shut them out. The poison they spat stuck to her skin, making her feel unclean. They didn't just want her to die. They wanted her to suffer. They promised to do unspeakable things to her dead body.

No longer soldiers. Any discipline they might have had was gone, replaced by something worse than hatred and violence. Laura had no words strong enough to describe it.

Shaking, her vision blurred with tears, Laura shut them out and focused on Finn, silently—powerlessly—willing him to look at her and remember.

He raised his gaze from the ax and looked straight through her. No warmth in his eyes. No hint of recognition.

Up on top of his perch, Talon fired his weapon to get everyone's attention.

The crowd hushed down to a hum and the beat of stomping boots.

~

The ax was lighter than it looked, but the weight of its purpose forced Finn's arm down to his side as he waited.

Talon hushed the crowd and held them suspended in anticipation, milking the moment for all it was worth.

"Finn."

He glanced at the woman on his far right. Laura McNally, on her knees, her pleading eyes focused on him with such intensity it raised Finn's hackles. That goddamned guilt returned tenfold, nearly bringing him to his knees, and he wanted to hate her for it.

"Please, remember."

"Shut up!" Her guard grabbed the back of her neck and forced her down until her face was pressed to the floor.

Inexplicable rage suffused Finn at the sight, and he clutched the ax tighter.

Then Vega, still wearing his helmet, stepped into the guard, shoulder-checking him away from the prisoner. She spoke a few words to him, and Finn saw the guard shudder, clutching his weapon so hard his hand shook. But he stepped off and let go of his prisoner.

She raised herself up only a few inches. Head bowed, arms hugged around her middle, she was the picture of utter defeat, and Finn couldn't bear the sight of it.

He looked away, focusing on the Shadow traitor in the middle of the row. Two guards held him up by his arms. His head hung forward, obscuring his face, but blood dripped to the floor in front of him from newly inflicted wounds.

He must have tried to escape again and gotten his ass handed to him a second time. Whoever had delivered his beating had lacked any semblance of mercy. John Wayland looked broken, if not dead, then hanging on by a thread. More guilt, coupled with something that might have been grief or regret—Finn couldn't tell which.

The wrongness of all this wasn't lost on Finn, but without any kind of internal compass to guide him in a different direction, he was at the mercy of whatever tides had swept him this far out of familiar territory.

Behind him, up on his platform, Talon spoke up at last. "By the power vested in me as the commanding officer of this unit, on the charge of desertion, I have judged the prisoner, John Wayland…*guilty.*"

The Shadows roared their approval.

"On the charge of treason, I have judged the prisoner, John Wayland…*guilty.*"

Another deafening roar assaulted his ears.

As it quieted, Finn caught the soft strains of a humming song. He frowned in Laura McNally's direction. Her guard bristled again but checked himself when Vega hissed at him.

"Both of these heinous crimes against the Shadows and all they stand for carry the penalty of death."

On the tail end of Talon's sentence, a soft feminine voice undercut the crowd's cheer. "Row, row, row your boat…"

If anyone else heard, they gave no sign of it. But Finn's heart beat double time as he strained to hear more.

"…gently down the stream…"

"I charge our newest member with the honor and duty of carrying out the execution," Talon said. It was Finn's cue.

"If Miss Laura should command…"

Finn's hands shook as he stepped up to John Wayland. The guards yanked Wayland into position, shoving him farther forward so his neck lay exposed and within striking range. Finn raised the ax, his breath turning choppy as the crowd chanted for Wayland's death. He had the weight of fifty-odd gazes trained on him, including Talon's, hungry expectant. Their frenzy infected his soul and met with a strange kind of resistance.

Finn couldn't move until he heard the rest of that damned song. He knew the original, of course, but more than the altered lyrics, there was something different about this version. Shaky, tearful, and desperate, it was a swan song that felt incomplete. It lacked something vital that teased his mind with an almost-memory. Something not quite tactile and not quite auditory, but somehow both.

Something he wanted so desperately he couldn't think about anything else.

"On my mark," Talon said.

Ax raised over John Wayland's neck, Finn waited.

"…life is what you dream," she finished at the same time as Talon barked, "*Execute!*"

Finn closed his eyes for a second and swung the ax to the redhead's horrified scream.

~

Laura looked up when Emma screamed. The whistle of the ax was somehow louder than any other sound. She saw it arc through the air as Finn's posture twisted, altering its trajectory. In one swing, a white-helmeted head toppled off the shoulders of John's guard. Finn followed through the swing, turning a full circle to come back again for the second one.

Their bodies were slow to fall. When they did, they buried the unconscious John beneath them. Shock suspended the Shadows in a split second of silence that felt eternal.

"*Now!*" Emma shouted, throwing herself at Laura, grabbing her hand in both of hers.

A sudden flare of awareness forced Laura's mind wide open, flooding it with too much information she understood instantly. The sensory overload yanked her attention away from the macabre sight she'd just witnessed and shoved her full tilt into the one task she couldn't afford to fail. With everything she had and everything Emma gave her, Laura gathered all of her will behind her command, shoving it outward in every direction as far as her mind could reach: *FIGHT!*

White hot lightning struck out at her instantly, searing through her brain and leaving darkness in its wake. The last thing she saw before her mind and body shut down was Finn charging up the platform toward Talon.

34

The dam broke. Vega felt warmth cap her skull, and a split second of deafening silence later, the Shadows erupted into a roar of violence that had no rhyme or reason. The guard next to Vega cursed just before they bowled him over, and she had less than two seconds to turn around and start shooting as the sea of maddened soldiers spilled toward her.

She shot three before her gun died, but it gave her a few extra seconds to pull her knives. They weren't only coming for her; they were fighting each other and mostly ignoring the telepaths on the ground. Vega threw one of her knives, buried it in a Shadow's forehead, and pulled another one, slashing at anyone who came too close.

She saw the three younger telepaths and a helmeted Shadow drag Emma and Laura away from the worst of it, then the gap closed, and the vault floor became a battlefield. Soldiers fought their fellow soldiers, teaming up to take out one, then turning on each other. Blood turned the stone floor so slippery every step became precarious. Vega lost her bearings, then her helmet was gone, and she was on her own in the thick of it, fighting for her life.

A tall Shadow came at her with a knife of his own. Vega ducked under his swing and felt the whoosh of a percussion blast displace the air over her back. The knife guy went down. Vega turned for the shooter, but he shot again, the weaker blast striking her in the chest. She dropped, clutching her knives as her vision went dark for a split second.

The shooter must have run out of charge. He came at her with his bare hands, pinning her to the ground with a knee to her sternum. Vega stabbed him in the side, but it was as if he didn't feel it at all.

He punched her hard enough to rattle her brain, and she lost hold of that blade, leaving it buried in his kidney.

A deep roar boomed over the chaos, and suddenly the soldier was gone, struck by a crate flying at the speed of a projectile. Vega heard his bones crunch on impact, the crate bowling four others off their feet before it crashed into the opposite wall.

Big boots thumped down on either side of her, and a giant shadow obscured the light above. Hands the size of hams grabbed her shoulders and hauled her up as if she weighed nothing.

Vega blinked into Quinn's pallid face.

"Now we're even," he said, setting her down on her feet, and then he was gone again, hurling soldiers out of his path as he went.

She wavered, shaking off the dizziness. The horde had thinned considerably. Bodies littered the floor. None of the fighters had a helmet anymore. The towers on the south side were toppled, but two remained standing to the north.

Vega raised her arm to block an attack, buried her blade in the soldier's neck, and yanked it out. She whirled on her heels, slipped, and crashed to her knees, facing Talon's platform.

~

Finn pumped his legs, sprinting up the stairs at Talon as the commander raised his gun. Two stairs from the top, Finn hurled himself sideways onto the platform. The blast knocked the ax out of his grip, but he was unharmed.

He rolled to his feet as Talon took aim again. This time, he didn't zig or zag. Finn launched himself straight forward and felt the plasma blast scorch across his shoulder blade as he bore Talon to the ground.

The gun clattered down the stairs to where the prisoners had retreated. No sign of John Wayland, but Finn spotted Laura right away. She was unconscious, with blood oozing from her nose. *Wrong!*

His moment of inattention cost him an advantage as Talon heaved up and threw Finn off. They came up at the same time, and Talon grinned. "Gotta say, I was kind of hoping I'd get a chance to kill you."

He twisted something on the thick cuff covering his right wrist, and a metallic disc came loose.

Finn reacted on instinct, diving for the floor as Talon threw the disc. He rolled and came up in a crouch, tracking its trajectory. Having missed its target, it came around in an arc and spun downward into the mele of battling soldiers.

While Finn waited for the gizmo to reemerge, Talon came at him with a shout, and he just barely avoided a blade to his neck. Twisting away, he came up swinging. Talon was shorter but much stockier, and he was out for blood. Finn met his attacks, breathing down a wave of fury that threatened his concentration. He couldn't let Talon get the upper hand.

They knocked over the couch and rolled to the edge of the platform, Talon on top of Finn, snarling down as he put his whole weight behind their locked elbows, and it was all Finn could do to keep the tip of Talon's blade away from his neck.

"How's it feel to lose to a Hound, Hawk?"

What the fuck was it with the animal references?

Finn dropped one foot to the next stair down. It gave him better leverage, and he grinned up at Talon, slowly pushing up, forcing him back. "I don't lose." With enough room to maneuver, he shoved Talon off him and followed. His opponent was on his feet again, his cuffed wrist raised before him, and in the next blink, there was a translucent blue plasma shield in front of him.

Finn straightened from his battle crouch, tilting his head. He tossed his knife up and caught it by the blade, then hurled it overhand at Talon, who, predictably, moved his shield arm into the throw to block it.

Except plasma shields were made to stop blunt force impacts, not pinpoint projectiles. The knife struck the cuff, and the shield disintegrated. Finn charged again, blocking Talon's blade and driving his fist into the man's face with all of his weight behind it. Talon's crooked nose shattered, and he fell back a couple of steps, bringing his heel to the edge of the platform. He was cornered.

Spitting blood, the madman snarled at Finn and charged. They met in a flurry of blows. Finn, now without a weapon, expected to feel Talon's blade sink into him at any second, but he was holding his own with surprising ease. Talon was nowhere near the challenge John Wayland had presented, and it occurred to Finn that he must have known it on some level already. Otherwise, he never would have risked attacking Talon's high-ground position the way he had.

He allowed himself a small smile as he ducked under Talon's wild swing and knocked his feet out from under him. The knife went flying, Talon crashed onto his back, and Finn pinned him there.

Talon laughed. "Look at you! Still fighting a lost war." He truly had lost his mind.

Finn punched him hard to shut him up. It wasn't enough to kill the son of a bitch. And it no longer mattered that Finn didn't remember his crimes. He knew Talon had perpetrated a slew of them, the most recent still raging a few stairs down on the main floor of the vault, and Finn wanted to make him pay.

The laughter turned into a bloody chuckle. "I already won."

Another punch knocked out a couple of his teeth.

Talon groaned. "What I took from you, you will never get back."

"Kill him!" Vega's voice cut through the rage in Finn's mind. He spotted her down below, on her knees, righteous fury twisting her mouth.

Talon roared and threw Finn off down the side stairs.

Finn caught himself and got to his feet in a hurry, charging back up. He saw Vega climbing the stairs from the front with her knife clutched in a tight grip. Finn was closer. He held his hand out for the blade, but she didn't throw it, wholly intent on taking Talon out herself.

Her prey, now sitting on his heels and listing sideways, took in the two-pronged attack and slapped a hand to the side of his neck like he was swatting at a bug.

Vega screamed and collapsed.

Too close now. Finn slammed full force into Talon, and the two of them tumbled off the back of the platform into a shadowed part of the vault floor off the main hallway. Finn felt every stair on the way down, a sharp pain stabbing through his ankle as his foot twisted the wrong way.

They landed apart, Finn's ears ringing. He struggled to get up, expecting Talon to fall on him, but he didn't.

He was getting away.

Finn swore and lurched to his feet, hobbling as fast as he could after him. Off the main hallway, Talon slipped into a hole in the wall and disappeared into darkness. Finn followed and almost took a long roll down another set of stairs when his foot met air. He caught himself, feeling along the wall to make his way down.

The stairway spat him out on a wide ledge on the north side of the mountain, and Finn got blasted with a cold breeze carrying the mineral scent he'd smelled on Vega last night. Before he could think to analyze it, his hand slid across exposed rock, and sharp needle-thin shards of crystal sliced open his palm. The pale moon above provided enough illumination for him to make out Talon's shape as he headed toward one of a set of dark forms that could only be escape vehicles of some kind.

Finn threw the knife. His bloody grip messed up his aim, and the blade struck Talon in the shoulder instead of his spine. The impact turned him around, but he didn't go down.

Laughing, the madman saluted Finn with his right hand, then did something with his left that caused sparks to flare off his cuff. "Send Vega my love!"

A massive percussion blast slammed into Finn and knocked him off his feet. By the time he got himself upright again, the transport was wobbling in the air. He watched it take off toward the west.

The hell that was happening.

Still three transports left. Finn lurched toward the closest one, keeping an eye on Talon to track his escape. There was a white helmet on the driver's seat. He knocked it away and got inside. The second he turned on the engine, the transport shot up toward the sky. Finn overcorrected, dropping halfway down into the ravine. "Fuck!" He had to battle the controls into submission and by the time he got the damned thing moving in the right direction, there was no more sign of Talon.

He kept going, eyes peeled for any sign of movement, but a dark transport with flight capability in the middle of the night was practically invisible. This was a civilian vehicle; it had no tracking equipment, no weapons, not even headlights. Finn was flying blind, with the controls fritzing out on him more than not.

He fiddled with the screen until a communications module popped up. "Anyone read me? I need a tracker on two transports flying the roost. Confirm command."

No answer. There was a comms station in the main vault. Either it had been destroyed, or the fight was still going on.

"Someone answer me, goddammit!"

—*He's gone.*— The voice was too young and female to be a Shadow and definitely not coming from the transport's console.

Finn swerved wildly off course and rolled the transport over, trying to correct. The bottom of it scraped across rock and missed an outcropping by a few inches. "What the fuck?"

His mind brought up an image of a young girl with dark skin and big glasses wearing a lab coat. His inner vision zoomed in on the name tag that read, "Jessica The Brain, M.D." He instantly knew things about her. She was sixteen years old and had been the lead medic in Gray Dublin's branch of the Special Unit since age ten. The information carried the weight of far too much authority for someone so young.

What was this, some kind of telepath introduction? He didn't have time for this shit!

—*The Shadow machines are destroyed. We were tracking him our way, but he disappeared a couple of minutes ago.*—

The helmet. Son of a bitch must have had one in every transport on the ledge. "What was the last thing you saw?"

—*The valley. Moon on his ten o'clock. He knows he's being hunted and will go to ground.*—

Then he planned to lay low until the dust settled.

—*You need to come back now.*—

No. The trail was already going cold. He needed to find Talon and take him out while he still had a chance. If Talon disappeared—

—*He already did. He's gone, and we need you here.*—

She gifted him with an image of blood and chaos. Shadow soldiers were killing each other; the vault was littered with corpses, the floor covered with blood. Lights were failing, and the telepaths were cornered behind Talon's platform with two soldiers standing guard. But Vega was on her own, in plain view of the fighters, and incapacitated.

She'd screamed at him to kill Talon. If she could talk, Finn knew in his gut she'd tell him to keep going.

Jessica showed him another image, a close-up of Laura McNally lying unconscious on the floor, blood oozing from her nose.

"What the fuck is this?"

No answer. The young telepath was gone, leaving him to make the decision on his own.

Finn's hands clenched hard on the transport controls. He needed to keep going after Talon, but that goddamned guilt tore him up inside, forcing him to turn around. The night was almost over. The sky to the east was already growing a lighter shade of midnight. Logic said Talon wouldn't risk flying in broad daylight. He'd go to ground like Jessica had said, at least until it got dark again.

But Talon wasn't a logical kind of guy.

Blood dripped from his cut-up palm, the droplets drumming out a steady rhythm on his thigh. With each one, Finn tensed a little more.

He'd failed—again.

And this time, he wouldn't get to forget.

July 7, 3039

Laura saw the world around her through a pale pink cloud of Emma's love for John. The two of them sat shoulder to shoulder and hand in hand, leaning on each other for the comfort of physical contact and the assurance that they were still alive. It didn't do her migraine any favors, but Laura was grateful for their peace soothing over the terror in her mind.

They'd had to walk through the carnage to get out onto the hover pad, and though it was now literally behind her, Laura still felt all the death and violence at her back, and it made her shudder in the cold morning air. She hugged the blanket closer around her and hunched down a little more, focusing on the gorgeous valley sunrise instead.

It didn't work for very long.

The soldier who'd helped guard them during the fight made his way out from the vault. He'd ditched the helmet at some point, leaving himself wide open to telepathic probing. She didn't know what the others saw in him, but Laura was picking up on a whole lot of, *GET ME THE FUCK OUT OF HERE!* "Hover's prepped and ready to go. Eskel says Quinn needs a doctor STAT." His name was Brent Catton. He couldn't wait to get out of the uniform and burn it at the earliest opportunity.

Laura braced herself before turning to look behind her. Quinn had collapsed off to the side, too big and too weak to move without a lot of help. Eskel was with him now, along with two soldiers who radiated fear in mini orange supernovas. They wanted to get out of there as much as Catton but were too afraid of the telepaths to try making a run for it.

Farther back, on the other side of a battlefield littered with dead soldiers, Finn sat with Vega and the Brain halfway up the stairs of Talon's platform, deep in an intense soft-voiced conversation. Vega had been curling up in full-body spasms for the last hour, and she'd screamed at them to fuck off when they'd tried to help her get out, so they'd left her there with the Brain to keep an eye on her. She'd only recovered enough to sit up on her own moments before Finn's transport had landed out front.

He hadn't even looked at Laura when he'd come out, so intent on talking to Vega, so determined not to notice anything or anyone else that Laura hadn't dared to stop him as he'd marched past her and into the vault.

Whatever he was saying now made Vega flare with a furious, murderous red, but the starburst fractured with teal-gray when another spasm seized her limbs.

The Brain said something to both of them and left them to it.

Laura tried hard not to be jealous of the solicitous hand Finn put on Vega's shoulder to offer comfort. His actions made it abundantly clear that he wasn't her Finn anymore, and Laura had no claim on him if she'd ever had any in the first place. A couple of nights and a few words didn't mean much in the grand scheme of things. Finn had had a whole life out there as a Shadow soldier and it was all he knew now that they'd stolen everything else from him.

He would not be coming back to her a second time.

Hugging herself against the pain, she turned back to Catton, who currently represented her fastest way out of there. "We should leave as soon as possible." If she spoke softly and kept her jaw clenched, her voice almost didn't shake at all, and it didn't make her head pound as much. "Can you help Eskel with Quinn?"

"Already taken care of. Zigmann's bringing a gurney." He hesitated, then asked, "What will happen to the others?"

He was referring to the seven Shadows who'd survived the fighting. The five who were awake and still able-bodied were falling all over each other to make themselves useful, trying to prove they deserved a chance to live. They'd escorted the telepaths out of the vault as soon as Emma and Laura had come to, brought them blankets and bottles of water, and jumped to obey any and all requests with so much zeal it made her flinch.

They were all desperate to get the hell out of there and put the whole atrocity behind them, same as Catton, and Laura was torn.

As a champion of lost causes, she wanted to believe everyone deserved a second chance. But these were Shadows. It wasn't as if they couldn't have chosen another path after the war. They'd chosen to sign on with Talon and followed every order he'd given them. Having been on the receiving end of some of those orders, she couldn't look at them with an eye toward redemption. They were responsible for the years of misery and pain her family had endured. She blamed them for every single death—including William's.

But she couldn't see their thoughts or memories like the others. All of the prisoner telepaths had scanned the surviving Shadows, and whatever they'd seen had convinced them to let the soldiers live. Laura didn't like it, but she was in no condition to argue.

"They have choices now," Emma said.

They didn't before?

"And we have their mental signatures."

That was better.

"Whoever wants to fly the roost is welcome to nest with us," John added. "Whoever tries to harry one of us again will wake up in ashes." He had a hard time talking with his face all swollen and bloody, but now that he'd fully regained his senses and gotten the all-clear from the Brain, Emma was satisfied that he'd make a full recovery.

It didn't make the redhead any less murderous toward the soldier who'd beaten him up, but, alas, his head had been the first to fall, and she couldn't kill him a second time.

Eskel was guiding Quinn's hovering gurney out toward them.

Laura got up slowly, enduring Catton's steadying hand on her as icepicks of pain stabbed through her head. She was exhausted, but the thought of closing her eyes terrified her. The Brain had examined both her and Emma and said they were stable but needed to be checked out at a hospital. They were all going to the Avencore clinic along with Quinn.

Laura took Quinn's hand in hers as soon as he was out past the entry, reassuring herself he was okay.

He gave her a reckless grin. "Check us out. Bunch of unlikely heroes. Gonna have war stories to tell now."

Laura would have laughed if it didn't hurt so damn much. "No one would believe us."

Quinn sighed. "Yeah, not sure I would, either." He was worn out, in dire need of rest and proper medical care. But a tiny spark of magenta flared into life in his halo of blue when he looked away from Laura.

She turned to follow his gaze to where Finn was guiding Vega toward them. Quinn let go of her hand, and Laura prudently stepped aside to make way. The soldier was leaning on Finn, stiff with anticipation of another spasm, her colorful aura throbbing. She would ride this out the same way she always had—alone.

"The hell was that back there?" Quinn demanded as soon as Vega was close enough.

Vega made a face. She didn't say a word, but her colors brightened a little beside Quinn. Curious.

Quinn spoke as if she'd answered him. "Worse than death, eh?"

"Something like that." Vega let go of Finn and braced herself on the edge of the gurney. Quinn's spark jumped out toward her, and one from Vega reciprocated. They circled each other in the space between the two in a strange kind of firefly dance Laura had never seen before. "You off to get that new heart?"

Laura was so absorbed in the scene she was startled to feel a touch on her shoulder. A series of blinding flashes that had nothing to do with her telepathy almost knocked her out when she whirled, and the ground started to tilt under her feet. She immediately brought up her mental shields and flailed an arm to catch herself on something solid. Her arm lined up with Finn's as he put his hands on her ribs to steady her until she found her balance again.

He drew her a little ways away from the group toward the valley side of the saddle. "Are you okay?" His voice was a low rumble full of solicitous concern and nothing else.

Laura burned to know what he wanted from her, but, at the same time, it was the last thing she wanted to see. Her shields stayed firmly in place. "I don't know. I'm alive." Sort of.

He caught a strand of hair that had fallen over her eye and tucked it behind her ear, then immediately let go of her and took a step back as if burned. "Good. That's… Good."

Laura couldn't bear to look at him. "Still can't believe it worked. I thought for sure Emma and I were dead when we got zapped."

"Yeah, I, uh, cut a couple wires earlier. Probably weakened the collective field." Finn shrugged as if it was no big deal.

"Then you saved our lives," she told him. None of them would be standing there now if he hadn't done it, and she needed him to know how important the seemingly small action had been.

Finn dipped his chin in an awkward nod.

"You really don't remember me?" Such a small question, with so much buried in the words. Damn, and she'd tried so hard to keep her voice steady, too.

Finn met her gaze. "Who were you to me?"

Were, not *are*. Laura's throat closed up, and she shivered. It took her a few tries to find her voice again. "I g-guess you were still figuring that out." And now Talon had made the decision for him.

He raked a frustrated hand through his hair. "Why can't I remember?"

She pulled on his wrist to let go, then took his hand in hers. "Come with us. Emma's people have some experience with this sort of thing. They might be able to help you."

Finn tensed. He didn't pull away, but his face shuttered into a blank mask. "I can't."

"Right. Telepaths." Like her. She let go of his hand.

"I don't know where to go from here, but I don't think it's with them."

Laura nodded. It made sense for him to be suspicious of them again. But he had helped free them, anyway. He'd retained enough of himself to doubt his orders. Maybe, in time, he would recover more. "What will you do?"

His shoulder hitched toward his ear. "Clean up the mess. Learn the world. Figure out my next move. You?"

"There's nothing here for me anymore." Laura swallowed back her tears. She couldn't quite bury the hurt, but after a breath or two, she was able to keep her voice steady. "I'm taking my family off-world. With any luck, we'll be gone in a few days and never have to think about Anamtaigh again."

Finn's chest hurt listening to her, watching her try so hard not to fall apart. She was holding back secrets he was sure would answer a hell of a lot of questions for him. But, by the looks of her, she was on the verge of collapse, and if he pushed, she'd break. He didn't want that. Bad enough to know she was hurting already when he couldn't do a damned thing about it. "Do you know where you'll go?" If she didn't tell him, he could always track her down on his own.

"Torrey, for now. Emma offered to take us in until we get ourselves straightened out. After that, I don't know. I'll send you my new address to the Avencore post depot once I get settled."

She wasn't planning to stay with the telepaths. Finn could go with her if that was the case. He could keep an eye on her, make sure she was okay and had everything she needed to make a fresh start.

But he couldn't do anything for her while Talon was still out there. Vega was determined to hunt him down, and she was right. As crazed as he was, Talon presented a real threat they couldn't ignore. They had to take him out before he had a chance to regroup and launch an attack. He seemed to be the type to hold grudges, which meant he'd strike at all of them where they were most vulnerable. Finn and Vega could take care of themselves. The telepaths would be safe by virtue of their numbers and organization. But Laura would be on her own.

For some reason he still couldn't puzzle out, the idea of her alone out there bothered him. She should have someone to watch her back, and it felt like his responsibility—one he wanted very much. "What would you have me do?"

He couldn't hunt Talon and go with Laura at the same time, but both felt equally important. There was a right answer here, and Finn had no idea what it was, but something inside him coiled with eagerness to have Laura tell him what to do. He needed her to tell him what to do.

"Remember me," she said miserably.

"Then tell me what I forgot."

She shook her head, wincing on a sob. Her nosebleed had stopped, but her eyes were still bloodshot, and she was still visibly in pain. If she asked him to comfort her, he'd never let go. Instead, her next words put up a barrier that might as well have been a mountain range. "If I did, how would you ever know it was the truth?"

Truth. A declaration and a demand. From her. The sound of her voice fell into place inside the void of a forgotten lifetime, setting a baseline for something monumental he couldn't build out on his own. But it did spark one small detail. "You're a persuasive telepath."

The look on her face told him he'd guessed correctly. Yet, despite knowing she could order him to do anything and he would do it as if it'd been his idea all along, he felt none of the apprehension he had toward the others. Once again, he was left with more questions than answers.

"Tell me something. Anything." *Give me a clue here!*

Eskel cleared his throat, intruding where he wasn't wanted. "Laura, it's time to go. You ready?"

Finn almost decked him.

"Yeah, just a second," she told the medic, then turned back to Finn. "I can tell you one thing. Something you told me recently." When she beckoned, he leaned closer, automatically putting his hand on her waist like it belonged there as she raised up to whisper in his ear, "*I love you.*"

Finn shuddered, his fingers curling to hold on even as she stepped back, forcing him to let go.

"When you're ready, you'll know where to find me," she promised, then put her arm around Eskel and let him help her to the waiting hover.

Wrong. All wrong. Everything felt out of place, unfinished, and Finn didn't know how to fix it. He just knew it should have been him guiding her across the hover pad. He should have been the one flying the hover—he was pretty sure he could do it better than Catton. He should be there to guard her while she was with the telepaths and scope out her new place to make sure it was safe and well-fortified before Laura moved in.

I failed her. Another small piece of the puzzle falling into place—the source of his guilt, walking away. The need to make amends was so intense he almost stalked across the hover pad to stop them.

But she'd chosen to walk away. She didn't want him with her, and he had to respect that. He went over to the vault entrance where Vega stood, braced against the wall to see them off. She didn't look any happier about it than Finn. "You could have gone with them," he told her.

"After you," she invited dryly.

Finn put his hands behind his back before they curled into fists.

Vega noticed. "Catton's solid. He'll get them to the Avencore clinic and make sure they're safe until they're ready to leave."

The hover raised off the platform and took off toward the west. As soon as it cleared the nearest mountain peak, Vega slid to the ground with a sigh worthy of the battle she'd fought in the night.

Finn lowered himself next to her, feeling a hundred years old. He frowned. "It just occurred to me, I don't even know how old I am."

Vega groaned. "Boo-fucking-hoo."

"Excuse me?"

"All the shit we've been through—years of torture and isolation. Every horrid thing you've ever done in your life, every sin, every regret—it's all gone. Talon did you a favor. Took the nightmares away, and now you get to go to sleep and dream again. I'm supposed to feel sorry for you?"

"Agree to disagree." He'd rather have bad memories than none at all. Every terrible thing he'd done had still happened, whether he remembered it or not. How was he supposed to make any of them right if he didn't know what they were?

As for nightmares, there were all kinds of those, and some of them followed you into the waking world. Finn walked by one every time he passed the infirmary, and it gave him chills whenever he thought about it, even when he didn't remember why.

He raised an eyebrow at Vega. "What about you?"

She closed her eyes. "I don't get to rest. My demon's still alive."

Finn tried not to read too much accusation into her words. He'd let Talon get away. It was his fault Vega still had a target on her back. "We'll find him," he promised. As soon as Owens got the tracking equipment up and running again, Finn would start canvassing the region for Talon's transport. How hard could it be to find a high-tech machine in what looked like a rural landscape as far as he could see in any direction?

But first…

"Where you goin'?" Vega asked. She was already half asleep where she sat.

"To slay a demon."

The infirmary had been cleaned to a state of order Finn hadn't seen anywhere else in the vault. Eskel's work, no doubt.

The chair's metal pipe base was anchored to the floor with crude bolts. Finn hefted the ax he'd picked up on the way and swung it hard at the pipe. Sharp as it was, the alloy blade cut through inferior steel and wiring in five ear-splitting strikes. When the chair toppled, Finn tossed the ax and grabbed hold of the backrest, dragging the contraption out the door. Wires tore loose, and jagged steel edges screeched across the ground. Soldiers paused in the process of picking up the dead to watch him trail sparks in the chair's wake.

Vega raised an eyebrow as he passed her. "Clean slate factory going out of business?"

"Damn straight." The Shadows had fucked up, and they didn't get to set it aside and move on with their lives. They needed to own it and start making amends.

He hauled the chair to the edge of the hover pad and hurled it down into the northern ravine. It struck an outcropping and broke in half, each one shattering into smaller and smaller pieces as it bounced off the rockface on its way down.

The sun peeked out from behind a wandering cloud when the last of the echoes fell silent, and Finn lifted his face to it. A new day. A fresh start.

Hope.

September 30, 3039 – Karsengale Valley

Sunshine speared down through the tree canopy in thin shafts that cast the forest into ethereal color, yet somehow still managed to hide his query. Finn followed the sound of running footsteps, soft laughter teasing him from just out of reach. He caught a sweet hint of perfume on his next breath and knew he was getting close. Anticipation coursed through his veins, making his heart beat double time as he shot through the underbrush to emerge in the dark of night on an abandoned dirt road.

Movement ahead, a shadow slipping into the cornfield. He followed, fighting his way through the tall stalks, drawn by whispers he couldn't make out. A feather-light brush against his mind turned him toward the right. He could almost see her up ahead, flashes of pale flesh in the darkness, beckoning.

Finn flanked outward and put on a burst of speed, heedless of the long leaves slapping at him and the thick, humid air clinging to his skin. Cutting back toward the path of his query, he collided with a woman's form and turned to take the impact as they tumbled.

Soft sheets billowed up around him. He was in a bed, limbs tangled with hers, her body pressed to his. Her sighs scorched his ear, and her long hair draped around them, an inescapable, sensual prison for his senses. Finn hooked his ankles around hers and reversed their position to pin her in place so she couldn't run from him again.

She didn't want to. He felt it in the way her body arched toward him. Her nails scraped along his skull as she clutched at his hair to guide him to her mouth, and he kissed her hard, the way he knew she liked.

Finn couldn't get enough. Air became secondary. The sheets, the *bed—everything disappeared, except the woman in his arms, and Finn lost himself in the taste of her on his tongue, the feel of her against him, and the sense of her in his mind.*

She needed, and her need guided him to trace kisses down to her breasts. She moaned, but it wasn't enough. Finn continued his path down to her belly button, savoring the way her muscles quivered beneath his lips. Her silent command for more raised goose bumps along his skin, and he grinned against her abdomen, not above teasing her a little. The longer he stalled, the more insistent she became, and he wanted to feel her take full control, tell him exactly what she wanted. He craved it like an addict who'd been denied for far too long.

When it came, her need wrapped him up in a fog that made him desperate to sate her, and he growled, clutching her thighs as he—

~

Finn bolted upright, wide awake and hard as rock.

The sun was up, and noises in the house told him he'd overslept again. He cursed in a long, vicious, and highly creative string as he got up and dragged on a clean set of clothes. This could not keep happening in a house full of former Shadows.

He'd been having dreams like that for the last month and always woke up from them disoriented, frustrated, and wanting. If he didn't know better, he'd think there was a telepath in the area with a sick, kinky sense of humor. But all the telepaths had left back in July, and no one came into Finn's territory without him knowing about it.

The only people left in the valley were the handful of soldiers who'd walked out of the mountain vault, minus Zigmann and Catton, both of whom had chosen to go to Torrey with the telepaths. They were occasionally visited by a scared shitless farmer who kept dropping off produce on a repurposed levpad. Finn had told him to harvest the corn across the road for himself the first time he'd come by. Not like any of them knew what to do with it. He hadn't expected the man to return a second time, but he kept coming, even after there was no more corn to harvest, and always brought more produce. Almost as if he couldn't help himself.

Finn opened the window to let in some air.

The room he'd chosen was on the ground floor with a view of dirt in the back. It'd been evacuated in a hurry, same as the rest of the house, but there were still a lot of things left behind that told him it had previously belonged to a woman. He liked it, but the frequency of his dreams suggested he should probably move.

Out in the main space, the men were already seated around the long table, quietly eating their morning rations. Finn served himself from what was left in the kitchen and brought his plate and a glass of juice to his usual spot, currently occupied by the surly Matsumoto.

The former soldier had ditched the cast on his right arm last week, but his hand still shook when he grasped small things. The High Crown village doctor who'd treated them all after the fight had said Matsumoto would need weeks of physical therapy to regain fine motor function but, despite living six hours out of the region, where none of the soldiers had ever stepped foot, he'd somehow guessed their former Shadow affiliation and refused to do any follow-ups.

They weren't likely to find any more sympathy anywhere else on Anamtaigh, and most of them had nowhere else to go.

"Move," Finn told him.

Matsumoto rolled his eyes and shifted one seat over. "Can't you just sit at the head of the table like you obviously want to?"

"What do you mean?" The head and foot of the table were always left empty. The men preferred to sit facing each other along the sides, as did Finn.

"You keep sitting in the same spot, but you always stare that way when you eat. So just sit there and take command already."

"I honestly don't know what you're talking about." Finn liked his spot. It was his spot. And he didn't stare in any direction—that he was aware of.

Although he did like the painted little cabinet set against the wall there. And maybe he'd looked up once or twice when one of the others joined a meal, expecting them to take the seat and ready to snap at them if they did. That didn't mean anything.

The men around the table snorted and chuckled.

"What?"

Owens shook his head. He'd lost an eye in the fight, but aside from some depth-perception issues, he was in better shape than most of them. "How long are you gonna sit there and pretend you're not in charge."

"Until you assholes get the hint that *I am not in charge.*" The last thing he wanted was to get saddled with this lot of broken vets. The only reason they were there was because the vault had been rendered no longer habitable, and they weren't exactly welcome in any towns. And yes, maybe he'd asked Owens and Galakis to set up some of the Shadows' surviving equipment in the room adjoining Finn's in a way that might have been construed as an order. But he claimed no responsibility or authority over any of them.

If Owens wanted to spend his time in said room, screening off-world chatter, it was his choice. If Matsumoto wanted to run perimeter security checks three times a day, that was on him. The only person with whom Finn worked directly was Vega. Having found no sign of Talon anywhere in the region in the days following the battle, they'd had no choice but to assume he'd slipped through their fingers somehow. Finn was expanding his search to the neighboring regions, but Vega was convinced Talon had made it off-world, and she'd left three weeks ago to track down a possible lead on Persephone 5.

Galakis gingerly leaned back in his chair and crossed his arms, then changed his mind and rested his forearms on the table. He'd taken a hell of a beating in the vault, including multiple low-level gunshots. His ribs were still healing, and he was covered with bruises in all colors of the rainbow, but he'd gotten lucky and avoided damage to his internal organs. "Yo, Owens. Why'd you go up to the Roost last week?"

Owens frowned. "Finn sent me to see if there's anything left to salvage up there."

Galakis turned to Massimino on his other side. "Mass, what'd you do yesterday?"

Massimino grinned. "Finn asked me to give the transports a check-up." Multiple stab wounds had taken him out of commission for two full weeks of bed rest. If the others hadn't stepped up to take care of him, he would have died.

Finn rolled his eyes. "All right, I see where this is going."

Galakis wasn't deterred. "Moto-man, you got any plans today?"

Matsumoto cast Finn an apprehensive glance and ducked his head, shoveling the rest of his food into his mouth to make a quick exit. He was supposed to go down to the lake and supervise the landing of the last Shadow satellite. Finn had assigned it to him the night before because he couldn't stand the guy's restless pacing anymore. He figured giving him something to do other than perimeter checks would be a welcome distraction.

If he'd known they'd use it against him, he wouldn't have bothered.

"As for me," Galakis added, "I'm going to sit my asshole self in front of the monitors and spend my day going over shuttle flight registries."

"I didn't tell you to do that," Finn pointed out.

The soldier shrugged. "Guess that makes me a take-initiative kinda guy. *Sir.*"

"Okay, enough. I am not your commander. We are not going to reform the Shadows. That shit is *done*. Do—you—get—me?"

Galakis exchanged looks with Massimino and Owens. "Shadows ain't done, Rowe. *We* might be, but you really think Talon was the only brainwashed dick out there who ever had the idea of starting shit up again?"

Massimino grunted. "He was looking for others like him. Found 'em, too. What do you wanna bet, he'll go straight to one of the other outposts and try to take over?"

Finn's face must have betrayed some of his thoughts because Galakis gave him a look like he was stupid. "We're Shadows. War is all we know. It's all they allowed us to know. *You* may have lucked out in the memory department, but the rest of us still sleep with guns under our pillows and boots on our feet."

"The fuck am I supposed to do about it?"

Galakis stood from the table and picked up his dishes to take back to the kitchen. "I'm not gonna tell you what to do. Figure out your own shit. Same as the rest of us."

So helpful.

The meal concluded a few minutes later with everyone taking their own mess to the kitchen. There was no chores chart, but the five of them had self-organized to split them up fairly. Today, it was Galakis' turn to wash the dishes while Massimino inventoried their remaining supplies and made a shopping list of items that were running low.

"Any word from Vega?" Finn asked.

Owens answered between sips of coffee. "Not that I've seen."

Finn handed his plate and cup to Galakis. "I'll need to make a trip off-world."

Everyone stopped.

Finn rolled his eyes. "Now what?"

"Nothing," Owens said, not meeting his gaze.

"Mass, you heard 'em!" Galakis snapped. "Saddle the fastest horse to take His Majesty to the shuttleport. He's going off-world."

Done with their antics, Finn retreated to his room to pack a bag. On his way out, he heard Massimino murmur, "Fifteen credits says he ain't going to Persephone 5."

37

"Rusty took a bath today," Laura said. "No adverse reactions. You should have seen how happy she was."

She didn't get a response—stone didn't talk back—but she liked to think William was listening and sharing in her excitement.

"Oh! And the medical wing is finally finished. I hired four full-time doctors and still can't get Eskel out of there. I told him he needs to finish his treatment before he's allowed to see any patients."

As soon as they'd landed on Torrey, Laura had begun to make arrangements to ensure every one of her family would be cared for medically and financially, no matter what they chose to do next. But, despite the entire universe now being open to them, many of the adults and all of the children had chosen to stay together rather than go off on their own. She was grateful to have them with her. It just pained her that so many were there in spirit only.

They'd lost Georgiana, Alexis, and Darax in the attack at the inn. Penelope had never woken up from her brain surgery, and the twins had succumbed to their illnesses a week later. All of their names were lovingly inscribed on two small monoliths underneath a constellation of glittering black jewels made from their ashes. Between them, the tallest monolith was reserved for William.

Laura sighed, breathing in the scent of blooming trees. Golden hour on Mai was different than anywhere else, with its white sun providing illumination and the red one casting a soft pink hue over everything. But the sky remained a gorgeous light teal, studded with three pale moons in static orbit above the snow-capped mountain range.

New Shangri La was a verdant and very exclusive valley surrounded by those mountains on all sides. It was a retreat for the incredibly rich and the deeply spiritual. The estate Laura had acquired had been a majestic mansion belonging to some politician she'd never heard of in the time before Shadows. When the war had broken out, the politician had left one day and never returned. She'd spent several sizable fortunes to find out what'd happened to him—killed three years ago—track down any living relatives—there'd been none—and clear all the red tape so she could legally transfer the deed to herself.

Then she'd spent another one on expediting renovations to build out thirty independent, private suites within its walls, landscape the grounds, and install a glen on the moon side of the garden with the three monoliths commemorating their fallen friends and family for all time.

It hadn't even made a dent in the sum total of her resources.

Now that it was all finished, Laura looked around and couldn't be happier. She'd built her family a paradise and given William and the others a beautiful resting place where everyone could see them from the house and visit them as often as they wished.

"I miss you," she said. "Everything is so much easier for us now and so much harder without you. I wish you were here to see the miracle we accomplished."

Her bracelet vibrated with a reminder alert.

"Time to go take my medicine." She kissed her fingers and pressed them to William's likeness carved into the center monolith. "Sleep well, darling. I'll see you again tomorrow."

The medical wing alone was as large as the compound they'd all shared on Anamtaigh. It was hermetically separated from the rest of the mansion, equipped with the latest, most advanced medical tools, and fully stocked with supplies that were set up on automatic reorder every week to ensure nothing ever ran out.

Two of the new doctors were on call at all times, with Eskel supervising more than he should. Like the rest of them, he was making progress, and it already showed. His face wasn't as gaunt as it'd used to be, and the shadows under his eyes had disappeared. He was more lively and energetic than Laura had seen him in a long time because he now slept a full five hours each night. Last time she'd broached the subject, he'd told her he even dreamed now.

"Laura McNally, reporting for treatment," she announced.

Dr. Lucy grinned. "Hey, Laura. Come have a seat."

Like clockwork, as soon as she did, Eskel stepped in with, "I got this, thanks."

And, like always, Dr. Lucy gave Laura a long-suffering look and let him take over.

"How are you feeling?" Eskel asked.

"You first," Laura countered, making him scowl. It was a ritual they went through every day, each of them mother-hening the other because neither could let it go and just be. She supposed there were worse ways to say, "I love you."

Eskel had her lie back on the exam table and lift her shirt so he could inspect the rectangular patch on her abdomen. "Any side effects?"

"A little nausea, but I'm getting used to it." The patch had microneedles stuck in her skin to deliver a steady dose of cancer-prevention medicines and hormone therapy. The doctors on Torrey hadn't been able to do anything about her ruined ovaries, so they'd removed them to make sure the damaged cells didn't mutate into cancer. Her treatment was supposed to "rehabilitate" her remaining organs back into proper health and stabilize her hormones to hold off early menopause.

Eskel checked her skin for adverse reactions, then pressed the refill device to the patch. "Your test results look good. I think it's safe to decrease the dosage. That should help with the nausea." When he finished, he adjusted the table into a chair so they could sit facing each other. "How are you doing, really?"

He wasn't asking about side effects anymore. Laura shrugged. "Okay, I guess. I'm still annoyed that Quinn won't return my calls." The big guy had taken off as soon as he'd recovered from surgery after his heart transplant. He'd barely said goodbye before going off to deal with some unexpected family issues, and none of them had heard from him since. "I'm this close to siccing the SU on him."

It was an idle threat. Laura loved all of her adopted family, and she knew they loved her, but that didn't obligate them to stay together forever. The adults had had full lives before the war. Of course they'd want to return to them.

Even so, after three years of taking care of one another day and night, not having everyone under the same roof made Laura anxious. Despite knowing that Quinn was now perfectly healthy, stronger than ever, and fully capable of taking care of himself, Laura worried herself sick about how he was doing out there all on his own.

"I just miss him, that's all. I miss all of them."

"You know I'm here for you if you want to talk."

"I know. And I appreciate it. But I don't really have much to talk about." Everything she'd wanted to accomplish was finished now. Her family was safe, taken care of, and provided for. Laura had a beautiful home and a new alliance with the Special Unit that ensured none of her blessings would ever be taken from her again. And with Emma sending lost causes her way for help and rehabilitation, she had a new purpose and a full schedule to keep her busy almost every day.

Everything was as it should be.

And yet her boots still chafed.

"Well, if you change your mind, you know where to find me."

"That goes both ways, you know. Just because I have a house full of people to look after again doesn't mean I don't have time for a cup of tea and a catch-up every now and then."

"Noted. Are you coming to dinner? First one for the newbies."

Laura hopped off the table. "I think I'll let Rusty take this one. She's been talking my ear off about taking a more active role in the house, and I could do with some time to myself." It was a luxury she could finally afford, and took advantage of every chance she got. After three years of sharing close quarters with so many people, sometimes it was nice to have a place of her own where she could be alone with her thoughts.

Eskel nodded. "I'll let you make your escape, then. See you next week."

"Better not make me wait a whole week," she warned, walking out. "I mean it. I'm still your boss, you know. I can fire you for disobedience."

"Yeah, yeah."

Her private suite was on the ground floor with a separate entrance and direct access to the garden. Aside from that, it was no different than any of the others. Two bedrooms, a bathroom with a tub, a small kitchen, a cozy living room, and lots of windows she never closed.

Mai only had two seasons: Summer and winter. One day soon, she'd wake up to a blanket of snow covering the green garden, and it would stay there for five months until it all melted in a day again to reveal new growth and flower buds eager for the suns to tease them open.

Laura couldn't wait to see it. Snow was a different kind of magic when one didn't have to worry about things like the roof caving in, or the heating system breaking down in the middle of the night or the last harvest of the season freezing before it could be collected and stored for the winter.

She made herself a light dinner of greens and a steak made from a local fish-like creature she'd become mildly addicted to and listened to children playing outside in the garden. Peace had become such an unfamiliar concept it was sometimes hard to come to grips with. Every so often, Laura got an anxious feeling that she'd forgotten something or left something undone. But she was determined not to let it spoil her night.

So, when someone knocked on her door, and she got the familiar flare of worry that something was wrong again, Laura smothered it with a glass of wine before padding barefoot across the polished wooden floor to see who it was.

Had she taken the glass with her, it would have shattered at her feet the moment she opened the door. "Oh," was all she could manage for a greeting, and even that came out barely audible.

"Hello," Finn said, standing there as if he's just stopped by for a chat. He looked the same way he had months ago when he'd shown up at the compound, only this time, there was no weight of a complicated history in his gaze.

"I…" *didn't expect to see you again,* she wanted to say, but that didn't feel right. She'd hoped he'd come find her. Actually, she'd hoped he'd come visit her in Avencore before they left. And when he hadn't, she'd hoped he would at least see them off. But Laura had had no word from him since stepping onto the hover outside the Shadow's Roost. Not one call to Torrey, even though she knew he'd spoken to Emma and John at least twice. No response to the message she'd left at the Avencore post depot a month ago with her new address and all contact information.

Last time, it'd taken him twenty years to find his way back to her. She supposed part of her had expected another twenty to go by before she saw him again. "Do you remember now?" She held her breath, waiting for his answer.

Finn studied her face with a slight tilt to his head for a long moment before he slowly shook it in the negative and broke her heart a little more. "But I know you. You're the widow of the late Lord William Belden. You inherited a massive fortune, and the first thing you did with it was to create a refuge for war survivors. You have a lot of in-laws who don't acknowledge you and a big family of people who dote on you, and you take care of all of them tirelessly." He smiled a little. "You're the patron saint of lost causes. So I figured I'd come to see if I qualify for a rescue."

Laura swallowed back her disappointment and opened the door fully. "If anyone deserves it, it's you," she said. "Please, come in."

He glanced down at her bare feet and toed off his shoes before stepping across the threshold. As soon as she closed the door behind him, the suite shrank to a third of its size, and Laura suddenly felt as if all the air had escaped out the open windows. She felt his gaze on her like a physical caress as she led him to the kitchen. "I was having dinner. Are you hungry?"

He shook his head.

"Maybe some wine, then?"

Another wordless no.

This was quickly turning more awkward than Laura knew how to handle. Her cheeks heated, and her palms turned sweaty. She was dying to know what he wanted, but the second she thought about taking down her shields, she remembered the look on his face outside the Roost when he'd realized she was a persuasive telepath.

Should she just ask him? He wasn't being very communicative at the moment, and she couldn't read his expression or body language when both remained neutral.

"Um, I found something for you." Laura edged around him to the living room and passed her palm over a sensor by the doorway to close and darken the wall of glass windows out into the garden. The lights turned on automatically to compensate. It only took a second, but it was enough for Finn to close in on her until she felt the heat of his presence all along her spine.

Her mouth went dry. When she felt his breath puff against her nape, it propelled her toward the bookcase to put some space between them. She clenched her abs to contain a whole lot of butterflies tickling her belly as she pulled a glass tablet screen off one of the shelves. "Please, sit," she invited, turning on the device. When he lowered himself onto the couch, she handed the tablet to him and took the far seat, facing him.

"What is this?"

"I figured you were the suspicious type, so I went straight to the source. Or what's left of it, anyway."

Finn started the recording.

"Oh, Romeo, Romeo, wherefor art thou Romeo!" The voice was hers, much younger, projecting the words from a small, high school stage.

"A play?"

Laura nodded. "An excerpt for the school vlog. Our high school put on a production every year. That particular one was scheduled for right before your graduation, and the director chose *Romeo and Juliet*, so I talked you into auditioning with me."

On the screen, the eighteen-year-old version of Finn intoned his part of the dialogue in overblown, amateur drama, making the audience laugh. "Why?" he asked. "I wasn't very good."

They watched together as Romeo scaled a ladder cleverly disguised as a trellis to reach Juliet on her balcony. "It was the only way I could get you to kiss me," Laura confessed. "Which, by the way, you didn't. Not once during any of our rehearsals. Until the live performance on opening night."

She'd been in love with Finnegan Rowe for as long as she could remember, but they'd been so young—Laura, too shy to tell him how she felt, and Finn, too much a teenager to notice the true depth of her feelings for him.

The audience in the recording cheered when the couple kissed on stage. The kiss, as innocent as it was, caused a visible change in Finn.

He delivered the rest of his performance with so much feeling the audience was rendered breathless.

She knew he noticed it now. Though he tried to keep his face neutral, his brows twitched together in a frown, and his body tensed as he watched. The recording cut out after the balcony scene to the very end when the entire cast came out on stage. Finn and Laura stepped out from the line to accept their accolades. When they straightened from a bow, something came flying out of the audience, straight at Laura's face. Finn caught it before it could strike her, and his mouth pressed into a thin line as he squinted against the lights to find the person who'd thrown it. So protective, even back then.

Now, Finn straightened as if preparing for an attack. "Who threw that?"

"A classmate of yours, Emily Kadee. She was president of the drama club and a shoo-in for the role of Juliet before I, uh, *intervened*."

"So I would kiss you."

Laura nodded. He was looking at her again with that sharp intensity like he was trying to see into her mind, and it made her feel the same way she had as a lovesick sixteen-year-old. Only now, she had the memories of him walking away from her, years of struggle, and all the turmoil of the last few months to complicate everything, and it froze her into indecision.

She didn't know what to expect from him anymore. He didn't remember her, but he'd come anyway. Was he only here looking for answers? Would he be gone again by morning?

Why was he staring at her like that?

"Do you still want me to?"

Finn didn't remember any of what she'd shown him, but the recording felt real enough that he had trouble reconciling the carefree youth on the stage with the man he was now. There'd been an openness to him in the way he'd thrown himself into the role to please the young Laura—something he couldn't see himself doing unless he'd cared for her, too.

She'd *intervened* to get the part of Juliet.

Finn didn't need to know what that meant to understand the implications. If Laura could have manipulated the director to get herself into the cast, she could just as easily have manipulated Finn to kiss her without the bother of a stage project.

It said something about her character and her ability. And it brought up the same guilt he'd felt since what he'd come to learn had been a deliberate memory wipe.

He and Laura had a history, and they weren't finished with each other. But he didn't know what their relationship was anymore, and Laura was taking her sweet time answering his very simple question.

Finally, she gave him a small nod, and the tight knot in his gut loosened the slightest bit.

He set the glass tablet on the side table. This was a precarious situation, and his instinct told him to tread carefully. The couch was a three-seater, and she'd put the middle seat between them. Finn shifted over, giving her time to change her mind and make a run for it if she wanted, but she didn't.

A pretty blush turned her cheeks bright red. He could hear her breathing speed up.

When he leaned in, she haltingly met him halfway, and Finn pressed his lips to hers in a chaste touch not unlike the one they'd shared on stage decades ago. It felt like a benediction.

He pulled back to gauge her reaction and lost himself in her eyes for a second. Finn must have spent a great deal of time staring into them because he knew every speck of their color pattern as if he'd memorized them ages ago.

She was the one to breach the distance next, and their second kiss was nothing like the first. Finn let her set the pace and matched her hunger with a surprising amount of his own. She clutched at his shoulders, and he itched to strip her down, but flashes of his dreams kept coming back, making him feel like something was missing.

Laura straddled him and pulled his shirt off over his head, then took off her own, leaving her half naked in his lap, her modest breasts concealed by a simple bra. She kissed him hard, guided his arms around her, and he was more than happy to tug her into him, spreading her legs wider to bring her down on top of his hard-on.

Her shyness melted away on a lusty moan. Laura kissed and touched and moved on him with full enthusiasm, and he could already tell she'd be a little bossy in bed, which pleased him immensely. But, "You're holding back." Finn didn't know how he knew. He just did.

She pulled away enough to meet his gaze, searching. Then her eyelids drooped lower, and he felt her spine soften a little under his touch, and something changed.

When she slowly brought her parted lips back to his, Finn's awareness of her intensified a hundredfold. He didn't just feel her physical presence; he felt her every need and a strong desire to sate it. And he knew exactly how to go about it as clearly as if she'd handed him step-by-step instructions. The sensory overload filled his mind and brought him almost to the precipice like a teenager with his first crush.

Finn locked his arms around her hips and surged to his feet to take her to the bedroom. The rest of their clothes came off there, and then he had her beneath him on the bed, squirming and arching with need. He brought his nose to the crook of her neck and breathed in deeply, recognizing her perfume.

"What is that scent?" he asked, trailing kisses across her skin as he hunted for its source.

Laura hummed. "Moonbloom essence. I put it in the soap I use."

He knew the flower. It was the official symbol of Anamtaigh because it didn't grow anywhere else. "It's home," he decided, pressing a kiss in the valley between her breasts.

He could tell his words pleased her. She speared her hands into his hair and pulled him up for a kiss but, just like in his dream, it wasn't enough, and soon her desire demanded that Finn provide some much-needed relief. The thrill of *knowing* was a heady thing. He felt no hesitation, no indecision. It was a gift he wanted to savor for as long as he could.

Laura's bedroom was awash in the most beautiful shade of bright magenta. It made her lightheaded and hungry for more. She wanted all of it—now. Forever. Banking that thought before it became a command, she tilted her pelvis up, silently asking for Finn to get to it already. For someone who wanted to be commanded, he sure took his time obeying.

He lavished her body with kisses, rubbed his palms over her in long, luxuriating strokes of a sensual massage that drove her mad. With her ankles locked at the small of his back, she clutched him to her, afraid he would come to his senses any second and remember that Laura represented everything he'd been taught to hate and fear.

When he suddenly stopped at her abdomen, even knowing for a fact how much he wanted her, Laura was sure it was all about to be over.

"What's this?" She could hear the frown in his voice.

Looking down at herself, she saw the patch he'd discovered. "Medicine."

A sharp spike of bright orange flared out through the magenta. "You're sick?"

He was about to retreat. That was the last thing Laura wanted. "Not anymore," she assured him, silently urging him back. She wasn't an invalid or a charity case, and she didn't want him to think of her as too fragile to love.

For the first time in their lives, Laura put the full force of her ability behind a direct command, squashing his sudden hesitation and the need to back off. She knew he felt it when he shuddered, closing his eyes. Had she gone too far?

Then he pressed a kiss to the center of her patch, lingering for a sweet moment in which she felt his desire to make her better somehow. When he made his way back up her body to bring them face to face and heart to heart, his eyes held a silent promise so intense Laura's breath hitched on a silent half-sob.

He kissed her and impaled himself inside her at the same time. Laura gasped at the sudden intrusion, then melted as her body adjusted to his. He pulled out almost all the way, then drove back as deep as he could go, setting a slow, intense rhythm that gave her no opportunity for hesitation, no time for doubt, and no corner to retreat—as if she would. He possessed her so thoroughly, it felt like having *her* Finn back, and she took everything he gave because life was too damned short and opportunities for true happiness too few to pass up a single one.

Her climax almost lifted both of them off the bed, and Finn watched her the whole time, savoring it, committing her to memory, determined not to forget her, them—*this*—ever again. "I love you," she said, making sure the memory would stick.

Finn shuddered, pumping his hips harder, faster.

"I love you, I love you," she chanted between gasps, climbing toward another orgasm, even more intense than the first.

He kissed the words from her lips, swallowed her cries as he rocked her to climax again, and another time after that, until she was left boneless and replete, purring as he finally took his own release, burying his shout in her shoulder.

When their bodies began to cool, Finn pulled the duvet from under them and tucked them underneath. He fit her against him to keep her close, but the look on his face held little of the post-coital bliss Laura felt. His intentions didn't give her any clues as to what he was thinking. It worried her.

"What's wrong." She imbued the question with the lightest of commands to answer truthfully.

Finn hugged her close and pressed a kiss to her forehead. "Nothing. It's just... I thought something this big would trigger some kind of memory."

"Was that why you came back?"

He frowned. "I don't know."

Well, she'd wanted the truth.

"I wanted to see you again. I've been watching you for weeks now, and—"

"You've been watching me?"

Finn shrugged. "Recon. Since I couldn't remember you, I needed to learn about you. And the more I learned, the more I wanted to know."

It wasn't exactly a declaration of love, was it?

He must have seen something in her face. "For the record, this, with you, wasn't about getting my memory back. It was… A need."

"I didn't—"

"I know," he rushed to assure her. "I felt it when you let your guard down. I know you weren't manipulating me into it. But you could, right? You have persuasion. You could command me to remember."

Her heart broke for him. "You don't have amnesia, Finn. You didn't misplace your memories in some dark closet in your mind; the Shadows took them from you. If I did try to command it, you would drive yourself insane looking for something that isn't there."

Laura expected him to pull away then and shored up all her remaining strength in preparation for watching him walk out the door for good. She'd die if he did. Her heart would stop, and she'd end then and there.

Instead, he shifted so they lay on their sides, facing each other. He brushed his nose against hers, pressed a sweet kiss to her lips, and said, "Then you'll have to help me make new ones."

She knew he didn't understand when she burst into tears. But he held her, anyway, crooning to her and rubbing soothing circles over her back. He stayed with her until she cried herself to sleep and when she woke up the next morning, he was still there, watching her.

"Did you sleep at all?" she asked, blinking sleep from her eyes.

Finn shook his head. "Didn't want to wake up and find out it was all just a dream."

Warmth bloomed in her chest and teased a smile from her.

He smiled back. "I feel like I've been waiting my whole life to watch you wake up next to me, and now I don't ever want to leave."

Laura traced his brow, the bridge of his nose, his cheek, willing her heart to slow its frantic beat so she could take just one steady breath to say something she hadn't dared to since she'd been sixteen years old, watching her best friend walk out of her life: "Then stay."

Bright light flared around him, and she couldn't tell if it was sunshine or his intent, but, for once, Laura didn't care. Finn pulled her into him and rolled onto his back so she'd straddle him. "Make me."

39

It had taken Finn all of five seconds after Laura first let him into her home to decide he wasn't going to leave again.

But staying with Laura and integrating with the large, tight-knit family she'd built were two different things. Meeting them all after everything they'd suffered because of the Shadows was daunting. With her insight into his mind and soul, Laura didn't try to convince him otherwise. She simply accepted his need for a little time and suggested they keep his presence quiet until he got used to the routines of everyday life in her community.

It turned out to be easier than either of them thought.

A week after their first night together, heavy clouds rolled in, shading the midday suns. As if a global timer had gone off, the flora outdoors broke out in a loud hiss of movement as flowers closed, complex leaf structures curled up, and branches folded downward. It took minutes. And then the indoor heating turned on, and all the windows fogged over as the temperature outside suddenly dropped, and frost bloomed in great big patches, covering everything in white.

Winter had arrived, and everyone retreated into the warmth of their own homes to watch snow fall from the sky in half-inch flakes. It would be another week before they braved the outdoors again, and by then, even Finn was starting to get a little stir-crazy. It was time to come out of hiding.

Communal dinner was a monthly affair at the house. Since everyone had their own space and their own schedules now, it was the one time when they all decided to set everything else aside and just be together.

"Like the old days," Laura said.

Tonight, they would welcome four new people into the group: an orphaned brother and sister, a young woman who'd started using drugs to make her telepathic visions go away, and Finn. He was unaccountably nervous getting ready for it. These weren't a bunch of strangers for him to blend in with; they were Laura's family.

But when they finally got to the dining hall, the grand catered affair he'd been expecting turned out to be a rowdy group of people in casual dress, stirring pots at side tables, putting out serving bowls, and talking animatedly to each other across two tables curved into half-circle arcs.

Everyone cheered when Finn and Laura entered. Finn stepped back to let them greet Laura with enthusiastic hugs and exclamations. He didn't expect the squealing redhead teenager to throw herself at him or the medic, Eskel to come shake his hand and say, "Took you long enough." Or the half-dozen others who greeted him as if they knew him but introduced themselves anyway, as if they knew he didn't know them.

Instead of taking her seat, Laura went to the side tables where a group of pitchers had been set out with water and other things. She took two and brought them to the table, all the while chatting with one of the women.

Finn mirrored her to give himself something to do to feel less awkward. But these people talked to him. They told him all about their home because it was still as new to them as it was to him. They included him in discussions he actually had an opinion on, having observed them all for weeks before knocking on Laura's door.

It wasn't always smooth—Finn had little experience with this type of camaraderie—but it felt *right*, something Laura had echoed the other day when she'd stopped in the middle of their nightly walk through the snow with an odd look on her face and said, "My boots don't scratch."

When all the dishes were completed and set out, Laura finally drew Finn to their seats. "Thank you all for being here," she said, and though she kept her voice soft, it carried to the far side of the table. "It means something for us to come together like this, and I want to honor that with a good, hearty meal and all the love in my heart. I also want to honor those who can't be with us today with a moment of silence."

He heard the catch in her voice.

When he reached for her hand, she clutched it hard and leaned into him for the full minute of silence before she invited everyone to be seated and dig in.

The dinner itself wasn't formal in any sense of the word. People changed seats every so often to catch up with their friends. Children chased each other around the tables, hiding under them and popping up behind Finn to reach for something that happened to be laid out in front of him.

It took him over an hour to shake his apprehension and relax a little into the ebb and flow of conversation around him. He kept expecting someone to accuse him of being a Shadow and start the cutlery flying at his head, but no one did. Finn figured it was in large part because of the way Laura had shifted her chair closer to him so their arms brushed and their legs touched and how she would peck a kiss on his shoulder to get his attention to pass her something from his side of the table—and then exploit the opportunity to steal a bite from his plate.

She was comfortable with him, so her people were, too.

By the end of the second hour, the sun had gone down, and someone had opened the garden-side wall to expand the space into the outdoors and let in some cold, fresh air. The heating kicked up a notch to compensate, but no one seemed to mind the occasional chilly breeze that swept through the hall or the frost that started creeping in along the floor.

He was laughing at a cute but ineffective magic trick one of the children was showing him when the pleasant cacophony of conversation suddenly hushed.

Finn went instantly on alert, surging to his feet and pulling the child behind him as an uninvited guest walked into their midst. She was limping, and, despite wearing clean clothes, her hair was a mess, and the scent of smoke clung to her skin.

People gave her a wide berth when she passed them, frightened by the look on her face and the way she focused so intently in Finn's direction.

Next to him, Laura stood up slower. She didn't take his hand, recognizing he'd need both if the worst should happen, but she stood by him, letting him know without words that she was with him, no matter what.

Then Vega stepped up to the inside of the table circle, right in front of Finn, staring him down as she dropped something mechanical and very much broken on the table in front of him. "We need to talk."

To Be Continued...

ALIANNE DONNELLY is an avid lover of stories of all kinds. Raised on a healthy diet of fairy tales in a place where they almost seemed real, she grew into a writer who seeks magic in the modern age and enjoys sharing a little bit of it with the world through every story she writes. Her books span the spectrum from fantasy to science fiction with varying degrees of romance sprinkled throughout. Alianne now lives in California, where she spends her free time reading, writing, and daydreaming. For more books, news, and updates, visit aliannedonnelly.com.

Keep turning the page for
an excerpt from Wolfen!

Man's quest for genetic perfection has led to the creation of new subspecies. Wolfen were the pinnacle of scientific achievement, redefining the limits of what it means to be human. Their counterparts, in turn, grew into the ultimate predators. Incapable of higher thought, converts were unstoppable in their need to breed and devour, and when they escaped, they brought the world to its knees.

Almost two decades later, humanity is on the brink of extinction and only the heartless survive. Rescued by two Wolfen brothers, Sinna must now brave the treacherous wastelands of North America in order to reach safety and the promise of a better life. But when an unexpected gambit forces them to separate, a genetic advantage becomes a liability, and the worst monsters turn out to be the ones who don't have claws.

In the game of survival, Wolfen were created to be champions. No longer. The enemy keeps evolving, rendering old tactics ineffective, and the only rule left is to endure at any cost.

THE END

2015 Common Era, Chernobyl

"You can always tell the Wolfen children from the inerts. Although the term is misleading, given the broad spectrum of animal traits mixed in vitro, they truly do behave like a pack. The two oldest of this batch, Alpha Seven and Beta Twelve, are growing like weeds, and their intelligence quotients are off the charts."

Dr. Leslie Gerome watched the two boys on screen, playing quietly in one corner of the playroom, while the rest of the children chased each other and fought for toys. Her smile ebbed. "It worries me sometimes. I can see it in their eyes, they just…know."

She set her voice recorder down, popped a piece of gum into her mouth, then tossed the wrapper in the general direction of the trash bin. Orderlies normally kept the lights on in the room, but Leslie preferred the dark. It was more intimate, and it forced her to pay attention to the monitors and nothing else. "Dr. Hallemann's file said that during the last round of tests, Alpha Seven noted a mistake in his serum formula. He'd pointed out that, at those levels, the acid content would burn a hole in his arm when injected." Leslie chuckled to herself. "Hallemann's recordings show him arguing proper test administration techniques with a ten-year-old. The child turned out to be correct."

Alpha Seven and Beta Twelve were brothers—the genetic equivalent of fraternal twins, born three years apart, and the only instance in which a particular cocktail of DNA fragments resulted in more than one viable embryo. Now, they were Chernobyl den's pride and joy, playing with construction puzzles, building intricate towers and castles. Every so often, one of them looked up to survey the playroom, his eyes catching the light like an animal's.

Such serious children they were. They never smiled anymore, not since the regeneration experiments had begun. And although Leslie knew them to have vast vocabularies on par with college students, the brothers never spoke, unless absolutely necessary, as in the case of the mistaken formula.

"The psych team has declared them at risk of being compromised, but fit to continue being tested—with caution. They're to be monitored closely during interactions with other children, but they rarely play with anyone else."

Sometimes a younger child would approach them for help with a puzzle, and they would help. But once the puzzle was solved, they'd turn their backs and let the child wander away. "They're deliberately setting themselves apart," Leslie said. "I'm sure they have a reason for it, but I can't for the life of me figure out what it is. It goes against their social nature, and has to be hard on them…"

She trailed off when one of the inert boys pushed a Wolfen girl, making her lose her balance and fall over a pile of hard wooden blocks. When the girl broke into tears, the brothers paused and looked up at the same time. The culprit faced them immediately, and as the brothers stared at him, he stared right back.

None of the other children noticed the three holding preternaturally still, but Leslie gaped, held her breath, and waited.

After a full sixty-seven seconds, the brothers exchanged a speaking look, then ducked their heads back to their own game. Too easy. This was in no way over.

Leslie frowned. "Their protector instinct is strong. They do not tolerate dissent within the group, but pick their battles and only engage when they can get away with it. Technical note: Move cameras in the play den. They've found them again."

The lights flicked on, blinding her for a moment. Leslie rubbed her eyes and swiveled away from the monitors to give the intruder a piece of her mind, but stopped short when she saw her colleague darkening the doorway.

Dr. Sallinger was a distinguished intellectual with a pair of glasses on his nose and another on top of his head, overdressed in a starched white lab coat. His real name was Dimitri Andreyevich Roskoff, but he liked to pretend he was a man apart. Tablet in hand, he barely looked up when he announced, "Sigma Nine is to start testing today. Have her prepped and ready in an hour."

It took Leslie's mind a moment to redirect and catch up. "So soon?" she asked. "She's only just transitioning."

There were certain biological thresholds which marked the end of childhood in all things. In humans, it was puberty. In these children, it was a little more complicated. Generally speaking, a conversion could be considered a threshold to failure. Children who converted were the result of a destructive combination of DNA flaws; they became more animal than human, incapable of higher thought function. They were incredibly fast when they wanted to be, yet had a lumbering gait that bespoke of an inner ear defect, which also accounted for their poor hearing. Having observed several of these for a number of years, Leslie recognized them for what they were. Monsters.

Another threshold distinguished Wolfen from inerts, and it was determined by a measure of pheromones. A higher level in one or the other usually predicted which way a child would develop.

Sigma Nine had only shown an imbalance of pheromones last week. It was tentative at best, so they'd been holding off further testing until she'd matured a little more.

"Apparently there's some confusion in her blood tests," Sallinger said. "We need to know where she falls."

"Why?" she demanded, mentally preparing for an argument. She couldn't help it. Sigma Nine was only four years old.

"Don't know, don't care." Sallinger lowered the tablet with a put-up-on sigh, and deigned to look at her. "Will you do it, or shall I call in Michito?"

Leslie frowned. "Michito is here?"

"Tick tock, comrade." Sallinger made a face and tapped his wrist. He didn't close the door behind him when he left, a signature Roskoff passive-aggressive jibe to get her moving.

The voice recorder was still on. With a sigh, Leslie spoke into the mic. "I've just been informed that Sigma Nine's timeline has been expedited, so… I guess I better get going." She was reaching for the stop button, when the Wolfen brothers caught her eye. Jonah had stepped out on break, and the brothers were putting their puzzles aside, watching the inert boy who'd hurt the Wolfen girl.

An odd thought occurred to Leslie. "Observer commentary: A few months back, we received a message that the Fukushima den was having issues. I know the protocol is to limit contact, but we haven't had any updates or progress reports since then. Now one of the Japanese team leaders is here, and this thing with Sigma Nine…" She rubbed her brow. "I don't know, maybe I'm being paranoid, but something just doesn't feel right. My gut tells me Michito wouldn't be here unless something was wrong." She chuckled at herself. "Listen to me. A seasoned geneticist having *feelings*. Ignore that last remark. It's apparently been a longer day than I realized."

Leslie turned off the voice recorder as Alpha Seven and Beta Twelve closed in on the inert boy. The others instinctively moved out of the danger zone. Fights like this occurred regularly among the subjects, and they were allowed, considered as an integral part of development. Unless blood flowed, the orderlies did not interfere.

But this was different. When the first blow came, it wasn't the childish slap Leslie would have expected. Alpha Seven drew back a fist, fingers tucked in like a champion boxer, and drove it into the boy's midsection. The inert boy went down, curling in on himself, and already the brothers were easing away.

It should have ended there. But instead of staying down and accepting defeat, the inert boy pulled himself up and faced off with Alpha Seven, a mean gleam to his eye.

Beta Twelve cocked his head and leaned in to sniff the inert boy. He met eyes with his brother and both nodded.

Leslie frowned. Had she missed something?

She was about to page Jonah to get back into the playroom, when Beta Twelve curled his fingers into claws and slashed them across the inert boy's neck. Quick as a snap; one swipe, and blood sprayed, sending the other children into a screaming panic. Leslie gaped. She couldn't have just witnessed a seven-year-old commit cold, calculated murder against another.

She zoomed in on the inert boy gurgling blood on the floor. The pool spreading around him was too bright to be healthy. Pressing a shaky hand to her mouth, Leslie sat back. He'd converted. And the Wolfen boys had smelled it on him.

But he'd tested safe!

Children weren't allowed into social units until doctors determined them either safely inert or Wolfen. How could he have converted so late?

By the time Jonah came back, the brothers had wiped off the convert's blood and returned to their game. Though still visibly shaken, the other children seemed to sense the threat had been eliminated, and following the brothers' example, quieted as well. They went back to their smaller groups, giving the now-dead boy a wide berth. Inert or Wolfen, they all trusted the apparent alphas of the pack, instinctively adhering to the subconscious social structure. Amazing.

Jonah herded the children out of the room and away from the corpse. He looked uneasy, as well he should. None of the children moved until the brothers did, recognizing their authority over them as greater than Jonah's.

Leslie was still pondering this as she walked down the Green corridor to the nursery. The hallway was quiet. This level didn't usually see much activity, what with nothing here but the guts of the facility—control rooms, nurseries, and incubation chambers. A horizontal green line ran its length as a directional. At the next intersection, a red line ran down another hallway that led to the convert testing rooms and loading/unloading docks.

Leslie glanced sideways at it as she passed, and waved to an orderly jogging to get somewhere. He didn't see her. She shrugged, and kept going to the nursery. This chamber was separated into halves, with the far side walled off for newborns and an antechamber that served as the sleeping quarters and playroom for the one- to five-year-olds. It had gray walls and black floors; a deliberately bland environment to encourage imagination and mental development, while curbing overt excitement.

Sigma Nine sat at one of the plastic tables, coloring with crayons. Her brown curls fell over her forehead and she kept blowing them back with frustrated huffs. The cutest little angel. She still had her chubby cheeks, but Leslie could tell it wouldn't be long before Sigma Nine hit her growth spurt, and when she did, the girl would be a show stopper.

"Hey, Sinna," she said.

Sigma Nine looked up and gave her a ten million megawatt smile. "Hi, Gerry! Are you here to play with me?"

Oh honey, how I wish I could. Leslie struggled to maintain her own smile. "Not today, sweetie. I need to take you to do some tests. Is that okay?"

Sigma Nine pouted. "Will it hurt?"

"Maybe a little."

"Do I have to?"

Leslie nodded.

Sigma Nine bowed her head, put down the crayon, and came forward, holding out her hand for Leslie to take. She kept her gaze on the floor, but didn't drag her feet, as docile as a trusting little lamb despite her apprehension, and it broke Leslie's heart.

When they reached the lab, Leslie lifted Sigma Nine onto the exam table and performed a quick routine physical, noting the results on her chart.

She was just finishing up with the initials when Dr. Sallinger arrived. He checked the chart, scrubbed up, and held his hands out for gloves. His face mask, as always, hung around his neck, ready to be donned in a hurry. He pulled it up, saying, "You may begin, Dr. Gerome."

Leslie stared at him. "Me?"

"Did I not make myself clear?"

Leslie swallowed hard. Sigma Nine was watching her with an eerie calm. She couldn't make herself move.

"Are you unfamiliar with the procedure?"

Leslie shook herself. "No. I mean, I know what to do."

"Then what are you waiting for?"

She stepped up to the table and pulled the instrument tray closer.

"Secure the arm," Sallinger instructed, and she did, hating that he felt the need to talk her through this. "Now, disinfect the area. That's right. You'll want a number eighteen scalpel. Make a six-centimeter incision parallel to the ulna, beginning one centimeter from the styloid process."

Leslie's head snapped up. "Six centimeters?"

"Need I remind you we have two hundred and forty-seven other children to see to? I do not have time for this. Now, make the incision. Six centimeters parallel to the ulna, beginning one centimeter from the styloid process."

Again, Leslie swallowed hard, and tried not to look at Sigma Nine's face when she pressed the blade tip to the inside of the girl's arm. She made the cut smooth, but not fast enough to spare the girl pain, and Sigma Nine gasped and moaned. She started crying, but like all of the children, she was trained not to move during testing. With a scalpel so close to her delicate skin, a sudden twitch could kill her.

"Starting timer," Sallinger said, as blood began to flow. "Five seconds… Ten seconds…"

Leslie frowned. "She's not healing."

"Give her time. Fifteen seconds…"

Sigma Nine sobbed, her heart rate rising with her distress. And she kept on bleeding.

"Twenty seconds…"

Leslie shook her head. "Enough of this." She grabbed a bunch of gauze and pressed it to the wound.

"What are you doing? I did not tell you to arrest the—"

"She's not healing! I am not letting her bleed out on the table."

Sallinger tore off his mask and gloves. "You have just contaminated the test and wasted my time, and you have achieved nothing except to ensure the test will need to be repeated."

"Get out," Leslie snapped. She'd been careful to make the cut shallow, but Sigma Nine was still losing too much blood. Pinching the girl's skin together, she applied a clear solution to glue the edges closed. It wasn't normally used for lacerations this long, but Leslie didn't want to mar the poor girl with rough stitches and an ugly scar. It would have to be enough.

"I will see you fired for this—"

The lights went out with the disconcerting sound of a power-down as the entire facility sighed into darkness. Five seconds later, emergency generators kicked in and red bulbs flared, illuminating the room and the corridors outside.

"What's going on?" Leslie demanded, winding a sterile bandage around Sigma Nine's arm.

Sallinger cast her a dirty look. "Probably just a power outage. Stay here."

"Gerry?"

"It's okay, Sinna. Just hang tight for me, all right? I'm so sorry I hurt you. I promise it'll never happen again." There was no reason; her lack of regenerative abilities confirmed her status as inert.

That's what you thought about the dead boy, too.

She pushed the thought aside. If she studied the boy's behavioral history, she'd probably find clues about his convert tendencies beginning from an early age. Sigma Nine was too gentle, too sweet. No, she was inert—for all intents and purposes, human.

When she finished with the girl's bandages, Leslie freed her arm and sat her up, pushing her curls away from her face. "How are you doing, sweetheart?"

Sigma Nine's chin wobbled, and more tears spilled.

Leslie hugged her tight, rubbing her back for comfort.

That was how Sallinger found them when he came back. His hair was disheveled and he was missing one pair of glasses. Gasping for air, he slammed the door shut and locked it. "They breeched the holding pens," he said, heading for the security console.

"What?"

It took him three tries to enter his code, then the screen split into nine, showing security feeds from their wing. "I knew I shouldn't have signed off on the transfer," Sallinger rambled. "My God, they'll kill us all!"

The break in his voice sent a chill down Leslie's spine. "W-what are you talking about?"

Sallinger rubbed his sweaty face, shaking as he watched the screen. Two of the nine feeds showed groups of scientists herding several children in one direction. Two more showed the convert holding pens—empty. "The crazy Japs! Michito didn't come alone. Fukushima den was compromised. They were storing too many fully grown converts, and they broke free. Michito didn't want to lose twenty years of research, so he captured several of them and brought them here."

"Is he insane?"

Sallinger trembled so hard, he knocked his glasses off his nose trying to adjust them. He wheezed, on the verge of tears, and his distress sent Sigma Nine into wailing fits. Sallinger froze, staring at the child. "She knows," he said. "She can sense them. We can use her to get out."

"Don't you dare!" Leslie twisted to keep Sigma Nine away from him, but her gaze was fixed on the screen and all of those people nervously looking over their shoulders.

"Didn't you hear what I said? We're going to *die* if we don't get out."

Leslie circled around Sallinger to get to the screen. Her thumbprint would be enough to signal distress in the lab. "You're panicking over nothing. The guards will take care of this." They were highly trained mercenaries, paid well for their service, and their response time was usually less than seventy seconds. Of course they could handle this. She was certain of it. They'd come and escort the three of them to safety.

But Sallinger shook his head. "They're all dead! Fully grown converts are not like the children, Gerome. They feed and they breed, and they're unstoppable when the urge hits them. It's like a hive mind effect. The Fukushima ones were starved, and their frenzy riled up the converts here. The den is overrun!"

No. That couldn't be. He was in hysterics. When he calmed down, he'd realize how crazy that sounded. A small army of guards, dead? No way. She'd show him.

Adjusting Sigma Nine in her hold, Leslie typed one-handed, looking for a duty roster. Everyone on active shift could be reached directly in an emergency through a tracker in their radio unit. She called them with her digital page, one after the other, but no one answered. Throat suddenly dry, Leslie shook her head and tried again. One by one, the signals disappeared as if deactivated. Either every one of those radios had gotten smashed, or someone—some*thing*—had damaged the main controls in the lower level server hive. She couldn't call out. No one was coming. They were on their own.

Apprehensive and irritated by the red lighting, Leslie backed away from the screen. "What about the others?"

Sallinger hesitated.

"*What!*"

He jerked his chin toward the screen just as the last group disappeared from the shots. "They're already evacuating. The researchers and orderlies are gone, along with whatever children they had with them at the time. The rest they left for dead."

Leslie's knees buckled and hit the floor so hard, the impact jolted through to the top of her head. Sigma Nine clutched her, whole body shaking with sobs.

"Listen to me," Sallinger said. "There's an escape hatch at the end of the corridor. We can make it. If we can get to the surface before they detonate the charges, we'll be fine. We just have to get there. Give me the child."

None of his words had penetrated Leslie's haze of fear, but when he reached for Sigma Nine, something snapped. Why did he want her so badly? "No." She moved out of the way. "I'll take her."

Though he looked ready to throttle her, he somehow pulled himself together and nodded. "Very well. But you must calm her down. They will hear us."

A flicker of movement on the screen caught her eye, but she refused to look. "Give me a minute."

Removing herself to one corner, Leslie rocked Sigma Nine, crooned to her. "Easy, sweetheart. Breathe. You're okay. You're going to be just fine. I won't let anyone hurt you."

"Hurry up," Sallinger hissed, nervously watching out the window.

Leslie hummed and rubbed the girl's back until her sobs eased. "That's my girl. That's my brave girl. Now, we're going to play a game, okay? I want you to close your eyes, and stay as quiet as you can. We're going to pretend we're hiding from monsters."

"Will they hurt me?"

Sallinger gasped. "Move it!"

Leslie glared at him. "No, baby. No one's going to hurt you again, I promise. Are you ready?"

Sigma Nine sniffled and nodded against her shoulder.

"Good girl. On three, okay? One…"

She signaled for Sallinger to open the door. He did it slowly, peeking out to make sure the path was clear.

"Two…"

Silence out in the hall—no hum of artificial lights, no pitter-patter of rushing feet, not even alarm sirens. Just total, dead silence. And that terrified her. They were truly all on their own. Gritting her teeth, Leslie walked when Sallinger beckoned, and stepped out of the room.

"Three," she whispered.

The race was on. Leslie focused on the ceiling hatch some thirty yards away. She headed straight for a wall ladder leading up to it, heart pounding, and Sigma Nine sitting heavy in her arms.

Of course, Sallinger noticed her readjust her hold. "Let me take her," he offered. "I can carry her more easily."

Leslie shook her head and quickened her step. Almost at the ladder. Shuffling noises from the other end of the corridor made her look back. "Oh, no…"

Two converts, an adult and a child, lumbered toward them. They looked marginally human, with patchy hair and thin bodies corded with lean muscle. But their long limbs ended in clawed fingers, and they had fangs instead of teeth. Because of their cold-blooded nature, their skin held a grayish tinge, but this condition didn't seem to affect their metabolisms in any significant way, acting as a cloaking mechanism only. Matching body temperature to their surroundings made them invisible to heat sensors and infrared cameras.

Monsters. Boogeymen out of nightmares. Mindless, ravening beasts.

And they were coming closer.

"Climb!" Sallinger shouted.

"Hold on to me," Leslie told Sigma Nine, and then she climbed.

The converts stopped and sniffed the air. Although their hearing was impaired and their eyesight compromised by the flashing emergency lights, their sense of smell remained unequaled. The moment it scented prey, the adult convert tossed its head back and screeched.

Several others answered from a distance.

Then it ran forward.

"Climb! *Climb!*" Sallinger shrieked.

Leslie climbed as fast as she could, arms burning with strain, Sallinger right on her heels. But they could only go so far before Leslie had to stop to open the latch. Sallinger clambered on top of her as high up as he could manage.

It wasn't far enough. He screamed as the adult convert sank its claws into his leg and dragged him down to the floor.

"Keep your eyes closed, Sinna." Leslie trembled, vision blurry with tears, but she didn't dare take her eyes off her target as she touched the thumbprint pad to activate the latch mechanism. *Don't look down. Don't look down!* "Just hold on, baby girl," she whispered as monsters tore into Sallinger below. The sounds he made…

Please, God, get me out of here.

The heavy escape hatch slid open, and she moved, climbing higher to reach the pad on the other side. *Don't look down.* Just a few more rungs. Almost there. *Don't look down…*

Got it!

The three-inch metal hatch slid closed, sealing off all sight and sound. Leslie pressed her forehead against the ladder, too shaken to keep going. They were still thirteen stories below the Chernobyl disaster site. To this day, few came to these parts for fear of radiation poisoning. Just as with Fukushima, it had been the perfect hiding place, with all contingencies accounted for.

Except for the crazy Japanese.

If Sallinger had been right, then somewhere on the surface, a researcher had his twitchy finger on a detonator that would entomb this place forever. Leslie had to get moving or she and Sigma Nine would be buried right along with it.

"Gerry?"

"It's okay, Sinna, we're safe. You can open your eyes now."

"I can't see anything."

"That's because it's dark." Leslie looked up. Twelve stories above, a small green light marked the exit—her north star. "I'm going to get us out of here," she swore. "We'll get out, and catch a plane to San Francisco. We can go check out the sea lions at Pier 39, would you like that?"

Sinna nodded.

"Good. Now just hold on."

Keeping her eyes on that little green light, Leslie reached up for the next rung.

Look for Wolfen at your
favorite online bookstore!